WATERWAYS

by Kyell Gold

WWW.SOFAWOLF.COM

WATERWAYS

Copyright 2005-2008 by Kyell Gold

Published by Sofawolf Press
St. Paul, Minnesota
http://www.sofawolf.com

ISBN 978-0-9791496-5-8
Printed in the United States of America
First trade paperback edition: January 2007
Third printing, March 2019

Cover art and interior illustrations by John Nunnemacher

To any gay teens who feel like they can't keep their head above water.

Remember: you're an otter.

You can swim.

Contents

FOREWORD

It started with a challenge, a story I wrote in three weeks that was long, sprawling, and incomplete, but contained a few interesting things, one of which was a self-assured black fox character. A good friend of mine who happens to be an otter told me I should write more with that character. Like a story where he falls in love with an otter. The result, "Aquifers," in which Kory the otter realizes that he is gay, became (and remains) my most popular online story to date. I have been touched and deeply flattered by the many e-mails I've received from people about it.

My idea for the series was to show the different stages of a young man coming to grips with his sexuality in a potentially hostile world. An aquifer is an underground stream, and in "Aquifers," Kory wrestles mostly with himself. In the second part, "Streams," his hidden, underground secret has been exposed, leading to repercussions from his family and friends. And as all streams flow to the ocean, so do all of us live in part of a larger society, and as we explore and shape our own identity, we push out against those who share the world we live in. "Oceans," the last part, chronicles the effect Kory's decisions have on his world.

Thankfully, it is becoming more common for children to be able to grow up gay without the realization being a cataclysmic event. There are hints in this book that Kory's world is undergoing a similar transition, that his fears about the world are worse than it actually is. I hope that "Waterways" serves to reassure gay tweens and teens that there *is* a happy ending possible, that while there may be people who hate you, God never does, and that those close to you can be your greatest strength. I hope it may eventually also serve as a reminder of what we once were like, a relic for us to smile and shake our heads sadly at.

"Aquifers" and "Streams" have been edited and tightened since their postings online, improved not only by my editors, but by the lovely illustrations of John Nunnemacher, to whom (in addition to a certain otter friend) I am deeply indebted. If you are new to the stories, I hope you grow as fond of them as I have, and my thanks for trying them out.

-Ky, January 2008

AQUIFERS

Under the water, everything else disappeared. The heavy, dry world dragged him down, but the water was his element. Kory wished he could go to school in the water; in the northwest, he'd heard, there were aquatic schools for otters, beavers, mink, and water rats. But he didn't live in the northwest, and there were no aquatic schools in Hilltown.

Only two public pools, even, and they were always crowded with non-aquatic kids, splashing around and screaming in the shallow water. He cut from one side of the deep end to the other, holding his breath as long as he could so that he could knife through the water, eyes open but unfocused, reveling in its rush through his fur, the low rumble that was all the outside world filtered through its insulating layers. In the water, he could go anywhere, do anything.

He angled to the surface for only the space of a breath. The other swimmers in the deep end were laboring near the surface, struggling to do their laps. He slid under them with ease, swimming in circles, touching one wall after another.

A shadow lurched towards him. He changed direction fast, and stars exploded around his head as he hit something much harder than water. He pressed both his webbed paws to his head, bobbing to the surface. Kicking to keep himself afloat, he leaned against the edge of the pool. The shock wore off quickly, letting in sharp, searing pain. "Ow. Ow ow ow."

"Man, I'm really sorry," said a low tenor voice behind him. He smelled wet fur and musk. "You okay?"

"Yeah." He found the spot on his head that had hit the wall, probed with his fingers, and winced. Experimentally, he ducked under the water, but the coolness only soothed a little, and his head started to throb from the pressure. Time to get out, definitely.

He broke the surface again, hung there, and sighed. Behind him, the same tenor said, "It doesn't look too bad."

Kory 'd figured the guy would've taken off once he said he was okay. He turned and looked up.

Crouched on the side of the pool, a young fox about his age smiled back at him. His fur was the color of night, glossy with water, except just under his throat, where a shock of white dripped. His long tail lay curled behind him, plastered to the tile around his long legs. "I mean, there's no blood in the water," he went on. He had deep, dark eyes, but his smile was warm and genuine.

Reflexively, Kory sniffed his paw. "No, I'll be fine. Just need some rest."

4

"If there was blood," the fox went on, "you'd have to watch out for the sharks."

Kory blinked at him. "Yeah," he said slowly. "Those pool sharks are bad news."

The fox laughed. "A sense of humor is a good sign. You probably don't have a concussion."

"Concussion?"

"My mom's a nurse," the fox said. "Concussions can be pretty bad. And the victim might not know he's got one." He stroked his chin with a paw. "You probably shouldn't swim any more. I know it's not my business."

"Wasn't planning on it," Kory said. He rested his elbows on the edge of the pool, looking up at the fox.

"Then, uh," the fox looked away, "can I buy you a coffee or something? I feel really bad about that still. Besides, if you've got a concussion, you might lose consciousness in the next hour."

Kory was about to say no, but the clock on the wall behind the fox caught his eye. It wasn't even three yet, and he'd hoped to stay out until at least four, which would get him home just in time for dinner. And then he looked at the fox again, at the deep black fur and the patch of white fur on his chest, and the smile under the dark eyes, and something made him say, "Sure."

"Great." The fox stuck out a paw. "I'm Samaki."

"Kory." The otter lifted a paw and grasped the fox's. Samaki had a strong grip, confident, but not too hard.

"I'm gonna hit the shower," the fox said, releasing Kory's paw and standing in a fluid motion. "Takes me longer to dry than it does you, I bet."

Kory just nodded. Now that the fox was standing, he could see two other patches of white on the nearly-nude obsidian form. Dangling just above the floor, the tip of the long black tail was white, though grimy from resting on the dirty tile. And beneath the trim stomach on the left hip, a small patch of white fur poked out above the dark blue Speedos the boy wore, matched by two triangles below, one pointing down the inside of each thigh. Kory blinked, abruptly aware that he was staring at another boy's groin, and looked up. "Yeah, I'll, uh, I'm done too."

Clambering onto the side of the pool, he cursed the clumsiness he always felt when getting out of water. He still had to look up at the fox, he found; Samaki was a good foot taller than his five feet one inch, which left Kory's eye level right at the bottom of the white patch on the fox's chest. He must be an athlete, Kory thought to himself. Good chest, good shoulders, good arms, good heavens, am I really thinking this? But it was natural, he told himself. Rivulets of water drew his eye to the curves of the chest, and the shoulders that flowed gracefully into well-toned arms. Kory wondered which sport the fox played. All of the foxes he knew were in track, but Samaki was tall enough to play basketball, if he wanted.

"Haven't seen you at this pool before," Samaki said as they walked to the locker room. "New to town?"

"Nah," Kory's short legs had to hurry to keep up with the fox's long strides. "I usually go to the Caspian."

"Oh," Samaki said. "I hear that's nicer."

"It's okay," Kory said. "Pool's bigger, and there's a section just for aquatics there."

"Not many 'quatics in this 'hood," Samaki said.

Too late, Kory realized that Samaki must live around here. "This is a nice pool," he said. "Water's clean, and there aren't too many guppies."

"Guppies?"

They'd reached the locker room. "Non-aquatic cubs. Their parents bring them to the pool hoping they'll learn to swim, or just to get rid of them, and they splash and run around and shriek and get in everyone's way."

"Guppies." The fox laughed. "I was one once. I think I'll start using that."

"Be my guest." Kory was oddly pleased by the approval.

He hesitated outside the large group shower. Normally he'd take his suit off, but having met Samaki, he felt, ironically, shyer than he would if they were strangers walking into the shower together. He walked in with his suit, and was relieved to see Samaki do the same. They didn't talk in the shower; Samaki rubbed shampoo all over himself, while Kory just rinsed. This pool didn't carry the right shampoo for his fur, whose natural oils kept most of the chemicals off anyway, so a good rinse would have to do until he got home.

The dryers were individual booths. Kory selected one of the two that was not occupied nor marked out of order, stepped in, and closed the door. Now he took his suit off, stood in front of the blowers at the back of the stall, and hit the switch. Warm air poured over him in waves. The throbbing in his head even eased somewhat as he closed his eyes and enjoyed the warmth.

He peeked out of the door when he was done before emerging. Samaki was nowhere in sight, but over the scented dryer air, Kory could smell the fox's musk. He padded around a beaver who was cleaning his long, flat tail, and opened his locker.

Just as he was getting his shirt on, movement caught his eye. He looked up to see the black fox emerging from the dryers, naked and holding his blue bathing suit in one paw. With dry (or mostly dry) fur, he looked puffed-out and comical, and he must have known it, as he smoothed down his fur with his paws. Still, he was as striking as he'd been by the pool, especially his long, fluffy tail with a newly-clean bright white tip. Kory could also see the full patch of white between his legs now, but didn't allow his eyes to linger there long.

Samaki waved cheerfully to him and walked over his way. "I'm right here," he said, indicating a locker on the other side of the beaver, who was just finishing up. Kory turned back to his own locker, getting the last few things out of it, and when he looked back, the black fox was just pulling a pair of black briefs up his legs, hiding the white patch again.

He wasn't looking at Kory, but the otter didn't want to just walk out without saying anything. On the other paw, he didn't want to call attention to the fact that he was watching the fox put his underwear on. So he waited until Samaki had tugged on a pair of shorts that ended just above the knees, and then coughed and said, "I'll just hang out outside."

"Hold up, I'm almost done." The fox pulled out a white tank top and forced himself into it, then threw a light jacket over his shoulders. "Okay, let's go."

"Getting too warm for this already," he remarked, sliding the jacket off and swinging it over his shoulder as they stepped out into the street.

The light breeze felt good against Kory's damp fur, but the day was still surprisingly warm for late March. "It's been warmer lately," he said inanely.

"So, where do you want to go?" Samaki asked, turning to him.

Kory looked around the street. The half block between the bus stop and the pool entrance, which he'd seen for the first time that morning, was all he knew around here. He glimpsed a familiar green sign a block in the other direction. "Starbucks?"

Samaki's ear flicked. "Sure," he said. "But that one's kinda crappy. There's a better one a block and a half that way." He jabbed a finger towards the bus stop. "You mind?"

"Nah, go ahead. I don't really know the area," Kory said.

"It's not quite Caspian around here," the fox said as they started walking.

"But you've still got Starbucks."

Samaki laughed shortly. "They're pretty ubiquitous, don't you think?"

The four-dollar word surprised Kory. "Yeah, I guess they are," he said. He rubbed his head.

"Still hurt?" The fox's ears sank.

"Don't worry about it," the otter said. "Really, it's just a knock on the head. I've had worse."

"I still want to make sure it's not a concussion." They rounded the corner onto a smaller street, lined with closed metal gratings and faded awnings. Only two stores looked as new as the Starbucks at the other end of the block, and one of those was an adult book store tucked into an alcove, set back from the street.

They walked past a small pizza place whose smells made Kory's stomach growl. He glanced around at the litter on the street and the faded window signs, then back at the fox. Samaki's muzzle was turned slightly toward him, but even though the fox looked quickly forward when he saw Kory looking at him, Kory saw in the bright light that the dark eyes were not black, but a deep violet. He'd never seen eyes that color before.

"So what'll you have?" Samaki said as they pushed the door open and entered the cool, familiar coffee shop.

Kory took a moment to look around at the art, the scattered chairs and tables, the rack of newspapers and the items for sale. This Starbucks was much the same as all the others he knew. They were a comfortable, known environment, and he felt safer here. Even if he didn't know where he was when he walked out that door, he knew where he was in here. "Uh, just a tall coffee, I guess." He usually ordered a hot chocolate, but that sounded like a kid's drink.

Samaki shook his head. "No caffeine."

"Oh. Decaf, then."

"Milk and sugar? I usually dump a lot in mine."

"Yeah. Lots," Kory added with a grin. "Sounds good."

"Okay. I'll get it. Go ahead and sit down." The fox waved him toward the chairs and walked up to the counter.

Kory walked slowly to the only padded chairs in the shop, fortunately empty now, and swept his tail aside as he sank into one. He watched Samaki order, smiling at the barista as he leaned against the counter, big fluffy tail arched confidently behind him, and thought about the midnight fox with the violet eyes. He was good with words, no question, and he seemed earnest enough about his clumsiness in the water. The thing that bothered Kory was that the fox seemed a little too solicitous, as though he expected something from Kory.

Problem was, the otter had no idea what that might be.

All he could do, he decided, resting his aching head against his paw, was find out more about the fox. It wasn't as if he was fighting off friends with his claws these days, anyway. So when Samaki returned with two cups and set one down in front of him, the first thing he said after "Thanks" was "So what school do you go to?"

"Hilltown P.S.," Samaki said, blowing on his coffee. "You?"

"Carter," Kory said.

"So what brings you to Hilltown Municipal? Caspian closed today?" The fox took a sip and leaned back.

"Uh, no." Kory looked around. "Just felt like a change of scenery, you know." He certainly didn't want to tell Samaki about the poem, or about Jenny. "How about you? I don't see many foxes at Caspian usually."

"Oh, I like to mix it up. Got to keep in shape since I dropped track. Swimming's easier on the knees, anyway."

"So you used to run?"

Samaki nodded. "Along with every other fox in HPS. Dropped it when I started working last summer. You do any sports?"

"Nah." Kory drank his coffee. It was sweet and milky, but the coffee taste came through clearly, a nice nutty flavor. "Only thing I'm good at is swimming, but I never wanted to do it all organized with rules. That ruins it."

Samaki nodded and smiled. "I wasn't very good at track, if that helps. I never got to go to any of the meets, just the practices after school."

"I don't have anything against jocks," Kory said. "My best friend's on the swim team."

"Good. We're not all peanut-brains. Some of my teammates have actually learned to read."

Kory chuckled. "I know. Just…" He shrugged, taking another drink of his coffee to think of something else to say. "Never that interested in sports."

"Me neither, if you want the truth." Samaki tipped the cup to his narrow muzzle again, and then looked at the otter, his long tail twitching at the tip. "I'm just a decent runner. If you're good at something, you should go ahead and do it and not be ashamed of it, don't you think?"

Kory frowned, but the fox's eyes were casual and innocent, and it wasn't possible that the remark had been pointed. Still, the words made him squirm slightly. "Yeah, I guess." He looked back. "So what else are you good at?"

The violet eyes widened slightly. "This and that. I do okay in classes. How about you? If not sports, then what?"

"Classes. Books. I like to read."

The fox cocked his head. "What do you read?"

"Science fiction and fantasy. And some biographies."

"Nice." Samaki nodded and took another drink. "What's the latest thing you read?"

"Uh…I'm reading the Foundation trilogy. Just picked it up a month ago." Kory remembered that he was supposed to be asking the questions. "What about you? Do you read much?"

"Some science fiction. I haven't gotten to Foundation yet, though. Asimov, right? How is it?"

"Not bad." Kory relaxed. Telling someone you read science fiction often got you a glazed look, an uninterested nod, or a smirk. Either that or they would ask if you'd seen "Event Horizon" or some such drek. Most kids considered books something you needed to read to pass English, not something you wasted precious free time with. "Some interesting theories, I guess, for the fifties. Story's a little slow."

Samaki grinned, and they talked about books for another half hour. The fox knew Clarke and Heinlein, liked McCaffrey and Lackey, and adored Harry Potter, as Kory did. They discussed whether Hermione would end up with Ron (Kory's opinion), Harry (Samaki's), or neither, until Kory's cell phone rang.

He took it outside, flipped it open, and said, "Hi, mom."

"Hi, honey. Where are you?"

"Just getting out of the pool. I'm heading right home."

"All right. See you when you get here."

"Okay, mom." He snapped his phone shut and headed back in.

"Sorry," he said, picking up his empty cup. "Parents. I should get back."

Samaki stood and nodded. "Me too. It looks like your head's okay." He paused. "Just in case, though, maybe I should call to check up on you."

Kory hesitated only a moment. "Sure," he said, and gave the fox his number. Samaki took out his own phone and tapped the number into it. "How do you spell 'Kory'?"

"K-O-R-Y." The otter peered at the phone. "Can I get your number?" The question popped out and Kory couldn't quite figure out why he'd asked, so he added quickly, "So when I have to go to the hospital, I know who to call when they ask if there's anyone I want to sue."

Samaki laughed. "You got it." He rattled off his number and Kory tapped it into his phone, getting the fox's name right on the first try.

"Thanks for the coffee and for being concerned about me," he said as they walked back to the bus stop.

"Least I could do," Samaki said. "I still feel like a total stooge. Guess I need to practice swimming a little more."

"Come down to Caspian sometime," Kory said. "I'll show you our Starbucks there."

"Ooh, I can only imagine. Is it fabulous?"

"Oh, so fabulous." Kory grinned. "Hey, there's my bus."

"Nice meeting you, Kory." Samaki shook his paw quickly. "Take care of that head!"

"Thanks again. See you!" Kory ran for the bus and made it to the stop just as the bus pulled up. He got on, paid his fare, and sat down on the side of the bus facing the sidewalk. Samaki was standing on the sidewalk, one paw tucked in his pocket, the other waving to Kory, his black tail flowing behind him.

Kory settled back into the bus seat and smiled. It was worth the bump on the head to have met someone he could talk about books with, who was engaging and intelligent. Most of the people he knew like that lived in other states and were only reachable through his computer. Here was one who was a short bus ride away. He reviewed the afternoon in his mind, looking for something that might not be right, but all he could come up with was, again, the feeling that Samaki was waiting for something else from him that he hadn't given. He spent enough time worrying about this that he forgot to prepare for his arrival home.

"Where have you been?" his mother snapped as he walked through the door. He could see her craning her head from the kitchen to look at him. "Dinner's almost ready. Go clean up."

The lightness he'd felt on the bus vanished, and now he felt the throbbing in his head acutely. He walked across the living room, skirting the edge of the central pool that joined all the rooms of the ranch-style house, and walked across the bridge and down the short hall that led to his and his brother's rooms, opening the door on the left wall and closing it behind him.

Through the window to his right, he saw his brother walking up from the back yard. He dropped his stuff on the bed under the window and flopped down on it. Just lying in his own bed in his cozy room made his head feel a little better.

Outside, he heard the splash as his brother dove into the pool from the back yard, and a moment later the younger otter's head bobbed up in the small corner of his room that was open to the pool.

"Hey, Kory," he chirped.

"Hey, Nick." He turned his head to look at his brother. Nick had the same broad muzzle and dark brown fur that Kory did, but where Kory had his father's brown eyes and small ears, Nick's eyes were blue like their mother's, and his ears stood up over the tuft of fur on the top of his head even when it wasn't lying flat and wet, as it was now.

Last year, Nick had insisted that they stop calling him Nicky; at thirteen he wanted to grab whatever dignity he could. At the time, Kory hadn't thought he would be able to, but now Nick had grown into the name, both in stature and, surprisingly, maturity. Kory almost felt that the little screaming brother who told tales and threw dirt at him had been exchanged for a wiser, quieter brother when he'd dropped the 'y' from his name.

"Dinner's almost ready."

"I know. I'll be there in a minute."

Nick rested his arms on Kory's floor. "Where'd ya go today? I went to the pool but I didn't see ya there."

"I just wanted to get away for a bit. Who was at the pool?"

"Nobody. I just went there to look for you. I was over at Mickey's."

That meant Mom had asked him to check up on his brother. Kory lay back again. "You going to swim to dinner?"

"Well, I don't have time to dry off." Nick snorted.

"Mom'll flip."

"So what else is new?"

"Okay, hang on." Kory rolled out of bed and stripped down to his swimsuit. "Race ya," he said as he dove into the water beside Nick.

His brother yelped, but he only heard the first part of it as the water closed around him.

Nick was on the swim team, and had been faster than Kory for years. Only by tricking him could Kory hope to win. He did this time, barely, popping out of the water and scrambling to the kitchen table, dripping. His mother gave a little squeak, and turned to glare at them. "Kory James," she began, but Nick interrupted her.

"Cheater," he said, and stuck his tongue out at Kory.

Kory glanced at his mother, feeling the flush in his neck and chest he got when he'd done something fun that he knew was wrong. "Nick did it too."

"And how much older are you than him?" She dropped a dish of potatoes on the table with a thunk. "I wish you boys would get dressed for Sunday dinner. I try to put something nice on the table, and you're sitting there dripping all over the furniture."

"Mom, we dress up five days a week," Nick said, his wet tail slapping the floor as he rearranged his seat.

"Don't slap your tail," his mother said immediately. "Weekdays we don't have much time because you have homework to do. Sunday it would be nice to sit around as a family."

"We can do that wet," Nick said, shoveling potatoes onto his plate as his mother placed the fish next to them.

Kory shifted one of the fillets to his plate and scooped the buttery sauce over it, then took the potato spoon from Nick. His mother, meanwhile, had sat down with the bowl of green beans. "Don't forget your greens," she said, shoveling a pile onto Nick's plate.

"Mom," he said, "Not so many."

"Don't fill up on potatoes," she told him, and piled beans on Kory's plate as well before taking some for herself. They waited until she'd arranged her own plate and then bowed their heads.

"For what we are about to eat, for the blessing of each other's company, and for our continued happiness, may the Lord make us truly thankful," she said.

They chorused, "Amen," and dug in.

"Kory, Nick said he didn't see you at the pool," his mother said after a minute. "You said you were going to the pool, and when I called, you told me you were just leaving, but you didn't get home for another hour."

"I went to the municipal pool," Kory said.

"Why on earth would you do that?"

He shrugged. Nick said, "I know why."

Kory glared at him. His mother said, "Nick, let Kory tell me. Kory?"

"Just felt like going there," he said. "Okay?"

"Did it have anything to do with Jenny?"

"No." He chewed a bite of fish far longer than he needed to.

She looked down at her plate and took a dainty bite of green beans. "I ran into Jenny's mother at the market this afternoon."

In the pause that ensued, Kory knew she was waiting for him to tell her what she already knew. He took another bite of fish and said nothing. After a moment, his mother continued.

"She told me you and Jenny aren't seeing each other anymore. Is that right?"

He took another bite, but she wasn't going to let him off the hook this time. He swallowed. "I guess."

"I see. When did this happen?"

"Yesterday." He focused on getting his dinner down as fast as he could, so he could leave the table.

"We saw them in church this morning, and you didn't say anything."

He didn't see a need to reply to that, so he crammed potatoes into his mouth. "Don't bolt your food," his mother told him. "I just don't know why I had to learn about these things secondhand. Do you know how

embarrassing that was? Mrs. Kish asked if you were doing all right, and I didn't know what she was talking about."

"Sorry," he mumbled through flecks of potato.

"Don't talk with your mouth full." She paused. "Are you all right?"

"I'm fine, mom," he said. "Can I be excused?"

She looked at his plate, which was mostly clean. "No," she said. "We've got banana cream pie for dessert, and I want us to sit around and talk. Tell me what the municipal pool is like. Is it as nice as Caspian?"

"No," he said. "It's smaller and more crowded." Then he decided to give her something to worry about, to stop her asking more about the pool, because he didn't want to tell her about Samaki yet. "I banged my head on the wall. I was trying to get out of this kid's way..."

It worked. His mother gasped and leaned closer. "Where?"

He showed her the spot. "Oh, Kory," she said. "It's swelling up. Let me get an ice pack."

The rest of the dinner was spent with her fretting over him, because those municipal pools might be full of disease, you never know. He let her worry, not pointing out that he hadn't broken the skin. The ice did help, really, and the banana cream pie (from the market, not homemade) was delicious. He was in a somewhat better mood when he swam back to his room and lay on a towel on the floor to dry off.

Nick surfaced and rested his arms on the floor, his nose only a foot from Kory's. "You went to the municipal pool because of the poem, didn't you?"

"Shut up, Nick."

"Hey, I think it's cool," his brother said. "I couldn't do it."

"Nick..."

"Why do you care what those dipwads think?"

Kory rolled over and stared up at his ceiling, where he could just see the glow-in-the-dark stars he'd put up when he was seven. "It's complicated," he said. "You'll understand when you get to high school."

He knew that would irritate Nick. He hoped it would end the conversation. Instead, he heard a huff, and then Nick kept talking. "Well, I think it's dumb. What happened with Jenny?"

"Nick..."

"Come on, Kory. I liked her. Why'd you dump her?"

Kory closed his eyes. "I didn't, okay?"

"Oh," Nick said, his voice small.

"Please, Nick," Kory said, resting a paw over his closed eyes.

"Yeah, sorry, I..." Kory felt his brother touch his arm gently. "I'm gonna go to bed. Hope you're okay."

"I'm fine," Kory said, and then felt bad. "Thanks, Nick. I'll tell you about it later. Just don't feel like it now."

"Okay." He heard the soft ripples of water as his brother slid down and swam back to his room.

The truth was, Kory had thought he'd be relieved to be broken up with Jenny. They'd had a nice summer together, then slept together a few times, and that had changed their relationship. Suddenly she wanted to talk about other people's relationships, like how Sal and Allie were doing, and things Jake Conly had said to Amanda that Amanda didn't understand, and what did Kory think of all that? He didn't care, truthfully, and apart from their double dates with Sal and Allie, he started making excuses to avoid Jenny unless it was in a public place like the pool. He'd retreated to an online book group, until he looked forward to logging on in the evenings more than he looked forward to seeing Jenny.

So he'd thought he wouldn't be upset if she dumped him; in fact, he was almost trying to get her to do it so he wouldn't have to. But he hadn't expected her to do it Saturday, when he wanted to talk to her about the previous week of school, when he really needed a sympathetic ear. Instead, it had been all about her, and how this was really too much, and she'd been talking to Chris Stafford—Chris Stafford!—and he'd asked her to the prom and she'd said yes.

He was surprised by how hurt he'd felt. No, he didn't want to be dating her, but he wanted to be the one to decide to stop. He'd been in a funk for most of Sunday, except when he'd been swimming, and when he'd been talking to Samaki.

The violet eyes and easy smile of the black fox crept back into his thoughts. If their engaging talk had been any indication, Samaki would enjoy the online book group too. He turned his cell phone over thoughtfully and wondered if Samaki would really call him. He could call the fox; he had his number and it wasn't even seven o'clock yet. Would the fox be eating dinner? Maybe it was a little too soon to be calling.

Too soon? Kory laughed at himself and set down the phone. It wasn't like he wanted to date the fox.

Though…come to think of it, he wondered now if the fox wanted to date *him*. He'd certainly been very friendly considering they'd just met. And had he gotten dressed a little too slowly, maybe showing off for Kory's benefit? Kory pulled his tail to his chest and scritched through it with his claws, thinking about the luxuriant ebony tail the fox had. Maybe Samaki had been hitting on him. He should call up and set the fox straight.

But what would he say? He didn't really know any gay people that weren't in movies or on TV. It was odd to think of Samaki that way; until that moment, he'd just been a friend, with a vast unexplored landscape, as if Kory had landed on a new planet. If he were gay, then all his actions took on a different cast, and maybe he really was more alien. That didn't mean they couldn't be friends. He just couldn't ever tell his mom. But if the fox thought he might be gay...well, he should say something, he shouldn't let that rest. It wouldn't be fair to either of them. He picked up the phone.

But what if he were wrong? He weighed the phone and set it down again, continuing to stroke his tail. Gay guys had a gay-dar or something, didn't they, to let them know whether someone else was interested? Surely he'd have seen that Kory wasn't gay. No, maybe he was just another lonely soul, with nobody to talk to about the books he was reading.

Hard to believe, though, as handsome as he was. Kory couldn't believe the fox would have any difficulty finding any kind of companionship he wanted. So maybe he was gay, and that explained his loner attitude.

"Grrr." He clutched his head. Best just to finish up his homework and worry about it next time he heard from Samaki, which would probably be never. He'd probably just asked for Kory's number to be polite, and walked away thinking what a dork he'd just swum into at the pool.

Though he had waited and waved goodbye to the bus. He didn't have to do that.

Kory sighed and grabbed his math homework. He'd ask Sal about it in the morning.

Like Kory, Sal was smaller than the otters on the high school swim team. They'd been friends since Kory could remember, going to church together, movies together, even playing Ultima Online together a few years back. Then Sal had discovered girls.

Kory had been mostly blind to the changes going on around him, but Sal began to act like a tourist in a strange new land. "I got a date with Jessica," he'd hiss. "Check her out. No, don't turn and stare!" Her primary claim to beauty appeared to Kory to be the now-prominent breasts straining against her sweater, because otherwise her features hadn't changed. He didn't think that was such a big deal, but the next week Sal had gleefully reported to Kory how they felt, the first in a long string of kiss-and-tell incidents.

Kory listened with polite interest, but it wasn't until the summer that he finally realized that this wasn't just a new game Sal was interested in, but a change that was happening to all his peers, one he was expected to share in. It was even harder for him to keep up, since he was seeing less of Sal than he had in the years when they'd spent the whole day together.

Sophomore year had been the first year Sal and his friends on the vocational track left the school every afternoon to get training for real world jobs. Sal was going to be a computer technician. "I'm gonna be the guy the big guys have to call to get their machines fixed," he was fond of boasting. "For you, Spike, I'll do it free." Sal still called him 'Spike' after his Ultima Online character, but he didn't want Kory to call him 'Ike' any more.

This morning, he was in a particularly good mood, so Debbie, a pretty sophomore skunk who was his current girlfriend, must have spent at least one of the nights of the weekend. Sal refrained from telling him about it, though. "Hey, Spike," he said. "I heard about Jenny. You okay?"

Kory shrugged. "I'm fine. How did you hear?" It must be all over school by now, he thought.

"Debbie's older brother's dating Jenny's older sister's best friend," Sal said, stretching his lanky form and curling his tail up behind him. "So what did she say?"

Kory dropped into his seat. "She said she didn't understand why I didn't write poems like that to her."

"That's all? That's weak."

"That and Chris Stafford asked her to the prom and she said yes."

"*Stafford?!*"

"Yeah."

Sal shook his head, unable to muster any more words. "Freakin' Stafford," he said.

"Yeah." Kory saw one of his Warcraft buddies come in and waved to him across the room. Jason waved back and went to sit with Dev. The two of them were hardcore gamers, and though he enjoyed playing with them, they didn't consider him dedicated. He sometimes hung out with them; they were nice enough in small doses.

"Hey, Sal," he said into the silence. "Say I bumped into a girl at the pool, and she...slipped and banged her knee. If I bought her coffee after, and then asked for her phone number, you think she'd think I was hitting on her?"

His friend turned to him with a grin. "Did you get the phone number?"

"Uh...yeah."

Sal punched him on the shoulder. "Back on the horse already!"

"Ow." Kory grinned. "C'mon, would she think I was hitting on her?"

"Heck, yeah," Sal said. "But if she gave you her number, she didn't mind. You didn't call her yet, did you?"

"No. But what if she thought I was just being friendly, like I said she should give me her number so I could check up on her knee?"

Sal laughed. "She wasn't, like, thirteen, was she?"

"No!"

"Then she knew and she didn't mind. So here's what you do. Call her tomorrow night. Not tonight, that's still too soon. See if she's free Friday night. Me and Debbie will go to the park with you. What species is she? Otter?"

"Uh, fox." Too slow to think of another lie.

Sal cocked his head. "Fox? At the pool? It's not Sharisse, is it? Please tell me it's not Sharisse."

"It's not Sharisse."

"Good. So who is it? Gina's dating that tod from Westgate, Ellen's seeing Jim Brush, and Tanya Torick is dating that foreign exchange student, the fennec. Not one of them, right?"

"No, she, uh, goes to Hilltown P.S."

Sal raised his eyebrows. "She was at Caspian?"

"No. I went to the municipal pool. Just to get away."

Geoff Hill, a large raccoon, stepped into the room and ambled back to them. "Oh, great," Sal muttered. "Just ignore him."

"I know," Kory muttered back.

"Hey, Rainbow," Geoff said in a falsetto, and the class tittered. "I got a pome for ya. 'Roses are red, violets are blue, who's the biggest wuss in school? it's you!' Har har!" He dropped into his seat behind the two of them, still laughing at himself.

The sad part, Kory thought, was that several of the rest of the class were chuckling along with him. He sank down in his seat.

"Asshole," Sal muttered. Kory shrugged. "Don't worry. They'll forget it pretty soon."

"Not while Deffenbauer has it posted in the hallway cabinet."

"We could bust it..." Sal shut his mouth as their teacher walked in, and opened his math textbook. "So...did you do the homework?"

They talked about school while Kory thought about what Sal had said. So Samaki *had* been hitting on him—and by giving him his phone number, Kory had effectively said, "Sure, stud, let's get it on." Well, it was nothing a phone call wouldn't clear up, he was sure. The fox was friendly enough, and once he heard it was all a misunderstanding, he'd happily go on his way. Maybe they could even stay friends. Samaki didn't seem as obnoxious or predatory as most of the gay people he'd heard about.

That night, though, when he called up the fox's entry on his cell phone, he was unaccountably nervous. What was he going to say? "Sorry, I'm not gay?" What if Samaki wasn't gay? He paced back and forth in his room, and just as he'd decided to close the phone, that Samaki wasn't going to call him back anyway, it rang.

Looking down, he saw Samaki's name flashing, and automatically picked up the phone.

"Hi, Samaki."

"Hey there." The fox's voice was cheerful and light. "Good, I was worried for a minute you might've given me a bogus number. How's the head?"

"Oh, fine, as long as I don't think about it." The "bogus number" comment sounded like something someone who'd been hitting on him would say.

Samaki laughed. "Sorry."

"Oh, no, I didn't mean…" He laughed too, worry receding. "It's okay."

"No blackouts or dizzy spells?"

"No, I'm fine, really."

"Well, that's good."

There was a pause. Kory tried to decide what to say next, but the fox beat him to it. "Hey, I was going to try to hit that new movie on Friday, *Planet Death*." For a moment, Kory thought, *oh, no*, and then Samaki said, "It's supposed to be terrible. Want to come along and make fun of it?"

"Sounds like fun," Kory heard himself say.

"Great!" The fox sounded almost relieved. "You know where the Landmark 8 is?"

"I can find it online," Kory said.

"Cool. I'll call you later in the week when they have the show times up. It'll be the sevenish one."

"Okay. Or you could just e-mail."

Samaki hesitated. "Sure. What's your e-mail?"

They traded addresses. Kory entered Samaki's in his online address book. It looked like a generic cable address. "Do you do any stuff online at all?"

"Not much," Samaki said. "Some homework. We only have one computer in the house for all of us."

Kory looked at his computer and felt a little ashamed of having it. His family didn't have much, but they had DSL and they each had a computer. "You have a lot of brothers and sisters?"

"One older sister. She's away at college. Two younger brothers and one younger sister."

"Wow."

"You?"

"One younger brother, that's it."

"Nice not to have to wear hand-me-downs, huh?"

Kory grinned. "I thought you said you didn't have an older brother?"

"My sister wore jeans. And t-shirts with flowers. I shouldn't be telling you this, I just met you."

Kory laughed. "It's okay. My brother hates wearing hand-me-downs too."

"Why, do you wear t-shirts with flowers on them?"

"Worse," Kory said. "Dragons. Oh, I don't think I should be telling *you* this."

"You went through a dragon phase too?"

"Uh..."

He heard the fox's soft chuckle. "Still kind of in it?"

"Kind of." He looked at the dragon poster on one wall. "Do you ever play online games?"

"Not really. It's hard with not having much computer time."

"Oh yeah." Great, Kory. Nice guy you are. Why not tell him how great the rich kids' pool is while you're at it?

"I play some games. The guys on the team play poker once in a while. My brothers and I play card games too. I used to read to 'em, but since they got older they don't like that so much. I still read to my sister, though. She's four. How old is your brother?"

"Thirteen," Kory said.

"Cool," Samaki said. "You got any homework tonight?"

"Yeah. Working on a paper for English."

"Hey, me too. Want to hear what mine's about?"

"Sure." He sat at his desk and listened to the black fox talk about his English paper, and then he told Samaki what his was about, and they talked about homework for forty-five minutes.

The next night, Samaki sent him an e-mail with directions to the theater and a note: "Math homework tonight. Quadratic formulas. You any good at that?" And they spent another hour talking on the phone, letting math lead them into science and science fiction and other favorite books they shared.

On Wednesday, Sal asked him if he'd called his girl, and it took him a moment to remember what his friend was talking about. "Oh, uh, yeah, she's busy Friday night. Sorry."

"You going to see her Saturday? We could go out to Kern's maybe."

"No, she kind of, uh, blew me off. I don't think it's worth calling again."

"You give up too easy. I bet if you call again, she'd go out with you."

"Just leave it, okay?" Kory slouched in his seat.

"Tell you what," Sal said after a moment of silence. "There's this place I know, over by the college. College women like high school boys. I got laid a couple times there," he added nonchalantly.

"You never told me about that."

"You were dating Jenny. Didn't seem like you needed it."

"You're dating Debbie!"

Sal shrugged. "Yeah, well, what she don't know...so, you in? I'll take you there."

Kory realized that his friend was making a sacrifice, telling him about his "special place," but he found the whole thing rather distasteful. "Nah. You know Friday and Saturday are the only nights Mom lets me play Warcraft."

Sal gave him a long look. "So play Saturday night."

"I can't, I...look, there's this group I'm supposed to go out with and...do some mission. Planet Death, it's called. They're going Friday night. I...I'll go with you some other time, I promise."

And fortunately, Sal lost interest at that point.

Friday night, Kory told his mother he was going out to the movies with Sal. She told him to be back by 11.

"What movie?" she wanted to know.

"Uh..." She'd never agree to *Planet Death*.

"I don't want you seeing an R-rated movie, Kory. Even if you are seventeen."

"I know. I'm not. We're going to that Schwarzenotter movie, *Girlie Men*. It's PG-13."

Her muzzle turned down. "Isn't there anything better playing? Well, all right. A little more Hollywood decadence won't kill you, I guess."

He caught the bus a few blocks away and rode to the Landmark, feeling a little giddy. He kept seeing Samaki's jet-black muzzle and bright white smile in his mind. They'd talked on the phone every night that week, about homework and games and books and friends, and Kory was really looking forward to seeing the fox in person again, his worries about whether or not Samaki was gay pushed to the back of his mind, if not forgotten.

The black fox gave him that smile and a cheerful wave as he walked up to the theater. "Hey, you found it. I got our tickets already. How's your head?"

"It's fine, thanks." He shook the fox's paw and followed the fluffy black tail into the theater, watching the white tip bob back and forth. "How's it going?"

"Okay." They stopped in front of the concession stand. "Do you want popcorn?" Samaki asked.

"Sure." Kory handed him a ten. "That cover the ticket?"

"Yeah, it was eight...here." The fox gave him a couple ones back. "You know, it's cheaper if we get one medium instead of two smalls. If that's okay."

Kory grinned. "Sounds fine. But I won't share your drink."

He didn't know why he'd said that, but Samaki seemed unruffled by it. "I drink Diet Coke. Most guys don't like that." He stepped up to the counter and placed their order.

"Ugh." Kory stuck his tongue out as they walked away with popcorn, drinks, napkins, and straws. "I hate that aftertaste."

"Yeah, but it's healthier."

"I dunno, all those chemicals?"

Samaki took his straw into his muzzle and sipped on the way to the theater. "Mmmm, chemicals."

Kory laughed and sipped his regular Coke. They settled into two seats in the theater and chatted until the theater darkened.

Kory had never been big on people who talked in movies, but the first time Samaki leaned over to whisper a comment to him, it was exactly what he'd been thinking, only funnier. He coughed around a mouthful of Coke, and whispered back, and they kept that up through the whole movie.

It was a terrible movie, and Kory couldn't remember one he'd enjoyed more.

"Who," Samaki said as they left the theater, laughing, "would be frightened of little chipmunks?"

"They did have bright red eyes," Kory reminded him.

"And claws of...what was it?"

"Diamondine," Kory giggled. "The hardest substance in the universe."

"Still..." Samaki cocked his fingers into a gun and aimed at imaginary chipmunks on the sidewalk. "Pow! Pow! Pow! Problem solved."

Kory chuckled. "No kidding. Man. That was awful."

The fox stretched. "I don't feel like going home yet. You have time to grab a shake? I know a great place."

Kory checked. "Yeah, as long as I get on the 10:15 bus I'm cool."

"Forty minutes? Plenty of time. Come on!" Samaki dragged him down the street into a small shopping center, walking fast along the sidewalk to a small shop with a red and white-striped awning. He held the door and bowed. "After you."

Cool air ruffled Kory's fur. He swung his tail in to make sure it didn't catch in the door and breathed in the rich, sweet fragrance. Samaki led him through the small round tables to the ice cream counter, where a young goat raised a hand to wave. "Hey, Sammy," he said, looking over Kory's shoulder.

"Hi, Chuck," Samaki said. "This is Kory. First time here."

"Great!" The goat smiled. "You on the swim team?"

Kory shook his head. Samaki chuckled. "No, he can have the full milkshake."

"Usual for you?" the goat said, already starting to scoop some ice cream into a silver milkshake cup.

"Yeah." Samaki turned to Kory and grinned. "What flavor you want?"

"What's a 'full milkshake' mean?"

"Oh, when I ran track they made me these frozen yogurt shakes. Almost as good and half the calories." Samaki patted his stomach. "It's hard to break the habit."

"*Almost* as good." The goat grinned at Kory. "You get the real thing." He shoved the cup under the old-style milkshake machine, and the whirr of the mixer filled the room.

When it subsided, he poured the shake into a cup and set it on the counter. "So, what flavor?" he asked Kory.

"Just vanilla."

"Malt?" Kory hesitated. "If you've never had it, I recommend trying it," the goat said.

"Okay, sure." He returned Samaki's encouraging grin.

"My treat," the fox said when the goat slid Kory's shake next to his.

"I can get mine," Kory said, but Samaki waved a paw.

"I dragged you here, I insist. You take me to one of your favorite places and you can treat."

Kory had his wallet out, but the fox was handing a ten to the goat, saying, "Don't take his money, Chuck," and when the goat took the ten, Kory thought he saw a brief wink back at the fox.

They sat down, slurping the first cold mouthfuls as they went. "Wow," Kory said. "Nice."

"I haven't had a malted in a while." Samaki sucked another mouthful and then clutched his head dramatically. "Ow! Brain freeze."

"Don't gulp it," Kory said. "That's what my mom says."

"I know, I know."

Kory didn't know what made him do it, but he slid his shake across the table. "Want a taste?"

Violet eyes regarded him under one raised eyebrow. "I thought you didn't want to share your drink with me."

"Not when it was a Diet Coke. That stuff's nasty."

"All right," Samaki said, and lifted his straw from his shake, tapped it reasonably dry, and opened the top of Kory's shake to slide it inside. He took a gulp and lifted the straw out, closing his eyes. "Mmmm. That is heaven. Thanks."

He pushed the shake back across, and then said, "Want to try mine?"

"Sure." Kory took a taste in the same fashion. He let the frozen yogurt roll down his tongue, as sweet as the ice cream, but with an acrid flavor behind it. "You're right," he said.

"About what?"

"It's *almost* as good." Kory grinned.

He felt relaxed and loose, sitting across from the black fox in the ice cream parlor. They talked about school and friends, and he told Samaki about Sal and his string of girlfriends, and that led Samaki to ask if he was dating anyone.

"No," Kory said. "I got dumped last weekend." The words spilled out naturally. To his surprise, he felt only a small twinge as he spoke.

"Oh, I'm sorry."

"It's okay. It was probably for the best."

"What do you mean?" The fox's ears swiveled forward.

"Well, things just weren't going anywhere. I mean, I don't know if you're seeing anyone or if you know what I mean, but sometimes it's just like you stay together because you don't know what else to do, not because you want to."

"That sounds like the wrong reason to stay together."

"Yeah, it probably is." Kory sighed. "But it was easier than breaking up. Until someone else asked her to the prom."

"You didn't ask your girlfriend to the prom?"

"I didn't think of it until it was too late!"

Samaki chuckled. "Then 'scuse me, but I think you did the right thing."

Kory nodded. "I know. But it's not easy." He looked up at the fox. "You seeing someone?"

Samaki shook his head. "Nah."

"Really? I'da thought the vixens would be beating down your door."

"Why?" The fox tilted his head. Kory began to feel a little warm. He took a drink to stall.

"Well, you're an athlete. You used to be, anyway, and you still...I mean, all the jocks in our school have women hanging around them like...like a cloud of comets or something. You never know which one is going to be coming close at any particular moment, but they're always there."

Samaki leaned back and laughed. "That's great. I'll have to remember that one. No, the track team rates pretty far down on the list. Plus, uh…" He hesitated, taking another drink of his shake.

The nagging suspicions about Samaki returned. Kory didn't want Samaki to tell him he was gay, not now. It would ruin this nice moment. He changed the subject before Samaki put his shake down. "How long have you been coming here?"

"Oh, years. My mom and dad used to take us out here for a treat, and when I starting working, I always put aside enough for one shake a week."

"What's your job?"

"I help stock at the grocery store on weekends."

"I had a summer job at my mom's office, just doing filing and stuff. She won't let me work during the school year, though."

"Too bad." By now, Kory recognized Samaki's gentle sarcasm.

"Yeah, I…oh, no." He'd glanced up to his right. The clock on the wall read 10:13.

Samaki pushed his shake aside. "Come on," he said, jumping to his feet. "We can make it if we run."

"Maybe you can," Kory said, but he got up anyway, and waved to the goat as they ran for the door. "Nice to meet you!"

"Come back soon!" Chuck the goat said as the door swung closed behind them.

They ran together down the dark street, paws slapping the sidewalk in time. Kory, a few paces behind the fox, admired the fluid grace with which he strode, and the billowing of his tail behind him. *I bet he'd be a track star if he put his mind to it*, he said to himself. He felt clumsy and awkward by comparison, his tail a heavy weight behind him. It was very useful in swimming, but a burden to run with.

They dashed around the corner. The bus sat idling at the stop. I'll never make it, Kory thought despairingly, but the bus stayed there as they drew closer, and closer. Then it started up with a rough cough, lurched forward, and pulled away just as Samaki reached the back corner and slapped it with a paw, yelling, "Wait! Wait!"

To no avail. The bus chugged down the street. They saw it stop two blocks down, as if taunting them to follow, but Kory was already winded. He panted hard, paws on his knees.

"I'm sorry," Samaki said, his long tail curled under his legs. "Maybe my mom can drive you home."

"It's okay," Kory puffed. "There's…another bus…fifteen minutes. I'll be a little late."

"I'm sure she wouldn't mind. We're about a fifteen minute walk from here, and then it'd be about half an hour."

Kory considered. His mom would freak out, absolutely have a conniption, if she found out he'd taken a ride with a strange woman. Strange, to his mother, was anyone she hadn't shared a meal with. But his mom didn't have to find out. And he would get to hang out with Samaki a bit longer. "Okay," he said.

The fox's muzzle lit up with a bright smile. He put a paw on the otter's shoulder, rubbing briefly. "Great! Come on, this way."

They walked down the street together at a more leisurely pace, through a few blocks of the main shopping district, passing only a few people. Samaki turned down a dark street and strode confidently ahead, his light shirt and white tailtip bobbing ghostlike in the darkness. Kory took a couple steps in and hesitated, letting his eyes adjust. He heard the fox's steps stop, and saw eyeshine as Samaki turned.

"Oh, you don't have good night vision, do you? I'm sorry. Here." He reached out a paw. "It's just this one stretch. It's a shortcut."

Kory placed his paw in the fox's and felt the warm pads close around his fingers. The warmth was nice in the night air.

"It's not dangerous," Samaki said as he padded slowly down the street. Kory felt more confident with the fox's paw around his, and matched his pace. "The people who live on this street are all nocturnals—foxes, raccoons, mice, possums, one skunk family down that way--so they petitioned the city to get the street lights turned off on the street. It's not dangerous, either. They do a neighborhood watch. A couple years ago there were some drug dealers that tried to set up shop here, but they ran 'em off."

Drug dealers, like gay people, were something Kory read about online or heard about in health class, not something that merited only a casual offhand mention. "Are there a lot of drugs around here?"

"'Bout average, I guess," Samaki said, and Kory felt him shrug. "I don't bother with 'em."

After a long pause, the fox said, "You ever try 'em?"

"Jeez, no!" Kory shook his head. "I heard about one kid in my class, this mouse who tried some stuff, but I didn't know him real well. None of my friends ever had any."

"I know some guys on the football team who tried some steroids."

"Does that stuff really work?"

Samaki shook his head. His form was visible now as a dark patch in the grey twilight at the end of the dark street, resolving as they stepped further into light. "I guess it does, sort of. If that's what you want."

Streetlights, lit here, shone softly on a quiet, residential street that reminded Kory of his own, scaled down: well-trimmed lawns and low white fences bordered a small cottage. Plants and bird feeders adorned wood-fenced balconies on a four-unit apartment building. Kory hadn't seen many apartment buildings in his neighborhood. "Like budding houses, waiting to fully blossom," he said, inspired by the sight.

"That's great," Samaki said. "I really like that."

"Oh, it's just a thought," Kory said.

"It's a nice image," the fox said, and Kory shrugged.

"I used to know a kid in one of those apartments, but he moved away," Samaki said after a moment.

Walking past the building, the otter saw a masked face in one of the windows looking out at him, and realized that he was still holding onto Samaki's paw. He let go, as casually as he could, and Samaki didn't comment. Kory stuck his paw in his pocket.

"Just around here," Samaki said as they reached the end of the next block. They crossed the narrow street at the stop sign and walked half a block down to a small house with an old VW Fox in the driveway. Samaki led Kory up a small flight of wooden steps onto a white painted porch. Lights burned in the first story and the television flickered with a low murmur, but the second floor was all dark. As the fox opened the front door, Kory smelled the musk of several foxes, strong but not unpleasant.

"Hi, guys," Samaki called softly as he walked into a narrow hallway, leaning against an open door. Kory's paws sank into plush carpet, clean but worn. Over Samaki's shoulder, in another room, he could see the arm of a sofa and a television set showing an old movie he didn't recognize. He looked around the hall at the framed art prints, not as large or as elaborate as the ones his mother owned, but interesting: a photo of a hillside pocked with dark holes and red foxes, a still life with brilliant purple flowers, a family portrait where Samaki stood out black in a sea of red. A stairway directly in front of him led up into darkness, and the room to his left that smelled strongly of food was also dark. Before he could look around any longer, Samaki grabbed his paw and pulled him into the living room.

"Who's your guest, hon?" a female voice said from the couch before Kory even made it into the room. He walked in and saw a short, slender red fox on the couch, leaning against a pillow, the television reflected in her eyes. She turned to look at Kory and gave him a broad smile, then paused the movie and got up, smoothing down her jeans. She wore a blue shirt with a faded flower pattern on it and had several beads of various colors woven into the fur between her ears.

"Hi, dear. I'm Samaki's mother, Mrs. Roden." She said it "road-in."

"This is Kory, Mom," Samaki said. His tail was swinging from side to side.

"Hi," Kory said, and stuck out a paw. "Pleasure to meet you, ma'am."

She smiled and took his paw. She was barely as tall as he was. "The one from the pool, right? Pleased to meet you too, Kory. I didn't expect company this late."

"Kory missed his bus, Mom," Samaki said, his ears twitching at the mention of the pool. "Can you give him a ride home?"

"I think so, sure. Let me find my keys and leave a note for your father in case he comes home while we're gone. Samaki, you'll stay here to watch the kits." She walked over to a side table and rummaged through her purse.

"Do I have to, Mom? They're asleep, they'll be okay."

She considered that only for a moment. "No. I don't know when your father will be home."

"Oh, all right." He sighed. "Thanks for coming down, Kory."

"Thanks for the movie," Kory said, and smiled. "I'll talk to ya soon."

"Bet on it." The fox's tail was wagging, and he gave Kory a good shake of the paw that made Kory think of the dark street they'd walked down, paw in paw.

"Kory, where do you live?" Mrs. Roden said, closing the door behind them.

"Over in Westmont," he said. "On Strawberry Lane back of Lincoln Highway."

"I know about where that is, but you'll have to guide me when we get close." The vixen smiled. "You want to call your mom and tell her you'll be a little late, Kory?"

"Uh, no, that's okay." Kory would then have to explain where he was calling from and why it was going to take him half an hour to get across town. "I think we can make it in time."

Mrs. Roden laughed. "I appreciate your trust," she said. "All right, here we go."

Kory slid into the passenger seat and drew the seatbelt across, looking around the car as he did. There were several bare patches on the seat itself, and both the seat and the back of the driver's seat that he could see bore numerous claw marks and gouges. Kory pulled the seatbelt across himself, aware of the strong foxy smell in the car that was older and deeper than just Samaki and his mother. He inhaled again, searching for Samaki's scent, but it was hard to pick out of the mixture.

"So how was the movie?" Mrs. Roden asked, backing down the drive.

"Terrible," Kory said. "We had a great time."

"So you like bad movies too?"

"I liked this one," Kory said. "We had a lot of fun."

"You don't go to Hilltown P.S., do you?"

"No. Carter High."

"How do you like it?" She turned onto the main street.

"It's okay."

She glanced at him. "How's your head feeling?"

He shrugged. "Really, it was nothing. I wasn't used to the smaller pool."

"Samaki was really worried. I don't see any sign of swelling, though." She asked him about symptoms for a few minutes, and Kory remembered that she was a nurse. He asked about her job and the hospital where she worked, until his exit came up, when he had to focus on directions.

Kory guided her through the small suburban maze and to his driveway. The larger, nicer houses on his street loomed ostentatiously to him after walking through the smaller, pushed-together houses on Samaki's. Mrs. Roden only said, "Such a pretty lawn," her admiration free of jealousy as far as Kory could tell.

"Thanks so much for the ride, Mrs. Roden," he said when they stopped.

"You're very welcome, Kory. Come back and visit with us sometime. Samaki's been telling us about you and we'd be happy to have you over."

Kory grinned widely. "I'd like that. Thanks again.," he said, getting out and waving.

Mrs. Roden waited while he walked up the driveway and then left as he tried the door and found it open. He waited until they'd rounded the corner and glanced at his phone before opening the door. Good: 10:54. He sighed with relief and walked into his house.

As he closed the door, he heard his mother call from the living room. "Kory?"

She was sitting on the couch, paws folded in her lap. Only the lamp on the end table was lit; the circle of light threw shadows across her muzzle. Something was wrong; he knew it immediately, even before she said, slowly, "Sal came by looking for you."

It took him a moment to remember that he'd told her he was going out with Sal. "Mom..."

She turned large brown eyes on him. "Kory..." The words were difficult for her to get out. "Are you...are you on drugs?"

"Mom! No!"

"I know you've been going through a difficult time, losing Jenny. It's natural for a young man to feel alienated and turn to sinful things in an attempt to feel better. We can get help for you. There's a group I read about, they have a wonderful center and it's just ten miles away. They put you together with other boys going through similar problems." Now the words were spilling out unchecked.

"I'm not on drugs, Mom." He took a step forward. "Really."

"Then why..." She sniffed the air. "You smell like skunks."

"It's not skunk, it's foxes," he said, annoyed.

"Well," she said. "You're grounded for a week for lying to me. Now tell me the truth."

He said, "Mommmm..." to buy time while he figured out the minimum he needed to tell her.

"The truth, Kory, or it'll be another week at least."

Across the water, Nick's door cracked open. The light was off, but he knew his brother was listening. "I went out to a movie, Mom, just not with Sal."

"Whom did you go with, then?"

He could feel the current of the conversation, tugging him inexorably towards what he knew would be the result. He battled it anyway. "This other friend of mine."

"What's his name?"

He stalled for time. "You don't know him."

"That's why I'm asking you. What's his name?"

"Samaki."

"Samaki what?"

"Roden."

She mulled the name over in her head. "I don't know him."

"I told you," he said.

"Don't talk back to me, cub," she said. "Is he a school friend?"

"Not really." He squirmed under her stare. "No."

"I see. Where did you meet him? It wasn't church."

"No. At the pool."

"Hm." He could see her thoughts; the pool was at least a place you had to pay to get in, and it was a Good Place. "When was this?"

"Last weekend. We talked on the phone a bit and he invited me to a movie tonight."

"Which movie?" She said it casually, but Kory wasn't fooled.

"I told you," he said, uncomfortably aware of the ticket stub in his pocket. "'Girlie Men.'"

She relaxed a little more, and then said, "Last weekend...so it was at the municipal pool."

"Uh...yes." He saw her stiffen again. The municipal pool was not as Good a Place as Caspian. "He's really nice, Mom. We talk about schoolwork. We have a lot of the same subjects."

"What school does he go to?"

"The public school."

She didn't like that either. "There's a lot of drugs down there." He didn't respond to that. "So you've been helping him out? I'm sure your classes are more advanced than his."

They weren't, but Kory realized that she thought Carter was supposed to be better than the Public School System, even though it was part of it. "Uh...yeah."

"The Lord does smile on charity," she mused. Kory sighed. At this point, the worse of the two outcomes had been avoided. She would let him remain friends with Samaki. But she would want to meet him. And that meant dinner.

"Invite him to dinner next Friday night," she said. "I don't like not knowing your friends."

"All right," he said immediately.

"I just worry about you boys, growing up without a father. I can't be here all the time for you."

"I know, Mom," he said.

"I worry because I love you, Kory. You know that, right?"

"You and God, Mom."

Now her muzzle broke into a smile. "That's right." She stood up and hugged him. "Oof. Go clean that stink off you before you go to bed. And give me your cell phone."

Whatever lightness had crept into Kory's mood vanished. He liked the smell, and he didn't intend to wash before bed. He pulled the phone out of his pocket and handed it to her. "Good night, Mom."

"Good night, sweetheart." She kissed him on the nose, since she couldn't reach the top of his head any more. "Whew!" She waved at the air in front of her nose. "I hope he'll wash before he comes over."

Kory rolled his eyes and walked across the little bridge to his room. When he climbed into bed, he breathed in the scent of the foxes on his fur, and carried it into his dreams.

He was sitting in school with Samaki, and they were in a history lesson. He realized that he wasn't wearing any pants, and he hoped the fox wouldn't notice. Then he saw the fox's thick tail fall away from his lap, and saw that the fox was naked as well, his white patch gleaming in the midst of his black fur. Samaki was smiling at him. "You can touch if you want," he said softly.

"What about the teacher?" Kory said back.

"Let's teach each other," Samaki said.

Kory reached over and touched the gleaming white fur, and then felt the fox in his paw. He felt the same warmth he felt when holding the fox's paw, and an extra jolt. "It's all right," Samaki said, and Kory looked deep into the violet eyes.

"You can touch me too," he said.

The fox wasted no time, his paw reaching over. Kory felt an electric thrill and shuddered, and jerked awake in bed, panting.

His room was dark save for the stars on his ceiling and their reflection in the water. He looked around, the residue of the dream pounding strongly through him. It took him a minute to slide back from the dream world, but his body took longer. What did that mean? He didn't even know if the fox was gay. Was he? He scrabbled through his mind to recall the psychology chapter of his social studies class. Was it rationalization or projection if he was suspicious that the fox was gay because it was really what he wanted?

That was ridiculous, though. It was just a dream, it didn't mean that that was really inside him or anything.

But his body was still responding to the dream, no matter how much he thought about it. That doesn't prove anything, he told himself. I wake up like this most mornings. It's not related to the dream.

Even so, he tossed and turned until he looked up and realized that dawn had crept up on him without him realizing it. He went for a swim to clear his head, and when he came back and logged in, he found an e-mail from Samaki asking if he'd gotten home in time. Seeing the words typed on the screen, he could almost hear the fox's voice, and that brought back the memory of his dream. In the daylight, fully awake, it seemed much sillier to be worried that the dream represented secret desires inside him. Samaki was a friend, that was all.

He sent a quick response telling Samaki about his grounding and the invitation to dinner, and was excited to get a quick answer back. The fox must have been on the computer checking first thing in the morning. He said he would ask about dinner but he thought it would be okay, and sympathized on the cell phone loss, offering to be online at certain times in the evening so they could set up a chat. Kory thanked God for the small favor of his mother not yet knowing about IM.

Sal came over in the afternoon, but was intercepted by Kory's mother at the door. He heard only her sharp, "I'm sorry, Sal, Kory's grounded and can't have guests." He turned up the music in his room and nodded silently when she came to his room later to tell him about the visit.

Homework occupied him for only part of the day, even when he tried to work on some things due beyond Monday. He wasn't supposed to play games or surf the web when he was grounded, but his mother rarely checked and he felt he was being punished enough to allow himself a little bit of surfing.

It wasn't until that night, lying in bed, that the images of the dream flashed through his head again, unbidden yet unstoppable. *"Let's teach ourselves." A long, black tail whose white tip traced an arc to the ground. White island in a black sea. "You can touch." The feeling in his paw.*

His body strained painfully, feeling like it was about to burst. Fists at his sides, he stared at the ceiling, trying to focus on something else. If he touched himself while he was thinking about the fox, that would make his whole dilemma much worse. He tried to remember Jenny, the way her body had felt, but he kept seeing Samaki over and over, and finally he knew if he didn't do something, he would lie awake all night. He slid his paw inside his pajamas and gave himself a quick, panting release. After that, sleep came quickly and was dreamless. But the morning was troubled.

He got ready for church, the dream still on his mind. He knew that there was a whole parcel of sin tied up in having impure thoughts, let alone about other boys, and now it was worse because he'd not only had the thoughts, he'd acted on them. Kind of. Church, he hoped, would help him clear his mind and gain some perspective.

After Mass, his mother habitually stayed to talk with the priest, a tall Dall sheep who liked to be called "Father Joe." He'd come to their church only a couple years ago, single-handedly changing Kory's view of church from a duty to something engaging to be looked forward to. Nick still found the sermons boring, but Kory loved the sheep's animated manner and found himself reflecting on the sermons during the week. It helped that Father Joe never preached the doom and gloom that Kory'd grown up with, but focused instead on self-improvement and helping others.

Kory had, in fact, been somewhat startled to find that his mother preferred Father Green, the older priest, to Father Joe, who was part of what she disparagingly called "the new church." Over the past two years, her complaints had fallen off as she'd spoken to him more often. Now, she and the Jeffersons, a wolf couple who lived a few blocks from them, were talking to him about an upcoming bake sale. Normally, Kory would have followed Nick outside, but now he loitered by the door, hoping to get a moment alone with the priest before leaving. After his mother and Mrs.

Jefferson started in on who would bring the bran cakes, he lost his nerve and turned to go.

Father Joe's deep voice stopped him. "Kory?"

He turned and saw the sheep's large, dark eyes and gentle smile. "Yes, Father?"

"Would you help me pick up the hymnals? I could use an extra paw."

Kory shuffled. "Uh..."

"He'd be glad to," his mother said, pushing him towards the priest. "Go on, Kory, we'll be outside when you're done. Thank you, Father Joe."

"God bless, ladies, Mr. Jefferson," the sheep said, bowing his large curved horns gracefully.

The church was empty except for Kory and Father Joe once his mother left, still chattering with the Jeffersons. The sheep waved Kory down one row while he took the next one forward, keeping pace with the young otter as they collected the books. "So how's it going, Kory?"

"Okay." Kory's stomach was churning. One second he wanted to blurt out his problem, the next he didn't want to say anything.

"School all right?" Father Joe gathered books easily into his large arms.

"Yeah."

They reached the end of the pews and circled around to the next two. Father Joe didn't look at Kory, just walked along the row picking up books. "Anything bothering you?"

Kory's throat seemed to close up. He tried to say, "Not really," but it came out as a squeaking sound. He clamped his mouth shut, embarrassed, and ducked his head.

"It seemed like you wanted to talk to me. Are you having doubts about faith?"

"Uh, no." He breathed a little more easily.

"Rats. I was hoping. That would be an easy one." The sheep looked down with a smile that Kory couldn't help answering. "Problems at home? A lot of children with single parents have problems. It's nothing to be ashamed of."

"Oh, it's not that...I mean, it's okay." He reached the end of the pew and they turned one more time.

"Your mother really wants the best for you." Father Joe examined one of the hymnals before adding it to his stack. "Sometimes what parents think is best isn't always what kids think is best."

Kory nodded. "I know."

"So...is one of your friends doing something you think is wrong, and asked you to join them? Maybe you're wondering whether to turn them in, if it's illegal, but you still want to be a good friend?"

Kory shook his head. "No."

They turned to start the frontmost two rows. "Well," Father Joe said, "I do greatly appreciate your help with this, and I wish I could help you in return. But we're down to the last two rows, and if it's not faith, family, or friends, I'm not sure what's left. I can't imagine you'd come to me with girl trouble." His eyes twinkled a bit as he said that.

"No," Kory said. The comfortable banter helped him make up his mind. "I had...a dream," he said.

"Oh, dreams." Father Joe shook his head. "Nightmare?"

Kory shook his head. "Not really."

They reached the end of the pew and stood silently for a few moments as he struggled to find words. "It was about...doing something...I don't think I want to, but it was..."

"But in the dream, you enjoyed it?" Father Joe said gently. "And now you're wondering if that means you would enjoy it outside the dream?"

Kory stared at the sheep. His mouth had gone very dry.

"It wasn't anything violent, was it? No, I don't think..." and then he paused. "Did you have a dream about another boy?"

Kory felt his legs shake. "No!" he said, hearing the lie echo in the large space of the church.

Father Joe looked right at him. "It's all right to have dreams, Kory," he said. "They're messages, but they don't always mean what they show on the surface. Sometimes they're just God's way of asking us to think about some part of our life. I have some duties to attend to now, but if you want to talk more, come see me next Saturday morning, okay? I'll clear some time for you."

"Okay," Kory whispered, though all he wanted to do was run for the exit.

Father Joe put a hand on his shoulder. "Adolescence is a confusing time, Kory. Don't be afraid to ask for help."

"Okay," Kory said again, "thanks." He was afraid to say any more.

"Thank you for the help with the hymnals." Father Joe smiled and released his shoulder. "Don't worry, Kory. It was just a dream."

Kory nodded and backed into the pew, then turned and walked quickly out the door.

He nodded at his mother when she asked if he wanted tuna fish for lunch, and mumbled, "Nothing," when she asked what he'd talked about with Father Joe. He was remembering all the stories about Catholic priests molesting young boys and suddenly wondered why Father Joe was so eager to set aside time for him. He didn't seem like that sort, but then he supposed that they never did, that boys were easy prey for someone they felt they could trust.

But it didn't matter, because he wasn't gay.

On Monday morning, he found that explaining to Father Joe had been a walk in the park compared to explaining to Sal.

"So you blew me off for another guy," the other otter said after Kory had told him what happened, sitting alone in a corner of the cafeteria eating lunch.

Kory sighed. "I forgot," he said again. "I'm sorry."

"Look, none of the guys are picking sides or anything with you and Jenny. Debbie asked where you were Saturday."

He hadn't felt any great desire to hang out with the old group, but it hadn't occurred to Kory that he might not be able to. The thought sat uncomfortably in him. "Thanks."

"So why didn't you tell me about this guy? Is he, like, a spaz or something?"

"No, he's really cool." Kory told Sal about the movie, about the books they'd talked about, about the conversations over the phone and the ice cream parlor.

"You meet this guy, what, a week ago and suddenly he's your best friend?"

"Yeah, he's my best friend," Kory snapped. "I went back in time and grew up with him."

Sal squinted at him. "Hang on...a movie? Ice cream? That sounds like a date."

"Jesus, no!" Kory covered his mouth and looked around, but nobody was paying attention. Not that anyone in the school cared about taking the Lord's name in vain anymore.

"All right, all right," Sal said, "Just funnin' with ya." He started telling Kory about his weekend and what he and Debbie had done, to which Kory made as little response as he felt he could get away with.

Things with Sal remained cool all week, but the thugs who'd been harassing him about the poem seemed to finally grow tired of it, so Kory felt that things had balanced out. He talked with Samaki over IM and e-mail during the week, and got increasingly nervous about the fox's visit Friday night, for no reason he could determine. If his mom didn't like Samaki, it wouldn't be the end of the world.

Nevertheless, he paced around his room Friday evening as six o'clock drew nearer, and at 6:01 he began hovering in the living room, watching the doorway. When the doorbell finally rang two minutes later, Kory ran the five steps to the door and flung it open.

Mrs. Roden wore a pale blue dress and a bright smile. Samaki stood to her left, grinning in a collared white shirt and khaki slacks. Behind her, holding onto one black paw, was a small vixen who looked to be about four. She peered shyly at Kory from behind her mother's tail.

"Hi, Mrs. Roden. Hi, Samaki," Kory grinned.

"This is Mariatu," Mrs. Roden said. "Come say hi, sweetie."

Kory grinned, ushering them into the foyer. After some coaxing, Mariatu was persuaded to remove the paw from her muzzle and say a soft "hi."

"I shouldn't stay too long," Mrs. Roden said. "I left Ajani and Kasim out in the car."

Kory's mother came out and greeted the brush of foxes, and Kory was glad to see her smile as Samaki shook her paw very politely. He noticed that the black fox had combed his fur and was wearing some sort of flowery scent to conceal his musk.

His mother said, "Welcome, Samaki," but then turned to Mrs. Roden, whom she could look in the eye. "It's so nice to meet you. Kory doesn't tell me anything," she said.

"Oh, at that age they can be very difficult," Mrs. Roden said, ruffling Samaki's headfur. "Is he your only?"

"No, he has a younger brother. I don't know where Nick is."

"Probably in his room." Kory said, halfway to showing Samaki the living room.

"Well, I'm sure he'll be out eventually. So you live over in downtown, Kory tells me."

"That's right." Mrs. Roden settled against the wall. "Samaki, could you go keep an eye on your brothers?"

"Sure, Mom. Kory, wanna meet 'em?"

"Yeah." Kory followed the fox outside, listening to his mother lob more questions at Mrs. Roden.

"How you doing?" he asked, aware that he was wearing a big grin.

"Doing good. Glad to see you." The fox's tail brushed his as it wagged.

"Me too." He saw the old Fox at the foot of his driveway and a couple shapes moving around inside. Snarls and yips floated out through the open window.

Samaki trotted the last few steps. "Hey, stinkers, cut it out!" he called as he got near the car.

Two reddish muzzles poked out of the open window. "Where's mom?" the older one said. He looked about Nick's age.

"She's talking to Kory's mom. She told me to make sure you don't rip each other's tails off while she's gone."

The other cub, about eight, said, "Why did Mariatu get to go in and we hadda wait in the car?"

"Because you smell so bad," the older one said, kicking off an exchange of "Shut up!" between the two of them, which Samaki broke up with a grin to Kory.

"Hey, you two. Say hi to Kory."

"Hi." "Hi, Kory."

"Hi," Kory said. "You guys are..."

"Ajani," said the older one.

"I'm Kasim," the younger said, and tilted his head. "Are you gonna be Samaki's boyfriend?"

In the silence that followed this remark, Samaki's ears folded back, and Kasim said, "Ow!" as Ajani elbowed him and said, "Shut up, dipwad!"

"What?" Kasim said.

"No, he's not," Samaki said. "Why don't you both sit down now?"

They grumbled, but did so. The black fox turned to Kory. "Little brothers," he said with a grin that looked just a little forced.

"I know how it is," Kory said. "Wait 'til you meet Nick."

"Yeah." Samaki reached back and scratched his ear. He looked into the car, lowering his voice so they couldn't hear. "I love 'em, though."

Kory looked in, too, at the four shining eyes looking out at them. "They're cute. Are you the oldest?"

"Now I am. My sister, Kande, she's off at college."

"Where's she going?" Kory itched to ask him about his brother's remark, his heart speeding up a bit, but if Samaki didn't want to talk about it, he wasn't going to bring it up.

"State. Main campus, though, not Hilltown campus."

"That's cool."

"You looked at colleges yet?"

Kory shrugged a bit. "Mom sent me some links."

"I was thinking about—"

The door opened before the fox could finish his sentence. His mother and Mariatu walked out, with Kory's mother behind them. Mrs. Roden's words floated down to them. "Thank you so much, and thank you for having Samaki over."

"Pleasure to meet you," Kory's mother said, remaining at the door as the vixen waved and then walked down the driveway.

"I get to sit in front," Ajani said from inside the car, scrambling through the two front seats and getting halfway before his brother grabbed his tail. Ajani yelped.

Samaki reached in to hold Kasim. "Hey," he said, "Mom said Ajani could sit in front."

"I don't wanna be in back alone with her," Kasim said sulkily.

"She's your sister," Samaki said, and ruffled his ears.

Mrs. Roden reached them and opened the door. "Scoot over, Kasim, and help your sister in." Kasim slid across the seat and didn't otherwise move at first, then grudgingly reached out a paw, which Mariatu took. She kept looking at Kory with wide eyes, and then smiled and waved her other paw and said, "Bye bye."

"Bye," Kory said. "It was really nice to meet you."

She giggled as she climbed into the back seat, where she sat and watched him.

"Bye, Sammy," Mrs. Roden said, and kissed him on the muzzle. "Mrs. Hedley's going to drive you back home. That way I don't have to wait for your father to come home to come pick you up. I know you know the way, Kory, but I wrote down directions for her anyway."

"Okay," Kory said. "Thanks for letting Samaki come to dinner."

The vixen laughed, and her eyes sparkled as she put a paw on Kory's arm. "Oh, bless you, Kory, but I couldn't have kept him away. I think he'd have snuck out and taken the bus if he had to."

"Mom!" Samaki protested.

"Sorry, dear," Mrs. Roden said, but she gave Kory a quick wink and he grinned back widely. "I told your mother we want to have you over for dinner too, maybe next week or the week after."

"Thanks." The wink made Kory feel warm and confident. "I'd love to."

"All right then. Be good!" She waved to them and got in the car.

They waited until she'd rounded the corner and then went inside, where the smell of salmon was already pervading the house.

Nick showed up, dressed but still damp, right as the rest of them were sitting down at the table. When his mother had finished serving the salmon, she started on Samaki, asking him about his school and his family before she'd even gotten all the food on the table.

"And what does your father do?" she asked as soon as they'd said the "Amen," in which Kory saw Samaki join.

"He works at the Ford factory outside town," Samaki said, "and over at the Hilltown campus of the state U. at night."

"Oh? What does he do at the University?" Kory saw his mother's interest perk up a little.

"He's a Facilities Maintenance Technician," Samaki said. "He started there so he could get benefits for my sister to go to State."

"That's great." They ate in silence a little longer. "What's your sister studying?"

"Sociology," Samaki responded promptly.

"Do you know what you want to study?"

"Not yet." He smiled. "I'm interested in lots of things. Journalism maybe."

"Are you going to go to State too?"

"Probably." He gulped down a bite of fish. "This fish is terrific, Mrs. Hedley."

"Thank you." She smiled, but Kory saw her muzzle purse slightly. State was not one of the colleges she'd sent him to look at.

Over the rest of the meal, she asked about his church, his neighborhood, his family, and his school. Kory and Samaki told her how much overlap there was in their subjects, and Samaki said he was taking some advanced work in school, which she praised him for.

He remained poised, polite, and proper throughout the meal, and actually seemed to be enjoying talking to Kory's mother. Nick stayed quiet for the entire meal, except to ask to be excused, and Kory didn't say much more. He felt a strong relief when his mother finally said, "Well, you boys probably don't want to sit here talking to me all night. Go on. I'll clean up, Kory."

"Want me to send Nick in?"

She shook her head. "No, I'll be all right."

"Thanks for dinner, Mrs. Hedley," Samaki said. "It was delicious."

"Thank you, Samaki," she said. "Go on, go play."

"I think it is *so* cool that you have a pool inside your house," Samaki said as they walked back through the living room. He crouched by the edge and trailed his paw in the water, his tail resting on the living room carpet. "Why would you ever go out to a pool?"

"To get away," Kory said, trying not to remember Samaki crouching in his swimsuit at the side of the municipal pool. "This pool's small, too. Even the municipal is bigger."

"Caspian's pretty big, eh?" Samaki stood up. "I love this bridge, too. It's like a little Japanese garden."

Kory grinned. "Watch your footing. It's always wet."

"A railing would be nice," the fox said.

"Then we couldn't jump up onto the bridge from the water. I used to put my brother in jail under the bridge."

Samaki laughed, stepping safely onto the far side between Kory's and Nick's doors. "I used to make my brothers be chickens and put them in the 'coop'."

Kory felt a flutter of worry, opening the door to his room. He watched Samaki's muzzle as the fox stepped in and looked around, watched the violet eyes take in the posters, the computer desk, the bed, and the pool.

"This is awesome," Samaki said. "The pool comes in here, too. So you can just slip in and out through the water. It's like having a secret base!"

"Everyone else can get in, too," Kory pointed out.

Samaki grinned at him, padding from one side of the room to the other, looking at everything, his tail wagging. "I think it's really cool."

Kory saw only the room he'd grown up in. Then he looked again at Samaki's expression and looked around and saw the pool, the posters, the computer, and slowly, he smiled.

Samaki ran his fingers along the posters on the wall. "Cool dragon," he said with a grin, his tail wagging. "ELO... haven't heard them. Good?"

"I thought everyone knew them." Kory turned around to put on ELO's Greatest Hits, and when he turned back, Samaki was at his computer desk, looking at a scrap of paper. "Hey, uh..."

The fox read slowly, "Water spills from the morning / coating the grass to start the day / the night is washed away ..." He looked up. "That's good. You wouldn't let me read any of your poems before."

"Now you know why," Kory took the paper from him. "That's not good, really. Just some stuff I was scribbling."

"It is good." Samaki looked around. "You have anything else?"

Kory weighed the question. "I've got a couple things."

"I'll show you some of the stuff I wrote, if you show me more poems." The black fox leaned against Kory's desk and swished his tail.

"The articles you were talking about for the yearbook?"

Samaki nodded. "And some stuff from the school paper." He flicked an ear. "This is ELO? I like this song. I never knew who it was."

Kory nodded, and sat down at the computer. He stalled, pretending to decide which files to open, really wondering what he should show the fox. He badly wanted to show him *the* poem, but the fox might misinterpret it. After all, he hadn't even shown it to Jenny.

Of course, he hadn't wanted to.

No, he would start with some earlier ones, about dragons and swimming. Those weren't too bad. He pulled them up and let Samaki sit down.

While the fox leaned forward, eyes scanning the screen, Kory paced behind him. *If he doesn't like them,* he told himself, *it's okay, a lot of people don't like poetry.* He found himself pressing his paws together, and sat down on his bed, trying not to look anxiously at the fox and failing.

Samaki turned his head and saw Kory on the bed. He smiled, warm eyes setting Kory at ease before he even spoke. "They're good. I like them."

"Really?"

"Yeah! Why would I lie?" The fox chuckled. "You could enter a poetry contest or something. This is as good as anything I've seen in our school."

At the mention of a contest, Kory stiffened. "I, uh...I don't think I'm good enough to win a contest," he said.

"Sure you are," Samaki said. "I'll make it my mission to make you believe in yourself enough to win a poetry contest. I hate seeing talent go to waste."

"No, really, I..."

The fox slid from the chair and was sitting next to Kory on the bed in a moment. "I told you, I think if you're good at something, you shouldn't be embarrassed about it."

The proximity of the fox brought his musky scent back to Kory, full force. The otter tried to ignore it, but couldn't help jumping a little when the fluffy black tail brushed his long brown tail on the bed. His whiskers twitched, the dream returning to his mind until he forced it out. *Don't think about that now, are you insane??* But he had to keep his paws held firmly in his lap to keep them from wandering over to the soft black fur.

"It's just not..." He struggled for words, forcing his other thoughts down. "You're the first person who's really liked them."

"Your mom doesn't?" Samaki spoke softly.

Talking about his mom helped. "Oh, mom doesn't count. I could write 'the cat sat on the fat mat' and she'd think it was Milton. I mean, my friends...you know, maybe if I wrote poems about sports, or boobs..."

The fox laughed, and patted his knee. "You have to write about things you're interested in."

The warm paw on his knee, the scent, the brush of the tail, and the residue of his dream were making Kory's jeans tight. "Strange Magic" was playing on his stereo. "I'm interested in boobs," he blurted out. "Uh...I mean..." He looked at Samaki's expression as the fox withdrew his paw. The vulpine muzzle was smiling, but the smile seemed forced and a little sad.

"Look, Kory," he said. "Uh...I didn't want to bring it up, but I don't want you thinking and wondering about what Kasim said..."

"It's okay," Kory said. His heart was pounding.

Samaki was quiet for a bit. "I'm not interested in boobs," he said. Only then did Kory register the stiffness in his posture and the way his paws were clenched together tightly. He realized how hard it must be for the fox to tell him that, harder than it had been for Kory to show the poems to him. He reached out and rested a paw on the black-furred wrist closest to him. He could feel the fox's quick pulse beneath the warm fur.

"I was wondering," he said. "It's okay. I don't care."

Samaki's shoulders sagged, his smile brightened. "Really?" And then he chuckled. "You mean you can tell?"

Kory grinned. "You were kinda hitting on me at the pool."

The fox's large ears flicked and violet eyes smiled. "I tried to be subtle. I figured if you were interested, you'd pick up on it, and if not, you wouldn't notice. Most straight guys couldn't even imagine another guy hitting on them."

"I had to ask," Kory admitted. "I wasn't sure."

Samaki laughed. "You asked someone? Who? Someone online?"

"No," and Kory now found himself embarrassed to admit that he'd asked Sal.

"Your mom?"

"Oh, no." Kory looked at the bedroom door and his smile faltered. "She'd freak."

"So who?" Samaki poked his side. "Come on."

"Hey!" Kory giggled. "My friend Sal."

"Sal?"

"He is an expert in flirting. I kind of pretended you were me and I was a girl…he said I was getting a lot better at flirting."

"I guess that's a compliment." The fox swished his tail against Kory's again, and the otter felt that shiver. His tail was sensitive, that was all. Jenny used to like to stroke it, too.

"If you want to take a compliment from a guy who goes to college bars to get laid…"

"I'll take whatever I can get." Samaki smiled. "Hey. I appreciate you being cool. I know it could be awkward and all. But really, I won't hit on you any more."

"Okay." For some reason, Kory's heart was still racing. His paw still rested on the fox's wrist, warm black fur under his pads. He was remembering the fox taking his paw down that dark street.

"Too bad," he thought he heard Samaki murmur, and the fox certainly had a coy smile on his muzzle as if he'd said something like that. But Kory couldn't be sure, and the next thing Samaki said was about *Foundation*, which he'd picked up and started to read. "It's interesting," he said, "This whole theory about predicting large group behavior."

Kory's heart slowly returned to a normal pace. "Cool to think about."

"What I want to know," Samaki said, "is what if you want to predict what just one person is gonna do? Or two?"

"Individuals are unpredictable," Kory said. "That was part of his point."

"Are they? Or is this Seldon guy just too full of himself to bother with them?" The violet eyes sparkled.

Kory laughed. "I'll have to ask the group about that."

"Your online one?"

"Yeah. Hey, did you want to join?"

"Maybe. What kind of stuff do you talk about?"

Kory scooted to the computer to show him some of the old messages, kicking off another round of conversation about *Foundation* and about the friends in the online group. Before they knew it, Kory's mother was knocking on the door to take Samaki home.

Kory scooted into the back seat with Samaki rather than ride shotgun, their tails bunched up on the seat between them. They started off talking about books again, but his mother intervened at the first pause in the conversation. She took up where she'd left off at dinner, and the half hour dragged on, Kory staring at the fox's white tailtip on the seat between them, forcing himself not to reach out and touch it. Twice he looked at Samaki and caught the fox looking back with a bright white grin as he answered some inane question or another.

At the Rodens' house, Kory got out to say goodbye. As they shook paws, Samaki said, "My mom was serious about you coming for dinner. Let's set up a time."

"Okay. I'll talk to my mom and work it out. Maybe next weekend."

"Sure. Hey, Kory…thanks again. For being cool." Samaki squeezed his paw.

"No problem," Kory said. "I don't want to find someone else to talk to about *Foundation*."

Samaki laughed and waved, walking back to his house. Kory watched his tail wagging behind him as his mother pulled away. He felt warm and good, a feeling that lasted exactly halfway home.

His mother was talking about how nice Samaki seemed, even though she hoped he wouldn't visit often because the smell lingered. That made Kory think of the scent as the fox had sat on his bed and told him he was gay. He started to wonder if they could remain friends, with one of them potentially interested in the other, even though Samaki had said he wouldn't push anything, and he didn't even know if the fox *was* interested in him. The lurking feeling that his body was interested, even if he thought he wasn't, made him shift uncomfortably in his seat. He stared morosely out the window. Samaki *is* gay, he thought. I acted like an idiot, when I could have asked him...what? Not that I wanted to try something, he thought, though he knew he was only saying that to reassure himself. His body knew what he wanted more than he would admit to himself. Whenever Samaki was around, it told him so, loud and clear.

If this happened every time he thought about Samaki, he might have to stop seeing the fox, and he enjoyed the fox's company more than he enjoyed being with any of his other friends. To cut himself off from that friendship felt wrong. But the alternative...he didn't, he couldn't.

He barely noticed when his mother handed him his cell phone. "I'm tired," he said, but instead of going to bed, he sat at his desk surfing the web, looking for anything about high school kids attracted to the same sex. The only postings that made it through the parental filter were both stories of boys in high school talking about how they'd realized that they were gay. One was a wolf; one was a muskrat. Both of them said the same things. *I liked looking at boys. Girls didn't do it for me. I finally had to admit to myself that I was gay.*

Frustrated, he switched off the computer. That's not me, he said to himself, pacing around the room. Finally, he undressed and dove into the water, letting its silence surround him. His mother rarely swam anymore, and Nick was already in bed, or else had snuck out as he often did, so he had the indoor pool to himself. He swam round and round in circles, thinking about nothing, rushing through the warmth and looking around at the uniform blue all around him.

After a ten minute swim, he really was too tired to continue. He climbed out and lay down on his mat on the floor, and fell asleep while he was drying off.

Everyone else had brought their swimsuit to the pool, but he was naked. If he got in the water, he thought, they wouldn't notice. And nobody seemed to, until it was time to do the couples swimming. He looked around and grabbed Jenny's wrist, but when he looked into her eyes, they were violet, and her muzzle was black and slender. "Hey," someone said, "are you gay or what?" No, no, he tried to say, but he was holding Samaki's wrist and they made him get out of the pool. But when he got to the locker room, Samaki was Father Joe, looking sternly at him. The sheep said, "you know better than that, Kory. It's only okay if you come see me." He made Kory lie down. "No, no," Kory moaned, shifting back and forth on his mat. The pool, the locker room, he could smell them, and he just had to get up...

Dazed, he opened his eyes, expecting to see the big sheep's horns. Instead he saw his ELO poster and felt his own mat under his damp fur. He got to his paws and knees and crawled into bed, where he pulled the covers around himself, shivering. His room was dark; his mother must have looked in on him and turned out the light. He closed his eyes, willing himself to get back to sleep, but as soon as he did he saw the locker room again. His eyes shot open. He tried tracing the patterns of the stars on his ceiling, but they brought him no rest.

Jenny had given him a small stuffed dragon to hold at night because they couldn't stay overnight together. He found it under the bed, where he'd kicked it weeks ago, but it gave him no comfort. Samaki's scent overwhelmed even the faint traces of Jenny's that Kory wasn't sure he wasn't imagining. Kory shoved the dragon away and pulled his pillow over his muzzle. It wasn't fair. He wasn't equal to this kind of temptation.

He didn't sleep. All night he stared at the ceiling, wondering if he would be fighting his body and its urges his whole life. If not, if he gave in…*would that be so bad?* whispered a voice into his head, as the serpent must have whispered to Eve, he thought. He remembered reading stories about people who'd given in to temptation, how it was the first step on a slippery slope that led them to ruin. I like girls, he said firmly back. He thought about the great times he'd had with Jenny when his mom was away, rolling around on the bed, and the voice came back and whispered, *they weren't that great, were they really?*

They were, he told himself firmly, and besides, I was never attracted to other guys. I never wanted to sleep with Sal.

Oh no? the voice mocked him. *What about that time at camp when you got him to go skinny-dipping?*

That wasn't…

Or the time you slept over at his place and managed to work it so you were in the same bed?

I was nine!

Or the time…

Stop!

He pressed his paws to his eyes, feeling the dampness leak out through the pressure in his head. Was it…could it be? Could it be that he wasn't upset about Jenny dumping him, not because he didn't love her, but because he didn't like girls? That the signs had been there his whole life that there had been this thing inside him, and he'd never known? He wished he'd never met the fox, never gone to the municipal pool.

He would find out how to fight this. The dream was just a dream. As the pearly light of morning crept through his windows, he decided to go see Father Joe.

The church was very different on Saturday morning. Empty of the Sunday crowds, it felt larger and more imposing, yet at the same time more personal because he was the only one there. Father Joe wasn't anywhere about, so Kory took a moment to look around.

He'd never been in the church by himself. For years, it was just the place where he was dragged every Sunday. In the last two years, he'd begun to see what his mother saw in it, a repository of strength for the troubled, guidance for wanderers, love for all. He rarely acknowledged it, because none of his friends talked about church except to lament the loss of a Sunday morning or to cut short a Saturday night. Now, standing alone in the light of the stained glass and beatific muzzles, he felt their love focused on him. He looked up to the rafters far above and took a moment to fortify himself. They will help me, he thought. This is my trial.

Towards the front of the church, he found a sign that showed the way to Father Joe's offices. They were actually in a small building beside the church, he discovered when he followed the signs and found himself outside. He knocked on the door and heard the sheep's cheery, "Come in."

Father Joe smiled and motioned for him to sit down. Warily, Kory did, taking the small stool closest to the modest desk, reading Father Joe's name on the simple nameplate. The crucifix on the wall to his left depicted a Dall sheep Jesus, but the portrait opposite was a popular rendition of Jesus Lion, with the medieval-style halo and a tear visible on the tawny cheek ruff.

"How are you, Kory?" The priest moderated his booming voice to the small quarters of the office.

His idea that Father Joe might want to take advantage of him seemed ridiculous now, in this placid and proper setting. "I'm okay," he said automatically, and then said, "well, not really." Fatigue pulled his shoulders down; he slumped in the chair, confused about what to say next.

"Want to tell me about your dream?"

"No." He couldn't talk about that with anyone, not yet. He had to start somewhere, though. "I want your help. I want to fight it."

The sheep's large yellow horns bobbed sympathetically. "Why don't you tell me what's been going on?"

"I met this guy...this fox...I want to stay friends with him, but I keep thinking...see, he told me he's...you know..." He hissed in frustration, one webbed paw squeezing the chair arm. "He's, you know, he doesn't like girls."

"He's gay," Father Joe said.

Kory met his eyes, seeing no judgment there, nothing but understanding. "Yeah. So anyway, he, uh, I really like talking with him, but not…"

"Did he make a pass at you?"

"No. Well, sort of, the first day we met, but not like touching or anything."

"Are you worried that he will?"

"No." He looked at the sheep, begging him to figure it out so he wouldn't have to say the words.

Father Joe inclined his head slightly. "Are you worried he might 'turn you gay'?"

Kory squirmed in the chair, looking away from Father Joe, but that turned him toward the crucifix, which was no better. "No. I mean, I keep thinking…but it's not his fault, I know people are just born that way."

"Do you think you might be gay?"

There it was. He looked in the other direction, at the Lion on the wall. "I still like girls," he said defiantly.

"Kory," Father Joe said gently. "This is a confusing time of life for you, and a confusing issue to be dealing with."

"I don't want to deal with it," he snapped. "I want to fight it. I know what the Church says."

The sheep's horns bobbed again. "I know what the Church's official position is. I also know how I want to minister to my flock." He reached into his desk and pushed a small card across the desk. "I happen to hold out hope that the Church will moderate its views. In the meantime, these people can help you out. It's a Catholic group. I know David." He tapped the card. "He used to be a priest. He felt he could better serve by leaving the Church, though it was a hard decision for him. He's a good wolf."

Kory stared at the card. He could read the words Dignity/USA on it, but nothing else from his position on the chair. He made no move to pick it up. "You're supposed to tell me I'm going to hell if I give in."

"Yes, I suppose, but if you knew that, you wouldn't have needed to come see me." The sheep looked shrewdly at him. "You came here to ask my help, and it may not be what you wanted to hear, but it's the best I can do. In this day and age, it's not a crime to be gay. The best thing you can do is find out whether the Lord made you that way. Popular culture gives us all sorts of ideas that might be right for us or they might not. It might just be that in meeting a gay person for the first time, you're curious about what it's like. Or it could be that for the first time, you're opening yourself to something that's been hidden in you all along. What's important is that you find out what God's plan for you is. Remember the Gospel of John?" He grinned when Kory shook his head. "Upon seeing a blind man, the disciples asked Jesus whether the man was blind because of his sins, or the sins of his parents, and Jesus told them it was neither, that he was blind 'that the works of God may be made manifest in him.' Jesus was saying that his affliction was not a punishment but a part of God's plan."

"But doesn't that mean that it's something I should fight? I mean, don't blind people want to see?"

"They do, but sight may not be granted to them. In that case, of course, it was; Jesus healed the man and restored his sight. But I don't think homosexuality is an affliction." Kory winced at the word. "Yes, God does set trials for us. But I believe God loves us, and the trials he sets for us are designed to make us better people. I have seen the ordeals some people go through trying to fight their own nature. I do not believe that those trials are set by God."

"Then why would He do this to me?" Kory hated to hear himself whine, usually.

"It is not for us to know God's plan," Father Joe said. "It is for us to live the best we can. Please take the card, Kory. They can help you more than I will be able to."

Kory reached out and took the card in his fingers. It had a name and a web URL on it. He slipped it into a pocket and stood up. "Thanks, I guess," he said. He'd been hoping for more, something definite, something supportive, rather than just vague 'we can't know what God wants for us.'

"One more thing, Kory. I just want you to hear again: God loves us. Maybe this is His way of showing you love."

Unable to think of a response other than to repeat his thanks, Kory did so, and walked out.

Sal had invited him out to celebrate the end of his grounding, but he put him off 'til dinner. He wanted to be away from people he knew, and in the water. Samaki worked Saturday afternoons, so the municipal pool would be safe. Rather than swimming and racing through the lanes, he floated on his back with his paws behind his head and closed his eyes. Here, it was peaceful, and with his ears under the water, he couldn't hear the shrieking of the guppies running around. The water helped settle his thoughts, helped him organize and sort through them. He kicked lazily off of one wall, paddled gently to the other, turned around without using his arms, and kicked off again. For over an hour he drifted back and forth, tail waving lazily in the water below him.

He couldn't believe that Father Joe hadn't offered to help him fight. It was wrong, he knew it was wrong, and it was wrong of him to want it.

Wasn't it?

The black fox's image floated before his eyelids. He hadn't pressured Kory at all, except with his eyes, and his sleek black form, and that tempting patch of white fur…and that long, fluffy tail that begged to be stroked and held. It didn't feel wrong; it was the fact that he wanted it and knew it was forbidden…but why was it forbidden, exactly?

Samaki would, presumably, not mind. And Kory had finally admitted that he wanted to try. So what was he afraid of? God? Maybe, at first, but after talking to Father Joe, he wasn't so sure. His friends? They didn't have to know. Nick? Nick wouldn't care. His mother? Yeah, his mother would freak. If she knew. But since turning about eleven, had he let that stop him from doing anything?

He opened his eyes and stared up at the blue and white tiled ceiling, fifteen feet above his head. Could it be that simple? He could just try it once. He could try it, and then the dreams and the images would go away. And if they didn't…he would deal with it then.

The tiles of the ceiling seemed to come into sharp focus. Had he just decided to sleep with another guy? It had happened so smoothly and quickly that he hadn't even been aware of the decision; he'd just turned around from the other side to find himself looking back across the line. What surprised him, too, was how the tension had drained from his body, as though he were one with the water. He dropped his arms to his sides, felt the eddies ruffle his fur as his arms slid downward. Sleep with Samaki. Well, not necessarily that; at least let himself go a little further than just touching paws. He rolled the idea around in his mind, getting used to it, finding that the shivers of wrongness were fading. It didn't have to be anything sexual, even, come to that. Just hugging, maybe. He'd give the fox a hug.

Yeah, right. He snorted at himself. At least, he felt, it was important to draw the line between experimenting and actually being gay. He just wanted to experiment. Nothing wrong with that.

Having made the decision, though, he found that it was unexpectedly difficult to work out how to carry it out. Because of his clumsy protestation of heterosexuality, he felt embarrassed enough; on top of that, how was he to initiate anything in the first place? He tried to recall how things had started with Jenny, and was annoyed to find gaps in his memory. They'd gone to the movies, something they'd done many nights before, but that night, they'd kissed, and groped. After that it was natural that the next time his mom was away, Jenny would come over and they would go further.

What had happened at that dinner? Or just after? He couldn't remember. The time had just been right. Or maybe she'd made the first move. He tried to picture scenarios in his head, but each one seemed more awkward and bumbling than the last. When he realized that his thoughts were getting to the point where his swimsuit wasn't hiding them very well, he got out of the water and walked slowly home.

There was a message from Samaki, of course. It had arrived right after Kory'd left to see Father Joe, and he hadn't checked before heading to the pool. He smiled, reading it. The fox didn't ask if things were still okay in so many words; he talked about what a fun night he'd had and how his mom would be happy to have Kory over the following Friday night if he still wanted to come. That last part made Kory write back right away. *Of course I still want to come, silly,* he said. *I'm pretty sure as long as I'm not grounded I can come.*

The problem wasn't that he wouldn't be allowed to come over, the problem was that he wouldn't be allowed to stay over. It'd be easier if they had time, if they didn't have to separate by ten. Then he wouldn't be rushed into doing more than he wanted to. He thought about that while doing homework, and then chatted with Samaki for a couple hours after dinner about the second *Foundation* book, the one in which the Mule shows up and messes up all of Seldon's predictions. Only once did the previous night's topic come up, when Kory assured Samaki that everything was cool, even though they wouldn't be double-dating anytime soon. He said it jokingly, but Samaki responded seriously that if they both had dates, he wouldn't mind going out with Kory and his date, and Kory said that of course that would be cool, he just meant they wouldn't both be dating females (or males). Then he felt flushed, because Samaki seemed a little hurt, and also because that wasn't precisely what Kory had meant, so he changed the subject.

Sunday he went to a movie with Sal, the Schwarzenotter one for real this time. It was nice to sit with his friend and watch the film and push his other concerns temporarily away. They walked out of the movie laughing about it. After the movie, while swimming at Sal's house, only twice did Kory glance at his friend and think, wow, nice body. How many times had he thought that without realizing what it meant? The thought made him uncomfortable, so he pushed it away.

They talked about school, and about Debbie, but when Sal asked about Samaki, Kory steered the conversation away. That didn't stop him thinking about the fox, though, especially when Samaki called him on his cell phone in the middle of the conversation. He took the call without thinking about it, then realized where he was and told the fox he'd call him back later. The next time the phone rang, he just turned the ringer off, a little annoyed that Samaki was calling again.

He arrived home to find his mother and a cold dinner in the kitchen. "Kory, are you aiming to get grounded again?"

"No!" He checked the time. "Sorry, I'm a little late, but…"

"I tried to call and you didn't answer your phone." She had her arms folded, which was always a bad sign. If she had her paws on her hips, you were okay.

"I didn't hear it," he protested, and then remembered the call he'd shut off. Uh-oh.

"What did I tell you about the phone?"

He sighed. "Always make sure I can hear the ring. Always pick up if you call. I'm sorry, Mom. I really didn't hear it. We were in a loud place and I didn't think…"

She put her paws on her hips. "All right, Kory. Cold dinner will be your punishment. Then get right to your room and finish up your homework."

It was already done, but he didn't tell her that. He'd just gotten an idea. "Hey, Mom," he said as he walked into the kitchen, "Samaki's mom invited me to dinner this Friday. May I go?"

She considered that while he sat down at the table. "I suppose so. I'll call her and find out when I should drop you off."

"Thanks, Mom." He took a bite of the cold mackerel and peas. "This is really good."

She sighed. "Oh, let me heat that up for you." She whisked his plate away and tossed it in the microwave. "Don't chew your claws," she said as he put a paw to his muzzle to cover his grin.

After dinner, Kory went to his room and called Samaki. He told him that he'd be coming to dinner and that their mothers would be talking, and they went on chatting for over an hour. Eventually, the fox had to go get his homework done; working most of the weekend didn't leave him much time. Kory stripped to his boxers, feeling glad and guilty that he didn't have to go to work. He swam a couple laps before surfacing in his brother's room.

"Hey, Nick."

Nick looked up from his television. Kory didn't want a TV in his room, but Nick had pestered their mother for nearly two years until she finally broke down and gave him one. He had on some extreme sports show where a snow leopard was racing down a hill on what looked like a toothpick. "Hey, Kory," he said, turning the sound down and raising his eyebrows in mild surprise. "What's up?"

Kory floated on his back in the water, looking up at Nick's posters. He had sports figures on his walls, and Kory knew that in one drawer of his dresser was the swimsuit issue of Sports Illustrated: Otters from a year ago. He turned his head to look at Nick. "Remember those pictures Sal gave me that I wouldn't let you see?"

"Yeah?" Cautiously more interested, Nick slid to the floor and lay on the towel that he'd spread out there, facing Kory. The towel was wrinkled and stained, and hadn't been washed in a while. Kory was always surprised his mother allowed that, and that Nick could stand it.

"How'd you like to see 'em?"

"Yeah! I...what do you want me to do?"

"You got plans for this Friday night?"

"Uh-uh."

Kory spun lazily in the water. "I'll give you ten bucks to go see a movie and stay out past curfew."

"You're bribing me to be grounded?" Nick's tail curled up.

"Kind of."

"Make it twenty." Nick grinned as Kory stared at him. "I gotta buy popcorn. And a drink."

"Fifteen."

"Aw, Kory, that'll only buy a ticket and popcorn."

Kory sighed. "All right, all right. Twenty."

"Cool." Nick lifted himself up onto his elbows. "Why? What'cha got goin' on?"

"Oh, nothin'," Kory said. "I just want Mom to be worried about you and not me."

"Why? What are you gonna be doing?" Nick squinted. "Am I gonna get in more trouble after Mom finds out what you're doing?"

"No," Kory said. "I'm going over to a friend's for dinner and I...I don't want Mom to pick me up at eleven. I just wanna hang out longer. She won't leave if you're not home. You know how she worries."

"Yeah. Well...okay. Who you going to have dinner with?"

Kory hesitated. "Samaki."

"Oh, yeah. He seemed pretty cool. For a fox." Nick shrugged. "Okay, deal." He extended a paw, and Kory shook it. "You guys gonna play online or something?"

"Yeah." Kory let go and slid back into the water. *Or something.*

Kory coasted through the week, talking to Samaki in the evenings and Sal during the week. His poem had finally come down from the hallway display, the ripples it caused fading from the kids' memories. Life was returning to normal, except that it was anything but.

Twenty dollars was more to Nick than it was to Kory, but it was still difficult to hand over the crisp bill he'd gotten out of the ATM. His plan had seemed perfect when it was all conceptual, but the execution filled him with doubts. He was no longer confident that everything would go as he predicted, nor that he would be able to do anything with the extra time he hoped to buy himself. The thoughts were as hard to get rid of as the twenty, but he managed both before Friday night swept him up.

Samaki greeted him at the door, thick black tail wagging. "C'mon in," he said. "You already know the family, right?" Kory stepped in ahead of his mother and saw three russet muzzles upturned and looking at him in a row.

"Of course." He turned to his mother. "You remember Mariatu, and that's...Ajani and Kasim." All three little red tails wagged. Mariatu moved from the shelter of Ajani to stand behind her bigger black-furred brother, closer to the two otters.

"Hello," Kory's mother waved, smiling. Kory noticed with some annoyance that her nose was wrinkled. The strong scent of fox didn't bother him at all. He turned away to smile at the cubs as his mother addressed Samaki. "Is your mother in the kitchen?"

He nodded, and she said, "I'll just have a couple words with her. Um..."

"It's actually downstairs, Mrs. Hedley" he said. "Through the dining room there and down the stairs."

"Downstairs?" Her brow furrowed faintly, but she walked into the dining room. Kory heard her clump down the stairs a moment later.

"I'll have to give you the tour," Samaki said to Kory, smiling, just before a flood of noise broke over them.

"I wanna give him the tour!"

"Come see our room!"

Even Mariatu joined in, squeaking "Hi, Kory! Hi, Kory!" over and over.

"Hey," Samaki said, grinning, "settle down, everyone. I'm giving the tour, but you can all come along." He swept them into the living room and then beckoned Kory in. The cubs clambered all over the three well-worn sofas, Mariatu and Ajani bouncing on one while Kasim ran from one to the other.

"Look what I can do!" he said, and jumped from the arm of one almost all the way across the other one.

"Wow," Kory said. "That's great!" He couldn't keep down his smile at the boundless energy of all three cubs.

"Pff," Ajani said, tail twitching. "I can do that too, but I don't wanna right now." Kory suspected that he did want to, but was trying to mind his manners.

Samaki laughed. "Kasim's going to be a long jumper, he says."

"What do you want to be, Ajani?" Kory asked.

"An astronaut!" the cub said. "I'm gonna go into space and discover a new planet. Didja hear about the one they found around Gliese 876?"

"That was cool!" Kory said. "I used to be into astronomy too."

"He's got stars on the ceiling of his room," Samaki said, and Kory turned to look at the fox.

"I didn't know you'd noticed," he murmured.

"Let's go upstairs!" Kasim bounded from the couch to the floor, ran over to Kory, then to Samaki, and then out to the stairs. Ajani rolled his eyes and Samaki chuckled.

"Well, there's not much more to see." He waved towards the side table. "There's the computer."

It was an older desktop, not as nice as Kory's. The chair wasn't even comfortable; at least it didn't look it. He pictured Samaki sitting there, then looked around at the room. He met the fox's questioning glance. "Oh," he said, "just nice to know where you are when I'm typing online to you."

Ajani stood up and took Mariatu's paw, helping her down off the couch. "We going upstairs?"

"Yeah," Samaki said. As the cubs scampered out, he said to Kory, "I know what you mean. I can picture you in your room, now, too."

The otter swung his tail back and forth. "What's upstairs?"

"Just our rooms. C'mon."

Up the creaky staircase, where Kory followed Samaki's light step with a wincingly heavy (to him) tread, they came to a small hallway with three doors off it and a trap door in the ceiling. The worn hardwood floor felt smooth and cool under Kory's bare feet. On the walls, framed finger paintings showed off the talents of all five kits, apparently. He saw the one with the green signature "Samaki" on it and studied it.

"Oh, don't look at that," the fox said, trying to pull Kory away.

"No, it's cute. Is that the Six Million Dollar Fox?"

"Yeah." The fox rubbed his ears.

Kory looked at the violet eyes and grinned. "The Bionic Fox?"

"I wanted to be bionic too."

"I never even saw any of those."

58

"They were on channel 48 when I was growing up. I used to run home from school and watch them." His ears folded back over his shy smile. Kory felt a strange urge to hug him right there.

"Kory!" Kasim ran out into the hall clutching a pawful of cards. "Look! I got Renamon in all five phases."

"Digimon," Samaki murmured to the otter. His ears had flipped back upright.

Kory nodded. "Nick was into that for a little while. Cool." He took the brightly colored cards from Kasim and examined each one before handing them back. "Are those hard to get?"

"Yeah." The cub nodded. "I do chores so Dad will buy me the cards. Wait, you gotta see the Giga Claws, I just got them!" He raced back into the room excitedly. Kory and Samaki, smiling, followed.

After the strong scent of fox, the first thing Kory noticed about the room was how full it was. Little bigger than Kory's room, every inch was packed with beds and desks, hardly an inch of wall space left for decoration. To the right, Ajani was sitting on the top bunk of a pair of bunk beds, straightening up a stack of comics on the small board attached to the side of his bed that served as a night table. Kasim was rummaging through the bottom drawer of the tall, thin dresser wedged between the beds and the wall. Clothing lay scattered on the floor; Kory thought most or all belonged to the two younger cubs, from the size. Opposite the bunk beds was an unstable looking structure that Kory could only describe as bunk desks: one desk stacked on top of another, the top desk attached to the wall, and the chair hung from the ceiling. An old pillow had been strapped to the front of the chair, its purpose immediately evident: Ajani jumped casually from the bed to the chair, his momentum sending the chair into the desk where the pillow muffled the impact. He put two comics away in a drawer and held one down to Kory. "You ever read Red Lightning? He's in the League of Canids."

Kory shook his head, leafing through the comic. "I collected the X-Men for a while, but haven't been into comics lately."

"Oh, the League of Canids is cool. They used to be the League of Crimefighting Canids until a couple years ago, then they changed their name. There's this one episode where…"

"Here's the Giga-Claws!" Kasim was thrusting a card up at him.

"Hey, hey," Samaki said. "He's my guest, okay? Settle down."

"I want to see the comics," Kory said, adding, "and the Giga-Claws," because Kasim's ears had fallen at Samaki's remark. He threaded his way through the clothes on the floor to the back of the room, where a wardrobe filled the space under a homemade but sturdy loft, leaving just enough room for the window. Another window opened high in the wall above, letting more light into the room than Kory would have expected. He looked from the sunset's crimson-orange brilliance to Samaki. "Pretty."

Red light gleamed in the black fur as the fox nodded. "I get the nice view," he said. "Come on up, it's big enough for two."

Kory froze for a moment, but Samaki was already on his way up the ladder. What did that mean? Kory thought frantically, then looked back at the cubs. Samaki wouldn't do anything with his brothers in the room. Kasim was rummaging through his dresser drawer again, and Ajani was reading a comic at his desk, kicking back and forth on the dangling chair. Kory chided himself for being twitchy as he followed the swinging black tail up the ladder.

The loft held more than just the bed. Around the futon mattress, the wood was padded with carpet remnants. Kory sat there, careful of the ceiling, while Samaki sat on his bed. A small alcove with a slanted roof, looking like it fit the eaves of the house, extended beyond the other side of the futon, piled with papers and a small alarm clock.

"Where does Mariatu sleep?" Kory had caught sight of the little vixen cub standing in the doorway, clutching a small stuffed rabbit and chewing on its head. He waved to her and she wagged her tail and waved back.

"In our parents' room. She used to sleep with them and Kasim slept on the cot there, until Kande left. Then Kasim moved in here."

"Kory!" He heard his mother downstairs.

"Oh, Mom's leaving." He clambered quickly down the ladder, with Samaki following. Kasim and Mariatu ran down the stairs with them, while Ajani kept reading his book.

His mother was looking at the pictures in the entry hallway. Happily, her nose wasn't wrinkling any more. She'd obviously enjoyed her talk with Mrs. Roden, or she wouldn't have stayed so long. Kory felt buoyed by that. "I'm going home. I'll be back at eleven sharp to pick you up, okay?"

He nodded. "Thanks, Mom. See you then."

She pecked him on the cheek and left, moments before a bell clanged somewhere in the house. "Oh, dinner," Samaki said. "You can sit down. I'm gonna run down and help Mom."

He showed Kory the dining room, with its large wooden table in the center. The table was beautiful oak, finely crafted and bare. Four of the chairs around it sported flowery carvings in the same grain as the table, but the other two were distinctive: a captain's chair with arms, made of a dark red wood whose grain was nearly invisible, and a small, light chair, higher than the others. Against the right wall, an oak sideboard with drawers held a vase of small white flowers and two silver candlesticks shaped like graceful foxes, a male and female nude with arms stretched overhead. The smells of cooking fish, some vegetables, and a spicy sauce wafted through the dining room from the far end, making Kory's stomach rumble.

Samaki pulled out the dark captain's chair. "This is Dad's, but he won't be home for dinner. You can sit there."

"I'll help too," Kory said.

"You don't have to," Samaki said.

"I want to." Kory felt a little flutter at the bright smile he got from the fox. That white-on-black crescent, the small upward curve of his lips, and the matching sparkle in his eyes that told Kory he was happy made Kory happy too.

Never got that with Sal, did you?

Oh, shut up, he told his inner voice. Just leave me alone for this evening, okay?

He followed Samaki down a curved set of stairs, toward the source of the mouth-watering smells. "Does your Dad make it home for many dinners?"

"Thursday nights, Saturday and Sunday," Samaki said. "Saturday is Family Night. I don't get to see him much. I work Saturdays, and Sunday mornings. He works two jobs Monday through Friday." He paused. "I wanted to work evenings too, but they wouldn't let me. Said I need to be able to get my homework done."

Kory pushed aside his recurring guilt over not having to work as he followed the black fox into the kitchen.

Heat and the aromas of food washed over him. On the island in the middle of the kitchen, two dishes full of vegetables and potatoes steamed, the spicy sauce aroma emanating from one of them. Mrs. Roden was just taking a large whitefish out of the oven, in between two large old refrigerators. A huge pantry as homemade as the loft in Samaki's room spanned the opposite wall. At the far end, another door stood slightly ajar, nothing but darkness visible beyond it. Mrs. Roden set the fish on the small kitchen island and looked up brightly at them.

"Samaki, get Ajani to help set the table. Kory, dear, just have a seat."

"No, I'll help Samaki," he said, and when Mrs. Roden turned around, he saw a little of where Samaki had gotten his smile from.

"You're a dear. Go on then," she said. "Then Samaki, come help me bring the food up."

Samaki and Kory set the table with silverware from the sideboard, and then Samaki asked Kory to get the cubs from upstairs while he helped bring the food up. The job was an easy one; alerted by the bell, Kasim and Mariatu were on their way down the stairs when Kory started up. He found Ajani still swinging from the ceiling chair in the bedroom.

"Dinner's ready, Ajani," he said.

"Kay." The cub tossed the comic book on his desk and slid off the chair, landing on the floor perfectly in a crouch. He grinned at Kory as he stood.

"Very nice!" Kory applauded, and let the cub scamper downstairs ahead of him, a satisfied smile on his muzzle and a proud arch to his tail.

Samaki and Mrs. Roden were putting the food out as they all drew up chairs around the table. "I don't know if you like halibut, Kory, but Samaki said you mostly eat fish."

"Anything's fine," he said. "Halibut's great. Everything smells terrific."

The mixed vegetables were cooked broccoli and green beans, with a light red pepper sauce. Kory wasn't used to spiced food, but he ate as much as he could, until his tongue felt like it was on fire even when he wasn't eating the veggies. "Is it too hot for you, Kory?" Mrs. Roden asked anxiously.

"No, no," he said, "it's fine." He found that if he interspersed bites of the vegetables with bites of the other food, that cut the heat down. The potatoes were wonderful, creamy and cheesy, and the fish was firm, well-seasoned, and just as delicious. The red pepper added a nice tang to the whole meal, and while it was a little strong, he was glad to have tried it.

That was nearly all he managed to say. The kids and their mother all talked at once, all over each other, and Kory didn't even try to get a word in edgewise, just listened to the raucous chaos with a smile. It wasn't until the meal was mostly over that he realized that they hadn't even said Grace, he was so busy listening and looking at the animated vulpines around the table. It was amusing to see Samaki's black fur in the middle of all the red foxes. Fox coats were odd things, he mused, but pretty. All the red foxes had black ears and paws with white underbellies; Samaki had only the black and white, as though the other foxes had had their ears and paws just dipped in ink, and he'd been dunked.

Mouth still tingling from the veggies, he thanked Mrs. Roden for the meal. She wouldn't let him help clean up, instead sending him and Samaki down to the rec room and recruiting Kasim and Ajani to help clear the table.

Samaki took Kory through the door on the opposite side of the kitchen, into a cool, musty, vulpine-scented darkness. He flicked on the light to reveal a worn couch and old gaming table, with an old console television set in one corner. "Feel like playing a game?" Samaki said. "We got checkers, Foxopoly, Careers, and Scrabble. I think it has all the tiles. Kande and I used to play Scrabble and Foxopoly all the time." He looked down at the boxes. "Foxopoly is missing some houses, but we could still play it. Or we could play checkers. Maybe you'd let me play red? The others never do."

Kory looked around. "Any video games?"

Samaki grinned, pulling out an old PS1 from beside the TV and spreading out a pad on the floor. "You wanna try Pounce Pounce Revolution?"

The game looked familiar, but the larger pad had more squares on it, with several strange symbols. "I'll watch you play first," he said. "It looks like fun."

"It is. You should see Kasim play it. He's better than I am." The fox fired up the PS1 and Kory watched an animated fox dressed in shiny purple clothes with gold trim appear on the screen and say, "Pounce Pounce Revolution!" While the instructions came up, Samaki took his shirt off and rubbed his paws together.

"Let's POUNCE!" the animated fox said. On screen, a mockup of the pad appeared as music started playing, a dance number with a driving beat. A small animated mouse danced out onto the pad on screen; Samaki leapt, coming down with both paws on the pad on the floor, and the mouse squeaked and vanished. Another one came out, then another and another, and soon the black fox was jumping all over the pad, spinning to change direction and pouncing on mouse after mouse. As he did so, the animated fox shouted out encouragement, like "Got 'im!" and "Nice pouncin'!"

The song ended, and the animated fox came back out, dancing a little himself, and said, "Amaaaaaaazin'!" Kory clapped.

Samaki turned, panting a bit, and bowed, tail arching behind him. "That was an easy level," he said. "I'll put on a harder one."

The otter grinned and settled back into the couch, watching the fox tap some buttons. "I like this song," he said over his shoulder, and when it came on, Kory couldn't resist tapping his feet to the infectious beat. The mice were dancing and spinning this time, even leaping in imitation of Samaki himself, and were harder to pin down. The shouts of encouragement now came interspersed with disappointed interjections, like, "Don't let 'em get away!" and "That mouse is playin' you!"

Samaki jumped and worked much harder at this level. Even when his thick fur was dry, Kory could see his muscles bunching and releasing. Reflexively, he shied away from thinking about them, then remembered his resolve and deliberately watched, enjoying Samaki's elegant grace and athleticism.

When the level ended, the animated fox didn't dance, just told Samaki to keep tryin'. Kory clapped again, but Samaki waved him off. "Nah, I'm no good. There's another level where you just hear them under the pad. That's insane. I can't react fast enough. Kasim can't even do the hard ones on that mode."

"Over the music, you mean?"

Samaki nodded. "Yeah, music's goin' and you hear scratchings under the buttons." He panted. "You wanna give it a try?"

"Is there a setting for 'blind and deaf'?"

Samaki laughed. "I'll put it on training mode."

"Well...okay." Kory didn't want to look clumsy in front of Samaki, but he didn't want to reject the fox's offer, either. He walked up to the pad where the fox was selecting a training mode, and said, "I'm gonna suck at this." Should he take his shirt off? He wasn't in as good shape as Samaki. He hesitated, then left it on.

"Nah, don't worry about it," Samaki said. "Just have fun." He showed Kory the controls and padded back to the couch to collapse.

The animated fox showed Kory the basic moves and let Kory practice them, then gave him a choice of training songs. Kory picked one, and the fox clapped his paws and said, "Let's pounce!"

The first mouse danced out slowly, and as he got under one of the buttons, the fox said, "Now, POUNCE!" Kory got both paws on the pad, and the mouse squeaked and disappeared. Another came out, and he slipped, but caught it on the second pad. By the end of the song, he felt more confident, and when he was done, the animated fox on screen and black fox on the couch clapped together. Kory saw from the stats that he'd gotten 27 of 30 mice.

"Not bad for my first time," he said, delighted that he hadn't embarrassed himself.

"Pretty good," Samaki said. "Do another?"

"Nah. I'm gonna quit while I'm ahead." Kory chuckled. "It's fun, though."

"Yeah." The black fox eyed the screen. "Mind if I do one more?"

"Go ahead." Kory enjoyed watching Samaki jump around, tail flowing behind him, springing fluidly back and forth around the pad. His decision colored everything in a new light. It was okay to stare at Samaki's arms and wonder how the fluffy chest would feel. It felt dangerous in an exciting way, wrong only in that they would be in trouble if they got caught. His fur tingled as his gaze traveled downward to the fox's tail, the firm lines of his rear and legs underneath it. Maybe he wasn't quite ready for that yet. He kept his eyes up, on Samaki's back and arms, while the fox finished the song.

"Sorry," Samaki said as he slipped his shirt back on. "That's the only video game we have."

"It's okay," Kory said. "We don't have to play anything."

"Great." The black fox wagged his tail and grinned. "Let me put on some music. Some quieter music."

Kory sat on the couch, curling his tail around beside his leg. He was starting to get nervous again, because he knew Samaki would sit down in a minute and the kitchen was right there, the door still open to it. He didn't feel private enough to be comfortable, but he felt like he wanted to talk to Samaki, at least try to reverse some of the image he'd presented the previous weekend. That would be hard with his mother still cleaning up upstairs. She could probably hear them as well as he could hear her. Better, with her larger ears.

Samaki plopped down beside him as the room filled with quiet classical music. "One of my dad's," he said. "Just wanted something kinda quiet." His tail came to rest between the two of them, resting on top of the otter's tail. Kory twitched his tail against the soft fur, his heart beating a little faster.

"That's nice," he said. "I know nothing about classical."

"It's Bach." Samaki shrugged and grinned. "That's about all the more I know."

"It's nice," Kory repeated. "So do you usually come down here to talk on the phone?"

"Nah. Reception sucks. I sit in the bedroom, up on my loft."

"It's pretty up there. I like your house a lot." He laughed. "You know what I just realized?"

Samaki grinned. "What?"

"Your family reminds me of the Weasleys."

Samaki laughed. "Yeah, I've heard that before. Kasim likes to pretend he's Ron. Ajani likes Fred and George, but I won't play them with him."

Kory dropped his paw in what he hoped was a casual manner and let it rest on Samaki's tail just below the white tip. It twitched below him but didn't move otherwise. He sighed inwardly at the soft fur tickling up against his webbing. "How was that test you had yesterday?"

For a while, they talked school, and then the cubs came in and climbed all over the couch and Mariatu fell asleep in Samaki's lap. Kory removed his paw from Samaki's tail, then, and fortunately it wasn't much longer until Mrs. Roden came in to collect the cubs for bed.

Putting his paw on the fox's tail was easier the second time he did it, and again Samaki didn't make any indication that he'd noticed. The conversation stayed away from relationships, but they talked about movies, books, and school, and though Kory had been tensely thinking about his mother's impending call when Mrs. Roden came in to collect the cubs, he was so lost in the conversation that he was surprised when Mrs. Roden came back, her ears down but not flat, a phone in her paws.

"Kory? Your mother's on the phone. She says your brother isn't back yet and she can't come pick you up."

He got up and walked over, feeling tense again. "If you need to stay here," Mrs. Roden said, "we can work it out."

He nodded and said, "Thanks," picking up the phone. "Hi, Mom."

"Oh, Kory, Nicky's not answering his phone and he was supposed to be back. I'm sorry, I don't want to leave in case he's hurt."

"Mom, I'm sure he's okay." Guilt flushed his neck. "He's got a key."

"But why isn't he answering his phone? Nicky always answers his phone."

"Maybe he's not getting good reception. I'm sure he's okay."

"God willing, Kory," she said, "but I just don't feel comfortable leaving. Listen, Mrs. Roden said you can stay there overnight. Will that be all right, sweetie? I'm sorry."

That was what he'd wanted. His plan had worked to perfection, and now that it had, he hesitated about accepting it. With Samaki sharing his room, it would be hard for them to get any time alone, and the worry in his mother's tone gnawed at him. "I guess…"

"If you don't want to, then I'll call you a cab and you can take that home. I don't want you taking a bus at this hour."

"No, no, that's okay. I'll stay here, and I'll see you in the morning?"

"Yes. I'll be there at nine. Can you put Cynthia back on? Mrs. Roden, I mean."

"Sure, Mom. And don't worry. I'm sure Nick's fine."

"God bless, Kory."

He handed the phone to the waiting vixen. "She wants to talk to you again."

"Okay." Mrs. Roden smiled encouragingly. "I'm sure he's okay, Kory. He probably just turned off the phone or something."

Kory nodded, and went back to the couch. "Samaki," Mrs. Roden called as she took the phone. "Can you figure out somewhere for Kory to sleep? He'll be staying with us tonight."

Samaki's ears were straight up as Kory sat beside him. "Sure," he said. As his mother went back into the kitchen, he grinned widely at the otter, violet eyes sparkling. "Change of plans?"

"My brother's late getting home and won't answer his phone." Kory sagged back against the couch, still feeling a little guilty. "Mom was really upset."

"I'm sure he's fine." Samaki's smile faded, but not completely. He put an arm around Kory's shoulder.

Kory leaned back automatically. "Do you have an extra bed somewhere? I don't wanna kick Kasim or Ajani out of bed."

"How about this?" Samaki gestured with his free arm to the couch. "I've fallen asleep down here a couple times. It's not bad."

"Yeah, that'd be fine," Kory said. "Too bad there's not another couch." His heart raced.

"Oh, I'll bring some blankets down and sleep on the floor. Actually, if you wanna help, I can drag the futon mattress down, but I don't need to." The fox grinned at him. "I wouldn't leave you down here by yourself."

"Cool." Kory finally realized that the paw on his shoulder was a response to his paw on the fox's tail, upping the ante. He started to get nervous again, which confused him because he hadn't been nervous when the fox put a paw on his shoulder, only when he started thinking about it.

Maybe you shouldn't do so much thinking.

Hey, he thought sharply. What did I say?

Sorry.

"Well," he said, getting up. "Let's go get that mattress."

They had no trouble getting the mattress down both flights of stairs, though maneuvering it through the kitchen was a little tricky. By the time they got it down, Mrs. Roden was bustling in with bedsheets for both the couch and futon. "Now don't stay up too late," she said.

"Just 'til Dad gets home?" Samaki said. "I want Kory to meet him."

"Sure. I'll send him down." She kissed him on the cheek. "If I'm too sleepy to come down too, you both have a good night." She gave Kory a hug too.

He was surprised at first, but it was easy to hug back and smile. "Thanks, Mrs. Roden."

They made the beds, and then Samaki picked up something else from the pile his mother had brought. "Heh. She brought you a spare pair of my pajamas," the fox said. "If you want."

He didn't really want to sleep in his clothes. "Oh, I…sure." As soon as the words were out, he was worried about putting on something of Samaki's. Well, it was too late, he'd said it already.

"I'm gonna go upstairs to brush and put on my pajamas. Back in a bit."

Kory watched the fox's tail wag as he disappeared into the kitchen. He took his time changing, half-hoping that Samaki would come back and catch him half-undressed. But the fox, for whatever reason, was not back quickly enough, and Kory lost his nerve, pulling the pajama bottoms on and then stripping his shirt off. He remained shirtless, trying to fluff his fur up so his lack of muscles wouldn't be as noticeable. Besides, he wasn't sure Samaki's pajama top would fit him. The pants were snug, and long; he rolled up the hems so he wouldn't be stepping all over them.

Samaki came in with two cookies in his paws. "Shh," he said. "We're not supposed to take these, but Mom's upstairs." He gave Kory a sly grin and one of the cookies.

It was chocolate chip, and delicious. "Didn't you just brush your teeth?" Kory asked.

"Mmmyeah, but these were too good to pass up." Samaki's grin was speckled with chocolate.

"Mm. No kidding." He licked the cookie crumbs from his muzzle. Samaki lay back on his elbows, also shirtless and looking pretty comfortable…well, looking pretty, too, his jet-black fur framing the white patch on his chest, a curl of white poking up from the waistband of his pajamas. Kory felt himself stirring in response, and that made him confused again. How was he supposed to try anything without climbing down into the fox's bed? He wasn't ready for that, not yet.

So he stayed on the couch and talked, trying not to wonder whether the fox was wearing anything under his pajama bottoms. Around 11:30, they heard footsteps on the stairs, and a deep vulpine voice said, "Samaki?"

"Dad!" The fox jumped to his feet and padded to the doorway as a tall fox emerged from the kitchen. He wore blue overalls, a Dragons baseball hat, and a tired smile. Like most of the rest of his family, his fur was russet red, though Kory thought he saw darker fur on the back of Mr. Roden's neck when the fox turned to greet his son. The otter got to his feet too, now wishing he'd kept his shirt on, but Mr. Roden didn't seem to care.

He and Samaki hugged, and Samaki said, "This is Kory, my friend from across town."

"The one from the pool, right? Nice to meet you," Mr. Roden said, holding out a paw.

Kory shook his paw, trying to match the firmness of his grip. "Good to meet you, too."

Though he looked tired, Samaki's father stayed to talk for a few more minutes before saying good-night. He turned off the light, leaving them alone in the dark.

No room in the house is quite as dark as a dark basement. Kory felt the darkness surrounding him like a soft black fox, but with no white patches to lighten the inky gloom. After a few seconds, he looked over and saw the faintest gleam of white a few feet away from him. Samaki's chest.

The fox rustled under his covers. Kory closed his eyes, willing himself to have the courage to reach down. He got his paw partway there, then drew it back. The fox's scent was strong. He was just a few feet away, wearing only pajamas. The white patch he could see made him think of the other one he couldn't, and his body took that memory and ran with it, until he had to press his muzzle into the couch, and now there was no question of reaching out to the fox, because Samaki would be able to tell just from his trembling what he was thinking of.

And yet…it wasn't like the nights he'd lain awake at home. The presence of the fox made him confused, but also made him happy in a way he couldn't quite figure out. He only was aware of that when the thought came that if he'd told his mother the truth, he would be at home in his bed and not lying here staring into the darkness and thinking about the white patch at the center of it. His reaction to that thought was strong and somewhat surprising: he rejected it as soon as he thought of it. He hated the confusion, but not the situation. Like the red pepper on the vegetables, it was new, different, and a little painful, but he was not sorry to experience it.

After a time, he became aware of Samaki's soft, even breathing. The fox was asleep, and he'd missed his chance. That didn't make the tension in his body—in one specific part of his body—go away, but it did remove the confusion somewhat. He fell asleep on his stomach, tail draped over the side of the couch.

He woke slowly to a touch on his paw. Gradually, he realized that he was still on his stomach, lying on the edge of the sofa with his arm hanging down onto the floor, paw pads up. On top of his paw, another warm paw rested. He cracked an eye open.

The darkness was less absolute than it had been the previous night, the open door to the kitchen a ghostly grey. Samaki lay immobile at the edge of his futon, a well of darkness in the room, neither his chest patch nor his tail tip visible. A curl of black snaked its way towards the couch, ending with his paw resting on Kory's. Kory watched him, not believing that the fox was actually asleep, but he was breathing slowly and Kory could see no eyeshine.

The otter stayed where he was, watching the fox's shape, enjoying the contact. The moment stretched on in a bubble in time, insulated by the stillness and darkness of the early morning. Time outside might be moving normally, but in the rec room, the warmth between their paws held them apart from the rest of the world.

Samaki stirred. The paw touching Kory's moved minutely, and then he saw the gleam of an eye looking into his. Eventually, time began to move again. "Kory?" Samaki whispered.

"Yeah," he whispered back.

"Morning."

The otter smiled. "Good morning," he said.

"What time is it?"

"Don't know. My cell phone's down there."

The paw lifted from his. He saw the light of a phone reflected in the fox's eyes. "Seven-thirty."

Kory nodded, leaving his paw where it was. "My mom'll be here at nine," he said. "Maybe we should move your futon back upstairs."

Samaki put his paw back onto the otter's, left it motionless. "We have a little time," he said. "Mom'll probably start breakfast around eight." They continued whispering, their voices as soft as the touch between their paws.

"Okay." Kory was happy to let the moment go on. This was nice, this was safe, and he didn't mind when the fox's paw rubbed his gently.

"You sleep okay?"

"Yeah. I had a funny dream." He paused and then decided it was harmless, he might as well tell it. "I dreamed I was a fox, in a pool full of other foxes. I didn't see you anywhere. I was just swimming around, but when I got out of the water, my fur and tail were still dry. I ordered some kind of candy bar at the snack stand, but they were out. So I went with some other foxes to play checkers."

"Were you a black fox or red fox? Or white fox?"

"I don't remember. I was just a fox."

"You'd make a good fox, I think."

Kory wondered whether Samaki could see his smile. Probably. Foxes had terrific night vision. "I'm too heavy," he said.

"I mean, you have the right spirit."

"I certainly don't have the right fur," Kory said jokingly, but he was thrilled at the compliment, or what he thought was a compliment.

"Try taking care of it in the morning," Samaki said. "I'll have to brush it before your mom gets here. Does yours get all matted and going every which way?"

"Not really," Kory said. "Too short and thick."

The fox's fingers rubbed the back of his paw. "I like that, though. Easier to take care of."

Kory nodded, remaining quiet. He was aware of the minutes ticking by; now that the small contact he'd hoped for had been made, selfishly he didn't want it to end. We held paws before, he told himself, realizing that two friends rubbing paws was not exactly normal.

Though I did put my paw on his tail. And he put his arm around me. Kind of. But that was all casual. He noticed with some surprise that the rubbing of the fox's fingers was very nice indeed, making his tail twitch and provoking other responses in him that he didn't know could be elicited just from paws. Amazed at himself, he tried to hold his tail still, with little success. Jenny had never gotten this kind of reaction from him, just from brushing him like that.

"I guess we should get ready," Samaki said finally, his paw resting still on Kory's again. Kory gave it a squeeze, stronger than he'd meant to at first, and Samaki squeezed back tightly.

"All right," Kory said.

The light seemed much brighter and harsher than it had been the previous night. He blinked and shielded his eyes from it.

"Good," Samaki said, his grin just visible through Kory's protective fingers. "Don't look at me."

"You look fine." Kory squinted at the black figure, opening his eyes wider. He could see where some of the white fur was matted and disheveled. As he grew used to the light, he saw soft grey lines of irregular patterns in the black fur, too. "You look great," he said sincerely.

"*You*," Samaki said, "look fine. *I* look like I just woke up."

"You did," Kory pointed out.

"I know," Samaki said. "But I don't like looking this way." He grinned and put his shirt back on, as Kory did the same. "Help me get the mattress up? It's harder than coming down."

"Sure," Kory said, and as they were hefting the mattress, he heard noise from the kitchen and realized that this might be their last private moment. "I had a really good time," he said. "We should do this again."

The fox's smile reached all the way up to his eyes. "Me too," he said. "And you're welcome anytime. Or…I'd love to have a swim in your pool."

Kory grinned. "Sure! I'll talk to my mom. Maybe we could go to a late movie and you could stay over. There are some neat small artsy theaters close to me."

"Cool. I'll check the listings." Samaki's tail wagged. "Now, ready? Heave!"

They dragged the mattress up the two flights of stairs, with only one minor incident when Samaki's grip on the mattress slipped and Kory had to skip down a step quickly. When they'd heaved the mattress up onto the loft, Samaki said, "Bathroom's free. I'm going to duck in and straighten up."

Ajani and Kasim were already in the living room watching cartoons, so Kory climbed up to Samaki's loft, watching the light spread over the city outside the window. It was a nice view, and a nice room, he thought, an ingenious use of little space to allow three boys to live here together. Compared to Sal, who lived in a huge two-story house with two rec rooms, five bedrooms, and a hot pool and water slide in addition to the main indoor pool, Kory had always thought of his family as poor, or at least not well-off. Samaki's family would be much better suited to Sal's house, and yet they had less than even Kory and his family did, and they thrived.

He glanced at the pile of Samaki's papers, and levered himself over to peer at the one on top. It was an article by Samaki about a gay teen support center in downtown Hilltown whose funding was being reviewed, written from the perspective of one of the teens it had helped.

"Hey," the fox called some minutes later. Kory hadn't even heard him come in. He put the paper down guiltily, but Samaki was smiling. He'd not only brushed his fur; he'd changed into new clothes, or at least a new shirt, and Kory noticed then that the wardrobe was open. He hadn't heard that, either.

"Sorry," he said. "It was right on top. And you did read my poem."

"It's cool," Samaki said. "The article about the Rainbow Center?"

"Yeah. That's really neat. You went there?"

The fox nodded. "I'll tell you the whole story sometime. Not enough time now."

"I'd like to hear more," Kory said as he clambered down. "Do you still go there?"

"In summer." Samaki walked downstairs with Kory. "Helping other kids, doing projects."

"You'll be good at it." He grinned at the noise from the living room. "Cartoons for a while?"

"Yeah. Breakfast first?"

"Oh, sure."

Down in the kitchen, the smell of eggs and sausage filled the air. Mrs. Roden bustled from stove to sink and fridge, and back, and greeted Samaki with a kiss and Kory with a hug. "I've got scrambled eggs, chicken sausage, some potatoes, and orange juice. Anything else you'd like, Kory?"

"No, that sounds amazing." Kory patted his rumbling stomach.

They helped themselves to heaping servings of fluffy eggs, crispy sausage patties, and browned potatoes with onions. After the black fox had sprinkled Tabasco sauce on his eggs and potatoes and Kory had declined it, they thanked Mrs. Roden and trotted back upstairs.

"We can eat in the living room," Samaki said with his muzzle full. "The good cartoons are about to start. I don't get the Digimon type ones..."

Kasim cut him off. "This is Yu-Gi-Oh," he said, and he and Ajani exchanged superior looks.

"Whatever," Samaki plopped down next to his brother and ruffled between his ears. "I can't get into those. But they still run Looney Tunes at 8:30 and I make them watch before I head off to work."

"I love those," Kory said, and for half an hour the four of them watched Bugs Bunny and Friends together, the otter and black fox occasionally sneaking looks at each other and smiling. Kory tacked one more interest up on the list of things they shared, and that thought made his tail thump against the back of the couch. When Ajani, next to him, turned around, he covered by poking the cub in the side with his tail's tip, and this delighted the cubs so much that Kasim pushed over to get his share of pokes, and they ended up in a giggling heap in the middle of the couch when Samaki joined in and started tickling their paws.

At the end of the half hour show, Mrs. Roden walked in from the dining room. "Sammy, you should get going," she said. "We'll take care of Kory 'til his mother gets here."

The clock in the hall read 8:59. "She'll be here in a minute," Kory said confidently. Indeed, just as Samaki opened the door, his mother's car was pulling up to the curb.

And just like that, the visit was over. He gave Samaki a handshake and a friendly wave as the fox walked off to work, while his mother introduced herself to Mr. Roden and gave Mrs. Roden some recipe she'd apparently promised to bring. Kory was glad to see that. He wanted his mom and Mrs. Roden to be friends, because that would make it easier for him to see Samaki. And then he was in the front seat of his mom's car, they were pulling away from the house, and he was back in his own world.

He told his mom that it had been no problem for him to stay there, told her about the house, and asked if he could invite Samaki over again. His mother, of course, agreed, since they had let him stay over. She said that she liked the Rodens, but "I'm sure you'll be glad to get in the shower."

That dampened his spirits. He didn't respond, and he did not head right for the shower when he got home. He walked to Nick's room.

Nick held the little CompactFlash card gingerly in his paw. "You want me to copy it and give it back?"

"Nah," Kory said, "you can keep it."

"Really?" Nick's blue eyes widened. A moment later, they narrowed, as he searched for the catch, and then relaxed as he tilted his head curiously. "Hey, Kory... uh..."

"Yeah?"

"You already make a copy?" That obviously hadn't been the first question he was going to ask.

Kory turned around and sat on Nick's bed. For a minute, he fought with himself about what to say. To talk to Nick would make it more real, harder to deny. That was a big leap. He thought about the high dive at Caspian, standing on the edge looking down, knowing it would be fine once he jumped. It would be a relief to talk to someone other than Father Joe, and Nick was probably the best one to talk to. "Go ahead and say what you were going to."

"Oh." Nick fidgeted. "You think you're...you know...I mean, do you not like girls any more?"

"Any more?" Kory forced a grin.

"I don't know. You went out with Jenny for like a year, but you weren't ever really happy." He held up the card. "And giving this away...man, I'll *never* get rid of this. Then you wanted to stay overnight with Samaki."

He looked back at his brother's curious, astute eyes. "I don't know. Maybe."

Nick patted his arm. "Cause it's cool, you know. I mean, I won't tell Mom."

"She'd freak out."

Nick laughed shortly. "Yeah, no kidding."

"But you? I mean, if..."

Nick considered only for a moment before nodding. "Sure. You're my brother, right? So, whatever."

"Thanks, Nick." He wrapped an arm around the younger otter's shoulder.

"It's no big deal, really. There's a kid in my class, he's, uh..." He looked quickly at Kory. "A couple kids give him a hard time sometimes, but they only do it if nobody's around 'cause if other people see it they get mad."

"Like teachers, you mean?"

"Nah, just other kids. It's pretty stupid, picking on someone for that, don't you think? Jerry Tucker caught Stewy Marchand making a comment one time and told him to shut up or he'd paste him one. Robby's pretty cool. Everyone likes him, except Stewy and his buddy Frank."

Kory sat back on the bed. "He's thirteen and he knows?"

Nick shrugged. "I know I like girls." He kissed the CF card. "Don't worry about it. Except with, like, Mom and some of her church friends, nobody really cares."

"I think people care. I care."

"You know what I mean."

"I guess so. I'm not sure you're right." But Father Joe had said essentially the same.

Nick got up and put the card down over by his computer. "Well, I dunno. All I know is it doesn't matter to me. Samaki seems pretty cool. And you seem to like him a lot."

"Yeah." Kory had just been thinking the same thing. "I do."

He swam back to his room, doing extra laps under the water, reflecting how odd it was that his brother was so close and so far. They had a great bond, and he knew Nick would always be on his side, just as he would be on Nick's. Then there was the question of being gay, where somehow Nick had acquired an even perspective that Kory could only characterize as mature, more mature than even he had. Was it possible for four years to mark such a drastic shift in attitudes? Or had Kory kept himself insulated from the world around him, taking his cues only from their mother?

He sent an e-mail to Samaki, telling him again what a good time he'd had and including the next four weeks of Friday night movies at the theater near him. He hadn't expressed a preference for any one of the four, but the movie scheduled three weeks away fell on Memorial Day weekend and it was an old science fiction classic, *Forbidden Planet*, one Kory had seen a long time ago, with his father. He felt sure that Samaki would zero in on that one, and sure enough, when the fox popped onto IM that evening, that was the movie he picked.

The month of May passed in a blur. He met Samaki every Sunday, once at the pool and twice just at Starbucks. Sal dragged Kory into helping with prom preparations, once Kory assured him that he wasn't upset to be missing it. He was somewhat amazed at the amount of money Sal was willing to spend on the prom, until he finally figured out that it was not to impress Debbie—who, after all, was already sleeping with him—but to impress his classmates.

Nick took his grounding well, so well that their mother was almost suspicious about the amount of time he was willing to spend in his room. Kory suspected that his digital camera, the one he'd loaned Nick that read CF cards, had a lot to do with it. He didn't need the camera; he no longer felt ashamed to call up his memories of the black fox as he lay in bed at night. That didn't mean he was gay. After all, he wasn't doing anything regular teenage boys didn't do, no matter what images he held in his mind when he did them.

Memorial Day fell at the onset of finals, two weeks before the prom. Normally, Kory would have spent every waking moment studying for exams, but even before he left to meet Samaki at the bus that night, he was too keyed up to focus on his books. His mother had made up an old air mattress with sheets and set it up on his floor, and every time Kory looked at it and thought of the fox lying there, he couldn't even sit still.

At quarter to seven, he threw on a short-sleeved shirt and waved to his mother, then ran out into the hot spring evening. He spent seven minutes at the bus stop pacing, until the bus pulled up and the black fox stepped down.

He was wearing a white t-shirt that was a little too tight for him, and shorts that showed off his thighs and bare calves. As he stepped to the pavement, he slung his old backpack over his shoulder and clasped Kory's paw. "Hot one tonight."

"Yeah," Kory agreed, and bounced excitedly on the balls of his feet. "The theater has A/C, though. And it'll be cooler when we get out."

"It's already cooler here," Samaki said, falling into step beside him. "It was 95 at my house when I left."

"Wow." Kory shook his head. "With that black fur, I don't know how you manage."

"I wear lots of white and I stay indoors." Samaki brushed ruefully at the long fur on his arm. "Actually, it's not so bad once it gets short, long as I keep my tail moving. That fur doesn't molt. Stays long all year round."

"So I see." Kory swung his own tail over to brush the fox's playfully as they walked. Samaki brushed back, and they played tail-tag all the way to the theater.

Samaki had never seen *Forbidden Planet*, a fifties adventure in which a spaceship of adventuring wolves discover a planet where an old rabbit scientist and his daughter live, apparently alone. At night, the wolves are attacked by a huge monster crackling with energy, and they must discover its secret. Kory had seen it years ago, and was happy to find that Samaki loved it as much as he had.

Some parts of the movie were genuinely creepy, and as their arms were adjacent on the armrest, Kory found his paw entwined in Samaki's about halfway through the movie. That seemed comfortable enough, and they happily squeezed each other's paws during the creepy parts.

"Great movie," Samaki said, panting as they stepped back out into the barely-cool evening. "Wow."

"I'd forgotten a lot of it," Kory said. "Whew! Glad you liked it."

Samaki looked up at the marquee as if fixing the name in his mind. "I see why it's a classic, all right. When did you see it before?"

"Seven years ago. With my father."

"Oh." They walked on for a few steps, and then Samaki said, "How about Leslie Wolfson? A serious role, too."

"He was good, too!"

"No kidding." Samaki's tail brushed Kory's and Kory swung his tail back. They chatted all the way home about the movie, and when they got back, Kory's mom made them banana splits and they told her about the movie all over again.

"I'm going to bed," she said finally. "Samaki, I made up the air mattress in Kory's room. Do you need anything else?"

"No, thank you, Mrs. Hedley," Samaki said. "Oh, just a towel?"

"Kory knows where the spares are. You're going to swim?"

They both nodded. "Samaki wanted to try the pool," Kory said. "Just a short swim."

She glanced at the clock. "Wait another twenty minutes, all right? Good night, boys. God bless." She disappeared down the hallway.

"Your mom's really nice," Samaki said.

"I guess." Kory scratched his ears. "She didn't have to tell us to wait twenty minutes. I know that."

"She just cares about you."

"*Your* mom is cool."

Samaki laughed. "You should have seen her when I broke the living room window. Oh, I thought my ears were gonna fall off."

"How did you break the living room window?"

The fox looked sheepish. "Just horsing around. Kande was outside and I wanted to get her attention. I poked the glass a little too hard."

Kory snorted. "You need to make that a better story. Like you were practicing karate too close to the window and put your fist through it."

The fox stroked his muzzle. "How about… I threw my little brother through it?"

"Now you're talking." Kory grinned. His paw found its way to rest on the fox's tail again, almost without his guiding it.

Twenty minutes later, they walked around to Kory's bedroom. Samaki changed in the bathroom while Kory changed into his swimsuit in the bedroom. He didn't usually wear his suit in the home pool, but with Samaki there he felt he should. He wasn't sure he was quite ready to swim around with the fox in just underwear, and definitely not anything less.

When Samaki came back in his swimsuit, his ears were half down and he wore a silly grin. "This feels funny. I never swam in someone's house before."

Kory felt funny, too, but it wasn't from being in his swimsuit. He took in the black fox's body, the slender runner's muscles, the fluffy tail, the white patch on the chest and the other one spilling out of his swimsuit. All familiar, but here in the privacy of his room rather than the public pool, his thoughts felt more intimate. "Let's, ah, go ahead," he said, and slid into the water.

Kory led Samaki outside first, where they bobbed side by side and looked out at the dark yard. "Cool," the fox breathed into the warm night. "Don't you worry about people getting in through this?"

Kory shook his head. "The yard's pretty secure, and that doorway there?" He waved down into the water behind them. "There's a gate that slides down. I'll close it before we go to sleep."

"Nice." Samaki looked up at the moon and the stars. "Pretty night."

"Yeah," Kory said.

"Somewhere up there is a Forbidden Planet," Samaki murmured.

"Hm?"

"You ever think that? Somewhere out there is everything we've dreamed about and invented."

"Yeah," Kory said. "In an infinite universe…"

"Everything exists somewhere." He paused. "Like the search for the Second Foundation, that just led back to themselves."

"But there really was a Second Foundation out there," Kory said. Their eyes met for a moment, bridged by moonlight. Then Kory said, "Come on. I'll show you the basement. Take a deep breath."

They surfaced in a dark chamber. Kory turned on the light to reveal piles of sealed boxes and bags. He swallowed to pop his ears and saw the fox's flick as he did the same.

Samaki looked around. "There's no other way out?"

"Nope. Just through the water."

"How does it not flood?"

Kory waved a paw through the air. "Pressurized. We have it checked once a year."

"Wow. You have such a cool house. What do you use this room for?"

"Sal and I used to play secret base with it when we were X-Force. Those boxes were our fort, and we'd retreat here to plan our attacks on the enemy."

Samaki grinned. "Who was the enemy?"

"Jeff Barnes, across the street and down one." Kory chuckled. "Dunno what happened to him. He went off to some military academy or prep school or something."

"Nice." Samaki rested on the edge of the floor, his body still in the water, and looked around. "Kinda chilly down here," he said after a moment, and sank back into the water.

Kory nodded. "We don't heat it. Back to my room?"

"Sure." But when Kory swam back, the fox split off from him, headed for Nick's room, and Kory had to grab his foot to stop him. When they surfaced under the bridge leading to his mother's room, Samaki shook the water from his head and looked sheepish.

"Sorry," he said before Kory could say anything. "I was curious."

"That's my brother's room." Kory pointed. "That's my mom's room."

Samaki nodded. "I like these bridges, too. Perfect for hiding stuff under."

"Your house must be full of little hiding places." Kory remembered all the levels and stairs and angles.

"Oh, definitely. Got to be able to hide things from the others, and Mom and Dad." Samaki grinned.

Kory wanted to ask what kinds of things, but he knew what was in certain files on his computer, and hidden in a small file behind some boxes in his closet. He suspected he knew what sorts of things Samaki had, too, and grinned a conspiratorial grin. "So… ready to dry off yet?"

"Yeah." Samaki shook his head, spraying Kory with water.

"Oh, don't even think about trying that…" But the fox had already plunged back under the water. Kory followed him, catching him easily and yanking on his tail, then spinning around as the fox tried to turn and intercept him, grabbing the fox's sides from behind, and whirling him around and around before letting him go. Samaki flailed in the water, and it occurred to Kory that, unused to the water, the fox might not be used to the kind of playing he and his brother did. He backed off and watched, but Samaki righted himself quickly and surfaced in Kory's room.

"Whew," he said with a grin and another shake. "Remind me never to fight with you underwater!"

"You okay?" Kory hung next to him in the water.

"Yeah, just a bit dizzy. Can you teach me that move? That was cool."

Kory laughed. "I dunno if it's a move or what. Just something me and my brother do when playing around in the water."

"I see." Samaki flicked his ears. "I guess I'll have to come over here to play more often, then."

Kory wasn't sure what to say to that, but his heart jumped when he heard it. "Uh...we don't really have dryers, but we have nice towels...I think you can get mostly dry."

Samaki laughed. "Should've known otters wouldn't have dryers. That's okay." He got out of the pool and stood there dripping, blue bathing suit clinging tightly to his body. Kory didn't remember it being so revealing. He wasn't as shy about looking as he'd been at the pool, but he still didn't want to stare. He did get a good look, though, and it was enough to keep him hanging in the water for a bit longer.

"Can I shake in the bathroom?" the fox asked.

"Sure." Kory grinned and pointed. "Out there and to the right. The towels are in the cupboard just outside the bathroom."

"Will I have any trouble finding it?" Samaki looked down at him.

Kory shifted in the water, not quite ready to get out. "Nah, it's right there."

"Okay." The fox padded out with his tail arched, giving Kory a nice view that he could appreciate, since the fox couldn't see him. Fluttery echoes of the worry he used to feel danced around, but he told himself there was nothing wrong with looking. The black-furred legs with the white patch right up where they met were as nice as any girl's he'd eyed.

He got out of the pool himself and lay on the drying mat, stomach down. He closed his eyes and felt the mat slowly leach the water from his fur. After a few minutes of thinking about the fox and trying to make himself relax, he turned his thoughts away and tried to just blank out his mind until he felt comfortable enough to turn over.

Samaki came back several minutes later, still in his swimsuit, fur sticking up every which way. He was trying to smooth it down with his paws, and when Kory grinned up at him, he said, "Don't laugh. I tried to use one of your brushes, but it kept catching in my fur and I couldn't get it to work."

"You didn't use my mom's brush, did you?"

"Heck no. I can tell yours by the scent. I tried to clean it out, but there's probably still some fox fur in there."

"No problem," Kory said. He looked up and watched the fox watching him, and liked imagining that Samaki was eying his swimsuit, and then imagining that made him feel tingly, and he got up abruptly. "So, want to, um, play on the computer a bit?"

"Nah, I'm okay..." Samaki yawned. "Ready to lie down, actually."

"Okay." Kory turned down the sheets on the air mattress, then padded to the doorway as Samaki got into the bed. He turned out the lights and found his way to his own bed.

His fur was still damp. He listened to the fox breathing in the next bed, and all his tensions returned. Looking was all well and good, but now they were lying a few feet away again. He was more determined than ever to initiate some contact, but rather than giving him courage, his resolve just made him more nervous.

"Thanks for having me over," Samaki said, and Kory heard him yawn again.

"Oh, I'm glad to. I had fun. Hope you did too."

"Definitely. I like your mom and Nick. They're nice."

Kory smiled. "They seem to like you, too."

There was silence in the room. Kory stared up at the glow-in-the-dark stars on the ceiling.

"Kory?" Samaki said into the darkness.

"Yeah?" He wondered if the fox could hear his heart pounding.

"What happened to your dad?"

The otter exhaled. "Oh. He left."

Samaki sucked in a breath. "I'm sorry. You talk to him at all?"

"Nah. He lives out on the west coast." That was already as much as Sal knew, and more than he told most people.

"How old were you?"

"Nine."

The room was quiet for several minutes. "When was the last time you talked with him? I'm sorry, I don't mean to be asking all these questions."

"It's okay. I don't mind." And he didn't; the usual sharp corners of those thoughts now padded by gentle black fur. "I talked to him when I was fourteen. Tracked him down and called him. I'd just gotten my cell phone."

More silence, then the fox, softly. "Didn't go well?"

Kory shrugged. "It was okay. Awkward, you know? I wanted to tell him all about the stuff I'd been doing, and he...didn't really care, I know now. I tried calling him back later and he never picked up. So I stopped trying."

He'd never told Sal, or Nick, or anyone else about that.

"I'm sorry, Kory," Samaki said again, and Kory felt fingertips brush his shoulder. He reached his paw down and the fox grasped it gently.

Kory remembered the dark street they'd walked down, the warmth of Samaki's paw then. It was just as warm and comforting now. He sighed. "It's okay. I'm over it, I really am."

"Still." The fox seemed to be groping for words. "It just sucks."

"Thanks," Kory said.

"Your mom seems okay."

"Yeah, the church really helped her." There was a time when he would have felt teenaged scorn, saying that. Now he understood it, and not only meant it, but felt an odd sympathy.

"Glad you guys are okay." The fox gave his paw a squeeze. "You take care of Nick?"

"He pretty much takes care of himself," Kory said. "But I used to, early on." He remembered painful conversations when he'd been too young to understand how and why to cushion the truth for his little brother, nights when Nicky had fallen asleep crying in Kory's bed, sullen evenings that stretched into weeks.

"Glad he had someone to look after him." For a long time, Samaki's paw remained wrapped around Kory's, the touch enough communication in the silence. Then Samaki spoke again, and Kory was surprised to hear anger in his voice. "Your dad is a jerk."

Kory didn't move. The fox went on. "Look what he's missing, what a great son he has and he doesn't even care. He's..." He went quiet, his breathing harsh.

Go, you idiot.

Kory slid easily down to the floor, crawled up next to the fox, and pulled the fox's arm around him, then gently pulled his paw free and placed it right in the center of the white patch of fur on Samaki's chest. The fur was still damp. He smoothed it down, letting his claws trail through it. "Thanks," he said.

Samaki's arm tightened around him, and his head lifted slightly. His eyes shone in the dark. As the otter's paw dug through his white fur, rubbing and letting his claws scritch the underlying skin, he said softly, "I thought you were interested in boobs."

Kory grinned, and then the perfect line came to him at the perfect time, and if that wasn't a sign that he was doing the right thing, he didn't know what else could be. "I am," he said. "You boob."

Samaki laughed, happy and spontaneous, breaking the tension. Still smiling, he leaned his head forward until his nose was about an inch from Kory's, searching the otter's eyes. "Really?"

Kory closed the rest of the distance, touching his broad nose to the fox's narrow one. "Yeah. I...yeah."

Samaki rubbed his nose gently across Kory's and then nuzzled across to rest his muzzle on the otter's shoulder, pulling him into a closer hug. "I don't want to pressure you into anything."

"No," Kory breathed, "I'm just figuring things out."

The fox's paw stroked his side. "I'm happy to help."

Kory buried his nose in the soft, damp black fur. "You are," he mumbled. "You have." The scent was strange, all vulpine, musky and unmistakably male, not at all what he was used to pressing his nose into. He breathed in and let the smell fill him giddily, and it wasn't hard to put his arm all the way around Samaki and hug him back. No, not hard at all.

And it wasn't the fact that the fox was gorgeous, or hugging him back, or male, that made it easy, Kory realized in a flash. It was the fact that this was Samaki, his friend, someone who cared about him, whom he cared about in return. That had always been missing from his relationship with Jenny. He'd listened to her crises, told her about his, but she'd never said anything like what Samaki had just said about Kory's father. He'd never said anything like that to her, either. The connection just hadn't been there.

It was here, in force, crackling between them, pulsing like a living thing. He felt thrilled, terrified, and happier than he'd been in a long, long time.

He pressed his paw through the thick black fur, mimicking the trails the fox's claws were leaving in his fur. Samaki rubbed down to the small of his back, further and further, but always stopping short of his tail. Kory let his paw wander more boldly, pressing into the curve between the fox's back and his tail, feeling the bare fur and the reflexive push back against his paw. Then onward to the fluffy mass of tail, his paw sinking into it as the fox followed suit, his soft pads wandering over Kory's thick tail.

Twice, Kory tried to roll the lighter fox on top of him, but couldn't balance properly on the air mattress. Finally, Kory murmured, "I think my bed is a bit bigger."

Samaki gave him a bright white smile. "Probably softer, too."

"Uh-huh." He started to pull away from the fox, and Samaki grabbed his paw.

"Kory."

He turned, and got a soft kiss right on his nose. Samaki's eyes were reflecting the glow of his stars. He hesitated only for a heartbeat before kissing the fox back, his lips warming the cool nose. Then their lips touched, and he didn't want to do anything else. His paws found the fox's slender form again, pulled Samaki to him as he sat up and leaned with his back to the bed. The fox slid into his lap easily, strong arms sliding behind his shoulders to hold him in return, and the kiss seemed to go on and on and on.

"Wow," he said, when Samaki finally sat back and looked at him.

The fox smiled, one paw tracing the curves of Kory's chest. "Wow?"

"So *that's* what that's supposed to be like."

Samaki laughed. "I liked it too. A lot."

Kory was aware not only of exactly how much the fox had liked it, but also of the fact that the fox could definitely tell how much *he* had enjoyed it. He shifted, found that the rubbing was pretty nice, and did it again intentionally. "So…up on the bed?"

Samaki nodded, and got up. "Let me, um, do something first…" As Kory watched, the fox hooked his paws into the waistband of his swimsuit and slowly pulled it down. He watched Kory watching him, and said, "This was getting kind of uncomfortable."

Kory's breathing sped up. Slowly, Samaki's white fur came into view, as did its centerpiece, long and dark and very erect. The otter stared up at it, then up at the fox's muzzle, smiling down at him. He struggled to his feet.

"Yeah, uh…" It was hard to talk. "Mine too." He pulled his swimsuit down, trying to emulate the grace Samaki had shown. As he kicked it aside, Samaki reached out and brushed claws through his stomach's fur, one paw on either side of the otter's stomach. Kory slipped his arms up inside Samaki's and did the same, pressing his webbed fingers through the damp black fur, letting them stray down towards the white patch. As the fox's paws roamed across the outside of his hips, Kory let his fingers tease the edges of the white fur, venturing ever closer to the center.

Samaki seemed to be waiting for him. As Kory's paw circled ever closer, the fox's lazy caresses grew more intense, and his breathing quickened. Kory hardly knew what he was doing, but he couldn't keep his paws away for long. He looked up into the shining eyes and brushed the back of his paw against the fox's maleness.

Samaki leaned forward and kissed him, and Kory could see the white tip of his tail swinging back and forth behind him. Emboldened, he turned his paw around and brushed the pads up the fox's erection, feeling the curves and the slightly different shape. He smiled, and then smiled wider as he felt the fox's fingers brush him, sending tingles down his legs. Together, they explored each other's shapes, shivering at the feelings, until they ended up pressed close and hugging again, arousals buried in each other's fur. Samaki pushed Kory backwards gently until the otter sat down, then lay down on the bed.

The fox straddled him and then slowly lay down on top of him. Kory hugged the fox to him and they kissed again, while the fox's tail swept back and forth over them both.

"Mmm. What now?" Kory murmured, when they'd broken the kiss and were nuzzling.

"Whatever you want," Samaki said back softly.

"Well, you're the one with the experience."

Samaki laughed softly. "I just know what I want. I didn't say I had any experience."

"You don't?"

The fox paused. His breath ruffled Kory's whiskers. "Let's just say that I know enough to know we should do what comes naturally. We can keep it simple this first time."

"Okay. That sounds good."

"I mean," Samaki said with a grin, his tongue lolling to one side, "if we just keep doing what we were doing a minute ago, I think that will work just fine."

By way of answer, Kory brought his paw up between them, and did just that. Samaki panted over top of him, then squeezed himself off to lie on his side next to Kory so that he could return the favor, their paws working in unison as their breath came hot into each other's fur. Kory tried to keep quiet, a little self-conscious about his panting and grunts, but he felt less so as Samaki squirmed against him, making all kinds of little yips and squeaks. He kicked the wall once, and froze until Kory said, giggling, "That's just the hallway."

It was strange, having another paw pleasuring him while going through the motions on someone else. It was wonderful, too, to feel the effect his paw was having on Samaki, and to feel Samaki's paw and press against him to show how much he enjoyed it. Kory couldn't remember anything so intimate, so personal, in his past anywhere. He felt his breath coming faster and harder, but it was Samaki who jerked against him first. Warmth coated his paw and the musky smell reached his nostrils.

"Oh," Samaki was moaning, "Kory…"

He kept working on the otter while he moaned and climaxed, paw moving nice and quick, and Kory was so wound up that it was less than a minute before he was burying his muzzle in the fox's fur and moaning, "Samaki…" It was an awkward name to moan, so he moaned again, "Foxy…" and that felt much better, a nice thing to moan as the fox brought him off.

For a short span of time, they both just lay there. Samaki was the first to talk.

"I think," he said, "that was more than just fine."

"Oh, yes." Kory pulled the fox on top of him, ignoring the stickiness in their fur. They hugged tightly and nuzzled again and again, paws stroking each other's fur.

"So can I ask you something?" Samaki said, and when Kory nodded, went on, "What made you decide to try?"

"That's easy," Kory said. "You did."

"I hoped you might be gay, but didn't want to pressure you."

"You didn't. And I'm not sure I am gay."

Samaki tilted his head. "You know…I dunno how it is in Westmont, but back in the city, what we just did here is pretty gay."

"Well, I know." Kory's whole body felt like it was grinning. "I just meant, I didn't decide to sleep with you because you're unbelievably gorgeous and I'm attracted to guys. I wanted to sleep with you because you're…because you're you."

The fox smiled and stroked his cheek. "You're unbelievably sweet, you know that?" He kissed Kory's nose. "You want to know a secret?"

Kory nodded. "Mm-hmm. If it's about you."

Samaki's ears folded slightly back. "Um, that night we went to the movie…I took you through the dark street on purpose so I could hold your paw."

Kory giggled. "I bribed my brother to stay out late so my mom wouldn't pick me up and I could stay over."

"Really?" Samaki laughed. "That's cute."

"Then I didn't do anything." Kory sighed.

Samaki nodded. "We had a nice night anyway. And you weren't ready then. I'm glad you are now."

"Me too."

After another kiss, Samaki said, "I should tell you one more thing…"

Kory nodded. The fox looked up at the ceiling stars, and Kory felt his tension. Before the otter could ask about it, the fox recited slowly, "*Scarlet the passion, the color of my heart.*"

The otter stared at him. "*Coral a sunset, God's work of art.*" Samaki went on, and looked down into Kory's eyes.

"Oh, no," Kory moaned, a different tone from his moans of a few minutes ago. "Where did you read that?"

"The paper." Samaki pulled back the pillow Kory was trying to cover his face with. "Oh, come on. It's really good."

"How long ago did you read it?" The hot flush of embarrassment was fading, very slowly.

"When it came out. What's the matter? It really was good." The fox's paw brushed his cheek tenderly.

Kory sighed. "My English teacher posted it in the hallway of our school. I got teased for it for weeks, and my…the girl I was dating said why didn't I ever write anything like that for her, and, well, that was Jenny, you remember."

"Oh." Samaki rested a paw on his shoulder. "Well…I'm not that upset about you not having a girlfriend."

"I guess that worked out okay," Kory admitted.

"And…to tell you the truth…that's why I was at the pool that day." Kory felt the motion as the fox's ears flicked.

"Huh?"

"I read about you in the paper and the poem really touched me. I wanted to meet the otter my age who could write like that. I kinda had a crush on you, I guess, without even meeting you."

The warm embarrassment was returning. "Me?"

"Heck, yeah. I cut the poem out and put it up on my wall." He licked Kory on the nose. "But I hid it before you came over."

"So you were hoping to meet me at the municipal pool?"

"Nah." Samaki laughed, and Kory felt the vibrations in his own stomach, and couldn't help giggling along. "I was just trying to practice so I could be a good enough swimmer that when I went over to Caspian, I wouldn't embarrass myself. I'm glad I didn't know you have an indoor pool, or I probably wouldn't have even tried that."

"Wow. Well…I'm glad you did," Kory said. "Really glad."

Samaki paused for a moment, and then said, "Want to hear something kinda silly?"

Kory smiled. "Only if it's from you."

The fox nuzzled him. "When I read the poem, there was a note of…of something behind it, of longing, or searching…and I thought, uh…"

Kory poked him in the hip, tickling gently. "Go on."

Samaki squirmed and giggled. "I thought, he's looking for me. I felt like you sent that poem out into the world to find me, and I had to find my way to you."

Something was making it hard for Kory to talk, all of a sudden. "Maybe…maybe I did," he said, swallowing. He stroked his paw down the curve of the fox's back, over the swell of his rear, and pulled his tail up to bury his fingers in. "I didn't know I was doing it."

"That's okay," the fox whispered. "I did."

"I fell for you back at the pool, you know," Kory said. "When you laughed at my joke, and then walked out of the dryers, so pretty, so handsome…I just didn't realize it for a while."

Samaki smiled and kissed him. "It's not easy. But I'm glad you did."

"Oh, me too." They kissed, more warmly, and Kory felt the stirrings of interest awaken again. The fur between them was all matted and sticky, so when they parted, panting, he said, "Maybe we should clean up a bit?"

They scampered to the bathroom, naked, Kory looking around to make sure his mother and Nick weren't making a mid-night visit. In the shower, they cleaned up with soap, and in the process of cleaning, found that the soap was quite nice between paws and the parts they were trying to clean, and ended up kissing, and then presently they managed to get themselves sticky again, so they had to clean up all over, panting and leaning on each other and giggling giddily.

Back in Kory's bed, they snuggled up close, exhausted and happy. Kory found that his muzzle fit nicely into the curve between the taller fox's neck and shoulder, and Samaki seemed to like curling his tail around Kory's. They whispered goodnights to each other, nuzzled and yawned, and Kory drifted off to sleep with the feeling that he was floating, insulated from the world and borne up by something much more buoyant than mere water.

STREAMS

In the oppressive heat of August, Kory felt uncomfortable any time he wasn't swimming. While he loved to be in the water, he didn't particularly like having it dropped onto him, nor did he like the thunder and lightning that accompanied summer storms. In previous summers, he'd worked as a lifeguard in the pool to earn spending money, but this August, he'd found something besides swimming that relaxed him no matter how hot the air was.

This morning, that something was lying on his bedroom floor, the first rays of the morning sun illuminating the black of his chest fur and the white patch at his throat. He'd turned onto his side so that one of his large black ears was folded under his head, a problem Kory's small round ears never gave him. Below the fox's slender stomach, a loose white sheet covered his hips and legs. His long black tail lay straight out behind him, as far away from his body as possible, the faint luminescence of the white tip seeming almost detached from its owner.

Thirty or forty sleepovers, nearly an entire summer, hadn't diminished the magic of waking up in the same room with the black fox. He rolled over onto his stomach and turned his head to one side so he could still see Samaki's stomach rise and fall, and slowly dropped one arm to the floor. His paw came to rest on the fox's outstretched paw, where it would remain until Samaki woke up in a few minutes.

On this morning, their routine was broken by a loud splash and a soft chirp. "You guys decent?"

Samaki woke with a jump. Kory rolled back onto his side and propped himself up on an elbow, looking at the corner of his room that was open to the house pool. His brother Nick bobbed there, eyes squeezed shut. "Of course," Kory said, suppressing the shiver he'd felt at the intrusion, even though his mother never swam and Nick knew about him and Samaki. "What are you doing up?"

He could see Nick's eyeshine in the dusk. "I wanted to catch you guys before you took off. You want a ride downtown today? Me'n'Mickey are going to the card show before the game to get autographs and his dad's driving us. They've got a Durango so I'm sure he has room, and the show's in the mall just the other side of downtown."

Kory peered down at the fox, who was rubbing his eyes. "Can you stand to ride in an SUV?"

"As long as we don't go to the gas station." Samaki yawned, showing off a grin of perfect white teeth and a long pink tongue. "When are you leaving, Nick?"

"Quarter to eight. The show opens at nine but Digger Clawson is gonna be there so there's gonna be a line. I'm gonna go shower then you guys can go." He vanished under the water with barely a ripple.

"Hang on," Samaki said, too late. He turned to grin at Kory. "Should know better than to try to keep up with an otter in the water." He rhymed "otter" and "water," making Kory smile.

"What did you want?"

"My dad's a big Clawson fan. I was going to ask if Nick would get me an autograph."

Kory trailed his paw up Samaki's arm. "You have enough money?"

"Money?" The fox cupped his ears forward. "They charge money for autographs?"

"Sometimes."

Samaki wriggled his fingers. "I have ten dollars. I hope that's enough."

Kory leaned over the bed. Samaki met his muzzle in a short kiss. "I'm sure it'll be fine," the otter said.

The hiss of the shower started up. "Hmm," Samaki said. "I guess we have about ten minutes." He closed his paw around Kory's arm. "What can we do in ten minutes, I wonder?"

Kory giggled. "We can't. What if my mom walks in?"

"Aw, she never does, though." Samaki's fingers teased right in the crook of Kory's elbow.

The otter squirmed, already hard from waking up and feeling the familiar tingle in his groin. "We just did it last night!"

"Well, I can't stay over tonight," Samaki said. "Consider it an advance payment."

Kory laughed, hesitating. He knew it was a bad idea, but his body was already urging him on. *Come on, it'll only take a few minutes.* Samaki's finger trailed up his arm, two claws parting his fur and just teasing the skin beneath. "I, uh..."

The fox withdrew his finger with a grin. "All right. You're probably right, I think it's a bad idea."

"You were just getting me worked up!" Kory got up on his paws and knees, glaring at the fox, who was already scooting back and away from him with a big grin.

"I wasn't! But now we don't have time any more, so I stopped." His protest of innocence was severely undermined by his self-satisfied tail twitching, the motion of the white tip clearly visible.

Kory didn't say another word, just launched himself off the bed. Samaki ducked to one side with a yelp, only partially rolling out of Kory's way.

The otter caught his arm and scrambled into the water, pulling the fox behind him. Samaki yelped theatrically as he was tugged into the pool, his yelp coming to an abrupt halt a moment before Kory pushed his head underwater.

The fox had gotten much better at playing in the water. He squirmed out of Kory's hold and rolled on top of the otter, sending him underwater as well. No matter how good Samaki got, though, he was lighter than Kory, and even in summer when his coat was thin, his thick, bushy tail was a liability. Kory grabbed at it, careful not to pull too hard, and Samaki clutched one of his hindpaws in revenge, nibbling at the sensitive pads.

In the thrashing around, tails and paws weren't the only things that got grabbed. By the time they finally surfaced in Kory's room again, giggling and gasping for breath, neither made a move to get out of the water even though the shower had stopped. Arms resting on the floor, Kory returned Samaki's grin, conscious of the warm weight between his legs, his paw still tingling with the memory of the fox's. "Got to get decent for the shower," Kory said.

"Uh-huh," Samaki said. "Think of baseball players?"

"That never works."

"Think of girls?"

Kory giggled. "That doesn't work either."

"Does for me." The fox chuckled. "Wrap a towel around yourself?"

Kory eyed the pile of towels on his floor. "Maybe."

"Wait here while I go first?" Samaki rubbed his wet muzzle against Kory's.

"That works. I get a show that way anyway."

The fox clambered out of the water, grinning, and turned his profile to Kory before lifting his arms over his head and stretching. Taut muscles under black fur drew Kory's eye as much as the well-defined bulge in front of his swimsuit. Since he'd molted, muscles had seemed to pop out of the fox's body, hills and valleys revealed by the melting black snows. Though Samaki would protest he wasn't really an athlete, his lithe body always looked barely able to restrain the energy within, as if it would take no more than a touch to send him into motion. In chemistry class that spring, Kory's professor had explained unstable equilibrium to them with a diagram of a marble poised at the top of a hill, unmoving, but needing only a touch in any direction to plunge down the slope. That was how Kory thought of Samaki: balancing expertly on a summit, just waiting to choose his direction.

Samaki grinned, flicked a large ear, and then cocked his head, remembering. "Oh. My mom understands why I'm over here all the time, because of the pool and all, but she wants you to come over for dinner again sometime soon. And Ajani wants to show you his latest comic book."

"Another League of Canids?"

The black fox picked up a towel. "It's a Red Lightning solo story. He's read it, I would guess, something like five hundred times since he bought it. He quotes lines from it at the dinner table. I even know some of them by now. 'If you didn't want trouble, you shouldn't have messed with my family'."

Kory laughed at the imitation of Ajani's squeaky voice. "I like his comics."

"I know. I don't hold it against you."

Small streams of water trickled from Kory's elbows to Samaki's feet, meeting and puddling on his bedroom floor. "You can hold other things against me," he said softly.

Samaki glanced around the room, and at the door. He blew Kory a kiss and then padded to the shower.

Kory ducked under the water and swam quickly to Nick's room, surfacing with his eyes closed. "One, two, three," he counted, and when Nick didn't tell him not to, he opened his eyes.

"Hey," Nick said. He'd tossed on a pair of jeans with patched knees, which their mother hated. She'd bought him three new pairs last month for the summer.

"Hey," Kory said, "Samaki's gonna give you ten dollars for a Digger Clawson autograph. Just tell him that was enough. I'll make up the difference."

Nick pulled down a t-shirt with the Dragons logo on it and squeezed his torso into it. Like Samaki, Nick would protest that he wasn't an athlete. He claimed he just liked swimming and was on the team to meet girls, but in the last year, his frame had grown enough that his t-shirts could barely contain it. He liked the look, and the girls did too, from what Kory could tell. "I dunno if I have enough."

"How much is it going to be?"

Nick shrugged. "I'm bringing forty."

"I'll give you another forty in the car," Kory said. When he wasn't volunteering with Samaki, he did some work at the local grocery store that he'd added to his savings. Forty was not so much, not for something Samaki wanted.

His brother flashed him a smile and a thumbs-up. "Cool."

As he blinked water out of his eyes, back in his room, he saw a shape at his desk and thought for a moment that Samaki had gotten back early from his shower. Then he smelled his mother and his nerves flashed a quick burst of panic. He wiped his eyes hurriedly, ready to leap out of the water, but she was only looking at the pile of college brochures. Was there anything else on his desk, anything he'd left there? He didn't think so. He rested his elbows on his floor, his body in the water, and tried to slow the racing of his heart. He hoped Samaki's strong scent would cover the scent from last night. He and Samaki were careful, always cleaning up and de-scenting, but he didn't know how keen his mother's nose was. Not as sharp as Samaki's, he was pretty sure.

"Two more college brochures came today," she said, tapping her paw on his desk. "I thought you might want to look at them before you went off to your homeless shelter."

"Thanks," Kory said, his mind racing to figure out a way to get her out of his room before Samaki came back. "I'll take a look."

"Bruin College is a possibility. I don't think much of Havertown, but I brought the brochure in anyway." She looked disdainfully down at it.

"Okay, Mom. What's for breakfast?"

She looked startled. "I didn't make anything. Do you want me to?"

"I dunno. I think we have to leave pretty quickly. What do we have?"

She turned her head in the general direction of the kitchen, and started walking toward the door. "I'll check."

He slid out of the water when she'd left and walked over to his desk. She didn't come into his room uninvited, usually, but she seemed to be doing it more and more when Samaki was over, as though she sensed that something was wrong without knowing quite what it was. If she caught them together...

He drove that thought from his mind, and pawed through the ever-growing pile of college brochures. Some of them knew enough to send laminated brochures to an otter household; Forester University was one of those. He picked up their brochure again, dripping water on the less well-prepared Bruin College. Much as he hated to think about it, he was going to have to start applying to colleges and making a decision soon.

Samaki was almost certain to attend State, where his father worked and his older sister Kande was attending. They hadn't talked about it much, but State was conspicuously absent from the pile of brochures his mother had organized for him, even though he knew they had sent more than one brochure to the house. How they knew there was a high school senior living there, he hadn't figured out yet. Colleges just had an instinct for that, he guessed. He sighed and put down the plastic, having not really even seen the pictures of old brick buildings and lushly colored maple groves.

By the time Samaki returned, just as wet, but smelling of soap more than just fox, Kory had moved on to checking his e-mail, and the sounds of his mother and Nick moving around in the house filtered through his walls to him, a soft chorus that nevertheless set the unromantic mood as effectively as anything he might have chosen from his stereo. Samaki didn't say anything as he sat on the bed in his underwear and attacked his fur with his brush, and Kory flashed a chaste and friendly smile on his way across the floor to take his own shower. Already his room wasn't "safe" any more; the memory of his mother's presence there made sure of that.

After his shower, they scarfed down bowls of cold cereal in the kitchen with Nick, during which his mother emerged wearing a simple white robe. "Why did you ask me what we have if you were just going to have cereal, Kory?" she said. "We have toast, and oatmeal, and eggs." She took some slices of bread out of the breadbox as she spoke.

"Can't eat oatmeal in summer, mom," Nick mumbled.

"Don't talk with your mouth full," she said. "Well, we'll have Sunday breakfast tomorrow. Samaki, will you be here tomorrow morning?"

The fox swallowed, shaking his head. "No, Mrs. Hedley. Not Sunday."

Kory thought his mother didn't really look like she cared that she'd forgotten, even though Samaki had told her every weekend he was over that he spent Saturday nights and Sundays at home. She went right on preparing her breakfast, getting the butter and jam out of the fridge while the bread toasted. "Oh, right. How is your family?"

"They're fine, thank you."

"I'm sorry your mother couldn't make it to our church social."

"She wanted to, but Mariatu had an upset stomach. You know how it is." Kory knew that was a lie.

"I certainly do." His mother smiled. "Kory had all kinds of stomach problems when he was four. There was a two-week stretch where he had the worst diarrhea I'd ever seen."

"Mom!"

Samaki had the grace to look away, and Nick, snickering, came to the rescue. "We gotta get ready. Mickey's gonna be here any minute now."

"Don't bolt your food!" their mother cried, but it was impossible to know whom she was talking to, so they all ignored her. By the time she'd gotten Nick's name out, all three were already getting up from the table.

Kory knew Mickey vaguely, a short, muscular, chattery otter. His father, built similarly, proved that "the oysters don't stray from the bed," greeting Kory and Samaki with a hearty slap on the back. He ushered them into his large SUV with obvious pride.

"Nice truck," Samaki murmured to Kory, ducking his head to clamber up into the spacious back seat. Kory giggled and nudged the fox, but Mickey's father hadn't heard; he started chattering about the players he'd admired growing up as he started the vehicle with a roar that made Samaki flatten his ears dramatically. Kory grinned, and nudged him again.

While Mickey's father talked cheerfully about baseball, Kory leaned back and responded occasionally. Samaki looked out the window, but his paw crept over to seek out Kory's. Still jittery with echoes of his mother's visit that morning, Kory moved his paw into his lap and stared straight ahead. The fox didn't react, just left his own on the seat until they reached Badger Square. "Where you guys headed from here?" Mr. Donovan asked.

"The library," Kory blurted out. "Working on some summer projects."

"Pretty smart. You keep that up, you'll get into a good college. You see that, Mickey?"

Mickey looked considerably less enthusiastic. "Yeah, come on, Dad, let's get to the show."

"Thanks for the ride, Mr. Donovan," Samaki said, getting out.

"Yeah, thanks," Kory said. He waited until Samaki was out to press two twenties into Nick's paw. "See you tonight," he said.

"Seeya." Nick made the money disappear into his pocket in a smooth motion.

Samaki walked quietly beside Kory to the thrift shop they usually made their first stop. It wasn't open this early, but they stopped to look in the window anyway. "Library?" the black fox said.

"What? Oh. Well, they don't need to know."

"You could've said you work with homeless kids. You didn't have to say gay homeless kids."

The feeling that Samaki was disappointed in him was a new one. Kory's stomach fluttered. "I dunno. It was just easier to say the library."

"Easier?"

Kory looked up at the black fox's bemused expression. "I didn't want to get into a whole discussion."

Samaki nodded. "I didn't mean you should've said 'gay homeless kids.' I just wondered why you went to 'library'."

"It was the first thing that came into my head." Kory curled his tail down as he walked.

"I guess it doesn't matter." The black fox looked around, his ears perking up as he looked across the square. "Hey, Starbucks is open."

Kory's mood improved almost immediately. Ever since their first cup of coffee in the Starbucks by the pool, the little green coffee chain felt special to him. He could walk into any one and remember how the sun had hit Samaki's black fur and violet eyes that afternoon. It never failed to cheer him up.

By the time they had gotten their coffee and pawed through the dusty racks of the thrift store, where Samaki found a pair of pants for him and a shirt for his brother Kasim, the comment and Kory's queasy worry, as well as the jitters about his mother's morning visit, were long gone. The walk to the Rainbow Center, a short six blocks, was always nice even in the warm summer morning, and though Kory would always rather be swimming, walking through Hilltown early in the morning was a close second, especially with Samaki at his side.

Holly Street led away from the bohemian Badger Square along rows of brick and wood houses, relics of an older time. Faded paint and cracked wood showed the age of the buildings, but no fast food containers littered the street, no old clothes hung over the bare wooden railings, and the windows were kept clean and free of dust. Between the tightly packed rows of houses, they passed a hamburger joint, a taco stand that was their favorite lunch place (two tacos for a dollar!), a laundromat, and a few book and clothing stores that had yet to open. Left down the narrow Badger Lane brought them to a converted three-story house that had once been two row homes. Alone on the block, it sported a fresh coat of neutral ivory paint and a well-kept porch. The words "Rainbow Center" were engraved on the wooden plaque to the right of the door, and beneath that, a quotation: "Beneath my roof, let all gather without fear or hate; for if we are to banish them from the world, we must first begin at home."

Kory had looked up R. Carmine, the attributed author, on the Internet with Samaki one night and had enjoyed reading about the life of the arctic fox, poet and ardent gay rights activist. She'd died twelve years before, but it was thanks to a foundation she'd helped create that the Rainbow Center continued to exist. Only one book of her poetry had been published, and it was on back order everywhere he looked. The Rainbow Center library had a copy, of course, but he wanted to spend his time at the house helping, not reading, so he only stole a look at the book on his breaks.

Usually, he loved to look at the plaque as they walked in, but today it brought back the memory of him saying "library". Was it wrong to not want to tell Mickey's dad their whole life story? Maybe not. But how would Carmine have handled it?

Even though it wasn't quite nine, the house was bustling. Summer was a busy time for runaways, with school out of session, and the kids were used to getting up at seven or eight even in summer. The house had DVDs to keep them busy for a few hours, but Margo, the black squirrel who ran Rainbow Center, didn't like the kids to sit and watch TV all day, so she organized work projects, some more fun than others. Samaki, in his second summer helping out, was allowed to lead projects unsupervised, but Kory had to be with Samaki or one of the other experienced volunteers, which didn't bother him at all, truth be told.

True to its name, the inside of the Rainbow Center was a hodgepodge of different building styles. In places like the school or public library, the interiors were deliberately minimalist so as not to favor any one species over another. Even though the Rainbow Center received some public funding, the equal-access laws known as the Orwell Act only applied to the common areas of the building, and then only to specify that the area be equally welcoming to all. Margo interpreted that to mean "as welcoming as possible to all," a passion which showed in the ceiling rungs, for squirrels and other climbers, the hard salt licks in the walls, the shallow trough of water running along one side of each of the ground-floor rooms, the sheltered corner with the thick triangular shade stretched over it to block out the light, and dozens of other small touches. Kory, used to the simple one- or two-species houses of his friends and the bare public school and library, had been first overwhelmed and then delighted by the feeling that he was entering a space that was not just communal, but an intersection of several different private spaces. It contributed to the feeling of home, and in fact, when he'd suggested adding a loft-type structure to the common room, inspired by Ajani's suspended desk in the Roden boys' bedroom, Margo had not only taken enthusiastically to his idea, but had let him design and oversee the building of it.

"Good morning, boys!" Margo said as they walked into the common room. Two boys a little younger than Kory sat in front of the TV: a skunk and a porcupine. Up on the loft, a weasel, hung half off the frame, watching with the others. Below him, slouched against the wooden frame, a fruit bat surveyed the room with folded arms and over-affected boredom. Piercings glittered in both her large ears, echoed in the silver studs down the side of the black leather jacket that hung over her bony frame.

Coming in here and remembering what these kids were going through made Kory's problems seem trivial. He put them aside and waved to the bat. "Hi, Malaya." She snorted, but nodded to him before turning back to the TV. The boys continued watching, oblivious. Kory leaned against the "dark corner," after checking that nobody was curled up inside it.

"Did Marty get his placement?" Samaki asked after a quick scan of the room.

Margo nodded. "He left yesterday evening. I have his address if you want to send a card along."

"Yeah, please." The young fox had been Kory and Samaki's favorite all summer, a boisterous bundle of energy who'd been the first to help out with every project despite his broken wrist. The only thing he wasn't eager to talk about was how his wrist had been broken. Kory only knew that his father had been somehow responsible and that his mother hadn't done anything to stop it.

"All right. I'm just going to get some more e-mails sent out. It looks like Jeremy's situation might get ugly." She dropped her voice, glancing sideways at the skunk. "Don't say anything to him, though. Now, go get started on the back yard. I'll come out and join you later."

"Bye, Margo," they chorused, grinning at each other. Samaki reached for Kory's paw as they walked across the room, and here in the only other place that felt safe, Kory took it. With that grasp, their argument of the morning faded completely. He saw Malaya roll her eyes at them, and gave her a big smile.

A little over an hour into the backyard project, Kory noticed that Malaya was gone. The boys were working hard cutting the fence posts, Samaki was collecting the old pieces of the fence, and Malaya was supposed to be on the other side of the portion of the fence that was still standing, digging at the foundation to loosen it while Kory did the same on his side. Only he hadn't heard her digging in a while, and when he peeked around the wooden slats, there was nobody opposite him.

"She's probably up in her room," Samaki said. "Want to go get her? If you can't find her or if she won't come, then get Margo to help."

"Sure." Kory started to go in the back door, then reconsidered and walked around the fence, down the narrow space between the houses. At the side of the front porch he paused, looking out into the bright summer street, and then the acrid tickle of cigarette smoke stroked his nostrils. He looked down and saw the fruit bat sitting with her wings closed around her knees beneath the porch.

As soon as his eyes met hers, the lit tip of a cigarette came back into view. She puffed on it and exhaled a cloud of smoke. "Damn," she said dryly. "You won't tell on me, will you? Because then they'd kick me out and that would be terrible."

There was just enough room next to her for Kory to squeeze in, leaving his left shoulder and leg out in the sunlight. He could see why Malaya liked it here. Nobody could see you. It felt safe, almost like swimming. "If you don't like it here, you could just leave."

"And go where? They won't let me go home yet. I'd rather be here than living in a box somewhere."

"It's not so bad here."

She blew a puff of smoke into the dark space under the porch. "You don't have to live here."

He sighed. "What don't you like?"

"What, going to go tell Margo to fix it? Don't bother. It's shorter to tell you what I do like." She took another drag, and scratched at her wing with her left hand. "The free food. Talking to you. That's about it."

"Me?" He'd known they had a rapport, but he hadn't thought he was the only one.

She shrugged. "You don't live in some pie-in-the-sky fantasy world. Margo says I'll be placed with my grandmother, as if I want to go live in a swamp. The boys all think their troubles are over now they're in Lotusland here. And your boyfriend, no offense, makes Pollyanna look like a realist."

It still took a few seconds for the glow of having Samaki referred to as his boyfriend to sink in and dissipate. "He's..."

"Relax." Her laugh was too deep for her age. "You guys prob'ly balance each other out well. You know what the real world is like. You know that your mom isn't going to pick up some PFLAG brochure and read it and suddenly say, 'Oh, I've been wrong about faggots all this time.' You know that placing you in custody with your grandmother in some other state is going to mess you up worse than dealing with your asshole father."

Kory wasn't sure he knew any of those things. He just hated to contradict people. "Sure," he said. "But that doesn't mean you can't hope for things to get better."

Malaya looked at him. "You know what hope is?" She took a drag and opened her short mouth into an "O", puffing out a small cloud of smoke. "That's hope," she said. "It burns and it stings, and when you try to grab it," she waved a hand through it, "it's gone."

Kory watched the tendrils of smoke dissipate in the darkness. "But you keep taking another puff," he said, his voice quiet. "Why is that?"

Their eyes met for a moment. Then Malaya ground out the cigarette in the dirt and bumped his shoulder. "All right, let's get back to it," she said. "Man, it's gonna suck around here when school starts."

"Aren't you going back?" He got to his feet and extended a paw down to her, which she ignored.

"Sure, but I'll be coming back here at night with Margo Sunshine and I won't have you to bitch to because you're going back to school too."

"You're in Samaki's school. Don't any of the other kids go there?"

"I can't hang out with them at school. They're losers." She grinned at him. "Not your boyfriend. But he's gonna be a senior and I'm a junior. Doesn't work too well."

"You can still have lunch, can't you?"

Malaya paused at the fence. "Do I have smoke on my breath?"

The whole crew worked through the afternoon, only breaking to get tacos for lunch, and finished the fence fifteen minutes before Samaki and Kory had to catch their buses home, giving the fox and otter barely enough time to wash up. Samaki released Kory's damp paw as they left the Rainbow Center and walked to the bus stop. "I hope Jeremy will be okay," he said.

"I hope Malaya will," Kory responded.

"Once they work out her travel to Millenport, she'll be fine," Samaki said. "She just needs to get to a better home."

"I don't think she wants to go to Millenport," Kory said. "She wants to stay here."

"That's silly," Samaki said. "It'd better for her to go to Millenport. Did you hear what her father did?"

Kory shrugged as his bus rounded the corner. "This is her home. Why should she leave?"

"If she doesn't want to leave, she's crazy."

Kory looked at the vehement violet eyes. "Maybe sometimes people want things that aren't good for them."

The fox's intensity melted away. His first response was lost in the squeal of brakes from Kory's bus stopping. "Fortunately," he said as the doors opened, "the things I want are very good for me." Cool air washed over them both. "See you Monday."

"See you Monday," Kory said at the bus stop as Samaki's bus pulled up.

"Bye, foxy." Kory smiled, tilting his muzzle upward. They touched noses briefly, which was as much affection as he was comfortable showing in public, and then he stepped reluctantly onto the bus. Samaki waved one more time as the doors hissed closed, and then the bus pulled away, leaving Kory with only the lingering smell of fox on his nose.

Nick's swimming practice was starting up again, so this Sunday, their mother left with him immediately after the Mass was over to drop him off. Kory was in no hurry to walk home.

"Glad to see you smiling more, Kory," Father Joe said, shaking the paw of Mrs. Jefferson and wishing her a good day.

"It's been a good summer," Kory said.

"Want to help me pick up the hymnals?"

Kory grinned. "Sure." He walked through the now-empty church on the opposite side from the priest, collecting the books in his arms.

"Your mother tells me you're doing quite a lot of charity work this summer."

"Yeah, there's a shelter on the north side of downtown that helps homeless kids. I go over there once a week and hang out with them, help paint the house, whatever."

"That's wonderful to hear." The priest chuckled. "You know, if you have any leftover energy, the church could use a coat of paint as well."

"School starts next week," Kory said. "I don't know if I'd have time."

"I was kidding." Father Joe looked over at him and winked. "Mostly. So how did you find this shelter?"

Kory didn't answer immediately. "Oh, a friend of mine told me about it," he said finally, glancing outside at the empty doorway. His mother had moved on to talk to some other friends of hers.

"Someone in this church?"

"No," Kory said. "You don't know him."

When they reached the front of the church, Father Joe leaned against one of the pews. Kory looked up at him. "A few months ago," the sheep said in a low voice, "you were having some trouble. Did you get that all worked out?" Kory nodded. "Did you call the people I told you about?"

"No," Kory said. "I pretty much worked it out on my own."

The sheep waited, but Kory didn't volunteer any other information. "All right," Father Joe said. "I'm glad to hear it's worked out. But I think it's also important that you be able to talk about it. It doesn't have to be with me, but I hope there's someone you can talk to."

"There is," Kory nodded, saying it more to end the conversation than because he meant it. "Thanks."

He started to leave, but Father Joe put one hand on his shoulder. "These kinds of questions, Kory," he said, "they touch on how we think of ourselves as a person. They mingle with species and gender and age and class and all those other things the people these days call 'Orwell Act stuff.' But who we *are* as a person," he tapped his chest, "that's in here. That's what God looks at, and what He's talking about in all that stuff I read every week up there. You know those lectures about the Pharisees?"

"I know," Kory said.

"All right." Father Joe stood. "Forgive me for taking a little more of your time, but it's my job to think about things like that." He smiled. "Good luck in school this year."

Kory raised a paw. "Thanks." He grinned. "See you next week, Father."

On the way home, he thought about it. Of course, he could talk to Samaki about any problems, couldn't he? Or Margo, in a pinch? But Samaki was personally involved, and Kory was already worried the fox thought less of him for not being more forthright about their relationship. Margo was so energetic and well-meaning that Kory wasn't sure he could even bring up the subject with her. She would just tell him everything was fine, just as Malaya always accused her of doing. And there was Malaya, but she would go too far to the other extreme.

Of course, he thought, there was Nick. He could always talk to Nick.

The first week of school was always disorienting. It seemed that the last school year ended right when Kory got the hang of things, and none of that helped in the fall when he was starting with new classes. At least his friends were the same as they'd been in the spring. Jason and Dev had both spent most of the summer playing World of Warcraft, of course. Kory wandered over to say hi to them and felt glad to get a hello sandwiched between descriptions of campaigns and strategies and artifacts. He listened long enough to get a feel for the game and a brief twinge of regret that his days of immersive gameplay were behind him, and then took his seat next to Sal.

"Funny," Sal said as he sat down. "It feels like I didn't see you all summer."

Kory played with one of his brand new pencils. "Sorry I didn't come by your dad's office more often."

"You would've been way better than Teddy. I still can't believe you didn't take the position."

Geoff Hill, behind Sal, snickered. "Assume the position!" he said. "Get a room, you two."

Kory ignored him and shrugged to cover the squirming inside. "I told you, my Mom wanted me to do something spiritual. Charity work."

This was partly true. His mother wouldn't have been averse to Kory taking the well-paid internship with Sal's father's company, but she was worried that he and Sal would goof off all day, and she'd seemed relieved when he'd mentioned the charity work with Samaki. Had he told her the truth about Rainbow Center, he suspected she wouldn't have been as enthusiastic, but she was happy enough that he was doing the Lord's work that she didn't press. The grocery store had evening hours so he could still earn some money.

"So you were hanging out with Sammy all summer?"

"Samaki, yeah." Kory cast about for a subject to change to. "Hey, is Deb in any of your classes?"

He could tell right away that things had changed with Sal and Deb. His friend shrugged. "I dunno."

Kory didn't say anything right away, and after a moment, Sal looked at him. "I got tired of her whining, you know? She was always tryin' to drag me out to hang out with her friends."

"Like Sarah and..."

"Jenny, yeah."

"She's dating Yaro now," Geoff Hill put in. "They were lockin' lips at a party I was at in July." Clearly he wanted them to be impressed that he'd been to a party where Yaro, the star of the swim team, had been, or else to be jealous that they hadn't been invited.

Kory felt neither of those. The nine months he'd dated Jenny felt as vague as a dream now. He'd never felt as close to her as he did to Samaki.

"You're still doing the vo-tech thing this year, right?"

Sal snorted. "Course. My dad can pay me to spend the summer shuffling papers, but I told him I still want to fix computers. He said just decide at the end of the summer." His face stretched into the wide grin that Kory always found infectious. "A couple times a week I hung out with Dan. He's the IT guy at Dad's office, a weasel, and he knows everything. I told him what I'd been studying and he showed me a whole ton of stuff. He's got it so good there. Nothing gets done if he doesn't want it to, and he reads everyone's e-mail. He showed me one e-mail a guy sent where he was talking about boning his secretary. It was cool."

Kory grinned back. "Sorry I missed it."

"I'm telling ya," Sal said, "you're missin' the boat with this college thing. Why spend a hundred grand to get a degree when you could be out there working full time in two years. Dan makes fifty thousand a year!"

"I dunno. I just...I gotta go to college."

Sal nodded. "I'll buy you a dinner sometime while you're paying off your college loans."

"And fix my computer?"

"Well, sure." Sal chuckled just as the homeroom bell rang.

With Sal gone for half the day at his vo-tech classes, Kory chatted with a few other acquaintances in Physics, Calculus, and English. Of those, only English class promised to be interesting; they were actually slated to do a unit on poetry in the fall, and Mrs. Digginson, the young rat, confirmed that she was planning another one in the spring when he asked her, after class.

Walking out of her classroom toward the bus, he noticed that a skinny wolf had hung back to listen, pretending to fidget with the unbuttoned collar of his shirt and pushing his glasses up on his muzzle every other minute. Kory remembered after a moment that his name was Perry, and he usually hung out with the hackers, a group unusual in the high school in that apparently only one member of each species wanted to join. Besides Perry, they included an otter, a rat, a raccoon, a grey fox, and one of the only two coyotes in the school. Most of them attended the standard English class, but Perry had been in the advanced class with Kory the year before, and Kory had noted without noticing that he was there again this year.

"I'm glad we're doing more poetry," Perry said without preamble.

"Uh-huh." Kory didn't encourage or discourage conversation.

"We're probably the only two excited about it, huh?"

"Probably."

The wolf stayed a half step behind him, silent for a few more paces, until he said, "Uh, I really liked that poem you did last year."

Kory's stride broke, but only for a half-hitch before he started walking again, a little faster. "Thanks," he mumbled, his mind wrenched away from thoughts of calling Samaki, back to the present.

"No, really." Perry hurried to keep up with him. "You have a great vocabulary and you used meter and imagery really effectively."

"Thanks," Kory said again, canting his ears back to listen. The last thing he wanted was for that poem to be brought up again on the first day of the new school year, but for it to be complimented on its merits was new.

"I wanted to say something to you last year about it, but, you know, those guys...and you looked so uncomfortable. I tried, the one time, but you just ran away. I think you didn't hear me."

He didn't remember that, but he said, "Probably not."

"And I thought it really sucked that they picked on you like that."

"Thanks." Now he slowed. "Do you write any?"

Perry hurried to catch up to him, ducking his muzzle. "Oh, uh, no, not really."

Kory grinned at the wolf's flicking ears, stopping in front of his bus. "Hey, you saw something of mine."

"No, I don't...I mean, I'm not that good." He saw Kory's look, then, and rubbed one ear. "Well, maybe."

"I'd like to see it. This is my bus," Kory said, waving up to the driver, who was beckoning to him. "Nice talking to you."

"Yeah, I'll, uh, see you tomorrow," Perry said. "Oh, are you in that college prep group?"

Kory tilted his head. "What group?"

"My mom signed me up for it. It's every Thursday after school for an hour. We go over college applications and stuff." He shrugged. "If I want to get into N.I.T., I guess I'll need it. You should be in it. I mean, not that you need help, I'm sure you'll get into a good school, but..."

Kory paused on the step. "Yeah, good luck," he said, and waved as he climbed into the bus.

On the bus, he sat alone and looked out the window. There was really nobody on the bus that he knew well; most of the other seniors in his area proudly drove their cars to school just because they could. The juniors and sophomores he knew, but not well, and of course, Nick was a freshman this year, but he had his own group of friends and wouldn't have wanted to sit with Kory.

Halfway home, Kory used his phone to send an e-mail to Samaki, wishing the black fox had a phone that accepted text messages. Maybe for Christmas, he thought, but he knew it was a stretch for the fox to have a phone at all. His plan didn't allow for many calls, so they used e-mail most of the time, but Kory didn't want to wait until he got home. His school day had immersed him in the other world, the one which had receded all summer, and he wanted to re-establish contact with Samaki, to find out what the fox had been doing and what his first day at Hilltown P.S. had been like.

Nick talked about his homework as they walked to their house from the bus stop, past neat lawns that Kory had thought of as small until he saw the yards in Samaki's neighborhood. He hadn't taken this particular walk in three months, but he still knew it by heart: The Jeffersons' maple tree and warm lupine smell, Mrs. Liata's profusion of rosebushes overwhelming even the odor of a skunk family, the white house with maroon trim that glowed in the sunset light later in the fall, the old three-story blue house whose circular corner towers and turrets brought to mind a modern-day castle, and all the other familiar landmarks cemented his return to school and the world of his normal life, the world where he was just Kory Hedley, Nick's brother and Celia's son, high school senior.

That world was comfortable, with patterns that were easy to slip into. He knew what was expected of him and had no trouble conforming. Over the summer, he'd come to regard the Kory who was Samaki's boyfriend as a different Kory, one who flushed guiltily during some church sermons now, who obsessively watched everything he did around his mother or left in his room, who had thought of the old Kory as nothing more than a shell he wore, a chrysalis to be discarded when the time was right.

Now, with the warm fall air ruffling his fur and the familiar sights and scents, the smell of school still in his nostrils and that creeping anticipation that the evening was only a break from the never-ending procession of classes, he felt like more than a shell. It wasn't until he slipped into the sanctuary of his room, with Samaki's scent faintly lingering despite his mother's attempts to dispel it, that he remembered the Kory of the summer. Relaxing into his chair, he found a reply from Samaki, and the warmth of summer infused him as he read it.

They'd set up an arranged time to talk each night, when Kory's phone minutes were free and Samaki would make sure to be somewhere private. Even if they could only talk for five minutes, it was worth it. Reading about Samaki's first day back at school, Kory wanted to call the fox that minute, not wait until after dinner. He contented himself with writing a long reply. He told Samaki about Perry, about the extra poetry unit, and about Sal's summer.

Dinner was salmon, one of Kory's favorites, even though his mother had paired it with bland lima beans. He took seconds while Nick told them about his first day at school, and then he told his mother more or less what he'd told Samaki, shading it with nuances she'd favor about how challenging his classes were going to be. Briefly, he mentioned Perry, and the college prep class, and his mother flicked her ears back.

"I never got that paperwork," she said. "I wonder why."

"I don't really need it," Kory said. "I have all the brochures, and there's plenty of stuff online to tell me how to register."

"But it certainly wouldn't hurt," his mother said. "And what else will you be doing with your Thursday afternoons?"

"Homework?" Kory said, but he knew that wouldn't fly.

"You do well enough in your studies that you can spare one afternoon a week to prepare for your future. Thanks to your charity work, you're reasonably well-rounded, but these classes help you gain that extra edge. If you want to get into Whitford or Gulliston, you'll need that edge. Nick, finish your beans."

Nick grumbled, taking one lima bean at a time and chewing forever, a strategy he'd developed to try to outlast his mother at the dinner table. So far, it hadn't worked. Usually Kory would give him an encouraging grin, but tonight his attention was elsewhere. "Mom, I..."

"If you have time to do your charity work on weekends, you have time to spare one afternoon a week for this." He didn't respond to that, not wanting to jeopardize the weekend visits to Rainbow Center, and she nodded her head. "I'll call the school tomorrow."

And that was the end of that. It wasn't worth his time to argue, and the only thing he could think of to say was that he wasn't interested in going to Whitford, nor to Grick, nor to anyplace that was going to take him that far from Samaki. But this was not the time for that argument. That argument was going to take careful planning. That argument was going to last a long time.

After dinner, he helped clean up and worked on homework in his room until eight twenty-four. He opened his phone and closed it, fingers skittering impatiently across the buttons as he waited for eight-thirty.

At eight-thirty and two seconds, he dialed. Samaki picked up on the first ring.

Kory felt himself relaxing just at the sound of the fox's voice. He listened to Samaki tell him about his classes and classmates. He'd mentioned some of them in e-mail, but it was nice to hear them in person. Kory told the fox about his classes too, and about his mom signing him up for the college prep course.

"You're lucky," Samaki said. "I already know I'm going to State."

"You're lucky," Kory said. "You already know you're going to State."

Samaki laughed. "You don't want to go to State. You have to go to Whitford so you can send me your coursework."

"And you can come visit me on weekends."

"On the weekends that you're not visiting me."

"Or at home."

The fox chuckled. "Kande comes home once a month. I'll probably come with her."

"I don't really want to go to Whitford, though."

"They had a really good-looking brochure."

Kory paused. They hadn't really talked much about colleges, apart from looking at the brochures Kory's mother had set out for him. But something was crystallizing now, something he'd missed in all the casual glances at the brochures. The "school Kory" was the one looking at them to make a decision about his future, what he wanted to be.

What if he didn't want to be "school Kory" any more? What if he stopped trying to decide which would be the best school, and just picked the one he wanted to attend? If he said, 'I want to go to State with you,' Samaki would say...would say...

What?

"I want to go to State with you," he said.

He heard an exhalation on the other end, and then silence. "I mean it," he said.

"Your mom won't let you," Samaki said. "Anyway, you can go anywhere. Why would you go to State?"

"Because you'll be there," Kory told him that Saturday morning, as they were finishing up the work on the fence at Rainbow Center.

"You think I'm going to forget about you if we go to different schools?" Samaki grinned at him, paws working evenly to apply the white paint, up and down. Kory thought of how those paws had been moving just the previous night, and of the bright white patch of fur he loved to explore with his own paws, and shivered.

"No," he said, focusing back on his own painting work. "That's just where I want to go."

"What if I got into Whitford?"

"Could you?" Kory looked up, hopeful.

Samaki chuckled and shook his head. "On a full scholarship, maybe, but do you know how smart I'd have to be to get one of those?"

"Too smart to be wasting your weekend here," Malaya chimed in. She had elected to paint with them rather than go with Greg and the boys up to a baseball game, a rare treat for the kids. "Never liked baseball," she claimed. She painted apart from them, her black leather getting dotted with white specks, the acrid scent of cigarette smoke concealed by the rich paint smells unless Kory stood right next to her, which rarely happened.

"See?" Samaki said. "No chance. My dad's working hard to put us through State. Kande will be done by the time Ajani's ready to go, and I'll be done when it's Kasim's turn. He's allowed two kids at a time."

"But what if you could get a full scholarship to Whitford? I mean, I'm going to need some financial aid, too. We could research scholarships, see what's out there."

"If you want to," Samaki said. "But it'll be a lot easier for you to get into State. Which you shouldn't," he added quickly.

"Whitford's too far away."

"Forester, then." Samaki dipped his roller in the tray. "That's close."

"It's not as good as Whitford and not as cheap as State."

"No, but it is close."

"Isn't that where that gay kid got beat up by the football player?" Kory touched up the post Samaki had just painted, filling in the spots of brown with white until it was all uniform.

Samaki nodded. "That could happen anywhere, though. And it might have turned out to be a good thing, in the long run. The players got kicked off the team, and it raised awareness on the campus."

Malaya shook her wings out. Drops of paint adorned them too, white speckles radiating up from her hands like part of her coat. "I don't know why you two are so obsessed with college. Just move in somewhere, some cheap place in the city, and get jobs. It's not that hard."

Violet vulpine eyes peered around Kory at her. "Doing what?"

"Whatever you want." She shrugged. "My old man's dumber'n a pile of bricks and he makes enough to afford a house."

"What does he do?" Kory asked.

"Construction. Any idiot can stack bricks on top of each other."

Samaki grinned, rolling the paintbrush up and down the next post.. "I don't see me on a construction site."

"Except maybe to stare at the guys," Kory said.

The fox laughed. "Why would I stare at other guys if you're around?"

"Oh, God." Malaya snorted.

"This friend of Nick's," Kory said, "his dad runs a painting business and he offered Nick a job next summer, when he's older."

"Good money in that," Malaya put in, waving the broad brush. "Not here, but..."

Samaki nodded. "I don't think I want to just be a painter, though. I want to be a reporter. You kind of have to go to school for that."

Malaya didn't answer. After a moment, Kory said, "Well, I can apply to State, anyway. I don't have to make a decision yet. But you should apply to some other places too, just to see."

"Sure." The fox smiled at him. "It'll be fun filling out those applications."

"Oh, God," the bat said again, turning pointedly away from them as Kory laughed and leaned over to kiss the fox on his muzzle, a bold gesture, but safe in the confines of Rainbow Center, even if they did both end up with smears of white on their muzzles.

They kissed again in the foyer, just before leaving. "Think of me when you brush tonight," the fox said with a sly grin.

"And you think of me," Kory said.

"I don't know if I'll need to brush for a couple days, after last night."

He spoke in a low voice, but Kory still looked around to make sure nobody was listening before he giggled. "I could brush again right now."

Samaki leaned down to lick his nose. "If my bus weren't coming in four minutes, I'd take you up on that."

"Mmm." Kory felt himself getting hard again, so when he hugged the fox, he pressed his groin against Samaki's hip. The fox didn't comment, but the hips he pressed back against Kory were just as full of desire. They separated, and with a glint of regret in the violet eyes, Samaki tugged him out to the bus stop, where he had to stand and wave good-bye for another whole week.

He wandered back to Rainbow Center, up the stairs and onto the porch, but the sharp tickle of cigarette smoke pulled him to the side of the house before he could walk inside.

He leaned over the railing, where the smell was strongest. "Malaya?"

"Shit," she said, "I thought you were gone."

"I'm taking a later bus."

"Spending more time with your boyfriend?" She didn't wait for his answer. "That's sweet."

"I don't get to see him much, with school and all." He heard a noncommittal sound from her. "You ever have a girlfriend?"

A puff of smoke floated up past him. "Not really," she said.

It didn't look like she was going to come out, so Kory sat on the wood porch and rested his back against the house, mirroring the position he thought she was sitting in below. He ran his fingers over the paint of the porch and wondered which kids had painted it. It looked recent. Maybe Samaki had helped, last year. "But sort of?"

"There was this one girl." Indrawn smoke. Slow hiss of exhalation. "She was a bitch, though."

"Sorry," Kory said.

"Not your fault she was a bitch," Malaya said.

The fact that he couldn't see her made it feel like a confessional. "What'd she do to you?"

"Just about everything two girls can do to each other." She puffed again. "Including talk behind my back and fuck me over."

Kory didn't really know what to say to that. After a moment, Malaya continued. "She wasn't really in love with me. At least, that's what she said. She just thought I was cool, at first. I guess I'm not."

"Were you in love with her?"

The bat didn't answer right away. "Sure, why not?" she said finally.

"Are you still?"

"Yeah. Don't you have to have someone new before you can forget someone old?"

Kory looked out at the crisp, blue sky, and at the trees, whose leaves were still bright and green. "I don't know," he said.

She was quiet for two more puffs of the cigarette. The smell faded into the warm fall air after that, so she must have ground the cigarette out, but she didn't come out from under the porch. "Did you tell your mom yet?"

"No," he said. "My mom's pretty religious. She'd flip out." Of course, that wasn't all there was to it, was there? He was religious too. He went to church regularly because he believed in its teachings, just like his mother did. So why did he feel it was all right to be with Samaki, when his mother didn't? Fortunately, Malaya didn't give him time to dwell on the question.

"No dad?"

"Nah." He didn't want to say more than that, but felt he owed her more. "He took off."

He didn't expect the response he got. "Lucky."

When he didn't know what to say, he didn't say anything. Malaya didn't let the silence last. "My mom died when I was two. I never knew her."

"Does your dad know?" Kory asked.

"That my mom died?" She laughed a dry laugh. "I know what you mean. Yeah, he knows. Why d'you think I ended up here?"

"I don't know why you're here."

Her wings rustled. "My dad caught me with Jen. He chased her out of the house, took my door off its hinges, and said if he caught me breaking God's rules again, he'd break my legs. So I ran away. Stayed in a couple shelters, heard some kids laughing about the 'sissy shelter,' and ended up here."

"Jeez," Kory said. The matter-of-factness with which she accepted the threat of violence in her life made him terribly sad.

"He might've killed my mom," she said, with the same tone, as if she were telling Kory about a house her father had built, or a car he drove.

That concept was too much for Kory. He knew he was supposed to help the kids here and support them, but Malaya was only two years younger than he was, and he didn't have the words or the experience to help her. He wanted to ask how she'd lived in her home for fifteen years, how she hadn't run away before now, but he didn't know how to ask without insulting her and he didn't know what else he could say. So he got to his feet, brushed the seat of his pants off, and said, "My bus'll be here soon."

"Okay," Malaya said. "See you next weekend." Her long, narrow hand, leathery wing trailing down from it, reached above the porch to wave to him, white splatters of paint gleaming on it like bone in the bright afternoon sun.

"This is the most important decision you'll make in your life."

Kory had to try not to roll his eyes at the lanky red fox at the front of the classroom. Perry had told him that Mr. Pena was "a bit dramatic." The wolf, it turned out, was understating things.

"You are all standing on the cusp of adulthood. College is where you will make that transition. The college you choose will determine what kind of an adult you become. Go to Pemberton and you'll emerge a leader. Go to Race and you will be equipped with all the tools to make important scientific discoveries. Attend Whitford, and you may become one of the luminaries of our time in any field. So it's worth spending not just this hour, but many more hours at home, making sure that your applications are in order. There's still time to join extracurricular activities to make sure you're well-rounded enough to get into the best schools. Last year, Carter High sent six students to Whitford, Race, and Pemberton." He looked around for effect. "All six of those students took this college prep course."

Kory looked around the classroom at the fourteen other students there. He recognized most of them from his advanced English class, and knew that most of them were also in the advanced math and science classes he hadn't made it into. Of course, he thought, if any of Carter's kids were going to get into the top three schools in the country, it would be those kids anyway, and of course they were so studious that the thought of skipping the college prep course had probably never occurred to them. But he paid attention to Mr. Pena anyway, because his mother was sure to ask him what they'd talked about in the class.

"All right," he said after his opening remarks. "Let's go around the room and introduce ourselves. Tell us what schools you're applying to. Next week you'll bring in the applications and we'll start working on those."

"My name's Ryan. Whitford, Race, and Western Tech is my safety school."

"I'm Vera. Whitford and Pemberton."

Kory watched the other kids with growing unease. Each of these kids already had a list of schools determined. Even Perry got up and said, "Uh, Pemberton, Gulliston, and Northeast College is my safety school." Kory had skimmed his brochures, and he knew the names of the schools his mother wanted him to go to, but watching nervous Perry's confident demeanor as he rattled off school names made Kory feel unprepared, as if he were really a junior and these kids were all a year ahead of him.

"I'm Kory," he said. "Whitford, I guess, and...Gulliston. And State."

Mr. Pena gave a short, nervous laugh. "State? We can find you a better safety school than that, Kory." He flicked his large ears while Kory folded his small ones back. The rustling of the other students sounded like laughter at his back, though nobody followed Mr. Pena's lead in laughing outright. Kory sank down in his seat. At least they hadn't asked him why he'd picked State. He wouldn't know what to answer.

"Now, the earliest thing you're going to want to do is make sure you're well rounded enough," the fox said when all the kids had introduced themselves. "Colleges like to see applicants with a variety of interests. Some charity work is always good, sports if you have it, yearbook, newspaper, and so on. Math Club, Computer Club are good if you're going for a science major. And use those clubs as leverage to get into national events and competitions. There are plenty of smart kids out there, but if you can show how smart you are on a wider stage, you'll stand out."

Kory saw nodding out of the corner of his eye. All the other kids were looking as though this were just confirmation, not news. Where did they all learn how to apply to colleges? Probably on the Internet somewhere. He'd have to spend some time this weekend looking. "Now, you're going to have a lot of friends bent on enjoying their last year of high school. I'm here to tell you that that's not what your senior year is for. The college you attend will shape the rest of your life. Employers will be much more impressed if you graduated from Gulliston than," his eyes settled on Kory. "State. More kids from this class will go to State than anywhere else, those that go to college at all. That's not impressive. That doesn't tell someone that you're going to be worth hiring."

Of course he would have to pick on Kory, mentioning State. Kory added Mr. Pena to the list of people he would upset by attending State with Samaki. The prospect didn't bother him at all. In fact, imagining the older fox's reaction if Kory announced his enrollment at State had him smiling as he and Perry walked out, so that the wolf asked him what was so funny.

"Oh, nothing," Kory said. "So, it sounded like everyone already knew a lot of that stuff in there, right? Are you all prepared, too?"

"I don't know if I have enough extracurriculars," Perry said. He stood next to Kory on the curb, waiting for the bus. "I wish I were good at a sport. My dad played baseball in college. I just hate gym."

"Even kickball?"

Perry looked back at Kory mournfully. "I always just kick it right back to the pitcher, and everyone snickers at me."

Kory liked kickball, but he found most non-aquatic sports fairly boring. "I don't think they really want English majors to have sport."

"They like them to be well-rounded." Perry paced while Kory watched.

"You're in, what, the hacker club, and you're on the yearbook. That's plenty," Kory said.

"I can't list the hacker stuff on a college app. I should do some non-profit work," Perry said. "Help at the senior home or something."

"Does it count if you're only doing it to get into school?"

The wolf stopped at that, and looked miserably downcast. "I don't know," he confessed. "What are you doing besides having poems published?"

Kory's fur prickled. "I'm trying not to do that again. But I do some charity work on weekends."

"You should get another poem published! You heard what he said about the national stage. Just don't tell the teachers this time. What charity work are you doing? You mean you already started doing something?"

He hadn't thought about the words before saying them, and now regretted having mentioned it. "Just a project with a friend of mine. Working with homeless kids."

Perry's eyes widened. "Homeless kids? Like runaways?" Kory hesitated a moment, then nodded. Perry's ears perked up. "Where? Would it be okay if...I mean, maybe I could come along? They always need extra help, right?" Without waiting for Kory's answer, he started talking to himself. "Homeless kids. That's terrible. I really do want to help them. I just didn't know how. Can I come along when you go next time?"

"Um, you know, I don't know," Kory said. He looked down the front of the school, wishing his bus would get here already.

"Oh," Perry said, his ears dipping. "I'm sorry. It's because I'm just doing it to get into college, isn't it? I really..." He sighed. "Never mind. Sorry."

Kory felt like a heel, but really, what else was he supposed to do? Bring along this guy he barely knew to work with gay kids? Introduce him to (*his boyfriend*) Samaki? He might as well tie a pink ribbon to his tail and walk around school with a "FAG" sign on his back.

He told Samaki about Perry's request that night, indignant. "He just wants charity work so he can get into college." He pushed away the memory of Perry's earnest expression.

Samaki paused. "Well," he said, "does it matter why he wanted to help? The work would still get done."

"He wouldn't be able to understand the kids, though."

"There's things to do that he wouldn't have to interact with the kids."

A little puzzled by the fox's attitude, Kory responded cautiously. "I guess so, but then, what's the point? And I didn't know if he was," he lowered his voice, "you know, homophobic or something."

"That's a good point," Samaki admitted. "Does he seem like it?"

"I don't know," Kory said. "Maybe. I barely know him."

"He liked your poetry, though. He's right, you should get something else published."

Kory shifted in his chair, looking at his computer screen. He typed in another search for college entrance requirements. "He *says* he did."

The fox laughed. "Why would he lie about that?"

That was a question Kory didn't have the answer to. When the silence had stretched out long enough, Samaki started telling him about his day at school. At Hilltown P.S., they didn't have anything like college prep courses. Getting motivated to attend college was all on the kid's shoulders. "There's a good site here about college," Kory said as Samaki was complaining about it. "I'll forward it to you."

"Thanks." Samaki sighed. "I should get going and get started on my homework. Oh, I've got a surprise for you for tomorrow night."

"Oooh. Will I like it?"

"Of course you will, silly."

"All right, then. I'll see you tomorrow. Think of me when you brush," Kory said.

"I will. You too."

"I will." He heard the fox's soft kiss, returned it, and hung up.

He grinned and got to his homework, looking forward to "brushing" even though Samaki wouldn't be there to share it with him.

Dinner at the Roden household was as much of an adventure as always, but one Kory relished. Mrs. Roden, aware now of Kory's tastes, made him a less spicy side of the vegetable stew. He devoured it with the soft flatbread she made, grinning at the flavors he never got to taste at home and at the rapid-fire conversation, as Ajani and Samaki and Kasim all told one or the other of their parents what their day had been like. Mr. Roden, normally not home on Friday nights, had switched a shift with someone to make tonight's dinner and had started by thanking Kory for the signed baseball card and talking about the old days of the Dragons, and the World Series game he'd snuck out of school to go see.

"I wanna get dessert!" Kasim said, springing from his chair and taking his plate to the kitchen.

"Not yet," his mother called after him.

The cub looked at Kory and grinned. "But I wanna show Kory what we're having."

"You can show him later." His mother laughed, getting up and taking her own dishes to the kitchen. "Come on, you and Ajani can help with the dishes. The sooner they're done, the sooner dessert will be on the table."

Ajani lingered over his stew, sopping it up with the flatbread and chewing the bread deliberately. From the captain's chair, Mr. Roden grinned at him and then turned to Kory. "So, Samaki tells me you're taking a college prep class."

"That's right," Kory said. "It's pretty useless mostly."

"Oh, come on," Samaki said, "you met a fan of your poetry there."

"I met him in English," Kory said, shooting a mock-angry look at the black fox, who widened his eyes innocently in response.

"So what colleges are you looking at?" Mr. Roden said.

Kory opened his mouth to say, "Whitford," then remembered that Mr. Roden worked at the state college and was sending his children there. Whitford was beyond their ability and he didn't want to embarrass Mr. Roden by pointing out, however obliquely, that his prospects were better than Samaki's. "Uh, I haven't really decided yet," he mumbled.

"He's looking at Whitford," Samaki said.

"Very good school," Mr. Roden said. "Tough to get in, but I'm sure you'll have no trouble. Ajani, there's no more stew there. Go help your mother in the kitchen."

The cub sighed heavily, put down the bowl he'd been licking, and left it on the table as he slid from his chair. "Take your bowl," his father reminded him, and he trudged back to the table, retrieved it, and carried it dangling from one paw.

"I might be going to State," Kory said.

Mr. Roden raised an eyebrow. "From Whitford to State? That's a wide range. I'm sure you can do better than State."

"It's not that bad a school," Kory said.

The older fox leaned over the table and smiled. "Kory, if I could send my children to Whitford, I'd do it. I know Sammy would do well there. But just for him and Kande to be going to college at all is great. Maybe his children will go to Whitford." He sat back, looked at the two of them, and flicked his ears, but his discomfort lasted only a moment. "If you two choose to have kids," he said, grinning slyly.

"Dad!" Samaki protested. Kory felt his ears get very warm as he stared fixedly down at his plate.

"Well, it's not likely to happen by accident, is it?" his father said.

"*Dad!*"

Mariatu, who had been pushing her stew around in her bowl with a piece of flatbread, announced, "Two boys can't have a baby."

They all turned to stare at her. "They have to get a mommy, and then they take turns kissing the mommy and whichever one she likes better she gives that one a baby but they have to promise the mommy that she can see the baby because otherwise she cries and she takes the baby away."

Kory and Samaki looked at each other, caught between blushing and giggling. Mr. Roden just smiled. "Where did you hear that, Mari?"

"In school," she said. "Billy Tooman said he wanted to kiss me and have a baby and I said he should kiss Vincent and he said two boys can't kiss and have a baby. He said his daddy Allen and his daddy Forrest had to kiss his mommy but he lives with his daddies and not with his mommy because she lives out in, um, Mars."

Mr. Roden turned to Kory and Samaki and shook his head. "A month ago she didn't want to go to kindergarten. Now she's kissing boys and making babies. I hope Billy Tooman is a fox, at least."

"He is," Mariatu said. "Vincent is a porcupine."

"Por-cue-pine," her father corrected her.

"Porcupine," she said, and lowered her ears. "May I please be excused?"

"Yes, go ahead," her father said. "Take your bowl."

She slid away from the table and scampered into the kitchen with her bowl. Kory watched the small flip of her tail as she walked, marveling at her acceptance of his relationship with Samaki. This was like another world, populated by alien foxes who knew and approved of their son and brother dating another boy.

"Now, we were talking about colleges?" Mr. Roden leaned back in his chair, his tail twitching.

"I'm going to apply to Whitford," Kory said, relieved to have the topic move away from his relationship with Samaki, "but I don't really think I'll get in."

"You've got as good a chance as anyone," Samaki said. "You got a poem published."

"It was a good poem," the older fox said. "You've definitely got talent."

He'd been expecting Samaki's father to ask about the poem, not already have seen it. He felt another flush as he looked up at Samaki. "You showed it to your parents?"

"Well, yeah."

"Oh, jeez." Kory covered his face with a paw.

Samaki put a paw on his shoulder. "It was published in the newspaper, you know. Millions of people read it."

"But not people I know!"

The black fox giggled. "Silly. It was good, admit it."

Kory groaned. Mr. Roden said, "If it'll make you feel better, Kory, you can read the article Samaki had in the newspaper when he was ten."

"Dad!"

Kory peeked through his fingers. "You had an article in the paper?"

"There was a cub reporter competition," Mr. Roden said, "and they published the top five articles."

"What was it about?"

"I don't remember," Samaki said.

Mr. Roden grinned. "It was a fashion article. It was quite good."

Samaki grabbed Kory's plate and his own. "Hey, Dad, Kory and I were just going to go for a walk before dessert. Can I take the car?"

"Sure." His father handed the keys over. "Back before ten, right?"

Samaki nodded. "Sure thing."

Kory helped take some dishes to the kitchen, staring at the black fox as he did. Kasim tried to get his attention in the kitchen to show him the pie Mrs. Roden had baked, but Kory kept trying to get the grinning Samaki to meet his eye (though the pie did smell delicious, all cinnamon and apples and a couple less familiar spices). Finally, in the foyer, he nudged the fox and said, "You can drive by yourself?"

Samaki grinned. "Surprise. I haven't passed the official test yet, but my dad said I passed his test, so as long as I stay under the speed limit and get back by ten, I can take the car." He opened the door, letting Kory precede him outside.

"Does that mean we can drive to the Rainbow Center?"

"'Fraid not. My dad still needs to go to work and my mom needs to run errands. I'm only allowed when they're both home."

Mrs. Roden's car, the older of the two, smelled strongly of fox, the different Rodens' scents mingling in Kory's nose as he slid into the passenger seat. He always remembered his first ride in the car, and his mother's reaction to the scent of fox, whenever he smelled it strongly. By now, the flash of resentment towards her came and went easily, gone by the time Samaki turned the key in the ignition and the car sputtered to life.

Kory grinned, and Samaki's tail thumped the seat. "I've only taken the car out once on my own. You're my first passenger. So buckle up."

"Don't worry, I always do." His mom had drilled that into his head.

"All right. Here we go."

The car lurched only a little on its way out of the driveway. By the time they were on the streets, Samaki was driving smoothly, both paws on the wheel, only the flicking of his ears betraying any nervousness. "Where are we going?" Kory asked him.

"A little place down by the river," Samaki said. "With the moon and all, it should be pretty tonight."

"Where on the river? Is it near Tom's Landing?"

"I don't think so. It's on the south side of the city."

Kory settled back and watched the city go by as they drove. As he often did when visiting Samaki, he thought about how Hilltown was really five or six different cities. He only knew the one he'd grown up in. Samaki had grown up here, where the houses leaned up against each other, streets and sidewalks were narrower, and the scents mixed on air currents and jumbled together so that it was harder to tell where one property stopped and the next started. Samaki's more sensitive nose had less trouble, able to pull nuances of scent out of the air that Kory couldn't catch. But on the other paw, Kory thought, he still wasn't as good a swimmer.

"What are you grinning at?" Samaki said, looking over.

"Nothing." Kory grinned wider. "Keep your eyes on the road."

"I know how to drive," Samaki said, flipping his tail over to rest on Kory's leg. The otter smiled and stroked one paw along the soft, thick fur as Samaki navigated them along the dark streets of the city. The privacy of the car was unexpectedly secure, a small world in which the two of them might go anywhere without worrying about college or family or any of that. Even the ever-present worry about his mother poking her nose into his life receded to the point that he only noticed it by its absence. He looked out the window up at the stars, imagining that they could keep driving on past the river and out into the night.

"Is this area safe?" he asked as Samaki pulled into a dark parking lot. Behind them, the lights of the city cast long, faint glimmers into the darkness ahead. He waited for his eyes to adjust.

"I wouldn't bring you here if it weren't." The fox turned the car off. In the silence, Kory could hear the water of the river lapping nearby.

"I'll hold your paw even if it's not dark, you know," he said.

"I know." Samaki leaned over in the car and kissed him, and when Kory turned his head they kissed for real.

Kissing was awkward between the fox's longer muzzle and Kory's short, stubby one, not to mention the differences in height. The only other person Kory had ever kissed—the real, tongue kiss that started at the mouth and ran all the way down the spine to the sheath—had been Jenny. Two like muzzles came together more easily than the fox and otter did, but kissing Jenny had been black and white, muted, awkward. Kissing Samaki was hot, riotous color and passion.

Kory turned his muzzle to the side and parted it, meeting the fox's turned and parted muzzle over the middle of the seat. Their tongues brushed in the open space between the muzzles, teasing even though they couldn't seal their mouths together. Kory closed his eyes, the musky maleness of the fox now familiar and exciting, the kiss a passionate reminder of their bond. Even without holding or groping each other as they kissed, he felt his sheath harden as if they were, responding to the light, loving brushes of the fox's tongue along his muzzle and the cherished lines his own tongue covered in return. The kiss suspended them in a bubble of time, where outside the world slowed to a crawl while they said with licks and soft chirps what they rarely put into words.

"Mmm." Samaki leaned his head back and grinned, the violet of his eyes nearly as black as the night. "Come on. I didn't bring you here just to park."

"Aw." Kory grinned, getting out of the car as Samaki did and locking his door. The night did not seem nearly as intimidating now. "Why did you bring me here?"

He saw the white flash of the fox's tail tip circle the front of the car. Samaki took his paw and led him toward the sound of lapping water. "To get away."

They made their way down a short path to the riverbank, through a small copse of trees. The bank itself was grassy and clear, the river a dark plain beyond it that shimmered with movement in the thin moonlight. Ahead of them, a concrete arch spanned the water, and now that they were in the open air, Kory could hear the soft rumble of a car passing over it. Above the bridge, the quarter moon gleamed, dropping its reflections down onto the ripples of the water. "You come here a lot?" he asked, keeping his voice almost to a whisper.

Samaki shook his head. "Dad used to bring us down here for picnics in the daytime. Lots of families from our neighborhood did. I only snuck down here at night with a friend once, but I remembered how pretty and isolated it was." He turned his head. "It'd be nicer with the full moon."

"It's beautiful," Kory said. "The moon reminds me of the tip of your tail. It looks like there's a fox in the sky."

He took Samaki's paw as the fox chuckled. "Not one in the river?"

"A whole host of foxes in the stream," Kory said, pointing out the gleaming reflections in the ripples. "There, and there..."

"And where are the otters in the stream?"

Kory grinned. "Under the water."

"Under the foxes?"

"Sure. Foxes can't dive."

Samaki laughed softly and kissed him again, and this time they wrapped their arms around each other as they did, pressed close, sheaths rubbing through the fabric of their clothing. Kory's fur prickled with the nervous exhilaration of kissing outside, under the open air. He felt the swish of the fox's tail, curling around , and wondered how far Samaki intended to go. They wouldn't be able to do anything at his house tonight, so maybe he had brought Kory here to make love outdoors, in a more private place than his house.

But was it more private? There was the bridge; anyone walking across it might see a couple silhouettes kissing on the riverbank below. Someone might come across the parked car and wonder who was down by the river.

Samaki's intentions became clearer as his paw slipped past the waistband of his pants, slender fingers brushing Kory's sheath and then pressing against it, cupping and rubbing it. Passion dulled Kory's worries; he moaned softly and slid his paw down over the fox's rear.

Samaki's tail curled up to brush his wrist, the fox's paw still rubbing warmly. Kory shifted as Samaki's other paw came around to undo his pants, breaking the kiss to press his muzzle into the fox's shoulder. "Oh," he moaned softly. Passion surged through him, forcing him to brace his knees. Samaki's chuckle rang in his ears and the slender fingers tightened around him.

"Like that?"

"Mm-hmm." Kory grinned, rubbing up against the warmth between the fox's legs. In a moment, he thought, he'd have to reach down there himself, but not quite yet. He opened his eyes, looking down the river and sighing as the tingling between his legs rippled and glowed just like the water's surface.

Then his ears snapped back and he lifted his head, staring at the woods. "What was that?"

"Just an animal," Samaki said, but his paw hesitated. "Nobody ever comes down here. We'd have heard the car."

Exhilaration fled Kory. He took a half-step back, acutely aware that he was standing out in plain sight with a fox's paw down his pants. Samaki kept a grip on him, until Kory reached over to grasp his wrist. Slowly, he released the otter, his ears sliding downward as he watched Kory fasten his pants. "Sorry," Kory said. "I just…" He looked up into Samaki's dark eyes.

"It's okay," Samaki said. "I guess I should've warned you. Or maybe we could've done something in the trees instead of out here. I just like this spot. It's always so quiet."

"Some other time, maybe." Kory looked up at the bridge again. "Sorry."

"Hey. Don't be sorry." Samaki leaned forward and gathered Kory into a hug again, a chaste one this time. Kory slid his arms around the fox, feeling guilty for being so insecure, and at the same time relieved that they'd stopped. The magical and frightening quality of the night receded as if it had been borne away on the river, and he was just a guy out walking at night with a friend. Nobody coming upon them now or looking down from the bridge would notice anything out of the ordinary.

"So is there anything else down here?" he said, aware of how lame the words sounded but needing to break the silence and start a conversation.

"Not really." Samaki followed Kory's gaze up to the bridge. "I like being here under the bridge, though. It smells bad if we get too much closer, but there's a nice place with a couple benches a little further up. I didn't go there because that's where people would be if they'd be here."

His smile, in the moonlight, was a ghostly shadow on his black muzzle, his ears half-lowered as if apologizing. Guilt made Kory reach down and grasp the fox's paw. "Let's walk up there, then."

Samaki smiled, his tail swishing, and squeezed Kory's paw as they set off under the moon. The sounds of the river accompanied them, burbling along quietly while Kory took in the wet, earthy smell of the riverbank, the wild, woody smell of the looming trees. The scent of fox was familiar and comforting, and the brush of Samaki's tail against his, the paw closed warmly around his own, made him feel safe.

"This college thing is crazy," he said abruptly, in a low voice so as not to disturb the silence too much.

"What do you mean?" Samaki responded equally quietly.

Kory sighed and squeezed the fox's paw. "Everyone knows where they want to go, what they want to be. They've got lists and applications and application strategies and recommendations. Even you know where you're going."

Samaki didn't respond immediately. "If you're really set on State," he said finally, "I won't argue with you."

Kory shot a quick glance up at the fox, whose eyes were set ahead of him, gleaming with moonlight. "Really?"

Now Samaki did turn to look at him, ears up, smiling. "Sure. I mean, you can make your own decisions, right? Nobody else knows what's best for you."

Warmth suffused him, flowing outward from his heart. He returned the smile. "You're the only one who seems to understand that. Thanks."

"That's part of my job now." The fox rested a paw on his shoulder. "Though I admit to being swayed by the thought of seeing you more than just a couple times a month. Maybe we could room together."

"Maybe." The thought sent a giddy flash of joy to Kory's stomach, then a lurch as he imagined what the other people at school would think. Samaki wasn't exactly shy about their relationship, and he'd resent any attempt Kory would make to hide it. The otter shook his head and pushed those thoughts away. Certainly, he would much rather be near Samaki than not. They could handle the details in time. "I mean, yeah. Of course we would."

They walked on until they came to the benches, and it was there, sitting by the river with his shoulder against Samaki's chest, that Kory felt the knot inside him loosen. He didn't have to make a decision yet, after all; perhaps Whitford and all the other schools would reject him, and then he would have to go to State. In the moonlight, with the water lapping the shore by his feet, the rest of the world didn't matter; it was remote and insignificant compared to this reality, that he was here with Samaki (*his boyfriend*), who believed in him. He leaned his head against Samaki's shoulder, breathed in the scent of fox as well as the river and trees, and reminded himself that here were the important things.

He didn't say anything, but Samaki turned to look at him, and then it felt right to lift his head and kiss the fox's muzzle. Samaki hesitated at first, then pressed forward, resting one paw on Kory's leg, but going no further than that. And that was a nice place to stay for a few minutes, muzzles together, tongues touching, the slight chill in the air offset by the warmth between them.

"We shouldn't sit here too long," Samaki said when they broke from the kiss. "We need to walk back and get home soon."

Kory swung his tail behind the bench. "Just a little longer," he said. "It's nice and peaceful here."

The fox swung his tail back, curling it around Kory's hips. "All right, then." He paused. "I had something I wanted to ask you."

"What's that?" Kory turned to smile, but Samaki wasn't looking at him. The fox fidgeted.

"My school does a dance in the spring. Like a prom. They were asking for volunteers to help work on it this week."

The otter grinned. "You want me to help work on your dance?"

Samaki shook his head. "I...want you to be my date for the dance."

Kory didn't process the words right away. In the space that followed, he focused on the river and how calm it sounded. When Samaki said his name, gently, he said, "Is that allowed?"

"I don't see why not. Nothing says that I have to bring a girl."

"Has anyone else done it?"

"Does that matter?"

"I guess not." But it did, even though Kory knew it shouldn't. "So it'd be like a protest?"

"No." Samaki's tail slid away from the otter's hips. "I just want to go to the dance, and I want to bring you."

"I didn't mean it like that," Kory said. As strange as he'd felt when Samaki asked him, he felt worse seeing the fox's ears down. "I didn't say no. It's just strange. Maybe it's too soon."

To his relief, Samaki's ears came up, slowly. "It's a long way away," he said.

"That's true." Kory put a paw on the fox's leg. "We don't have to make a decision yet."

The fox's ears came all the way up at the 'we'. "All right. Just keep it in mind. I think it would be okay."

Kory nodded. "I will." He looked up, smiled, and met the fox's lips again.

Driving back in the car, the smells of fox replaced the river's wet, wild aroma. Now that they were safe in the car, Kory regretted having stopped Samaki earlier. His arousal blurred the memory of why he'd been so upset, and here in the closed car, he was half-tempted to take the fox's paw and put it in his lap. He shifted in his seat as he aroused himself further just thinking about it. Of course, Samaki was keeping both paws tightly on the wheel and seemed nervous about driving at night, so probably it wasn't the best of ideas.

All the same, it was going to be hard not to do more than a few gropes this weekend. Ironic that at Samaki's house, where his parents knew about their relationship and were happy with it, they had to sleep in separate rooms, while at Kory's house, they could both stay in his room and fool around as much as they wanted. Maybe they shouldn't have told Samaki's parents, Kory thought, though he hadn't been party to that decision, and he suspected they would have figured it out anyway. Samaki wasn't the sort to keep things secret.

They did have a few minutes alone in the basement, where Mrs. Roden had set up a bed on the couch for Kory. There, when Samaki slid a paw into his pants, Kory returned the grope, glad to feel the fox's matching arousal against his paw for the first time in a week. He couldn't give it his full attention, but it was still better than nothing. Too soon, his ears caught Mrs. Roden on her way down the stairs to announce bedtime, giving them time to extract their paws and assume a reasonably innocent position.

Once, Samaki had snuck down early in the morning, but they'd been faced with the problem that the only bathroom in the house was on the upper floor, making it difficult to clean up. Logistical issues like this were part of the reason Samaki stayed at Kory's house more often than the other way around. Which would only last, Kory reflected as he drifted off to sleep, as long as his mother remained ignorant of their relationship. Just another year, he told himself. Then off to college. That brought back his worries about rooming together. Should he say something to Samaki? No, the fox would be disappointed in him. He was right; the fact that they were together should be more important than anything else. But Malaya's view of the world seemed closer to his experience than Samaki's, and that thought made him toss and turn until he finally fell asleep, nose pressed into the fox-scented fabric of the couch.

At the Rainbow Center the next morning, Margo greeted them with a grim expression. "Jeremy's mother was here yesterday with her sister. She wants to take him to this religious camp that tries to make kids straight. I don't know how she found out where we are. She went from pleading to threatening to screaming to crying. We didn't let her in, or let Jeremy talk to her, but he's been crying all night. Samaki, can you go sit with him? Kory, can you just help me keep an eye on the others?"

As the black fox hurried up the stairs, Kory looked around, the previous evening's worries still lingering. "Is Malaya around?"

"I haven't seen her yet. If you like, you can go up to her room and call her down." The black squirrel wrung her paws. "I've got to get food ready for the boys, and I hope Samaki can calm down Jeremy."

"If anyone can, he can," Kory said.

"Of course." The assurance didn't seem to help Margo too much, but she did lower her paws to her sides before rushing to the kitchen.

He'd been up to Malaya's room only once. The boys all roomed together and came tumbling down the stairs together when it was breakfast-time, but as the only girl, and, what's more, the only bat, Malaya had a small room to herself up on the third floor. Kory passed the boys' room, where he heard Samaki's soothing tones and smiled. One more flight up brought him to Malaya's door.

Nobody answered when he knocked. She wasn't in the bathroom; he'd glanced in on the way up. He knocked again and tried the knob. The unlocked door swung open.

Malaya kept her room neat and tidy. Toward the ceiling, he saw the bar she hung from to sleep. Below that, books were piled neatly next to the overstuffed, decrepit chair. Chilly morning air played over Kory's fur from the open window on the other side of the room, the sickly maple tree swaying gently in the breeze.

He walked in and saw a piece of paper on the chair. The handwriting, though he'd never seen Malaya's, was exactly what he would have expected of her: sharp, angular, and precise. "*I'm going home. I can't stand the delusions any more. The lies have been exposed for what they are tonight. Good luck to all of you. You'll need it.*"

It felt like a joke to him at first, that she would come strolling languidly out from behind the door, take the note from his paws, and crumple it with a wry grin, saying, "You don't really think I'd do that, do you?" But no matter how hard he looked around, the room was empty and even Malaya's scent was weak. He wondered how long she'd been gone.

Margo was distraught enough about Jeremy that he didn't want to give her the note right away, but it was too depressing to wait in the empty room, so he wandered downstairs to the basement, where the aquatic room was vacant, as it often was. Kory sat on the rubber drying mat and dangled his bare feet in the two-foot-deep pool, letting the feel of the water relax him as he read Malaya's note over again.

What he wanted to do was go find her and tell her that whatever she thought she needed, going back to a violent homophobe wasn't it. He kept hearing her voice as she told him, "I think he might have killed her," and though he told himself it was likely childish exaggeration, that didn't drive away the worry. He knew that the familiarity and comfort of home seemed better to her than not knowing what would come next, where she would go from here, but had she forgotten the reason she'd run away in the first place? Maybe she hadn't. Her note contained no indication of it, but he could see her thinking that unhappiness was her fate. More than anything, he wanted to tell her that was wrong.

She'd thought that he was more of a "clear" thinker than the others, which in her mind was someone as pessimistic as she was. When it came down to it, though, he wanted to believe that people were destined to be happy. That might not be as easy as Margo and perhaps Samaki thought, but he thought it was possible and worth fighting for.

He set her note aside and closed his eyes, moving his webbed paws through the water and enjoying the eddies it generated, letting his thoughts swirl similarly around Malaya, colleges, and Samaki's school prom. It didn't help him reach any conclusions, but at least he found it pleasantly relaxing. Time drifted as languidly as the water, until he heard the door open and caught a familiar musky scent.

"Hi," Samaki said, stepping around the pool. "Thought you might be down here. Where's Malaya?"

Kory reached down beside him and handed the note to the fox. Samaki read it, and sighed. "She really seems determined not to be happy."

"I wish there were something I could do for her," Kory said.

"I'll see if Margo has an address. Maybe we could send her a letter." Samaki sat next to him and dipped his paws in the water. "I don't want to bother Margo now, though. She's stressed enough about Jeremy."

"How's he doing?"

"Sleeping, finally. She told me to hang out with you and Malaya for half an hour or so while she tries to get things organized for breakfast."

"We should tell her Malaya's gone." Kory sighed, and leaned against the fox. "Great day we're having, isn't it?"

Samaki slipped an arm around him and squeezed. "There'll be bad days and good days. Last year we had three of the kids get into a fight and two had to go to the hospital. That day pretty much sucked."

Kory nodded. "This feels...worse, somehow. Like everyone's giving up."

The fox nuzzled him gently. "We're not giving up."

And that just reminded Kory of last night. "I'm sorry," he said.

"For what?" Samaki's usual light amusement covered his concern only thinly.

"Last night. Stopping you and...I guess I just wasn't ready to be doing it out in public." He was apologizing, but also trying to convey how outrageous it still felt to him. Sort of "I'm sorry I'm not as crazy as you," but nicer, aware that he couldn't just come out and say, "you lunatic," like he would if Sal did something nuts.

"Is it something you want to talk about?" Samaki squeezed his paw.

It was, but the problem was that of all the issues Kory was worrying about, the whole public display of their relationship was precisely the one it was hardest to talk to Samaki about, because the black fox was squarely in the center of it. So he just shook his head, repeated, "Sorry," and hoped Samaki wouldn't press.

He didn't. "It's my fault. I should've warned you. That's really a pretty secluded spot, and you can hear anyone coming with plenty of warning. Plus the river covers up most of the scents. Most." He wrinkled his nose.

"I didn't smell anything," Kory said, and reached up to brush one of the fox's large triangular ears. "And I can't catch every little sound like you can."

"Nah, but you can swim," Samaki said. "I figured if someone came along, you could just dive into the river and get away."

Kory drew in breath to retort, and then saw the twitching of the fox's tail, and grinned. "Oh, you did? Maybe I'd just drag you in with me."

"Oh no no," Samaki play-protested. "I know what happens to foxes who get dragged into water by otters."

Kory leaned closer to him. "Oh? What's that?"

"Oh, all sorts of things. They get those otter paws all over them in all kinds of private places."

"Do tell." He slid his paw up Samaki's leg. "You're in the water now, you know."

The fox glanced down at his feet and kicked up a splash. "Oh, dear." He turned to Kory and grinned. "You know, that door locks."

Kory's already excited sheath surged with warmth. "Does it?" He rested his paw between the fox's legs, lightly, but even so, he could feel the other's arousal, matching his.

"Uh-huh." Samaki's tail swished back against him. "Doesn't lock by itself, though."

The fox's violet eyes sparkled. Kory pressed with his paw and got up, suddenly worried that Margo would come to fetch them before he could lock the door. But he made it to the bolt and threw it, testing the door to be sure before running back around the pool.

Samaki was reclining back on his elbows, feet still dangling in the pool. Kory knelt beside him and reached around to bury his paw in the black fur at the back of the fox's head, leaning down for a warm kiss. As their tongues met, he returned his right paw to the fox's sheath, now warmer and harder than before, and rubbed through the cotton fabric.

His muzzle vibrated with the fox's soft moans. He opened his eyes so he could see the restless twitching of the long black tail. The sight sent the usual stirrings of delight through his chest at being able to make this wonderful person's happiness match his. He kept his muzzle close to Samaki's as he unfastened the pants with practiced ease and gently worked his paw inside, along the white patch of fur and the warm thickness in the middle of it.

Samaki made no move towards Kory's pants, and Kory didn't expect any, after a little while. Sometimes it was like this: one, then the other, rather than both together. Sure, it was nice to have Samaki's paw on him while he was stroking the fox, but it was nice to be kissing Samaki, his paw moving up and down and being able to focus on the reactions in the slender black form below him. He liked that feeling, that he was doing something nice for Samaki.

The fox was at least as worked up as Kory was. He reached around and hugged Kory with one arm, leaving the other behind him to support his torso, and it wasn't too long before he was making muffled moans and throaty yips at Kory's strokes. When he shuddered and tensed, Kory grinned happily and stroked faster, and was rewarded with a warm splash over his paw and a series of gasps, a tightened arm around his chest. Closed eyes opened as Samaki drew his muzzle back and smiled, panting.

"Mmm," he sighed, looking down at his shirt. He'd tugged it out of the way just in time, so only his black belly fur had gotten spattered. "Have to find something to clean up with."

In the corner by the sleeping mat, Kory spotted a worn brush and a pile of handkerchiefs. He chuckled and licked the fox's nose. "It looks like we've been painting again. Just stay here a second."

Dipped in the water, the handkerchief did a serviceable job cleaning up the mess. When Samaki'd done up his pants, he pushed Kory over onto his back and said, "Now it's your turn, you naughty otter."

Kory was only slightly surprised to see the fox's muzzle dip towards his pants. Samaki had taken him that way only twice, partly because he was worried about his teeth, and partly, Kory suspected, because Samaki didn't want Kory to feel bad about not using his muzzle himself. He didn't, really. Samaki had told him that he didn't want to pressure him into doing things he wasn't comfortable with, and for all the things Kory did feel ashamed of or guilty about, he'd accepted that he and Samaki were at different comfort levels, and that in time, he'd reach a point where he was willing to take the fox into his muzzle.

He definitely felt closer today, as he watched Samaki's long black muzzle bob up and down. It felt so good, the press of his tongue, the slide of his lips, that Kory wanted to let Samaki feel the same thing. And he wondered, what would it feel like in his mouth, the long, hard shape of it against his tongue, through his lips? That he didn't mind so much. It was more the idea of the fox coming, that musky liquid bursting in all in a rush, that worried him. What if he coughed and spit it out? What if he choked?

He abandoned that line of thinking as the sensations built up, his muscles quivering as they tingled. His left foot, dangling in the water, kicked to release the nervous energy he felt building up. Samaki's paw caressed his side, up under his shirt, the smooth brush of fingers overloading his brain even further. He heard himself making small cries and felt the material of the drying mat bunch under his clenched fingers. Samaki brought his other paw up under Kory's sac, holding it and squeezing the base of the otter's hardness, and that was enough to send him over the edge.

He cried out and arched his hips up into the waiting muzzle, feeling his release with electric intensity from the tips of his toes to the tips of his ears. It went on, forcing another moan out of his mouth and a tight curl to his tail, and then left him drained, panting on the edge of the drying mat.

A moment later, he lifted his head to see Samaki wiping his muzzle with the handkerchief. "Sorry," the fox said, ears still perked forward, a smile tempering the apology.

"For what?" Kory panted, and then grinned as Samaki gestured with the handkerchief. "Don't worry about it. Doesn't matter to me if you do that."

"It's not that you, y'know, taste bad. It was just kind of a lot." Now his ears flicked as his smile widened. "I need more practice."

"You can practice on me anytime," Kory said.

"Mm, good." Samaki stretched out next to him. "And we still have a few minutes before we should go look for Margo."

"Good. I think I'd be all twitchy if I tried to stand up now."

Samaki moved a paw lazily over Kory's tummy. "Don't want you to be twitchy, do we?"

"Definitely not." He leaned over to nuzzle the otter, but hesitated when Samaki moved his muzzle for a kiss. The scent of Kory's own musk was strong on the fox's lips. But after all, hadn't he gotten off in his own mouth more than once? He told himself it was silly to be that way, and leaned in to the kiss.

"I wonder if we're the first ones to do it in here," he said, when they parted.

Samaki laughed. "In a house for horny young unescorted boys?"

"Well, okay." Kory grinned. "Did you ever walk in on anyone?"

"No..." Samaki hesitated just a little. His paw paused on Kory's stomach.

Kory saw the tilt of the fox's ears and the shift of his eyes. In the afterglow, he felt relaxed enough not to mind asking, or hearing the answer. "Did you ever do anything with someone here?"

Now the violet eyes searched his. He smiled reassuringly. "Yeah," Samaki said. "Just once."

"You can tell me about it," Kory said. "I don't mind."

He watched Samaki decide, and then shrug. "There's not much to tell," he said softly. "He was all upset, talking about how nobody loved him, and we just ended up doing it. I just wanted to make him feel better."

"Oh." Kory nodded. The thought of Samaki being with someone else was vaguely troubling, but only vaguely. It was another Samaki who'd done those things, just as it was another Kory who'd slept with Jenny on and off starting, he realized, just about a year ago.

"It wasn't in this room," Samaki said. "And we just pawed. It wasn't anything serious."

"Did he feel better?"

The fox tilted his muzzle. "Yeah," he said. "I think he did."

Kory smiled. "Okay, then." He fastened up his own pants, and kissed Samaki on the nose. "We should go find Margo."

The squirrel was even more upset at Malaya's leaving than she had been at Jeremy's situation. Which made Kory feel guilty, because fifteen minutes ago he'd been enjoying himself with little regard to anyone in the house. He saw Samaki's eyes lower and knew the fox was sharing the same thought, so he swung his tail over to brush Samaki's, and smiled back at the look he got. Sharing the guilt made it easier. And after all, there was nothing either of them could have done fifteen minutes earlier to make the situation better anyway.

They played cards with the other boys for a bit, too distracted to organize any more productive activity. During one game, Kory saw the weasel leaning over and sniffing at Samaki, but if he smelled the evidence of their activity, he didn't say anything about it.

Margo had calmed down somewhat by the time they left. She promised to keep them up to date on Malaya and Jeremy, who was still asleep in his room, and they promised to come back the following weekend. "That's going to be hard," Kory said, walking to the bus stop. "We both have big tests week after next."

Samaki nodded. "I want to come back, though. I mean, if we disappear when she needs us...right?"

"Yeah." Kory nodded. "No question."

He hugged Samaki, leaning up to rub muzzles as they saw the bus pull around the corner. Even though he was leaving the black fox for another whole week, the memory of Friday night by the river and that morning in the aquatic room kept Kory smiling all the way home.

When he walked in the door, though, his mood faded, as the scent of his mother and their house brought back his fears. He would have snuck into his room without saying hello if she hadn't been in the living room. "You look happy," she remarked. "Did you have a good time?"

"Sure." He walked quickly towards the little bridge over the house's pool.

"Kory." She turned in her chair to look at him. Her tail thumped down as it hit the other side of the chair. "What did you two do?"

"Oh, uh, we just had dinner, and then he drove down to...around for a while. And then we helped at the Center yesterday."

"Samaki can drive?" He nodded. She sighed. "I know you want to. I'm sorry I haven't had time to help you practice."

"It's okay, Mom." He did want to learn to drive, but that wasn't really bothering him. He knew that when his birthday rolled around in the spring, he'd get his license. He had plenty of other things to worry about.

"Where did he drive? Just around the block?"

"Oh, around the city a bit." He waved his paws, the memory of the dark space by the river vivid as he did.

Her eyes narrowed. "The two of you, by yourselves? I don't like that. Some of those areas are dangerous."

"Samaki knows the areas. He wouldn't take me anywhere dangerous."

"I want his father to go along if you go driving in the city again."

Kory's shoulders sagged, but he felt stronger, relieved that she was pressing on a topic that he didn't care as much about, not on why he wanted to see Samaki every weekend. "It's perfectly safe," he said.

"I read the news, and I know that's not true. Promise me, Kory."

He sighed. "I promise, Mom."

"All right. I trust you to keep your promises."

"I will. Can I go do my homework now?"

"Just a moment." She looked at him harder. "Kory, at your age, I know a lot of boys get into trouble. They have friends who don't always make the right choices."

He rolled his eyes theatrically to cover the pounding of his heart. "Mommmm."

"I know we've talked, and I am confident that the Lord has set you on a moral path, but all the same..." She scraped the arm of the chair with a claw. "I worry about you when I don't know what you're doing."

"We drove around, and then we went to the Center this morning. That's all, Mom. I promise." *Please, please stop asking questions.*

"I read in the paper," she said as though he hadn't spoken, "about these boys who were taking...meth, was it? They did it in one boy's bedroom, upstairs, while the parents were watching television."

He noticed that their TV was off. Meth, he thought, and almost giggled. "I'm not doing meth, Mom."

"Or any other drugs?"

"No drugs." The relief was taking a long time to reach his heart. "I should get to my homework."

She nodded, waving him to his room and turning back to the book she was reading. The Bible, he noticed. Not a good sign. She only did that when she was worried about something. Even when he got into his room with the door closed, the relief that she'd been on the wrong track didn't come. She knew something was wrong, and he was going to have to be more careful about hiding it.

After English class the following Monday, Perry caught up with Kory. "Hey," he said, smiling, ears perked up.

"Hey. What's up?"

"Well, I hope you don't mind, but I looked up shelters for homeless kids on the Internet." He was struggling to keep the bashful tone, but clearly he was proud of having succeeded.

Kory's fur prickled. "Oh?"

"Yeah." Perry's tail wagged. "If you were worried about what I'd think, you know, you shouldn't be."

His heart beat a little faster. Regardless of what Perry said, this intrusive feeling of someone knowing his secret was starting at uncomfortable and getting worse. Was everyone he knew determined to find out what he was hiding? "You know," he said, "I don't really work there. I just, I said that so you would think I was well-rounded."

Perry tilted his head. "Really? I mean, I asked about you and they didn't know your name, so I kinda wondered. You didn't have to do that."

Kory felt a light-headed sense of relief. Margo had lied for him, then. He wouldn't have thought she'd be smart enough to figure that out. "Well, you know," he said, and shrugged. "So you're okay with helping the kids out?"

"Sure, I mean, they're people too, right?" When Kory nodded, Perry went on. "And I know what some people say about 'em, but I don't care. It's just ridiculous about them ruining society. It's those conservatives, they'll just go after anyone who's not like them. But these kids, it's terrible, you know, they just want to have a normal life and they've been taken away from their homes and mostly lost their parents..."

"Some of them would be better off if they had," Kory said.

Perry bobbed his head. "Yeah. I didn't want to say that, but they said there's a couple where the families are alcoholic and it's just a bad situation. You know, you think they all come to this country to get a better life, and then how do you go from that to being a drunk and abusing your kids?"

His ears were back now, a definite growl underlying his words. Kory's ears came up. "Come to this country?"

"Yeah. Most of them from down south, or the far east, right?"

The beating of his heart slowed. "Which shelter is this again?"

"Holiday House. That's where you meant, isn't it?"

Kory shook his head. "No, I've never heard of it. What is it?"

"It's a shelter for the kids of illegal immigrants. I thought that's why you didn't want to talk to me about it. But I called them and they said they always need more help. So I'm gonna go in this coming weekend. That'll look great on my application." His tail wagged, and then slowed. "I mean, uh..." He lowered his head. His tail curled under him, and it was only then that Kory realized that that was how he was used to seeing the wolf.

"I bet it will," Kory said.

"They really need help, too. I mean, this house got stones thrown at it a couple times over the summer. People don't like the kids being there. It's right on the edge of a new rich development, that's what Jolena told me, but they were there before the development and now the people are trying to force them to move, so one of the things I'll be doing is not just working with the kids, but also doing some campaigning, like writing to tell people how valuable the house is. That's pretty cool, and it works with my English major, too. So what shelter were you talking about, or did you just make one up?"

"You're going to be an English major?" Kory said.

Perry bobbed his head, ears flicking sideways and back. "Not for writing like you, but literature. I love reading, and Mr. Deffenbauer says I have a real talent for analysis. He's coaching me for the AP English test this year."

"Hey, cool." Kory stepped up to his bus and waved. "Let me know how the kids work out."

"Yeah," Perry said, waving brightly. "See you tomorrow."

On the bus, Kory wondered why he was so reluctant to tell Perry about Rainbow Center. After all, the wolf wasn't an illegal immigrant, but he was helping kids who were. Just volunteering at a house for gay teens didn't mean Kory himself was gay. Perry would just assume he was doing it to pad his college application. But was it the sort of thing he would have done last year? Probably not. Well, to be honest, definitely not. There was something strangely...contagious about being gay. All it took was association for you to fall under suspicion.

He huddled against the window and stared out of it. Lines of a poem flitted through his head. *You can have the symptoms but not the disease. It spreads by touch, by mouth, by sight. The outward signs don't mean a thing. The sickness is in the ones who point.* He rolled the lines around, rearranged them. There might be something for him to work with there. He actually hadn't written any poems specifically about being gay, which, now that he thought about it, was odd. He would have to work on that, like Samaki'd encouraged him to. The disease lines might be a little strong, though. Samaki definitely wouldn't like that. Maybe he'd just write this poem for himself, and another one for the fox. Something about being evaluated for college, your life reduced to a piece of paper with marks on it. That was a good thought. He made a note of that one, too.

His lie to Perry continued to nag at him, building on the worry about his mother and the issue with rooming with Samaki in college. The world was pressing to know his secret, and the more he felt it slipping out, the tighter he clutched it to himself. The problem was that more and more his secret felt like a mass of water behind an inadequate dam. Pressure and containment would be second nature to a beaver, but Kory was an otter, and he just wanted to let things take their natural course. *Just another few months, after the holidays, then it'll all be downhill.* College, and the question of rooming with Samaki, was months away, a problem hidden by the larger one of getting accepted in the first place.

He spent Wednesday night talking with his mother about colleges, another exercise in frustration as she was mostly concerned with him getting into Whitford. He had to pretend that he was actually planning to try to get in there, all the while presenting his other choices as "insurance." The whole evening had left him drained and frustrated, and when he told Samaki about it, the fox said, "So just tell her you don't want to go to Whitford." Which was impossible, knowing Kory's mother, so he changed the subject to talk about the schools he was planning to attend and the tricks they were learning in the college prep class.

"One of the most important parts of the application is one you may overlook at first," Mr. Pena said Thursday night. "I'm talking about the 'species and ethnic origin' page. I know a lot of you are used to just checking "fox," or "otter," and not thinking about it any more than that, but it's worth putting some extra time into this section now. A lot of schools have species quotas. Most of the ones you're applying to, in fact, have quotas, though they don't publish them. Those are laws you should have studied in Civics class. I bet you never thought your Civics homework would be useful, did you?" He chuckled, looked out at the silent classroom, and resumed his speech. "So if you are a river otter, for example, but one of your grandparents was a small-clawed Asian otter, you might be able to put "Asian river otter" in that space on the application. You'd qualify as a minority, and have a better shot at getting into school."

A grey squirrel, Jelena, Kory thought her name was, raised a paw. "My grandmother was an albino," she said. "Does that count?"

"With rare exceptions, color phases don't qualify for minority admission," Mr. Pena said. "There are exceptions—white tigers and white lions are culturally protected communities as well as being a different color phase, and would qualify."

Kory raised his paw. "What about black foxes?"

Mr. Pena shook his russet-furred head. "Maybe, but we don't have any of those at Carter. No, I don't think anyone here qualifies under fur color alone, but you do need to talk to your parents about your heritage. If there's anything unique in your background, don't be afraid to use it."

One of the other students raised a paw. "Isn't that a bit dishonest? Why aren't we just judged on our ability?"

The fox nodded. "I would love to live in a world where individuals were judged on merit. Believe me, it would be a vast improvement over the systems we have now, and would remove the need for you to attend this class. But as it is, all the other applicants are going to be doing the same thing you are, and there are so many kids out there with as much talent as you have that the smallest edge can mean the difference between Whitford and," his eyes fell on Kory, "State."

Kory flattened his ears to mute out the snickers. "Ah, I'm just kidding," Mr. Pena said, without much sincerity, Kory thought. "But really, kids, if you think someone's going to judge you on who you are, you're deluding yourself. Colleges have to weed through thousands of applicants and the people doing it are overworked and underpaid. You need to make yourself stand out in an easy, quantifiable fashion." His tail swished as he looked around. "You know what quantifiable means?"

"Easy to measure," someone said, behind Kory.

"Right. You've got to have characteristics that stand out on a list that someone can put together. If your grades are a half point higher than someone else's and you're the smartest kid in the class, you're still going to lose that spot if the other kid is more well-rounded than you are, in the sense of having the right number of activities on your application, or being a member of a minority group."

He kept on in that vein for a while, and Kory noted that among all the characteristics he mentioned, he never once talked about gay students. Isn't that distinctive, he thought? Wouldn't that stand out on a list? The difference, he told himself, is that it has to be a trait that colleges want.

As if they didn't have enough homework, Mr. Pena gave them an assignment as they were wrapping up. For the next meeting, they were to look at the essays on their applications and come in with three potential subjects. He'd evaluate them and return them the following week with suggestions for which was the best, and how to get started.

Kory left class wondering where he was going to find the time to do all of that in addition to his other work. When he called Samaki that night, they agreed not to have a sleepover for the first weekend since May. Samaki had just as much work as Kory, even counting the college applications. Kory made him agree to look at the application to State so he could pass along any questions to Mr. Pena under cover of his own interest. The thought of the class snickering at him was not bad enough to discourage him from helping Samaki.

They met at the Rainbow Center Saturday morning, but didn't have time for another tryst; Margo had recovered her poise and put them all to work painting. Jeremy seemed recovered from the previous week, though reluctant to talk about his parents. The atmosphere was cheerful, but Kory felt paradoxically depressed by that, because it highlighted Malaya's absence. Margo had found an address and given it to them with the caution that they should only send letters, not try to visit her. All through the day, the weight of the folded paper in Kory's pocket distracted him, turning his mind to what he'd say in his letter. Between the lack of quality fox time and Malaya's absence, Kory felt less fulfilled on the way home than he normally did on Saturday afternoons.

He spent the next day poring over his applications, shut into his room after church. They would take him a while to figure out. The Whitford and Gulliston applications had essays and neither of them was easy. "Pose a question and then answer it," was Whitford's. Gulliston just said, "write an essay," and didn't even give him that much. He pored over online essay examples until his eyes and head hurt, and then had to shut off the computer and sit down with a pencil and paper.

The question he really wanted to answer was, "What does it mean for me to be gay?" He didn't think he could write that and send it off to a college, though. Maybe something about poetry. He could write something like, "Where do my poems come from?" No, that was terrible. Maybe, "What am I trying to accomplish with my poems?" No, that sounded horribly arrogant. "Where should I go to school?" A valid question, but not very original. "Should I listen to my mother?"

He looked down at the paper where he'd written the question. Now, where did *that* come from? He crossed it out slowly and wrote next to it, "Does God love me?"

That one he looked at for a long time. It had potential: he could talk about the hardships he'd endured and the blessings he'd been given, and discuss some of the theology he'd learned through years of Sunday school. He could even talk about Malaya and her family, his mother's devout belief in the face of her misfortunes, and Father Joe's cheerful sermons, if not the talk he'd given Kory last spring, back when Kory was agonizing over his feelings for Samaki.

In retrospect, it was hard to believe he'd resisted the attraction to the fox. Samaki had been a steadfast friend as well as a boyfriend, closer than anyone save for Sal and Nick in Kory's life, and their lovemaking seemed so natural now that Kory couldn't remember why he'd spent a whole night in Samaki's basement sleeping two feet from the fox, terrified to touch him. Father Joe's reassuring voice had been a huge help in surmounting that wall of fear.

He couldn't use that in the essay, not without revealing his private life to the admissions officers and whoever else read the essay—he imagined it on the Internet next year at this time, available to all his friends. What he could use was Father Joe's calm assurance of God's love.

He jotted down some notes on that essay, and then set about coming up with two more subjects. Neither of the other ones felt as rich to him as his first question, and when he called Samaki that night to talk and told him the questions, the black fox agreed.

"It's really good to put a positive spin on religion these days," he said. "Just don't come off like some sort of home-schooled right-wing wacko."

"Like I normally do?"

Samaki laughed. "I know. Anyway, you could always just say you're gay. Gay and religious, that'd get you into any college. Talk about diverse."

Kory laughed too, but shortly, feeling the pressure on the walls of his internal dam again. After hanging up, he worked on some other homework, and didn't look at his essays again until he handed them in on Thursday.

Thursday evening, Samaki called him just as they were sitting down to dinner, well before the appointed time. Kory felt a prickling as he stepped out of the room to accept the call. "Kory, dinner is ready," his mother said sharply. "You can talk on the phone later."

"Just a minute," he said vaguely, staring at the phone. Samaki wouldn't call at this time unless it was important. He braced himself, and hit Talk.

"Malaya's in the hospital," Samaki said. "Margo just called to let me know."

"Which hospital?" he said numbly. His mother stepped into the room and held out her paw, glaring at him.

"Westfield General," Samaki said into his ear.

Instead of placing the phone in his mother's paw, Kory looked up at her and repeated, "Westfield General. Westfield's over past the river, right?"

"That's right. Can you go over there tonight? I'm going in a minute. Mom's just getting the kids dressed to go out."

His mother's expression had softened at the name of the hospital. "I'll try," Kory said.

"She'd probably like to see you the most."

"I'll try," he repeated. "We just started dinner." As soon as he said it, he was aware of how inane it sounded.

"What's wrong?" his mother asked. "Is it Samaki?"

He nodded, as Samaki said, "All right. I'll see you there."

He hung up with a warm flush that the fox understood him even when he said something silly. "Is he all right?" his mother was saying. "Why is he in the hospital?"

"He's not. Oh, no, I mean, that was him calling. One of the kids from the shelter is in the hospital. She was a friend of mine. Can we go, Mom?"

"It's a school night, and besides, there's nothing you can do for her, is there?"

He holstered his phone, and shook his head. "But I want to see her. I want to let her know that I'm there for her. She probably got put in the hospital by her father."

"Her father!" His mother's eyes looked sharply past him. "You don't want to get mixed up in another family's business."

"I just want to let her know she's not alone."

She wavered, looked back into the kitchen, and then put a paw on his shoulder. "Let's eat quickly, and then we'll go."

Nick came with them, following silently out to the car and into the back seat as his mother started it up. At first, Kory thought Nick was just seizing on an excuse to avoid homework, but as they pulled out onto the street, he reached along the window and patted Kory's shoulder.

Kory turned and smiled, then sat forward and watched the lights speed past the windshield. He shouldn't let his imagination wander, but he couldn't help seeing Malaya's skeletal hand reach up over the porch, remembering the fragile body she tried to conceal with her tough manner. He wished he'd taken that hand and held it then. What if it were shattered now, what if it was too late? He pictured her bleeding from the head, paralyzed, back broken, and shook the images from his mind.

"How did she end up back with her father?" his mother asked. They had just merged onto the expressway. "I thought your kids had been taken away from unsuitable families."

"She went back to him," Kory said. "She didn't have anything but her family, and she thought everything else was a lie."

"A lie? What does that mean?"

"We kept telling her she'd be okay, that she deserved to have a normal life, but she didn't believe it." He was too upset to give much thought to the words he used.

"Oh. Is she...special?"

He jerked his head to the side to look at his mom. "No!"

"Well, what do you mean, have a normal life?"

Now he was fully aware of how close he was to dangerous ground. Her stare probed for cracks in his armor. He looked straight ahead again.

"You know, because she was abused." Another lie, but only a partial one, at least.

His mother stayed silent after that, but he could feel her disapproval of anyone who didn't take steps to solve their own problems. *The Lord helps those who help themselves*, he knew she was thinking, even though she didn't voice it. Her sense that something about him was wrong might have been diverted, but surely it was only a temporary reprieve.

Kory's only experience with hospitals had been at St. Michael's when Nick broke his arm playing on the playground in second grade. Westfield General looked nothing like his gleaming white memory of St. Mike's. The carpet of the lobby, dull grey, felt tacky under his paws, and the antiseptic smell made his fur prickle, but he ignored that as he walked past the battleship-grey walls to the dimly lit reception desk and the tired-looking deer behind it.

"I'm here to see Malaya Bahar," Kory said, aware of the jangling of his nerves. His fingers drummed the desk; his tail twitched restlessly.

The nurse consulted her computer screen. "She's in 405, but visiting hours are over in fifteen minutes."

"That's okay, we'll hurry." He turned to his mother and said, "I'll be back down soon."

"Don't be silly," she said. "Come on, Nick." Taking Nick by the paw, she strode toward the elevator.

Kory squeezed his paws together, then hurried after her. "But Mom, you don't know her."

"I'd like to meet her. You're clearly important to her, aren't you?"

The elevator was taking forever to show up. He shifted from one foot to the other, and didn't respond. "Well?" his mother said. "Is she just a friend?"

"Yes!" Kory almost laughed at the thought of him dating the dark, grim Malaya.

"Well, I just wondered. You did spend so much time helping at that home, and it was right after you and Jenny split up."

Nick had wrested free of his mother's hand and now stood silently behind her. He met Kory's eyes and rolled his own. Kory nodded to him, and said, "She's not my girlfriend," just as the elevator arrived.

The elevator doors opened onto a jumble of bright reds, yellows, and blues. Cartoon characters cavorted over the walls, and in a corner of the large waiting room, yellow plastic toys lay strewn over the gaily patterned carpet and rounded plastic chairs. It took a moment to see the worn patches in the carpet, the white scars on the cartoon characters, the cracks in the

chairs. In one corner of the lobby, Mrs. Roden and Mariatu were playing some game with a little toy, while Ajani and Kasim sat nearby, kicking their legs. The two boys jumped up when they saw Kory and ran over to him.

"Hey there," he said, hugging back, looking down the hallway.

"Kory!" Ajani said. "I'm so bored."

"I'm not," Kasim said, the lie as evident as his pride in telling it.

"Ajani," Mrs. Roden said with gentle reproach. His ears folded down, his bushy red tail curling underneath himself. She greeted Kory's mother and Nick, and said, "I'm so glad you could make it. It'll mean a lot to her, poor thing."

"Mom, you want to wait here with Mrs. Roden?" Kory said.

"No, no, I'll come along."

"But maybe they don't want too many visitors there at once."

Mrs. Roden waved a paw. "She's stable and awake, if a little muzzy. They have her on Temerol. We just came out here because Mari and the boys were bored."

"I'm still bored," mumbled Ajani. "I wish I had my comic books."

"Just recite them to yourself, dear."

"Mom!" Kasim protested.

She smiled, one paw grooming the fur between Mariatu's ears. "We do need to leave soon, though. Would you tell Sammy when you get down there, Kory?"

Kory nodded. "Sure." He hurried off down the hallway, hoping that if he moved quickly enough, he could ditch his mother. What if Malaya called Samaki his boyfriend in front of her? The click of her claws on the tile floor followed him. For a moment, he considered giving Nick a look that would enlist his help, but then he drove the worries from his mind. They only had a few minutes, and Malaya was more important than him worrying about what his mother would think. Though it was a good sign that Mrs. Roden was in good spirits.

Though the hallway walls were white, each door was a different color. They passed a bulletin board with a number of crayon drawings tacked up onto it: "A leukemia germ," "Get well Marky," and untitled illustrations of home, hospital beds, and children in casts. Kory scanned the numbers and then heard Samaki's voice, and padded quickly toward it.

"I only had one other person in my room at St. Mike's," Nick said behind him as they entered the room. Samaki looked up from the farthest of the three beds on the left as Kory entered. The black fox gave him a wave and a brief smile. Kory padded quickly around to his side, looking down at the bed.

Malaya's eyes, half-lidded, followed him partway around and then gave up, drifting back to where his mother and Nick were approaching. Her right arm lay across her stomach, encased in plaster, and one of her ears drooped with the weight of taped bandages. The other still bore a silver stud, but that was the only trace of the old rebellious Malaya. In the hospital gown, she looked sick, not goth. "Hey," Kory whispered, then asked Samaki, "Is she awake?"

"Yeah," the black fox said, and looked up, acknowledging Kory's mother and Nick with a short wave.

Malaya stirred, now turning her head toward Kory, blinking slowly. "Kory?"

"Hey." He smiled.

"Told you," she said, "didn't I?"

"Told me what?"

Her eyes had drifted over to the other side of the bed. "Who's that?"

"Malaya, this is my mom and my brother Nick."

They both whispered hellos. The bat turned back to Kory and Samaki. "Kory knows," she said. "He wasn't trying...to sell me on a rainbow."

Kory exchanged a bewildered glance with Samaki, and then decided to ignore the comment. "So how are you feeling?"

"Feel..." She raised her arm an inch, let it drop, and winced. "Like shit. How's it look?"

"How did this happen?" Kory saw his mother flinch at the language. Maybe another swear or two would drive her out.

"*He* did it. Course."

Samaki whispered, "Margo said the hospital banned her father from seeing her. There's a social services worker coming to interview her." Kory felt a knot of anger form in his chest, bright and hot. He clenched a fist at his side.

"Social services," Malaya shook her head back and forth in a full one-eighty. "Bunch of fucking morons."

"You really don't need to use that kind of language," Kory's mother said reprovingly.

Malaya looked at her again and said, "Don't need to. But I like to."

"It doesn't serve any purpose."

The bat turned back to Kory. "I haven't had a mom in twelve years. I don't need one now."

"Mom," Kory said, louder than he'd meant to, but his mother had drawn herself up, whiskers twitching and mouth pursed shut, her ears flat back.

The nurse broke the uncomfortable silence, announcing that there were only five minutes left. Kory's mother grasped Nick's paw and turned to head for the door, then turned. "Kory, come on. Time to go."

Kory didn't move. His paw hurt from how tightly he was clenching it. "What happened?"

Malaya's rattling laugh made Kory's fur prickle. "Teen Vogue. Caught me reading Teen Vogue. Told me I had to cast Satan out. I told him...Satan has pretty dresses." She indicated the bandage on her ear with her good hand. "Hit me in the head. Knocked me down." She lifted her cast. "Broke my arm pulling me up."

Kory looked up at the nurse, an elderly wolf beckoning them with a gloved paw. His mother had listened to Malaya's speech and now was dragging Nick past the nurse and out. He wanted to tell Malaya that it wasn't right, that he'd help her and protect her, but she knew it wasn't right, just as she knew there was nothing he could do. Social services or not, once she was out of the hospital she would go back to her father eventually and this would happen again until maybe it wasn't a hospital she'd wind up in, but wherever her mom had gone. He wanted to tell her not to go back, but the words got jumbled together in his throat and nothing he could say would be more than a crayon "get well soon" drawing she could tack on the hallway of her mind and look at while her father was hitting her. "We gotta go," Kory said.

"We'll come back and visit when we can." Samaki leaned over and squeezed her hand.

Malaya nodded. Her eyes closed slowly as they followed Kory's mother out.

"Well, if anyone needs help, she does," Kory's mother said softly as they walked down the hall. "You're to be commended for your charity, Kory."

Samaki's tail brushed against his, safely out of sight. Kory worked to unclench his paw and relax. "I wish I could do more."

"Her father sounds like one of those Baptists."

"I don't know, exactly."

"He must be, to think Vogue is sinful. Talking about casting out Satan." She made a 'tch' sound with her tongue.

Kory had been wondering that himself, but the brush of Samaki's tail against his, reminding him of their shared secret, gave him the answer. "He thought she was looking at the women." He only realized after he said it that he'd said it loudly enough for everyone to hear.

They had just arrived in the gaily colored lobby. With one final tail-tag, Samaki left Kory and padded over to his family. Ajani said, "Can we *go* now?"

Kory's mother had half-turned to look at him, her brow creased. "The women?"

Mrs. Roden, holding Mariatu in one arm, distracted her before Kory could respond. "Are you all leaving now, too?"

"We have to," Kory said. "Visiting hours are over."

The elevator dinged. Doors creaked open. "Come on," Mrs. Roden said. "We'll all ride down together."

The two moms talked about recipes and pointedly skirted the subject of Malaya, while Ajani and Kasim both tried to talk to Kory at the same time, Ajani telling him about the latest comic book and Kasim trying to talk about one of his cartoon shows. He listened to their chatter with one ear, catching Samaki's eye and noticing that the black fox wasn't smiling, either. The violet eyes reflected Kory's pain, if not so much the anger. Kory tried to suppress his own, knowing it wasn't Samaki's way, knowing it wouldn't help, that what was needed was for him to be Malaya's friend and support her. It was hard to let go, and it was compounded by the black fox's presence three feet away, because all Kory wanted right now was to hug him and tell him how unfair it was for a bright, funny girl to be lying dazed and broken in a hospital bed, but with his mother in the elevator, he didn't dare. They shared the thought with their eyes, but eyes couldn't encircle him warmly, wrap a tail around him and squeeze him, rub a muzzle against his and kiss his cheek softly. His fur and skin ached for that touch, and to see Samaki so close just fed the small, hot anger he felt at Malaya's father.

It all came from the same thing, didn't it? His mother wouldn't knock him down and break his arm—probably couldn't—but she wasn't so different from Malaya's father. Not in spirit. He disliked her intensely for a moment, a spike of rage that simmered down as Kasim pulled on his shirt, distracting him. Perversely, his annoyance spread, encompassing his whole situation. Why did he have to be trapped in this life where he couldn't be honest with his family and friends about the people he loved? Why did Samaki have to come along and drag him into this? If he'd never met the fox, he'd never have met Malaya, and he wouldn't be here in the hospital in an elevator that felt more and more claustrophobic by the minute.

He met Samaki's eyes again, and instantly felt bad. If he hadn't met Samaki, then he wouldn't know Samaki. He wouldn't want that. It was everyone else causing the problems. Guilt flushed his ears, still warm as the elevator doors opened.

As they left the elevator, the Rodens all milled around one end of the lobby, away from where Kory's mom had parked. They said good-byes, Mrs. Roden promising to call, Kory's mother saying she hoped to see Samaki again soon. Kory and Samaki squeezed paws in a firmer-than-usual grip and said goodbye with their eyes. "Call ya tomorrow," Kory said, and Samaki nodded.

"What did you mean, she was looking at women?" his mother asked as they left. Kory groaned inwardly. Of all the things for her to latch on to.

"Nothing," he mumbled, feeling his paws tighten into fists again. *Relax*, he willed them.

"Is she homosexual?"

The carefully controlled distaste with which his mother said that word sent a jolt through Kory's chest. He snapped his head up and opened his mouth to say something noncommittal like "I don't know," but different words boiled out. "What does it matter?"

His mother blinked. "Of course, at that age she's still vulnerable to urges. If she was being approached by homosexuals, she could be confused."

"Her father beat her up and broke her arm."

"Lower your voice," his mother snapped. "You're too young to know what you're talking about. You have to protect children from those people while they're at an impressionable age."

"Mom, that's so lame." Kory had almost forgotten Nick was with them. His younger brother looked at Kory around his mother's dress, his eyes wide in warning.

"Quiet, Nick."

"He's right," Kory said. "It is lame. You think you can protect us?"

They had left the hospital and now walked along the sidewalk back towards the car. "The Lord knows I'm doing the best I can." When Kory snorted, not trusting himself to speak, his mother turned around, paws on her hips. "What is so amusing, young man?"

"Nothing," he said, glaring at her.

"Come on, let's get home." Nick tugged hard on his mother's arm, his eyes pleading with Kory: *Don't!*

She ignored Nick, staring back at Kory. "Have you been approached by homosexuals, Kory?"

"Oh, I sure have, Mom," he said, the words spilling out. He wanted to hurt her. His heart was pounding. "They got me. There wasn't anything you could do."

As soon as he said it, Nick groaned, and Kory wished he could take the words back. His mother didn't scream, or strike him, or gape in disbelief. She stared at him for a moment, then turned around and walked for the car again, Nick firmly in tow.

Kory stood, bewilderment overcoming anger for the moment, and hurried after them. His mother's ears swiveled back, hearing his footsteps, and she shook her head. "Father Joe said you'd go through this stage."

Now Kory's fur prickled and he felt a chill that had nothing to do with the crisp evening wind. "What?" Father Joe had told him their talks would be confidential.

"He said all teenagers go through a rebellious stage. You obviously feel sorry for that poor girl and...you're lashing out at me. That's okay. God gives me the strength to handle it. If you really are confused about homosexuals, you can talk to Father Joe about it."

"I already have," Kory said.

"Oh." This stopped her only for a moment. "I don't mind that you went to him first. It's natural for you to hesitate to talk to me. It's part of that stage you're in. Well, if he can't help, there's a camp you can go to that will clear it all up."

"I'm not going to be brainwashed," Kory said. He wondered how much Father Joe had told her. Not what he'd initially feared, it seemed. "And stop calling it a 'stage'."

"Oh, Kory," his mother sighed. "The Lord works in mysterious ways. The camp may be just what you need anyway."

"Just what I need? For what?"

They all climbed into the car. His mother didn't say anything until they were on the street. "A little discipline, a father figure. I know...I read about cases like this. You're missing a strong male authority figure. I tried to compensate with sports and that church retreat."

"That's what that was about?" Nick said from the back seat.

His mother continued as though he hadn't said anything. "But you never took to sports. I should have known you'd need more. I'll go find the information on those camps, and if you're still persisting in this fantasy, we can sign you up for the summer before you go to college. See? It's an easy problem to solve."

Looking across the seat, Kory fumed at her placid expression. "It's not a problem, and it doesn't need to be solved," he said.

"This girl in my class kissed another girl right in front of--"

"Nicholas!" His mother acknowledged Nick now, sharply.

"Seriously," Kory said, "I've read about those camps, you know. Have you?"

"I don't want to discuss that right now. I just want you to know that I'm willing to help you with this problem, Kory. I love you."

The words sounded forced out. Kory stared at her. "Yeah, Mom. You and God. Right?"

"I know it might be hard for you to believe."

"When you talk about sending me away to camp to fix me, it is."

She heaved an exaggerated sigh. "If you broke your leg, I'd send you to the hospital. Would you not want that, either?"

"Nothing's broken!" Kory yelled.

She stopped at a red light, slamming the brake hard. "Lower. Your. Voice," she snarled back. The light turned green. She rolled through in silence to the freeway on-ramp. "I don't know whether you're really feeling these things or if you're just acting out some kind of rebellious impulse because you know it will upset me, but either way you need to learn how to behave normally."

"Rebellious impulse?" he gaped at her. "You think this is about you?"

"Of course not," she said with false sincerity. "It's about your need to have your own space, to define your identity independent of me. I know I haven't given you everything you need, Kory, and I'm sorry about that. But it's important that whatever you think you're feeling, you talk about it and make sure we can head it off before it becomes any more of a problem. Nicholas, that goes for you too."

He folded his arms and stared straight ahead at the road. Lightposts and other cars sped by them while Kory tried to figure out how he would talk about it with his mother so that she would leave him alone. As they exited the freeway, she said, "It's that fox, isn't it? He's the one putting ideas in your head."

"His name's Samaki. You've eaten dinner with him."

She turned onto their street. "Well, you're not to see him any more."

Kory laughed. "You going to ground me all the rest of the year until I go to college?"

"If I have to."

"I'll sneak out of the house. I'll go directly from school."

She stopped the car in the driveway. "As long as you're living under my roof and eating my food, you'll obey me."

Kory found that his paws were shaking as he got out of the car, following his mother to the house with Nick close behind. "You're just like Malaya's father."

When she whirled to face him, her eyes glowed. "How dare you," she whispered. "I would never raise a paw to you. I have loved you, fed you, sheltered you..."

"Except when it mattered," Kory said defiantly.

They both knew he was not talking about being gay. Mouth open, she stopped, turned, and opened the door. Paw on the knob, she stopped just inside. "That was not my fault," she said. "I can only control what I do. I can't be responsible for the behavior of others."

"Except me, apparently."

"Of course, you. You're my son." She closed the door after Nick and locked it emphatically. "I'm just glad you talked to me before you acted on any of these so-called 'feelings.' Lord knows what might have happened otherwise."

Kory stared at her, and when she'd hung up her coat and turned around, she saw his expression. He made no attempt to hide anything from her. It was a relief to let the dam burst, all the things he'd hidden from her for the last six months plain to see on his face. He watched her eyes meet his, widen, and flick to his room, and he could tell the moment when she began counting up all the times Samaki had stayed overnight because her jaw dropped, slightly, and then her eyes narrowed. "Kory James Hedley," she said, "you had better not mean what I think you mean."

His heart pounded hard in his chest again. "What if I do?" he said.

"Don't be insolent with me, young man." She strode toward him.

"What are you going to do, break my arm?" He lifted his chin. "For being in...in love?" He'd never used that word to talk about Samaki, but he needed its weight in this argument, wanted to hit her with it as she was hitting him with her God and her motherhood.

"That is not love," she started.

He interrupted, yelling, "Didn't you tell me God is about love? Didn't Father Green preach that every Sunday, and Father Joe every Sunday since then?"

"Don't you throw the Lord into this. He is about love and this is not love." She matched his pitch. He saw Nick standing frozen at the door of his room, his eyes like saucers.

"How do you know that?"

"Because love doesn't make you defile my house," she cried, and then, as if to herself, "Oh, dear Lord, I'm going to have to get the carpet cleaned now. I always hated that smell."

"What smell? My *boyfriend's* smell?" He'd been mad enough when she was only judging him, but to bring Samaki into it set his blood racing faster still. "You...you goddamned bigot."

Her ears flattened all the way. "Don't you take the Lord's name in vain, you sinner," she hissed. "And how dare you sit in judgment of me. I clothed you, fed you, raised you..."

"And somehow I turned out okay anyway."

"You ungrateful child. You're not even repentant."

Kory folded his arms and shook his head, vaguely aware that part of him was shaking as badly as Nick was, but anger kept his defiance up. He looked his mother in the eye and said, "You're the one who should be repentant."

She breathed hard for a few heartbeats and then raised a paw and pointed at the door. "Get out of my house. Get out right now."

Kory spun on his heels and unlocked the door. He heard her yell after him, "And don't you come back until you're prepared to—, " but he never heard what he should be prepared to do, because he drowned out her last word with a loud slam that rattled the glass in the door.

He stood on his front walk, listening to the fan in the car engine. Crickets chirped nearby. Otherwise, his suburban street had settled in for the night, at the late hour of 9:32, by his cell phone. Slowly, his heartbeat eased. He was waiting, he realized, for his mother to come out and tell him to come back in, whereupon he could angrily tell her that he didn't want to come back in, could turn his back on her pleading.

He folded his ears down against the breeze. What had just happened here was a real event, not just a fight, the culmination of the past year of Kory's growth apart from the path his mother had so carefully laid out for him. He'd started to hide things from her, not just little things like the occasional beer or the pictures he found on the Internet, but big things like his relationship and his work at the Rainbow Center. She didn't even really know him anymore, not the things that were most important to him. He glanced back at the house and felt in his heart that it was just his mother's house now, no longer his home. That quickly, he'd cut himself loose.

Freedom felt terrifying and invigorating. He could walk down the path and up the sidewalk and make his own way through the dark neighborhood, the quiet streets. A car drove slowly down his street and turned at the end. He followed it with his eyes, wondering where it was going, and then wondering where *he* was going. The places he could stay tonight were few enough that he could count them on one paw while still holding his phone.

There was the Rainbow Center, of course, if the buses ran this late. He had his cell phone, and twenty-six dollars in his wallet. Not much to go on. The list of friends he could impose on for one night's stay, let alone an indefinite stay, was depressingly short. His aunt—his mother's sister—was out. His only option, really, was Sal.

Unless he wanted to go sleep at the bus shelter. He'd only seen people do that downtown. He suspected that if he were to try it here, he'd meet a policeman in short order, and then there would be explanations and his mother would be forced to be involved again. He dialed Sal's number and held his breath.

"Of course you can come over for the night," Sal said. "Just let me tell Mom. Why? What's going on?"

"I'll tell you when you get here. Can you pick me up at the Hilltop Shopping Center?"

"Sure. Be there in about twenty minutes."

Kory took a look at his phone. 9:38. He looked once more back at the house and then started walking.

His familiar street comforted him, the smells and the configuration of the yards, promising that outside his house, the world was going on as it always did. The people in those houses, relaxing after dinner, had no idea what had just happened, and if he knew his mother, they likely never would. That was fine. It crossed his mind that he might never call this street home again, but he recognized that that was his dramatic imagination. Right now he had no desire to come back, but what else could he do, in the long run? They had a college visit planned for the end of the month. College? How would he afford college without his mother's help? And anyway, he couldn't stay with Sal forever.

Forever was a long way away. He just had to get through tonight. He pushed away thinking about the fight and realized he had to call Samaki. He weighed the cell phone in his hand. It was late, he thought. He might be disturbing the household. And how would Samaki react? Would he tell him it was better to get it out in the open? He'd be thinking that, anyway. But he'd be sympathetic, too. And he had to call him. This couldn't wait until the morning.

Mrs. Roden answered the phone, panting slightly, and he could hear Ajani and Kasim arguing in the background; they'd just gotten home. She fetched Samaki without any questions, and when the black fox came on, Kory could hear the concern that he'd felt just a couple hours earlier, when Samaki had called him off their normal schedule.

"I got kicked out of home," he said.

The silence on the other end lasted for so long that he put one paw to his ear so he could hear the fox's soft breathing. "Samaki?"

"I'm here. What happened? Are you okay?"

Kory glanced around the street, standing at the corner where he had to turn away from the bus stop and his familiar morning route. "I'm fine." He started walking along Salmon, the winding street that would drop him behind the shopping center. "We had a fight about Malaya. I told her about us and she told me to get out."

"Just like that?"

On Salmon Street, the strange smells and lights quickened Kory's pace.

He began to realize how vulnerable he was out here in the dark. "I kinda told her what we'd done. I might have cursed, too." The memory of that word brought a flush of shame to his ears.

"Oh, hon. Are you okay?"

"I am now. I think. But she knows for sure, now."

Samaki sighed. "I guess we knew she'd find out sooner or later. Wish she hadn't taken it so hard. Do you need somewhere to stay tonight? I can come pick you up in a couple hours when my dad gets home. Or I could ask my mom if you need a ride right now."

"I already called Sal," Kory said, watching a car approach. A large Jeep, with a hare at the wheel who ignored him as he passed.

"Okay." Samaki was quiet for a moment. "I guess I won't be staying over for a while."

Kory chuckled. "Yeah. Me neither."

"Well," Samaki said, "I mean, you'll be back home in a day or two, right?"

Now Kory remained quiet, until Samaki said his name again. "I don't know," he said. "I don't want to go back."

"What did she say?"

He could see the words as though they were written in fire in the air before his eyes. "She said we defiled her house. She wanted to send me away to one of those ex-gay summer camps to 'fix' me."

"Just give her time to cool down..."

"She doesn't need time to cool down. She needs a complete brain transplant."

Samaki paused, and then said, "Well, you can stay in our basement if you need to. I'll ask Mom, but I'm sure she won't mind. And we don't have to worry about them finding out."

"You're lucky," Kory said with only a little bitterness. "She had that stuff about the camps all teed up. She must have been reading about it."

"But she didn't figure out about us?"

He scuffed his feet along the sidewalk. "She's freaking paranoid. She probably had drug rehab camps and alcohol rehab camps and weight loss camps and loss of faith camps and every other behavior modification thing for disobedient teens all ready. Probably she was happy just because now she knows it's not one of those other things. Now she knows what's wrong with me."

Samaki said instantly, "Nothing's wrong with you."

"No," Kory said, as another car rushed by him, on its way home, no doubt. "I know."

In the background, he heard their house phone ring. Samaki ignored it. "So you want me to come by tomorrow?"

"Maybe. I can probably stay at Sal's for a while. They have a lot of room there, and it'll be easier."

The pause that came before the fox spoke again didn't register immediately with Kory, distracted as he was with thinking about staying at Sal's place. Later, he would remember it. "Okay," Samaki said. "I'll still see you this weekend, right?"

"Sure." Kory's ears flicked against a chilly breeze. "I have to call Nick and get him to bring my stuff to school. I'll call you tomorrow night."

"Sounds good." Over the fox's soft voice, Kory heard Mrs. Roden, her voice raised as he'd never heard it. "I'll see you Saturday, too. And don't worry. It'll be okay."

"Thanks." He put his smile into the word.

He said good-bye, closing his cell phone and walking around the next curve. The night still seemed ordinary, the shopping center just ahead of him already closed for the night. The only cars in the lot were a few employees still closing up shop. Kory looked from the center down to his phone. He and Samaki had talked as if him leaving home was ordinary, was just something to be gotten over, not a life-changing event. The impact of it hadn't really hit him yet, but it was starting to, now that he was thinking of the one person he had left to call.

After hitting the speed dial (his brother was '3', just after his mother and voicemail and just before Samaki), he hesitated over the 'Talk' button. What if his mother was in with Nick now, monitoring the phone in case Kory called, or just taking out her anger on him?

There was no help for it; he had to get his schoolbooks and notebooks and some clothes before tomorrow morning. He couldn't—wouldn't—go back to the house, so he stabbed the Talk button and took a deep breath.

Nick answered almost immediately, his voice low but genuine enough that Kory knew he was alone. "Oh my God, Kory," he said before Kory could say anything at all. "Where are you?"

"Sal's picking me up," Kory said. "Don't worry, I'll be okay tonight. I just need you to grab my books and bring them to school in the morning." It was weird, talking to Nick on the phone. His voice sounded different, whether from the phone or from the stress of the evening.

"You're not coming back tonight?"

"Why would I come back? Did Mom tell you she wants me to?" It wouldn't change his mind, but it would give him a great deal of satisfaction to know that she regretted her words already.

"Nooo." Nick drew out the word reluctantly. "But where else are you gonna go? You can't stay at Sal's 'til September."

Nick was probably right, but when Kory looked ahead to the shopping center where Sal was going to meet him, he felt a burst of desperate confidence. "If I need to, I can. I'm not coming home."

"But..."

"You heard what she said about Samaki. What she said about me! I have to do the right thing for my life, and I'm tired of her roof and her rules and her narrow-minded bullshit!" The word felt dangerous and good to say. He threw in a "God damn it!" at the end just to punctuate it.

Nick didn't respond immediately. Kory's triumphant bravado faded, leaving him feeling a little dirty about the swears. Finally, Nick said, "I'll bring your books to school tomorrow. I can bring 'em to your homeroom."

"I'll meet you at the bus when you get there," Kory said. "Thanks, Nick." And then, because his brother sounded so tired and forlorn, he said, "Hey. I'm still your big brother. I'm still gonna look out for you."

"Maybe I should be looking out for you," Nick said, in a cheerier tone.

Rounding a corner, Kory saw another set of headlights, and this time recognized Sal's car. "Sal's here. I'll see you in the morning, Nick."

"Kory?"

"Yeah?"

"Love you."

His throat closed up for a moment. "Love you too, Nick."

His brother's words stayed with him, strongly enough that if the first words out of Sal's mouth hadn't reminded Kory of his mother, he very likely would have told his friend to drive him back home. But Sal said, "So what'd you say to get kicked out?" and Kory remembered his words, and his mother's, and the anger came flooding back as he curled his tail around behind him and settled back into the seat.

"I think I called her a goddamn bigot," he said.

"Wow." Sal chuckled. "Pulling out the name of the Lord in vain. That's, what, three Hail Marys?"

"None for me, now," Kory said. "You have to repent to do penance."

Sal whistled. "Harsh. What'd she say to get that?"

"Oh, um..." Kory looked out his window. "She was saying stuff about Samaki. And his family."

"The fox? You got kicked out of your house for a fox?"

He could see Sal's reflection, looking at him, more amused than anything else. His friend's equanimity helped him relax. "Well, she's been going on about them for months. I just got sick of it."

"So you cursed at her and she kicked you out? That don't make sense."

"We were fighting already," Kory said, "about..." He couldn't think of a plausible lie, and realized he didn't want to. He turned to his friend and sighed. "Sal, pull over here a second. I need to tell you something."

Sal listened to his confession, his eyes barely widening. He shrugged when Kory was done. "Dude, that's cool. You never really seemed happy with Jenny anyway. Makes me feel a little better, you know, about all those times you wouldn't come out with me."

"Huh?"

Sal grinned. "I mean, it wasn't me. It was just that you didn't like girls. Good thing you found out early, or you mighta been really fucked up."

"Thanks," Kory said. "I mean, really."

"Also explains your mom flying off the handle. I guess she just found out tonight too, huh?"

"Yeah." Kory laughed shortly. "The number of people who know just doubled. Well, not counting the kids down at the Center."

"The Center?"

And then he had to tell Sal about the Rainbow Center, and he was surprised at how good it felt to open up. Sal nodded, pulling back onto the road partway through the story. When Kory reached the part about Malaya being in the hospital, and came full circle to the argument that had led to him being in Sal's car, Sal was just pulling into his driveway. He parked to one side, both parents' cars taking up the garage, and they got out just as Kory was recounting the last things his mother had said.

"She said she was going to clean the carpets?" Sal whistled. "No offense, dude, but your mom is a little bit nutso."

"More than a little," Kory said, following Sal along the stone path across his lawn.

"S'okay, so's mine. Just not in ways that get me kicked out." Sal grinned at him. "I'd take you in by the pool, but if you've just got those clothes, we should keep 'em dry."

"Good thinking." Sal's family lived in a large three-story house on the side of a hill, with a yard that extended all the way around the house (Kory had sometimes helped mow in the summer) and a large outdoor pool that connected with their indoor pool but wasn't heated. The taupe-colored stone walls blended with the green grass to make it appear that the house had risen organically out of the hillside, an impression reinforced by the rounded corners and oval windows. 'A lot of personality,' Sal's dad said about their house, which also boasted pools on the upper floors and water slides running down through the walls.

Because of the upper-story pools, they had to climb almost twenty feet of stairs to get up to Sal's room. Kory waved to Sal's parents on their way past the rec room; they waved back, looking up from the TV for only a moment.

"You can stay here," Sal said, opening the door across the hall from his.

Kory stepped inside and looked around. "Your mom redecorated again."

"Yeah, she's all into this 'colors of the seasons' crap now. She tried to paint my room in greens and yellows for spring, and I told her no fucking way."

Kory looked around at the brown walls, the artfully bunched orange and red curtains, and the coordinated drying mat and bed with the maple leaf pattern. "I think it looks fine," he said.

Sal snorted. "It's not your room."

"Is now."

They grinned at each other, and then Sal punched him in the arm. "So how long you think before this blows over?"

Kory shook his head, tired of thinking about that question. "I don't know. I don't care if it lasts 'til I go to college."

For the first time in a night of revelations, Sal's eyes really widened, and his ears came up sharply. "Seriously?"

"Yeah. Seriously."

His friend whistled again. Kory rubbed a paw over his eyes and through his head fur. "Look," he said. "She can't accept what I am and she can't accept Samaki, and I'm not going to give any of that up just so I can live with her. I'm almost eighteen. I don't need her."

Sal nodded, rubbing his whiskers, and said, "So you're really into that fox, huh?"

"Pretty serious."

"Cool." Sal tapped his arm again. "I'd like to meet him sometime."

Kory punched back. "You will." He loved Sal for that.

"Well, I gotta finish some homework. I guess you don't have any books or anything?"

"Homework's mostly done. Nick's gonna bring it tomorrow."

"Cool." Sal waved. "Good night, then. Tell me if you need anything. Towels in the usual place."

Kory waved good-night, and when the door was shut, he took off his clothes and slid into the water. Its warmth surrounded him, penetrating and relaxing. More words circled round his head: *The prisoner escapes into the dark water, his chains lie piled on the shore. He flees the judgment from above, he runs from fear to love.* That word again: love. He thought it about Sal; he felt it for Nick; he remembered it for his mother. What did it mean for Samaki? Some combination of all of them? He set the word aside and played with the lines of poetry until they became abstract, and he stopped thinking about the fight with his mother. When he felt himself slipping out of consciousness, he slid up onto the drying mat and went to sleep, one arm stretched out as though searching for someone by his side.

For a moment, when he woke the next morning, everything was normal. Then he looked around at the turning leaves, the bookcase that was too small to be anything but decorative, the unfamiliar rough ceiling, and the posterless walls, and he remembered.

Trepidation warred with elation, a battle he was becoming familiar with and tired of. Freedom, not only to go where he wanted, but from his mother's expectations and prejudices, buoyed him, but the currents carrying him away from her didn't tell him where they were taking him. The river ahead looked huge and unfamiliar, making him close his eyes for a moment and wish he were back home in his bed. Then he wished Samaki were there with him, and he found that the anger at his mother was not all exhausted after all.

He used its fierce flare as impetus to get up and get dressed. School, at least, he could count on being constant. Nobody knew what had happened, except for Sal and Nick, and he could make sure they didn't tell. If it got out that he'd been kicked out of the house, there'd be explanations required. Being out to Sal was a good feeling, as if he'd crossed a chasm safely, but the rest of the school was unlikely to react as well.

Through breakfast and the pleasantries exchanged with Sal's parents, to whom he said only that he wanted to hang out with Sal more and work on their college applications, he thought about the black fox and missed him, wondering what breakfast would be like in their house, just the two of them. Maybe, he thought, he and Samaki could just get an apartment together, somewhere in the city. Get jobs, earn their own money, start their own life. Nobody would have to know what their relationship was. There were plenty of friends who rented apartments together. He and Sal had talked about it, jokingly and half-seriously, the summer before last, when they'd both been grounded for being caught with beer.

Sal punched him as they got into the car, because he'd mentioned college, but when Kory pointed out that it was probably the one thing that had stopped further questions, Sal laughed and agreed, not really mad. Kory envied him the freedom from caring about what his parents thought, but Sal had always been that way. Kory was the cautious one, the one most likely to ask, "What would your mom say?" Sal forged ahead on his own path, not uncaring of others, just independent of them. Even when he lost a girlfriend, he was more annoyed at the loss of sex than he was about the relationship. When Kory asked him not to mention to anyone else that he'd been kicked out of his house, much less the reason, Sal shrugged as though it hadn't even crossed his mind to talk about it.

Kory waited outside for the bus while Sal walked in to homeroom. When Nick got off their bus and saw Kory, he ran to him, but pulled up short a foot away. "Here," he said, holding out Kory's backpack.

"Thanks." Kory took it and slung it over his shoulder. He looked back at his brother's blue eyes. "How you doing?"

"Me?" Nick forced a grin. "I'm fine." He put out a paw and patted Kory's arm, as close as they'd come to a hug on school grounds. "You?"

"I'm good." He wanted to tell his brother more, but he didn't know what. "I figured I'd come home and get some stuff after school, before she gets back."

His brother's ears perked briefly at the word 'home,' then lowered again. "Okay."

Kory reached out and squeezed his brother's shoulder. "You want to come over to Sal's sometime next week? Maybe you and me could go out for pizza?"

"Yeah." Nick flashed him a smile as the five-minute bell rang, summoning them inside.

Fortunately, Kory's first class was trig, which he'd already done his homework for, and he was able to surreptitiously finish his homework for English while Mrs. Molken was droning on about sines and cosines in her high-pitched ferrety whine. By the time he got to the end of the day, he'd gotten the majority of his work done.

He actually stepped up onto the stairs of his bus out of habit before remembering that Sal was going to pick him up. "Not today," he said, waved to the driver, and stepped down. Nick came running for the bus, but stopped when he saw Kory.

"You waiting for me?"

"Nah, Sal's going to pick me up." Kory looked along the front of the school for Sal's old black car. "You want a ride?"

They rode back to Kory's house in silence, Nick in the back seat, Kory in front. Sal tried to start talking about his day, but Kory, running through the checklist in his head of things he was going to have to get out of his room, didn't encourage him, and Sal eventually shut up. Computer, of course,

Kory thought, and clothes. Some music and books, but only the essentials. His photo albums from growing up. He wanted to take his toy chest and box of mementos, but that was already going to be more than would fit in Sal's car. He asked Nick if he'd be willing to keep some stuff in his room to keep it safe, and his brother responded with a subdued "Yes."

The house already felt strange to him, like a copy of something he'd once known intimately. Kory walked with only a slight hesitation over the spot he'd stepped when his mother had told him to get out, and crossed the small bridge over the pool in the living room into his room, with Nick and Sal behind him.

"What do you wanna grab?" Sal was rubbing his paws together, looking around as though they were doing something excitingly illegal.

Kory tossed a suitcase from his closet onto the bed. "Can you pack this up?" He started pulling shirts, pants, and underwear out of his dresser. "Nick, can you get my other bag from the hall closet?"

His brother left the room without a word, returning a moment later with the big blue bag and throwing it onto the desk beside the first. Silently, he walked over to the bookcase and started taking Kory's books.

Of course Nick would know that he'd want his books. Kory leaned against the closet, just watching his brother, feeling the emotion swell in his chest. It would be so easy just to wait until his mother got home, wouldn't it? It would save him all this trouble, and he could stay with Nick. He swallowed. "You know," he began, but Nick's expression stopped him.

"I know," he said. "It's about her. And you gotta, you know, stand up for what's right. Don't you?" Kory didn't trust himself to speak, so he just nodded. Nick put the books on the bed, facing away from his brother, his ears and tail drooping. "You won't be that far away."

"Never," Kory said, and when Nick turned around, he hugged him tightly. He wanted to stay more than ever, but he would only be doing it for Nick, and Nick had just explained exactly why he had to leave.

While Sal and Nick carried his bags out to the car, he took his computer apart. With the wires packed into a plastic bag, he looked around his room, at all the trappings of his childhood. That was all they were now. He could take them with him, but they were mementos, not part of his life any more. The posters on the walls, the picture of his family at the ocean…he looked at that last one, picked it up, and put it into the plastic bag with the wires.

They carried his personal boxes into Nick's room, and then he and Sal carried his computer out to the car. Nick carried the small printer, lagging behind them. They stowed the equipment in the back seat, and then Kory gave his brother another hug. "See you at school," he said.

Nick nodded. "Get going," he said. "She'll be home soon."

Kory looked out his window at his brother, getting smaller and smaller in the side mirror, but the sight grew blurry and he had to look away before they'd even turned the corner.

Saturday morning, he walked down to the bus stop. Sal had offered to drive, if he were awake, and Kory, knowing he wouldn't be, had accepted with a grin. His friend hadn't been back at one a.m., when Kory had enforced his own bedtime, and there was no movement from his room at seven a.m., when Kory's computer beeped to wake him up.

Once he got to his accustomed transfer point on the bus, he got to the Rainbow Center as easily as ever, enjoying the familiarity of those surroundings. Margo, it turned out, had been to visit Malaya the previous day, and planned to go again in the afternoon. She invited Kory to come along, which he gladly accepted. Samaki arrived just in time to hear an update on Jeremy's situation: the skunk was doing much better and had told Margo that he wanted to go live with his aunt and uncle in the northeast. "It helped," she said, "that his aunt and his mother had a falling-out. I could just hear her thinking about boasting that she could take better care of Jeremy than his mother could. It's not the healthiest environment for a boy, but it isn't for long, and he did used to live in that town anyway." She shook her head. "Sometimes it takes a little crisis for a boy to come to a decision. How are you doing, Kory?"

"Oh," he said, "fine." He started to tell her about his own crisis, but he was too familiar with the questions that would raise, and he was tired of them already. He just wanted this day to be normal.

Kory couldn't wait until their first hug was done to ask Samaki not to mention his situation. "Sure," Samaki said, arms still around the otter. "It's your business. How are you doing?"

"Fine." Kory looked up and nuzzled his shoulder. "Sal's place is nice and I'm all set up there."

"How long do you think you'll stay?"

Kory shrugged. "I really don't know. I just don't want to think about that."

Samaki released him, stepping back. "Because you know, you could stay in our basement. Mom said she'd love to have you there."

Kory nodded. "I know. I just...Sal has pools, and his parents are..." Well-off, he started to say, but snapped his mouth shut before the words escaped. He didn't want Samaki to think it was all about the money. "...they're cool with it. And it's closer to school and stuff."

"Yeah, okay." Samaki's tail dipped, but his smile didn't fade too much. "Oh, I didn't tell you last night. When you were talking to me on Thursday, your mom called my mom."

Kory felt his fur prickle. "Why didn't you tell me last night?"

"Oh, we were talking about school, and I kinda forgot," Samaki said. "It wasn't a big deal. My mom hung up on her after about fifteen minutes."

Kory groaned. "What'd she say?"

"Mom wouldn't tell me. But I heard Mom saying 'we know, and we love our son'."

"Tell your mom I'm sorry."

Samaki squeezed Kory's arm. "Why? Not your fault."

"I know, but..."

Samaki kissed his nose. "She knows you're going through a rough time. She can't wait to see you tonight. Be warned," he grinned, "she's feeling really sorry for you. You may have to eat two desserts."

"I think I can manage." Kory smiled.

Delicate fingers caressed one of his ears. "You doing okay?"

"I guess." Kory closed his eyes.

He heard toeclaws clicking on the floor as someone walked by. "Get a room, you two," Jeremy said lightly, pushing open the door to the back yard.

"We'll be out in a second," Samaki called. "I can't imagine getting kicked out of my house," he said, more softly.

"Well, you like your parents." Kory opened his eyes, resting his chin on the fox's shoulder. On the opposite wall, a small rack of brochures for the kids hung. He could read the big black text on one: "YOU'RE OKAY." Next to it was a space that he knew was waiting for a new shipment of "YOUR PARENTS LOVE YOU."

"We always talked about your mother freaking out," Samaki said. "Was it bad?"

"It was a scene. Poor Nick was caught in the middle."

"What did she say, besides the camps?"

Kory shrugged. "The usual stuff about homos being evil. She wanted to protect me from them."

"I still can't believe she mentioned those camps." Kory felt rather than heard Samaki's low growl.

"Don't worry," Kory said. "I'd run away before I ended up in one of those."

"You already did." Samaki leaned back to look him in the eyes. "Anything you want to talk about while we have time here?"

Kory smiled and touched his nose to the fox's. "I don't want to ruin today. Let's work on the yard while the weather holds. We're going to go see Malaya this afternoon."

"Okay, lead on," Samaki said. "Oh, I filled out my application for State last night. It felt just like applying for a job at the supermarket."

"I haven't looked at mine," Kory said as they walked to the back, where the boys were already working on laying some paving stones. Kory could see that while the porcupine, Jano, was just laying the closest stones within his reach, Jeremy was trying to sort them by size and color. The stones had been donated, so this was not a simple task. "I don't even know if I can go to college now. Who's going to pay for it?"

"Your mom will. She has to." Samaki bent to lift a stone.

Kory paused, staring beyond the fence. "I don't know if I want to take her money."

The fox placed the stone down for the boys to tamp into place. He turned to look at Kory. "If it's a choice between going to college and not?"

Kory shrugged. "I can work for a year. Earn money. Maybe I'll join the Army or something, get them to pay for school."

Samaki giggled. "I can just see you in the Army."

Vic, the weasel, looked up. "I thought gays couldn't join the Army."

"I wouldn't *tell* them," Kory said. They stared at him until he pinned his ears back and reached for the tamper, pressing the stone Samaki had just laid into the sand.

Vic shrugged. "Who wants to go to college anyway? I've had enough school already."

Jano said, "You've gotta go to college. That's where you start the rest of your life."

"I'm ready now," Vic said. "Starting here." He fitted a stone next to two others and eyed it. "What do you think? Does that work like that?"

They all looked it over. He'd placed a reddish clay stone in between two slate-blue ones. "Looks great," Samaki said, and Kory nodded his agreement.

At the hospital, they found Malaya alert enough to roll her eyes as Margo, Kory, Samaki, and the boys trooped into her room. "They said I need peace and quiet," she grumbled, but Kory saw the hints of a smile under the bandaged ear.

She told them the story again, more coherently: her father, seeing her leafing through Vogue while talking on the phone about how pretty some of the models were, had assumed she was talking to a girlfriend, which she didn't deny because it was, in fact, true. "And maybe I was talking about how much I'd like to do some of those models," she said, "but it was just talk, that was all."

They laughed with her for a while, and she pretended to hate it. When Margo announced it was time to return to the Center, they all said their goodbyes, and she waved at them and told them to get out. Kory and Samaki, planning to take a bus, started out to walk down with the rest of the group, until Malaya called, "Kory?"

He turned and saw her beckoning. "Go ahead," he said to Samaki. "I'll be down in a minute."

When the others had gone, he sat by Malaya's bed again. "What's up?"

She shook her head. "Remember what I told you about hope?" He nodded. She waved toward her smokeless muzzle with one hand. "See? Given it up."

Her eyes defied him to contradict her. Normally he would have skirted around the issue, but his own recent wounds were too fresh. "I got kicked out of my house," he said.

"For a night?"

"I'm not going back."

He hadn't expected her to be shocked or impressed. If she was either, she didn't show it. "Seems like we're in the same boat. You staying at the Center?"

He shook his head. "With a friend."

"Well, hey," she said, "good for you. I don't know anyone I can stay with."

"Go back to the Center. That's what it's there for."

She coughed. "It's too much sunshine and brightness. Life sucks, and I'm okay with that, but it's bad enough without people pretending it's all gonna work out okay. I'll probably end up there for a little while, but as soon as I can find somewhere else to go, I'm gone."

"The Center's not so bad," Kory said.

She nodded at him. "What'd you do to get kicked out?"

"Blew up at my mom after we left here." He looked at the window, at the bright day outside, away from Malaya. It was hard, realizing he'd told personal details of her life to someone she didn't even know, but he owed her that explanation. She listened calmly as he gave it, and then nodded.

"She's probably a closet dyke," she said.

"What?"

"It's the closet cases that are really homophobic like that," Malaya said. "I read about it. They've got all this self-hatred going on and they take it out on other people. Kinda sucks for you, though."

"I don't really think...she's just really into religion, is all."

Malaya nodded sagely. "A lot of 'em do turn to religion. It helps 'em overcome their horrible urges."

Kory stood up. "I gotta get going. Glad you're feeling better. Uh, see you next Saturday."

"Sure." She waved a hand and gave him the ghost of a smile.

As if he needed one more thing to think about. His mom? He brooded over it all the way back to the Rodens' house, until Samaki asked him what was wrong. He said he was just thinking about Malaya, and they talked about the fruit bat and her family trouble, and he put the conversation about his mother out of his mind.

Mrs. Roden fussed over him without ever directly mentioning his situation, until Kory came in to help her do the dishes while Samaki was still talking to his father. The slender vixen put an arm around his shoulder then, her ears cupped toward him. "Kory," she said, "you know that whatever happens, you're always welcome here."

"Thanks, Mrs. Roden," he said. "I'm okay where I am right now."

"I know." Her voice cracked a little. "I just don't want you to think you have nowhere to go. We're an independent family, you know. Everyone makes their own way. So even if we don't offer help out loud, it's always here for you. You've been really good for Sammy, and we'd like to—we do consider you part of our family."

The last bit came out rather defiantly. Kory stood awkwardly, looking at her, and because he knew he was expected to, he said, "Thanks. That means a lot."

He didn't tell Samaki about it, but the brief exchange left an uneasy feeling in his stomach for the remainder of the night. He couldn't say why Mrs. Roden's kindness seemed unnerving. Perhaps it had gone too far, or perhaps he couldn't stop thinking about his own mother and the contrast between her and Mrs. Roden. He looked around at the house and tried to imagine himself living there, but it would never feel like home, he thought, and he still felt like an outsider in this family of foxes.

They lounged on Samaki's loft while Ajani and Kasim played some card game over on Kasim's desk. Samaki had propped up some pillows against the wall and was leaning on them, his tail draped over the otter's hip as Kory lay on his side, propped up on an elbow. He rested one paw on the fox's foot, rubbing the fur gently while Samaki trailed his fingers up and down Kory's calf. They had gotten out the applications to State, and Kory was filling out his in between conversations about school and science fiction books and anything but his living situation.

They finished the form in forty-five minutes. "This kinda sucks," Kory said. "I mean, not that I want to write those essays for Whitford and Gulliston, but at least it felt like they weren't going to let anyone in who can spell his name."

"It's a place to get an education," Samaki said. "It is what we make it. There's resources there we can use."

"At least I can afford the tuition," Kory said. For in-state students, the amount was ridiculously low compared to the other schools he'd looked at, something he could pay with his savings the first year, and a part-time job the rest of the time. Looking at the numbers made him realize for the first time how poor Samaki's family must be, if they couldn't spare the amount of money he had just in his savings.

That thought led him to wondering how much of his savings would be used up paying for food and clothes now that he was on his own. He had many years of birthday checks and a small inheritance from his grandfather, but he wasn't sure it was enough to last a year. He shook that thought aside and returned to the applications.

"You know," he said, "Mr. Pena's an ass, but he did say that there were lots of scholarships available out there. Some for ethnic minorities, but some just for talent. We should look around for some. Not for Whitford, or anything like that, but at least for something..." Other than State, he started to say, and then stopped himself. "...different."

Samaki chuckled. "Okay, I'm game. I think the computer's free. Want to go look now?"

An hour and a half later, they had a list of six nearby universities with likely scholarships, and a pile of applications. "Great," Kory moaned, "more paperwork."

"A few hours now could save us hundreds of dollars." Samaki pointed dramatically to the Esther J. Dobson Grant For Aquatic Writers, which awarded $250 per year to students at tiny Haverlawn College in the south of the state.

"Haverlawn's cool," Kory said. "They have a self-grading policy."

"They're cool, but they're also ten grand a year. Two-fifty isn't going to make much of a dent in that."

Kory rummaged through the printouts. "That's why you also go for the, um, Tilford Times Journalism Award. That's a thousand."

"Still not beating a free ride to State."

Kory shrugged. "This Drew Fortunas one for foxes looks good. Full tuition to Forester, and all you have to do is mentoring your junior and senior years."

"Thought you didn't want to go to Forester." Samaki held the paper as he said that, scanning it.

"You said it was getting more progressive."

"I said it might." He flipped to the second page. "'Submit essays on previous mentoring experience.' Hey, I could actually do this one." His ears perked as he looked down at Kory. "Is there a way you could afford Forester?"

"Maybe." Kory called up their financial aid package again. "They have a good work-study program, and if I'm on my own, I qualify for more loans."

The fox put the paper down and nuzzled Kory's small ears. "Okay. We'll have fun with those next weekend. Let's do something else fun now. Any good arguments going on anywhere?"

They read newsgroups and journals until midnight, then kissed and went to their separate beds. Kory lay alone in the darkness of the basement, wondering what it would be like to live here. It wouldn't be that much different from living in Sal's spare room, would it? Samaki's parents hadn't known him as long, but seemed more genuinely interested in his predicament and had said they regarded him as family. But he remembered, too, the small amounts of tuition for the state college, and he couldn't bring himself to take their food.

And it was really more convenient for school. Vacations and weekends he could come over here, but it would just be better off for everyone if he stayed at Sal's rather than here.

But when they got to school...he turned over uneasily. He'd want to be near the fox, of course, but could they keep their relationship secret from everyone in their dorm? Would Samaki even want to? Kory stared into the blackness, deeper than the fox's fur. Samaki wouldn't, of course. He wanted Kory to go to his prom, which Kory had not yet committed either way on. One day it seemed like a fine idea; after all, who down at Hilltown P.S. knew him there? If Samaki wanted them to know, they were his friends and it was his lookout. The next day it seemed insane to Kory. Gay couples at the prom were still news, they were strange and unusual and drew attention, often unpleasant. Why couldn't they just be boyfriends and not tell anyone about it?

The questions had no answers, but at least they could be put off by the merciful darkness of sleep.

Sal picked him up Sunday morning, greeting Samaki cheerfully when the fox walked out with Kory to meet him. They chatted only briefly, because Kory and Sal had to get to church, but Sal and Samaki shook paws firmly as they parted. "See you next weekend," Samaki said, waving as they pulled away.

"Nice guy," Sal said, watching in his rear view mirror, and grinned at Kory. "I guess I can see where you'd think he was sexy. Nice butt, if you're into that."

"Cut it out." Kory forced a grin, but felt himself flushing at the tips of his ears.

Church was a surreal experience. He was so used to Father Joe that going to a different church with Sal was like changing religions. The priest in Sal's church, an old lion, reminded him of the old Father Green as he wheezed through a sermon decrying the evil inherent in all people, whereas Father Joe's sermons had always focused on the love of God and the positives in life. Kory listened to the rheumy feline voice, whose words did nothing to help his general feeling of unease. When he tried to talk to Sal about the sermon afterwards, Sal's only comment was, "You stayed awake through the whole thing?"

For the rest of the day, he helped Sal with chores and then talked to Nick on the phone. His brother had calmed down since the night he'd left, but still held out hope that Kory could come home. When Kory asked whether their mother had cooled down, though, Nick was silent, and then changed the subject. They arranged to go out for pizza the following Wednesday night, and Kory hung up feeling homesick and angry and frustrated, all in one uncomfortable emotional lump that sat just above his chest.

Even though it wasn't their scheduled night, he called Samaki, needing something reassuring to counteract the rest of his day. The fox answered with some apprehension in his voice, which vanished as soon as Kory explained that he just wanted to talk about his day. He told Samaki about church, about his call with Nick, and about his general feeling of being adrift.

"You could always come here," Samaki said.

"It'd take me an hour to get to school," Kory said. It sounded stupid as soon as he said it, but fortunately Samaki didn't press.

"When do you learn to drive?"

"I don't even know how that's going to work now. I'll take the class at school, and Sal can take me over to get my permit, I guess." He pressed his fingers to his muzzle, rubbing his whiskers. "I don't wanna think about it."

"It's not that hard," Samaki said. "I can come pick you up this weekend. My mom has off for some holiday."

"Cool." Kory smiled at the warmth that thought brought. "I miss you."

"Miss you too," Samaki said, and they hung up soon after, with Kory's jumbled feelings only slightly better. He never thought he'd be thankful to go to school, but he was actually looking forward to class on Monday.

Wednesday night pizza with Nick became a regular thing, in the shopping center where Sal had picked him up on that night he'd left home. As they munched their anchovy and oyster with extra cheese, they talked about school and TV shows, and only rarely about their mother. Nick did bring up the subject a month after Kory'd moved out, when one slice of congealing pizza remained in the box.

"I guess you're used to living with Sal now," he said.

"I don't really see him a lot," Kory said. "Meals, and going to and from school. He still likes to go out at night, and I'm trying to get all these college applications done."

"How are they going?" Nick asked.

"Ugh. I'm glad I have Samaki to talk to. So much paperwork and they all want these stupid essays."

Nick grinned. "So use the same essay for all of them."

"I can, for some of them. The hard ones, anyway. And I have that college prep class, which is giving me some good ideas."

"Whitford has a swim team. If you go there, I could try to get a scholarship."

"I'm gonna need one to be able to afford to go," Kory said.

Nick acknowledged that with silence, looking away before asking, "Where else are you looking?"

Kory rattled off the schools, and saw Nick take mental note. "Wherever I end up," he said, "it'd be great to have you there in a few years. Just make sure you're well-rounded." He made sarcastic air quotes for that last phrase. In Physics, he learned that fluid materials like liquid and gas would naturally flow to a spherical shape, and whenever Mr. Pena said "well-rounded," he imagined some kind of spherical otter who was the perfect college candidate, all his skills the same perfect distance from his perfectly centered core.

"We should order another pizza, then." Nick patted his stomach.

Kory laughed. "I'm glad we get to have pizza together."

"I miss you at dinner," Nick said.

"I miss you all the time," Kory said. "Dinners and breakfast, and whenever I sit down to watch "Dr. Otter," and Rob Travis says something funny and I want to turn and laugh with you about it. I miss being able to swim over to your room. Sal's pool is big and complicated and I slid downstairs by accident three times the first week. I even miss..." He paused. "You know I make myself eat all my vegetables now?"

Nick shook his head. "I get even more vegetables now. Plus I get lectures if I don't eat 'em."

"Stuff like, 'careful you don't turn out like your brother'?"

"Nah. Just, 'I try so hard to put good food on your plate.' That kinda stuff." He eyed the last slice. "You miss that, too?"

"I miss her," Kory said. "Just not when I think about Samaki. You can have that slice if you want."

Nick didn't need any further encouragement. "How's he?" he mumbled around a mouthful. "Surprised you didn't move over there already."

"Yeah," Kory said, remembering the silence when he'd first refused that offer. "Sal's place just works better for school, and I don't feel bad eating their dinners. They can afford it."

Nick looked up. "You going to get a job?"

"Huh?"

"To pay for your dinners."

Kory poked at a piece of anchovy in a pool of congealing cheese. "Maybe."

"Jerry Tamrin's older brother is a waiter at DeMarco's and he gets his dinners for free."

"I don't have any experience being a waiter."

"Well, I mean, then you wouldn't have to eat the dinners at Samaki's. You could just stay there." Nick chomped down the last couple bits of crust.

"Maybe," Kory said. "It's still a pain to get to school."

Nick licked his fingers and shrugged. After a moment, he said, "You guys basically lived together all summer. I felt like I had another brother."

"That was different."

"How?"

A skunk couple Kory didn't recognize from his high school sat down at the next table with their pizza. Kory watched them share smiles and pizza, watched the boy's paw creep over to rest on the girl's. He lowered his voice. "I dunno. It just was."

Nick glanced over his shoulder at the couple, then back at his brother. He matched Kory's near-whisper. "It's not a big deal," he said. "You know that, right?"

"I know," Kory said automatically. Then he looked at his brother's earnest expression. "What if it is a big deal for me?"

Nick grinned. "Then you need to get over it. What would you have done if Jenny said 'I want to go out with you but we can't tell anyone'?"

"It's different," Kory said. "Anyway, you know."

"Yeah, but I know a lot of things." Nick grinned.

Kory brushed his claws through the fur on his arm. "And Sal knows."

"What about Aunt Tilly?"

He snorted, so loudly that the skunks looked over at him. He lowered his voice again. "I'm sure Mom's told her."

"What about—"

"What's your point?" Kory leaned back and folded his arms.

Nick shrugged. "You left home for him."

"That's Mom's deal."

"So you had nothing to do with it." Nick rested his elbows on the table. "You were furious when you called me about what she said about him. Remember?"

"Yeah." Kory looked his brother in the eyes. There wasn't anyone else he could ask this question of. "So...Nick, why do I feel so weird about going to live at his house?"

"I dunno," Nick said. "But you should maybe figure that out, huh? Hey, ask Father Joe. He asked me to invite you to come see him on Saturday. He said something about your issues. I think he knows, too. Maybe Mom told him."

"This Saturday?" Kory asked. "Did Mom ask him to?"

Nick shrugged. "Maybe. He's been trying to corner me for a few weeks now."

They walked out together to where Kory would have to catch the bus. "Okay," Kory said finally. "I'll go see him."

Afternoon light set the trees in the churchyard blazing a bright, fiery red. Kory's paws crunched through piles of yellow and reddish leaves on his way to the small office in the back. When he knocked, Father Joe came around the corner of the building, dressed casually in an oxford shirt and jeans. "Hello, Kory," he said, and extended a hand. "Thanks for coming to see me."

"I guess my mother asked you to talk to me," Kory said, grasping the large white hand in his brown paw.

Father Joe shook his head. "You think I wouldn't notice when you stopped coming to church? I asked your mother, but she...well, she didn't tell me how to get in touch with you."

"Oh." He knew he shouldn't feel disappointed, but he had been hoping, without realizing it, that his mother had asked the priest to talk to him. He kicked some leaves and shrugged. "So you heard the story?"

"Not from you."

"Oh," he said again. Father Joe put a hand on his shoulder, gently.

"Let's walk. I like to be outside this time of year, to enjoy the weather before it gets cold."

They walked around the churchyard, Kory telling his story over the rustling of the leaves. He referred to Samaki only as a 'friend,' but told all of Malaya's story and his mother's reaction, his mounting anger, her sharp words and his reaction. In Father Joe's silence, he felt a judgment, and reliving the story after so long, he felt the old anger surface again. With it now, at the priest's side, he also felt unsure of himself. "I guess I sort of overreacted," he said, and when Father Joe didn't respond, added, "Are you going to assign me penance?"

The Dall sheep shook his head. "This is not the confessional, Kory. I'm disappointed that you felt you had to resort to harsh language, and that you failed to honor your mother, but I won't assign you any penance. I suspect you're living your penance."

"But she was wrong too, wasn't she?"

Father Joe sighed. "I presume you would not want me to render my judgment of you to your mother, would you? Then allow me to reserve my judgment of her for a time when she comes to seek it."

"Sorry." Kory folded his ears down.

The priest returned his hand to Kory's shoulder. "I am sorry for you, Kory," he said. "I wish I could say that the road ahead will get easier."

He looked up and saw resolve in the wide brown eyes. "I will give you penance, of a sort, after all," he said. Kory nodded. "But no Hail Marys, no Our Fathers. Your penance is to love your mother."

"The prayers would be easier," Kory said, joking to overcome his surprise.

"Of course they would. But this should not be hard. I am not asking you to forgive her, or even talk to her. I'm asking you to love her. Understand her actions. Don't carry hate in your heart. That is not for her sake; it's for yours. Okay?"

Whenever he thought about his mother, his chest tightened and he felt his paws want to clench. But he nodded and said, truthfully, "I'll try."

"You don't try to do penance," Father Joe said with half-playful sternness. "You do it. You're still going to church, right?"

Kory nodded. "St. Lutris."

"Oh, Father Brewer. I do hope you'll say my sermons are better than his."

"I miss your sermons." Kory grinned back up at the sheep.

Father Joe nodded. "I know it's uncomfortable with your mother, but I'd be glad to see you here once in a while."

"I'll try." He grinned. "I mean, I will."

He'd thought that would be the end of it, until Father Joe made no move to dismiss him, instead looking up at the trees. "How are things with your friend?"

"Huh? Oh...fine."

"Does he have your best interests at heart?"

Kory tilted his head. "I think so."

"What I mean is, he's allowing you to make your own choices, and not pressuring you into something you don't feel comfortable with?"

"Oh." He shoved his paws into his pockets. "Yeah. I mean, yes, we talk about stuff all the time. He didn't tell me to yell at my mom."

"No, that sounded like it came from your heart. I just want to be sure that the decisions you're making are your decisions. It is often easy to become tempted into alluring unknowns when we are fleeing a too-familiar known."

"Better the unknown than the known, sometimes. Like for Malaya," Kory said.

The tall sheep bent his head gracefully. "I hope the worst is over for her as well. She's lucky to have friends to help her."

"It's hard to get her to take help, though." Kory sighed. "She's so stubborn and independent."

"So many young men and women are." Father Joe smiled. "That is our delight and our frustration with the young. Did you tell her what I told you about God, this spring?"

"Once," Kory said. "She said it sounded like your God was nicer than hers."

Father Joe laughed. "She sounds like quite a personality."

"She is," Kory said. "I don't know what she's going to do now, though. She won't be happy at the Center, and she can't go back to her father. She has grandparents in the south, but she's already threatened to run away again if she's sent there."

"Often," the priest said after a moment, "God selects the challenges he sends us for a reason. They are not to punish us, nor to test us, but to make us stronger. But it is up to us to meet the challenge, to face it and respond to it, not to flee it."

The word 'flee' reminded him of the door of his house—his mother's house—slamming behind him. He shifted from one foot to the other, rustling the leaves. "She's had a lot of things to deal with," he said.

"So have you." They had reached the churchyard fence. Father Joe stopped to lean on it, looking out over the houses below. "I gather you're living with a school friend now, not your other friend?"

"No," Kory hesitated. "He wants me to move in. They have room in the basement and they say I'd be welcome."

"But you haven't made that decision yet."

Kory shook his head. "They're not that well off. I don't want to take their food unless I can pay them for it."

Father Joe turned his head towards Kory. "That's remarkably considerate. I don't know many young people in love who would have that much restraint."

Kory fidgeted, looking at the reddish leaves over the green grass. "It's also just not convenient. For school and stuff." After the conversation with Nick, his arguments sounded hollow, but the more direct question lodged like a lump in his throat. He swallowed.

A bird sang in the tree above them. Father Joe and Kory both craned their necks to look at it. When it was silent again, Father Joe said, "I think you might want to spend a little time thinking about yourself. It's difficult to let yourself love another if you don't feel you yourself are worthy of love. It's always good to start with God at times like that. He always loves you, Kory."

"I wrote an essay about that." Kory had revised and revised it, only stopping because he was tired of reading it.

"Really? I would like to see it."

"I'll bring it over."

The sheep bobbed his head. "Thank you. How are the college applications going?"

Kory snorted. "I don't know. I think I need to eat more."

"Eat more?"

He held his arms out at his side, as if curved around a wide belly. "I need to be more well-rounded."

Again, Father Joe laughed, and Kory shared his smile. "I think you're going to be a fine student," the priest said. "You are already a fine young man."

Kory's ears flicked at the unexpected compliment. "Thanks."

Father Joe pointed a finger at him. "I believe that. And you should, too."

He didn't. But as he walked home, he remembered the earnest openness in Father Joe's warm, brown eyes, and he resolved to try.

"I liked your essay," Perry told him after the college prep class.

Kory nodded. "Yours was better." He'd finally given in to the wolf's pestering the previous week, and had been depressed to read the clever essay Perry had written on how Star Trek related to the current political climate. It showed a breadth of experience—a well-roundedness, Kory would have said if he didn't hate the phrase so much by now—that the otter desperately hoped for.

"You think so?" Perry's tail wagged.

"Sure," Kory said. "I mean, mine was all just this introspective garbage."

"No, I thought yours was good. I mean, you got all that philosophy stuff in it, and you included some life experiences." Perry bobbed his head. "And then you added that bit from Dostoevsky that we did for extra credit in English. I think it really showed your well-roundedness. I just, if I had one suggestion?"

Kory stopped himself from rolling his eyes. "Uh-huh?"

"Why didn't you include some stuff about the homeless kids you work with? I mean, they've got great stories, at least the ones at my shelter do, and I've only been there a month."

"Oh." Kory pretended to think about that. "I didn't even consider it. Thanks."

The wolf's tail wagged. "If you add those in, I think it's a real winner."

"Thanks," Kory said.

Perry tugged at his polo shirt. "So, uh, what would you change in mine?"

Kory pushed open the school doors, stepping into the late afternoon sun. "I don't know," he said. "It all looked good to me."

"There has to be something," Perry persisted.

Kory shook his head. "Really, it was good. I'd just go with it." He walked past the bus he'd used to take home, feeling only a little strange about it now. Sal had pulled up in the student parking lot across from the buses and waved to him. "I gotta run, Perry. See you in English."

"Yeah, okay." The wolf raised a paw. Kory didn't look back as he crossed to Sal's car and got in.

"Who's the feeb?" Sal said.

"I told you about him," Kory said. "Perry. He's in the college prep class with me."

"Figures." Sal snorted and pulled the car out of the lot.

Kory tossed his bag in the back seat. "He's not bad. Just a little too, I dunno, eager to be my friend."

Sal grinned. "Maybe he's hot for you. Is your gaydar going off?"

"Shut up!"

"What? I thought all you guys had that."

Kory folded his arms. "Look, I'm not...don't do that."

Sal made the turn onto the main road toward his house and glanced sideways at Kory. "What, don't call you gay because you're dating a guy?"

"It's more complicated than that."

Sal laughed. "Really? Cause I learned if you're straight, you date girls. If you're gay, you date guys. This isn't like experimenting in summer camp, you know. You're, like, serious about him."

Kory stared out the window and didn't respond. After a moment, Sal continued. "Spike, I told you there's nothing wrong with it. I'm cool, totally."

"You experimented in summer camp?"

"Only with girls." Sal leaned back in the seat, steering with one paw, his tail swishing lazily through the seat behind him.

"That's not experimenting. Experimenting is like when your mom makes kidney paste."

"I can't believe it tasted like vomit, it really did."

And the conversation moved on from there, even if Kory couldn't leave it quite so easily.

He studied the essay again that evening. Perry was right. It needed more of his personal experience with the kids from the Rainbow Center. It needed more of himself in it.

"So put in Malaya's story and the stuff with your mom," Samaki said on the phone that night. He sounded tired. "I don't think that's a big deal."

Kory stared up at the ceiling. "I think I can do that. Did I tell you Father Joe wants to see it when I'm done?"

"That's nice. You going to let him see it before you send it off?"

"I think so. I'll try to finish it before Thanksgiving."

"I'm looking forward to that." Samaki perked up as he mentioned Thanksgiving. "Mom said you're not allowed to say no."

Kory grinned. "I've already said yes. Hey, would it be okay if Nick came over too, for a bit? He'll have to be home for dinner, but..."

"Course." Samaki replied immediately. "Just let Mom know when."

Kory settled back in his bed. "Ready for your history final? Want to go over anything?"

"I'm good. How about your math test?"

"I could run through some of it if you have time." He settled back in his bed and talked math for the next fifteen minutes.

"I need to get going," Samaki said. "Going to finish up the form for that Drew Fortunas scholarship."

"Okay. I'll think of you tonight when I brush."

"Me too. Be sure and brush very thoroughly."

Kory grinned, resting a paw on his sheath. "You too."

November rolled into Hilltown with surprising force, a howling winter storm that Kory and Sal sat watching, guessing back and forth how many inches of snow would drop. The light flurries promised more to come, but when they got up in the morning, there was no accumulation and the buses ran as normal. Outside school, Kory found Nick and asked him when he could come by to get his winter clothes. "I wanted to use the snow day, but..." He gestured out at the barren, snowless lawn.

"Tonight's good," Nick said. "I'm not going out 'til later and Mom's going out to dinner with the Jeffersons."

"She's letting you get dinner on your own?"

"No, she's making dinner before she goes." Nick shrugged. "She lets me come to pizza with you, at least."

"I'll come by after dinner, then." Kory couldn't help but marvel at how well he and Nick had adapted, together, to their new situation.

Nick's gaze slipped up over Kory's shoulder. "Okay. See ya tonight, then. I'll call when she leaves." He moved forward to embrace Kory, and then walked off with a quick, "Seeya."

Kory caught the smell of wolf and freshly laundered shirt before he turned. "Hey, Perry," he said.

Perry's ears flicked up. His tail started wagging as he fell into step beside Kory. "That's your brother?"

"Yeah, Nick."

"So, uh, he still lives at home?"

Kory stared fixedly ahead. "Yep."

Perry swallowed a couple times. "You know, uh, you never said what happened. I mean, I just thought you were getting a friend to pick you up. When Jessica said you weren't living at home anymore, I said, I said that wasn't true. I thought you'd tell me if something happened."

"It was no big deal," Kory said. "I'm just staying with Sal for a while."

"But why?"

Perry even followed him to the door of his homeroom. Inside he could see Sal looking past him at the wolf, and rolling his eyes. "My mom just has to get some things in her life together," Kory said, "and it's better for me not to be around, and I'd really rather not talk about it. Okay?"

Perry's ears folded down, and he ducked his head. "Sure, I understand. Thanks for telling me. And if y'ever want to talk, y'know."

"Thanks," Kory said curtly, and raised a paw to wave, turning to go to homeroom.

"Looks like he has a crush on you," Sal said, first thing when Kory sat down.

"Bite me," Kory said, pulling out his books to check on his homework.

"Can't believe the stupid weather." Sal doodled the logo of Limp Foxxkit on his math book cover. Kory wouldn't have known the band a month ago; now he was quite familiar with the pounding chords he heard issuing from behind Sal's door. "Not supposed to be this cold without snowing."

"This happens every winter," Kory said. "Hey, speaking of, can you give me a ride over to my mom's place tonight? I need to grab my winter stuff."

"Sure. Right after school?"

"Nah, she's going out to dinner, so she'll be home early. Nick said he'd call when she's gone."

"Oh." Sal dug his ballpoint pen into the paper. "I was gonna head over to Life of the Party."

That was the bar over by Forester, where Sal liked to go to pick up college women. Kory had found that his ideas of his friend's success at that had been wildly overblown. Sal had gone to that bar six times since Kory'd been living across the hall from him, and had come home alone each time. He'd claimed once to have gotten a hand job from a cute ringtail out behind the bar, but the sketchy details and Sal's overconfident tone had failed to convince Kory that he was telling the truth. "Well, you can go after, can't you?"

"Why don't you come along?" Sal said. "You can be my wingman."

"Wingman?"

"You know, tell girls how cool I am."

"You don't need a wingman," said Geoff Hill behind them. "You need a complete makeover. Maybe you could get on Queer Eye."

Kory bristled at that, and Sal saw it. "Just ignore him," he said. "Seriously, come with me tonight. You never come out. It'd be good for you."

After one more glare at Geoff, Kory nodded. "Yeah, okay."

The twinges of homesickness when he visited his mother's house were fewer now. Going into his closet, he felt like an archaeologist exploring old ruins. *A-ha, a valuable trove of woolen protective clothing. This civilization was obviously quite familiar with the change of seasons.* He didn't voice that aloud; Samaki would have appreciated it, but Nick and Sal wouldn't have understood. He threw the winter gear into a bag and hugged Nick, then drove off with Sal.

"We going to stop for dinner somewhere?" he asked as they pulled away.

"The bar has appetizers," Sal said, navigating smoothly. "We'll just eat there."

Appetizers, Kory found, consisted of bowls of pretzels on the counter and half-congealed fried cheese sticks with ketchup. Squinting at the menu, he thought he saw fish strips, but the music was so loud that he ended up having to point to the menu to order from the bartender, and what the bartender handed him was a pile of something greyish with curls of sickly steam rising from it. It smelled of vegetables, with maybe potatoes, and there was cheese involved, of course. Everything at the bar was either fried, or covered in cheese, or both.

After trying to decipher what on the menu their dish could possibly be, and seeing Sal survive a mouthful, Kory decided that whatever it was would be better warm than cold, and he was hungry, having let Sal eat most of the cheese sticks. For an otter, Sal certainly didn't eat a lot of fish, but then, Nick didn't seem to want much fish when he wasn't at home either.

Kory took a mouthful and found that it tasted mostly like greasy cheese. He got half the plate down before disgust overwhelmed hunger, even with frequent drinks from the beer Sal had bought him.

Sal, on his second beer already, had pointed out a female otter halfway across the bar and was now doing his best to appear completely disinterested in her. "Tell me when she looks at me," he muttered to Kory.

At least that gave Kory something to concentrate on, though with all the natural musks and artificial scents in the bar, his eyes were starting to water already. The ceiling, though at least attractively dotted with wooden beams, was too low to allow for much ventilation. Even through his watering eyes, he had to admit that the girls here were way better looking than any of the ones in his high school. The one Sal was interested in had light streaks in her fur and two silver earrings in her right ear that glinted in the dim bar light. She and her friend, a grey squirrel, both wore low-cut dresses with shoulder straps that disappeared into their fur. Her light dress (yellow? cream? mint?) looked better on her than the squirrel's dark one did, or else she just had a better body, tight and slinky. She looked like a dancer, shifting her feet back and forth as she talked to her friend at the bar.

Around the room, the mix of species was almost as even as the boy-girl ratio. He and Sal weren't the only otter pair; two tall otters in Forester University hoodies chatted up a pair of female raccoons over by the dance floor, and a pair of female otters giggled together under a big neon sign for Huffenbrau Beer. Foxes, wolves, hares, weasels, and rats mingled, shared drinks and laughs, danced under the garish red and blue lights, and leaned against the bar. The bartender was the only bear in the room, a large brown bear who shambled from one side of the bar to the other and never seemed to ask anyone for their ID. None of the foxes were black, none as handsome as his fox. He wished Samaki were there, because he'd appreciate the silliness of this place.

"Hey!" Sal elbowed him in the ribs, hissing. "Is she looking?"

Kory snapped his attention back to the otter. Oddly enough, she was looking at them, at Sal in particular, while her friend, who had been looking at Kory, lowered her eyes to the bar as soon as he looked in their direction. "Yeah, she is."

Sal nodded and lifted his head, tipping the bottle of beer casually to his muzzle. He licked some of the foam away, lowered it, and started tapping his paw on the bar. "Still looking?"

"Yeah." The squirrel was still studiously ignoring him. Kory looked at his friend. "What are you doing?"

"Shh. Okay, get ready now."

"For what?"

Sal's tail tapped against Kory's. "When I finish talking, laugh like I told you something funny. Go on, now."

"Huh?" Sal was grinning at him in an odd, forced way, and Kory tried to find that funny enough to laugh at. He succeeded at least in opening his mouth and forcing out a "ha ha" kind of sound, and apparently that was enough.

"Cool. Now look at her and smile and nod."

Kory blinked. "I thought you were interested in her."

"I am. I mean, smile and nod like I just told you that and you're saying, 'yeah, she's hot'."

"Oh." Kory didn't quite know how to look at a woman like she was hot, but he gave her a smile and an approving nod. She met his eyes and smiled, and then turned to talk to her friend.

"What's she doing?"

"They're giggling. Can't you hear that squeaking? That's her friend. She's a squirrel."

Sal snorted, finishing his beer and signaling for another. "I thought that was someone's barstool. You sure it's her?"

The squirrel squeaked again, piercing the background chatter like a train whistle. "Positive."

"Okay, just keep an eye on them and if she looks over here again, let me know." The bear slid a mug over to him, and Sal took a drink. "This is way easier with two people. You gotta come again."

"We'll see." Kory was still on his first beer, reluctant to drink any more for fear of how it might mix with the lump of grease in his stomach. "Oh, there. She just looked over at you again."

Sal gulped down half his beer, gathered himself, then finished it. He plunked the mug down on the counter and slid off the barstool. "Let's go."

As they walked over, he muttered to Kory, "Talk to her friend."

"It's okay," Kory said. "I'll be fine on my own."

"Not for you," Sal said. "It's so she doesn't get bored and bug her friend to leave. Tell her she's pretty, pretend you're interested."

"Okay." Kory followed his friend, bewildered by the complexities of this game. At the same time, he could see why Sal enjoyed it so much. When they'd played the online RPGs, Sal had always been the one leading the hunt, figuring out the rules and going after the monsters. This was just a different kind of game, and although he found nearly every element of it distasteful, the gritty reality clearly appealed to Sal. As did, of course, the more tangible prize.

"Hi," Sal said to the female otter. "This is kinda weird for me, I usually don't just walk up to pretty girls, but...my name's Sal."

"I'm Divinity," she said.

The squirrel was looking at Kory. He shook off his amusement at the name and edged around Divinity to get closer to her. "I'm Kory," he said.

"Hazel," the squirrel said. Her scent was a strange mix of liquor, artificial musk, and her own scent below it. Kory could also smell her friend, who'd chosen a much more flattering artificial musk that enhanced her natural scent rather than trying to conceal it. "Do you go to Forester?"

"No," Kory said. He remembered just in time that he wasn't supposed to say that they were in high school. He opened his mouth, but Sal came to his rescue.

"We're at Lake City College," he said. "Home for the weekend."

"Oh, cool," Divinity chirped. "I love Lake City. I go to LakeFront Mall all the time."

"I've never been to Lake City," Hazel said, and just like that, the conversations were separate again.

"It's pretty nice." Kory, who had only been to Lake City once, was anxious to get off the topic. "So you grew up around here?"

She had actually grown up in a small town fifty miles north, whose name Kory forgot the moment after she told him. Hilltown was a sprawling metropolis to her. They talked about the quaint Badger Square, because Kory knew it from his trips to the Rainbow Center, and Hazel went on about the cute little shops that she liked. She'd never been down Holly Street to the Center, of course, but Kory had been to enough shops on the Square to keep the conversation going.

At a break, he looked over for Sal and Divinity, but they'd gone. Hazel saw his look. "They're dancing," she said. "See?"

Beneath the flashing blue and red, two otters gyrated amidst the crowd. Kory had to stare to recognize his friend's compact form and characteristic dance. When he turned back to Hazel, he saw red and blue gleams reflected in her dark eyes and felt the creeping dread that she was waiting for him to ask her to dance. "Uh," he said, "you want another drink?"

She looked down shyly. "Sure."

"I hurt my foot," Kory said, feeling the need to explain himself.

"Oh! Sure. I'll have another Cosmo."

He put it on Sal's tab, and ordered a Coke for himself. Hazel asked how he hurt his foot, and he'd made up a story about twisting his ankle before he realized she was fishing to find out whether he played sports. As the conversation dragged on, he marveled at how anyone could ever hook up in this kind of place, how Sal could know so many of the rules. It certainly looked like Sal and Divinity were getting along well; they were bumping together now, locking arms and tails with their paws all over each other. He missed Samaki.

Samaki! He was late for the call, but on Friday night it shouldn't matter. Claiming he had to use the bathroom, he made his way to the back of the bar and flipped open his cell phone.

"Sorry I'm late," he said when Samaki got on the line.

"Sounds noisy. Where are you?"

"Oh, Sal dragged me out to this bar. We'll be here for a while. I guess until Sal hooks up or something."

Samaki sounded worried. "Then what? You ride with him in the back seat to her place?"

"I don't know. I never thought of that."

"Call me if you need a ride, okay?"

Kory grinned. "Well, maybe her friend will give me a ride."

"What friend?"

"Sal's conquest came with a squirrel. Her name's Hazel."

"Hazel the squirrel. Is she cute? Should I be jealous?"

Kory leaned back into the corner between the phone cubicle and the wall. "Absolutely. We're dancing and kissing and everything."

"Slip her some tongue for me." Samaki chuckled.

"I miss you," Kory said.

"Miss you too. I'll see you tomorrow though."

"Bright and early. Starbucks?"

"Wouldn't miss it. I'll let you get back to your dream date now."

It was amazing how talking to Samaki was so effortless, not like the strenuous uphill efforts of keeping Hazel engaged. Just hearing the fox's voice and knowing he'd see him again soon relaxed him and made him smile.

Hazel was waiting for him, looking restless, and her Cosmo was empty. "Get you another?" he said, indicating the empty glass.

"Oh, no, I'd better not. Maybe just a Diet Coke."

"Good idea. I'll refill mine." He signaled to the bartender.

"Oh, well, maybe one more," she said, as he was ordering the drinks.

They carried their glasses over to a corner of the bar where the music was slightly less loud. Kory positioned himself so he could still see the dance floor, while Hazel groomed her cheek fur with quick, jerky motions. Kory had decided that he was going to ask her what college life was like, so he could at least get something worthwhile out of this evening for as long as Sal needed him to pretend to like her.

An hour later, the pretense was getting harder to maintain. Hazel's college experience, to hear her tell it, consisted mostly of her wandering around the campus with her jaw open, gaping either at the size of the buildings or the size of the boys. By this time, it had become apparent even to her that Kory wasn't interested in her, but she was clearly too timid to tell him to go away, so she kept looking around the bar at any unattached male who came within five feet of their little corner. Kory, for his part, was searching his brain for things to talk to her about, and found himself mentioning the football team.

"Well," she said, "they kicked off two of our best players just because they got in a fight with some faggot. Sorry—homosexual." She dangled her wrist as she said it, and then covered her mouth and giggled. "Oh, I'm so bad when I'm drunk! I hope you're not one of those PC cops. Take me away, officer!"

"No," Kory said, "don't worry about it." He debated how much Sal would hurt him if he went and dragged his friend off the dance floor at that moment. He didn't really believe Hazel was drunk, but he didn't know how much she'd had before the two Cosmos. His fur had prickled with the way she'd said, 'homosexual,' a warm flush of shame creeping through him even though there was no way she could have known.

Another hour dragged by. Hazel switched to Diet Coke and took out her cell phone, checking messages and sending texts to friends. Kory lost sight of Sal on the dance floor and wondered if he'd gotten some action out behind the bar. He went to get a refill of his own Coke, stopping at the bathroom first, and when he came back, Hazel was gone.

Good riddance. He scanned the bar for her quickly before remembering that he didn't really care where she was. Sal might, if she'd taken her friend with her, but after a moment of panicked searching, he spotted the two of them on the dance floor, so Hazel had clearly taken care of herself. He settled back against the wall and sipped his Coke, thinking of all the homework he could be doing or all the things he could be saying to Samaki, and growing steadily more annoyed at Sal.

Well past midnight, his friend appeared in front of him, swaying slightly even though his tail was waving quickly back and forth to balance him. "There you a-are," he said.

"I've been here all night," Kory said. "You ready to go?"

Sal nodded. "Let's get the fuck out of here."

He wasn't slurring that much, but he stumbled on the way out and his tail smacked the door frame. Remembering an endless drone of safe driving commercials, Kory said, "Hey, maybe you shouldn't drive."

"What, you want to drive?"

Kory held up his paws. "I just think..."

"Look, I wanna get home and...dammit, it's cold out here." Sal got into the car and started the engine.

Kory opened the passenger side door, but didn't get in. "Let me call a taxi."

"S-sure, with whose money?"

"I'll pay for it." Sal just looked at him and revved the engine. "I'm serious!"

"A-all right. Look. There's a d-donut shop down the street. One block. We'll get some coffee."

The large "24 HOUR D NUTS" sign was more like two blocks away. "Let's walk."

"It's cold out! I don't wanna have to walk b-back for the car."

"I'm going to walk." Kory slammed his door and started walking.

Sal drove past him, staring straight ahead even when he was right alongside. When Kory got to the donut shop, fluffing up the fur on his paws to keep warm, he didn't see Sal inside. It took him a moment to locate the car, parked in the shadows around the side of the small building. Sal was already sitting in his car, the windows fogged. "Enjoy your walk?" he said when Kory got in. The car was warm and thick with the smell of coffee from the one cup in Sal's paw.

"You didn't want to sit inside?"

Sal shrugged. "Car's warm and I got my tunes in here." He'd put on one of his favorites, something loud and blaring with lyrics that Mariatu could have written.

"So it didn't work out with Divinity?"

"Damn cock tease," Sal said. "She danced with me all night and then just took off. Got me all worked up, too." He took a sip of the coffee and put it down in the cupholder.

"Hazel was so boring," Kory said. "And when she wasn't being boring, she was being offensive. I don't think college girls are all they're cracked up to be." He looked at the steamy window, missing Samaki's company. The phone call with the fox had been the highlight of his night.

"You kidding? They're mature, they're hot, they've got a nice rack on 'em...they know how to bump and grind and p-play the game. Ahhhh."

"It's sure a different game. I guess I never really learned..." The slow rasp of a zipper interrupted him. He turned to look at Sal. "What...?"

His friend was leaning into the angle of the driver's seat and the driver's door, his right arm across the back of the seat while his left sat in his lap, lazily stroking his unzipped erection. "That c-cock tease...fucker, I'm all worked up. Just got to take care of some business."

Kory's mouth hung open. The scene was so surreal: the steamed car windows, the glow of the "D NUT" sign through the windshield playing over the hard pink length under his best friend's paw. He'd seen Sal naked before, but never hard. The self-indulgent grin was familiar, the same expression he'd worn when he'd suggested cheating on a test in ninth grade, or when he talked about not working at his father's company. "You can whip it out too, if you want," Sal said. "Or, wait, you get to see your boyfriend tomorrow, right? Better save it." He continued to stroke himself. "Christ, that feels good."

Kory couldn't shake the dreamlike feeling. He reached for the door handle and even started to open it.

"Hey, don't go," Sal said. "S-sorry if I surprised you."

"Yeah," Kory said. "You want to wait 'til we get home?"

Up and down, stroking. He tried not to look, but it was impossible to avoid in the small confines of the car. "I was gonna," Sal said, "but you s-said I can't drive yet."

"Well, go in the bathroom in there, or something." Kory let the door handle go to gesture at the donut shop.

"It's warm in here," Sal said. "Whassa matter? I thought you liked to look at cock. Go ahead, look. You seen it before."

"That's not the point." Kory said.

"Ain't we friends?"

"Sal..."

"Ain't we?" Sal persisted. Kory couldn't keep the motion of his paw completely out of his vision. He wished Sal would finish already.

"Yeah, but..."

"And ain't I lettin' you s-stay at my house?"

"Yeah..."

Sal shrugged and leaned back again. "So just settle down. Free show." He grunted and worked himself a little harder.

Should he stay? Should he leave? Drunk, Sal might drive home without him if he left the car now. He stared straight ahead through the windshield and curled his tail under the seat. If Sal drove home without him, still drunk, he might get in an accident. *Is that your responsibility? He's probably driven drunk before.* Before doesn't matter, Kory thought. I'm here now. Just wait 'til it's over and then never talk about it again.

"Damn it," Sal said softly. Kory didn't respond. "Spike," Sal said. "Hey. You're good at this. Give me a paw."

Kory ignored him. Sal raised his voice. "Come on, I'm fuckin' serious here. I can't...my fingers aren't doing this right."

"What? You forgot how to jerk off?"

"Not forgot, just...c-can't make myself come. Come on, gay boy, I know you jerk off your fox enough times, right?"

Now Kory turned to him, ears flushed and folding down. "That's not..."

Sal grinned. "How m-many other boys you done? Like at c-camp, that time you were trying to get me to strip. Did you do that with all the boys?"

Kory froze. *He remembers that?* There was no reason he shouldn't, of course, but they'd never discussed it after, and Kory had come to regard it as his private memory. "Hey," he started weakly, "let's go home."

"C-come on." Before Kory could react, Sal grabbed his paw and brought it to his groin.

Hot flesh, not as hard as Kory would have thought, but getting harder. He jerked his paw back. "Jesus, Sal." The impact of using Jesus's name made barely a blip.

"You ruin my night and n-now you want to go home and s-sleep in my house and you won't even help me out?"

"Ruin your night?"

"You were s-supposed to keep her friend happy."

"I talked to her for three freakin' hours!"

Sal kept stroking himself mechanically as he talked. "Divinity took off, just like that, she must have seen that you weren't interested. Couldn't pretend to be interested in a girl, could you? Not even for me?"

Kory sorted through the pronouns and shook his head. "She was an idiot!" he said. "And her friend wasn't any better! If you couldn't get into her pants in three hours...let go of me!"

Sal had grabbed his paw and wrapped it around his erection again. "Come on," he said as Kory yanked his arm back. "You'll do it for him but not for me? How long we been friends? Just this once."

Samaki. Kory thought about the gentle fox and how he would handle this situation. He'd make a joke, laugh, put everyone at ease, and in a few minutes they'd all be driving home, this whole tableau just an embarrassing blot on their memories. "Sal," he said, trying to calm himself down, "you know, if you wanna be gay, there's a whole list of forms you have to fill out."

His friend's eyes narrowed. "*I'm* not gay," he said. "Just askin' for a favor from a friend. Least, I thought you were a friend."

So much for the joke. Maybe he should just close his eyes and do it. What harm would it do? Sal was probably drunk enough that he wouldn't remember too much later. Kory could get him off and they could go home and forget about it.

Except that Kory had a boyfriend.

He wasn't sure what was considered "cheating" in gay relationships, but jerking off someone else was probably on the list. What would he tell Samaki?

"I am your friend," he said. "Not your experiment. I'm sorry." He put his paw on the door handle, and again imagined Sal, drunk and angry, careening home in his coupe, wrecking the car, or killing himself or someone else.

"Some friend," Sal said. His paw jerked up and down, now matched with little grunts. Kory pressed his gaze to the passenger window and tried not to look, listen, or smell.

The inside of the car became stifling. Sal's grunting was punctuated with pants now, and little mutters. "There we go," he said, and "oh yeah," and, once, "who needs you."

"At least," he rasped, panting harder, "get me...tissues...glove box."

Kory popped the small compartment open and found a flat box of tissues. He grabbed four and held them out. Sal took them without another word. Kory fixed his attention on the patterns of steam his breath made on the chilly window, ignoring the louder and louder grunts and the final "Uhhhhhhhhh," which he was sure was exaggerated for his benefit. He put a paw to his nose to cover up the sudden sharp musky odor that overwhelmed the coffee smell, with only partial success.

A zipper, Sal clearing his throat and repositioning himself, and the prolonged, "Ahhh," all went ignored. What got Kory to turn around was the rumble of the engine starting.

"You sober now?"

Sal rolled the car forward. "Enough to get back to my house."

Kory resumed his study of his window, fighting a growing frustration. It felt as though his relationship with Samaki was slowly bubbling through the rest of his life, tearing it down, washing old friendships and family relationships away, leaving him with nothing. At each turn, he was faced with the question of whether he would give up the fox for his mother, for his house, for his best friend. Each time, the answer was no, but if he looked at all of those things together, would he have made the same decision?

Sal would be okay when he sobered up. Kory didn't know if things would ever be the same between them, though.

Indeed, when he got back from Samaki's on Sunday, Sal came into his room without knocking. "Hey," he said, leaning against the doorframe.

Kory looked up and waited. Sal looked away. "My mom says, uh, you should probably move out next weekend."

"Okay," Kory said evenly.

They looked at each other, and then Sal turned and left.

If that had been the end of it, that would have been bad enough, plunging Kory back into the turbulent issue of where he might possibly live. With his mother? Absolutely not. With his aunt Tilly? Even if she didn't live further from school than Samaki did, she was if anything more religious than his mother, and would have been filled in on all of his sins by now. With another relative in another city? The only one he might look up was his father, somewhere on the West Coast, the father he hadn't spoken to in almost eight years. He didn't have any other friends close enough to impose upon. That left Samaki's house, or the Rainbow Center. He settled on the Rainbow Center, at least temporarily, because he knew that the aquatic room was still vacant.

Tuesday morning homeroom brought more turmoil to his life. As he and Sal spent the second morning in uncomfortable adjacent silence, Geoff Hill cooed nastily behind them, "Oooh, trouble in paradise? Lovers' quarrel?"

"Screw off," Sal said.

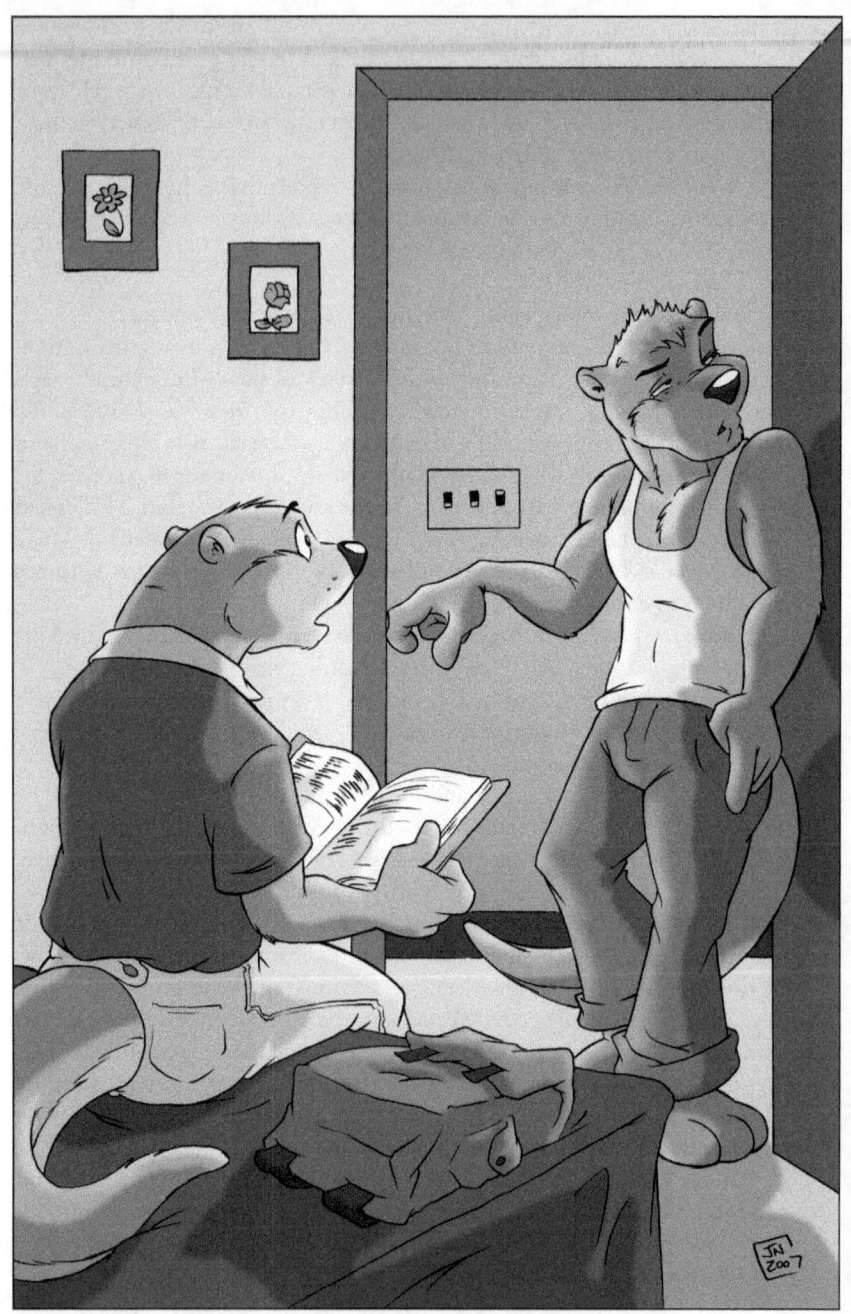

"Come on now, ladies," the raccoon said, chortling. "Kiss and make up."

"I said, screw off," Sal said, turning to face Geoff.

Clearly delighted to have provoked a reaction, the raccoon flipped his wrist limply forward. "How butch! Way to defend your boyfriend."

Sal got half out of his seat. Their teacher snapped his name sharply.

Kory turned as he sat back down. He gave Kory a sideways look and said, "He's not *my* boyfriend."

Kory could have punched him, and if he hadn't known that the homeroom teacher was looking right at them, he might have. His only hope, that Geoff hadn't heard him, was dashed a moment later.

"Oh, it's like Romeo and Juliet, but with faggots!" he whispered just before the homeroom bell rang.

At least he could ignore Geoff, Kory thought. But on Wednesday, he noticed some other kids staring at him. After English class, Perry scooted quickly from the class, where he usually hung back to chat with Kory. The otter didn't want to think it was related, but sitting in the silent car with Sal on the way home, he couldn't come to any other conclusion. His relationship with Samaki was spreading, rippling out further, out into the light.

"You told someone about me, didn't you?" he said to Sal.

His friend didn't immediately answer. When he did say, "Why would you assume it was me?" the pause was so long that Kory knew he'd had to think of what to say. "Maybe it was your friend the feeb," Sal added.

"It wasn't Perry," Kory said. "He didn't know anything. You did. Nobody else at school did."

Sal paused again. "I don't see why it matters," he said. "You're an English major, and everyone kinda half-thought you were gay anyway."

"What does that mean?"

Sal went on as though Kory hadn't spoken. "But my friends...I got a reputation to protect."

"So you sold me out."

"I didn't get any money for it, if that's what you're thinking. I just had to set the record straight. Well," he added, smirking, "at least set *my* record straight."

"You're such an asshole," Kory said.

"Fuck you too."

He didn't talk to Sal again that night.

Nick noticed right away that something was wrong, of course, even before Kory'd gotten out the money to pay for the pizza. "What's going on?" he said as they sat down to wait.

The thought of denying it flickered only briefly across his mind. "School," he said. "You haven't heard?"

Nick inclined his head. "Nah."

Kory summed up the rumors and the way he was being looked at, and, he suspected, talked about. Nick listened, leaning forward on the table. "I dunno," he said. "It's just not that big a deal in my class. Maybe they're just wondering why you didn't want to tell anyone."

"It doesn't feel like that."

"I told you about the gay kid in my class, right?" Kory nodded. "So why should it be a big deal for you?"

"It's just...why does everyone have to know? It's my business." He bit down hard on a breadstick.

Nick laughed. "Everyone's in everyone's business. My friends get on my case if I'm not on IM every night. They think I'm grounded or something."

Kory shrugged. "It's not like I have a lot of friends." He watched Nick devour another breadstick and took a small bite of his own. There were probably about twenty kids he could list who Nick considered 'friends.'

"What about, um, what's-their-names, Jamie, Jason?"

"Jason and Dev? I haven't played online with them in ages."

"Oh." Nick leaned back to let the weasel drop the pizza on their table. He had two slices on plates and was back behind the counter almost before they could say "thank you."

Kory took a bite, while Nick kept rubbing his muzzle. "Well, what about Griff and Heko?"

"They were Jenny's friends more than mine."

Nick flicked his ears and his grin angled up at one corner. "So who do you talk to at school? You've still got Sal, right?"

Kory chewed his pizza and didn't answer. "Hoo boy," Nick said. "You and Sal had a fight?"

"I think he was the one who told people about me," Kory said.

Nick took a bite, considering that. "Why would he do that?"

"We had a fight. Friday night. I'm moving out this weekend."

Nick paused with the slice halfway to his mouth, his ears straight up. His eyes widened, and the fur around them creased with worry. "Where are you gonna go?"

"To the Rainbow Center," Kory said. "At least for now."

"Still not movin' in with Samaki, huh?"

Kory took a bite, chewed, and swallowed before answering. "Rainbow Center's more convenient to school, and they're set up to help people. Plus

Margo has connections to help me get a job, which I'm gonna have to do."

"I don't like the idea of you living at a homeless shelter."

Kory grinned. "Come visit sometime. It's a pretty nice house."

"Oh, I will."

Watching his brother gulp down his third slice of pizza, Kory felt the urge to hug him. Even if everyone else in school despised him, even if Sal was afraid of being turned gay or whatever it was that was going through his head, at least Kory still had Nick. "Thanks," he said.

Nick looked up. "Mmf?" He swallowed. "For what?"

"Just...for being there."

The young otter grinned, his ears flipping back bashfully. "Ah, well, someone's gotta look out for ya, right?"

"I'm glad someone is." Kory grabbed another slice, feeling better and hungrier.

"Not just me," Nick said.

"I know. Samaki is too."

Nick pointed up. "And Him."

"Yeah." Kory let the taste of tomatoes and anchovy roll around in his mouth. "I hope so."

The next day, after the next to last meeting of the college prep class, Kory followed Perry out and caught up to him, despite the wolf's quick pace. When it became impossible for Perry to ignore Kory without being overt about it, he sighed, ears back and tail down. "Hi."

Kory was in no mood for pleasantries. "What's up?"

"Nothing." The wolf's eyes darted back and forth.

"You've been acting weird around me the last couple days."

Perry refused to look directly at Kory. "I'm just busy, ya know. Essays and...and applications..."

"Right," Kory said. "And listening to rumors about me?"

Now Perry stopped, looked furtively around, and lowered his voice. "Is it true?"

Kory wanted to shake him. "Is what true? Who told you?"

Perry looked at his paws, twisting his fingers around and around. "I heard Dilly Carlisle say that you and Sal are gay but you broke up recently. But then Flora McGuister said that Sal wasn't gay, that it was just you and he kicked you out."

"So, what? You afraid of gay people?" Kory took a step forward.

Perry cringed. "No, no," he said. "They're fine! Only I can't...I mean, they already call me loser, bitch, p-pawfu..." His ears were flat back now.

"Other stuff. I can't hang out with you. It'll just make it all worse. They'll call us butt-buddies, or c-cocksuckers." He whispered the last word.

Kory's stomach lurched. He waved a paw at the cowering thing. "Fine," he said. "Go. Don't be seen with me."

"I'm sorry," Perry said. "I'm just not strong like you." He scuttled to the door, and out.

Strong? At the moment, the otter felt anything but. The prospect of going from that conversation to facing the silent car ride home with Sal depressed him. Kory leaned against the wall and closed his eyes.

Clicks of claws on the tile floor echoed through the hallways, receding. It wasn't that Perry had been a particularly good friend. It was just that the school year wasn't even half over, and already he'd lost most of the people he'd spent time with at school. There were casual friends, more like acquaintances, and none of them had acted any differently toward him this week, but they weren't the kind of friends he could talk to about college, or relationships, or life. When he'd broken up with Jenny, he'd stopped going to parties and movies, stopped hanging out with them Friday nights at the Big Boy, stopped talking about TV shows. Odd, indeed, that it was the conversation with his newest "friend," Perry, that had brought home how far he'd drifted from his older ones.

He opened his eyes and looked back down the long, empty hallway. Outside the glass doors, across the parking lot, Sal sat in his car, waiting. Walking across the bus lanes, the feeling in Kory's stomach was the same feeling he'd gotten going back to his room to get his winter clothes. He was in a place that had once been a part of his life, where he no longer belonged, an archaeological curiosity, a legacy of a past civilization that had crumbled and died. He wondered, fleetingly, whether Hari Seldon could have predicted how fast his life would have changed.

Dreading the conversation that would ensue, he hadn't told Samaki about leaving Sal's, but on their nightly call, he knew he couldn't put it off any longer.

"Why do you have to leave?" Samaki sounded angrier than Kory'd ever heard him.

"I guess I just overstayed my welcome here. I knew it couldn't be forever."

"No, but they could give you more warning than a week. Did something happen?"

He drew his legs tighter against his chest, sitting on the bed. "No," he said, and then the wave of guilt over the first lie he'd told Samaki forced him to take it back. "I mean, yeah, kind of, but it's a lot of things."

"Like what?"

Kory sighed. "Can I tell you Saturday? I don't want to go into it now."

A short pause greeted that remark. "Okay." Samaki sounded gentler. "I'm just worried for you. So did you want to move over here?"

That was the question Kory was dreading. "I want to," he said, stumbling, "but I talked to Margo and she said they have room. I thought it would be less trouble."

"It's no trouble."

"I know, but..." Kory sighed. "It's just easier. They don't have a lot of people there. I don't want to be a burden."

When Samaki spoke again, his voice sounded tight and pained. "All right. I'll see you there Saturday and we can talk about it."

Kory sat on the bed after they hung up, just staring at his cell phone. It had never occurred to him that he might lose the one person he'd lost everything else in his life for, but he'd never heard that tone in Samaki's voice. His refusal to move in there was obviously hurting the fox. Why couldn't he understand what Kory was going through and respect that? He couldn't believe that would be enough to drive them apart, but hadn't he and Jenny also changed and broken up? Hadn't there been a time when he'd believed they'd be happy forever? No, he thought. Not like with Samaki. Never like that.

But if Samaki needed him to move into the Rodens' house to save their relationship, then what?

Packing didn't take long, so even though he'd left most of it until Friday night, he was done within an hour after dinner. When he went across the hall to see if Sal would give him a ride, he found his friend's door open and his room dark.

"I think he went out, dear," Sal's mother said, coming upstairs as Kory was staring into the empty room.

"I guess so." Kory turned around and looked at the five boxes in his room, plus the computer. All his life fit in such a small space.

Sal's mother glided down the hall. Her paw rested on his shoulder. "I'm so sorry you have to move on. We've enjoyed having you here. Even if Sal hasn't quite picked up your dedication to education."

"I really appreciate you having me here for so long," he said, aware that he could mess up Sal's scheme by confessing that he didn't really want to leave. If he did, though, Sal might refuse to drive him to school, and he'd certainly be unpleasant. Anyway, Kory *was* anxious to leave at this point, as bad as this last week had been.

She had applied perfume today. "It was no trouble," she said, the pine scent wafting over him in waves as she spoke. "Do you have a ride to where you're going?"

"No," he said. "I was thinking of just calling a taxi."

"Oh, don't be silly," she said. "We'll drive you over. Joey!"

Sal's father called from downstairs. "What?"

"Come help Kory load his things into the car."

"You don't have to..." Kory began, worrying about them seeing the Rainbow Center, but it was too late. Sal's father was already on the stairs.

"It's no trouble," Sal's mother said. "And until things are better with your mother, you call on us if you need anything."

He was too startled to answer that, too startled to do anything but watch as Sal's father hefted a box of books and carried it down the stairs. He hadn't realized that they knew that much. Either Sal had told them or they had called and asked of their own accord. Really, how naïve would he have to be to believe that they wouldn't realize something was wrong when their son's best friend moved into their spare room for over a month? That they hadn't asked him questions had been a mark of tact, not of indifference, he realized guiltily.

"Did you talk to her?" he asked, picking up his computer while Sal's mother took a light box of clothes.

She shook her head. "Sal told us you were having a fight over some family business. It's for you to work out. We don't want to intrude."

In his experience, she didn't intrude much in matters that concerned her own family, either. Whether Sal's father felt the same, he didn't know, even after the twenty-minute ride to Badger Square. He tried to get them to leave him there, but they insisted on driving him to the door of the house, and because he couldn't figure out how to carry five boxes and his computer down a block and a half, he finally directed them to Rainbow Center.

Margo flung the door open and embraced Kory. "You poor thing," she said. "Stay as long as you need to." To Sal's parents, she said, "I'm Margo Cinturis. I..."

"Margo lives here." Kory jumped in. "I met her over the summer and she, um, has a little kind of hotel here, I called her this week and she said she can keep me here for a while."

"Joe DiAngelo, and my wife Alia." Sal's father extended a paw, which Margo shook, turning her attention away from Kory.

"Thank you for bringing Kory over," she said. "I'll take care of him here."

"I like your plaque," Sal's mother said, brushing a finger over it.

Her husband glanced at the burnished bronze, then back at Margo. "Do you have a phone number here?"

"You can call my cell phone," Kory said quickly, but Margo had already disappeared back into the house. She emerged a moment later with a scrap of paper, which she handed to Sal's father. It wasn't her business card, Kory saw with some relief, even though the business cards were very plain.

They helped him move the boxes inside and then left, after asking him one more time whether he'd be okay. He and Margo moved the boxes down to the aquatic room, where the bed had been freshly made and the water lightly scented. Kory looked down at it. "Can't wait to get in there," he sighed.

"Malaya's very excited that you'll be living here," Margo told him, piling his clothes on the bed.

"Really? Hey, you don't have to do that."

She waved away his objection and continued emptying his boxes and bags, her tail flicking. "Well, as excited as Malaya gets. I don't know what to do with that girl sometimes, but I'm happier to have her back here than with her father. She absolutely won't go to her grandmother's and I don't know what else to do. She can't stay here for another year and a half."

Kory started putting the clothes away in the worn dresser. "Well, when I figure out what I'm doing, maybe she can come with me."

Margo chuckled, making Kory want to smile back at her, despite his mood. Her beaming smile radiated genuine warmth, making him think of Mrs. Roden. "I think she'd like that, I really do. Do you want me to tell her you're here?"

He thought about that. "I think I just want to go to sleep. I'll see her tomorrow."

But when he thought about tomorrow, he thought first about Samaki. He hoped the fox would understand his decision. More than that, he hoped he himself would understand it.

He didn't sleep well that night for any length of time. When Samaki arrived the next day, Kory was lying in the water, paws linked behind his head, staring at the ceiling. He heard the door open, and smelled fox.

"Hi," he said, not moving.

The door closed. Blue jeans, a black t-shirt, and a beige jacket moved into his vision, surmounted by a white under-muzzle and violet eyes, looking down. Two large black ears cupped down. "Hi," Samaki said. "How you doing?" He placed a Starbucks cup on the floor near Kory and sipped from another one as he sat on the floor.

Kory flipped over and crawled out of the water, sitting upright on the floor. Samaki sat a foot away from him, keeping his clothes dry. "I'm okay," Kory said, smiling with a little relief at the fox's calm demeanor. Samaki would understand. He always did. "It's been a hard week. Thanks." He raised the Starbucks and took a drink.

Samaki nodded. "So what happened with you and Sal?"

Kory closed his eyes. The warm latte filled his muzzle with coffee smell and milk sweetness. "He wasn't as okay with our relationship as he thought he was."

"Asshole," Samaki growled.

"I mean our relationship, me and him. Well, it was more that he wasn't okay with thinking that he might be gay."

"And that's your fault? He can't be a good friend, because you're gay?"

Kory shook his head. "It's...there was some stuff." He didn't want to tell anyone about the previous Friday night. He wanted to put it out of his mind. It was Sal's secret, and whether he thought he was gay or whether he just wanted to experiment was his business and nobody else's.

"What stuff?" When Kory didn't answer, Samaki leaned forward. "Did he come on to you?"

Kory looked back at the fox's eyes. Was it that obvious? "Uh, well..."

Samaki shook his head. "I've had three of my straight friends try to experiment with me in the last two years. It always ends badly. They think, I don't know, they think being gay means you'll do anyone. They think it won't change anything." He growled the words. "I'd think he would know better, though. Wasn't he your best friend?"

"Yeah." Kory shrugged. "He was drunk, he'd been dancing with this girl the whole evening, and she got him all worked up."

"Still." They sat and contemplated Sal and other "curious" straight friends, until Kory sensed that the currents of Samaki's thoughts were drifting in a new direction. The black fox's tail was curled up tightly around his legs, his tail twitching. "So," Samaki said. "Margo set up this room pretty nice."

Kory took another sip of the lukewarm latte and set it aside. "Yeah."

"How long you figure to stay here?"

He inhaled, exhaled. "I don't know."

"If it's the water, you know, we can get Mariatu's kiddie pool and put it in the basement."

Samaki was smiling, his ears perked. "It's not the water," Kory said.

"Then what?" The smile faded, slowly. "Mom said you can stay. I want you to stay. Don't you want to?"

"It's not that simple." He curled his tail up around his body and rested his head on his knees.

"Then tell me why it's complicated."

"I don't know!"

Samaki sat, watching him. Kory avoided looking at those violet eyes because he knew the hurt in them would make him want to cry, and he didn't want to cry. "Is it getting to school? We can work out something where I could--"

"It's not that." He kept his voice flat.

"Is it me?"

Kory couldn't stand the twisting in his heart. He stared at the water. "I don't want to take your family's money. You need it to go to college."

"Money?" Samaki sounded incredulous. "This is about money?" He reached out and grabbed Kory's shoulder. "I don't believe you."

Kory turned. "I've never lied to you."

Violet eyes widened, ears folded back. "I'm not accusing you of lying. Is that really it? That's all there is?"

"I told you, I don't know! It's not simple! It just doesn't feel...it doesn't feel right!"

The paw dropped away from Kory's shoulder. Samaki's eyes narrowed. He studied Kory, searching the otter's face. Finally, he uncurled his tail and got to his feet. "It feels right to me," he said. "Maybe I'm just imagining things, then. Maybe you'd rather be with Hazel the squirrel?"

Kory jerked his head up. "Why would you even think that?"

"I don't know. What am I supposed to think? You don't want to be seen with me in public, you still haven't answered about the prom, you don't want to be close unless you can leave. Am I just an experiment?" Samaki's tail lashed against the bed. He wasn't looking at Kory. "I know you don't like it here, but you'd rather be here than with me? Tell me what that means."

"I like it fine here." After all they'd been through, Samaki would really think he was just an experiment? He wanted Kory to protest that, was manipulating him into a corner where Kory would have to confess his feelings and that he was the one being irrational. He splashed a paw in the water.

Samaki got up from the bed and paced back and forth. "I really do care for you, Kory. I know you've gone through a lot with being kicked out of your house, and I tried to be patient. I just can't understand why you keep me at arm's length. I've been waiting for you to let me get closer, but I don't want to wait around forever if it's never going to happen. Is it? If this isn't going anywhere, maybe we should just..."

"Closer? Do I have to move in with you to be your boyfriend now?"

Samaki's ears flicked. "Of course not. And you should know better than to think that."

"I should know a lot of things I don't. Like why I'm going through all this for you if you're not going to help me."

"For me?" The fox raised his voice. "I didn't ask you to curse at your mother."

"I wouldn't have been kicked out of home if not for you," he snapped.

The fox stared at him, moisture gathering in the corners of his violet eyes. "So you want to go back home." His tail was curled tightly underneath him, his ears flat. "Is that what you really want?"

His whole body felt hot. He stared down at his paws. "No," he said, but his voice was shaky. He curled his own tail around his legs and squeezed the tip.

"Maybe we shouldn't be seeing each other. Then you could go home, and I could find someone..." Kory didn't have to look up to see the tears in the black fur of Samaki's muzzle. This was going all wrong. But maybe Samaki had a point. If they couldn't be together, what was the point of fooling themselves any longer?

"Kory?"

He looked up reflexively at the sound of his name. Samaki was leaning against the doorframe, his head angled forward into the room. The large black ears had come up. "Am I wasting my time?"

Why did he have to make all the decisions? "I don't know! Give me a little space!" As soon as he said it, he knew it was the wrong thing to say, but he couldn't take the words back.

Samaki sagged against the frame. He wiped his muzzle, and then spoke in an oddly calm voice. "Maybe you're right. Maybe you do need some space. I'm sorry I thought differently."

He was gone before Kory could think of anything to say.

His first reaction was anger. After the week he'd had, getting kicked out of Sal's house—the second house in as many months—and after the issue with Sal himself and the kids at school, what he needed was a sympathetic boyfriend, someone who'd hold him and say everything was going to be all right because they were together. He didn't need to have his faults pointed out, or the decisions that even he didn't quite understand second-guessed.

He slipped back into the water and lay there looking at the ceiling, brooding and hurting. How much easier it would be if he weren't really gay after all. What if it had just been Samaki who'd entranced him? He still thought girls were pretty. Maybe he just hadn't met the right one. It occurred to him that perhaps his reluctance to move in with Samaki was due to his not being comfortable with the relationship, that that was a sign that he wasn't really gay. And if he wasn't really gay, then Samaki would be right, and he had no business being at Rainbow Center. That would just be perfect. His stuff was already packed to move. He could go home.

What happens to foxes who fall in the water? Looking up at the ceiling with the water flowing around him reminded him of the afternoon Malaya had left, when he and Samaki had done it here in the room, partly in the water. His body tingled with just the memory of the sensations, from his sheath down to the tip of his tail and up to the tips of his ears, settling in his heart. The smell of Samaki still lingered in the air, or was it just his memory? Kory remembered their caresses, how bad he'd felt about Malaya and how Samaki was able to take that all away and make it better. He wanted that, he did, but he didn't want anyone else to have to know about it.

So why did it feel so good when Malaya called Samaki his boyfriend? Was it the danger, the thrill? Was it that it was safe for her to acknowledge their relationship? And why couldn't he talk to Samaki about this?

All the things he'd gone through were no excuse. Why couldn't he just let Samaki make him feel better? Why did things have to spiral out of control like that? Maybe it wasn't that he wasn't gay; maybe it was that he wasn't suitable to be with anyone. Maybe he needed to find someone else like himself, someone content to keep their relationship in the shadows, out of the light.

Someone else who was as ashamed of him as he was of them. The throbbing in his heart moved up into his throat, closing it off and squeezing his eyes shut. He turned over out of habit so his tears would leak into the water, pressing his paws to his eyes and shaking with quiet sobs.

Maybe Malaya was right after all, and the world was not a nice place. It had taken a remarkably short time for Kory to lose everything: home, friends, boyfriend. He envisioned Margo's smiling face telling him it was going to be all right, and for a moment, he understood Malaya's running away perfectly.

Long after the sobs had drained from him, leaving him weak, he lay in the water. Eventually he pulled himself up and rested his elbows on the mat, laying his head on his forearm. He was hungry, too, but had no desire to leave the room. Upstairs, they were serving lunch, or would be soon, but even through his hunger, the thought of food made him nauseous. All he could see was Samaki cheerfully slicing a sandwich, making one for Kory just the way Kory liked it, laughing at him for choosing the American cheese over Swiss.

If he didn't go upstairs, he'd never have to face that memory. And Samaki might still be up there, and what would he say then? Better to wait until dinner. Or breakfast tomorrow. Or dinner tomorrow. Dully, he tried to make himself focus on the ache inside his stomach, but he suspected that it was an emptiness that couldn't be filled by food.

Steps clicked at his door, but the smell was cigarette smoke, not fox. "Welcome back," Malaya's husky voice said.

He lifted his head. She'd gotten some of her wardrobe back: the black leather vest and mini-skirt, and the piercings in her left ear. The right bore ragged scars along its edge, and no silver at all. On the cast on her arm, he recognized the signatures of the kids from the center, around which she'd drawn skulls and daggers in thick black marker. The other wing was stretched to its fullest across the span of the doorway, as though compensating for the broken one.

"Same to you," Kory said.

"What'd you say to Blackie?" she asked, staying in the doorway. "He sulked around upstairs not saying two words to anyone and then he took off."

Kory closed his eyes. "We had a fight, I guess."

"You guess?" She chuckled. "If you don't know, then it wasn't a fight." When he didn't answer, she walked in and stood over him. "So? Was it a fight?"

He lay back, glaring up. "I never had a fight in a relationship before."

"Then you were never in a real relationship. Didn't you date anyone before Samaki?"

He closed his eyes. "Go away."

She laughed and sat on the bed. "Dream on. Are you mad at him but mad at yourself, too? Wish you could take back some stuff and wish you'd said more?"

Now he opened his eyes and turned his head to look at her. "Kind of."

"Okay. Congratulations, you've had your first fight. If you stay together, you get to have make-up sex, which is pretty awesome if you don't ruin it by having another fight in the middle of it."

"I dunno," Kory said. "Maybe this whole 'gay' thing was just a mistake."

She just stared at him. "Are you serious?"

"It would make things so much easier. Maybe this isn't what God wants for me. Maybe this was just a test."

Malaya opened her good wing. "What God wants? You wanna talk about what God wants? Look at this." The leathery skin rustled as she shook the wing. "I got wings. Can I fly? Can I glide more than twenty feet? This is some kind of joke. What does God want me to do with these wings? Fuck what God wants. What do *you* want?"

His depression withered under her vehemence. "I don't know. That's part of the problem."

"Okay, then, here." She pulled a rolled-up magazine from inside her vest and tossed it onto the nearby mat. "Take a look at that."

B.A.T.s, blared the cover in bright red letters like a theater marquee. On the front, a buxom female bat pinched the nipples on breasts the size of her head, her wings strategically hiding her sex, but not much else. Kory looked up from the cover at Malaya. "You just carry this around with you?"

"Bushytail confiscates 'em if I leave 'em in my room. Go ahead, look through it."

He pulled himself all the way onto the mat and flipped the pages, past photo after photo of different kinds of bats showing off their immense chests, plump rear ends, and full-lipped genitals. As he flipped through, he found himself more interested in the different species; most were large-eared, small-nosed bats, not like Malaya. The few fruit bats who were in the magazine had more attractive faces, he thought. He got to the last well-worn page and tossed the magazine back to Malaya. "And?"

"There you go," she said, picking up the magazine and tucking it back into her vest. "You're gay."

"Huh?"

"Well, first, you didn't stop to stare at any of the pictures. Second, those shorts you're wearin' don't look any tighter now than when you started. So I'm guessing none of those really did anything for you. Me, I can't get four pages into this without getting all wet. So, y'know, don't sweat *that*. You're better off anyway. Women are bitches."

"Thanks. I don't really know if I feel better."

"Hey, us faggots have to look out for each other." She leaned back on the bed, cradling her broken arm in her lap.

Kory rested his head on his folded arms. "So what now?"

"Hell, I don't know," Malaya said. "Maybe you get back together, maybe you don't. You're gonna break up eventually. Maybe this is it. Better to get it over with, eh?"

Kory lowered his head. "I wish it were that easy."

"Make it easy, then. What's the problem?"

"The problem is I don't know what the problem is!" he cried.

He listened to the ripples of water and the rustle of bat wings fill the space until she said, "You want me to tell you?"

Kory snorted. "Go for it."

"You and I got the same problem. We're trying to figure this whole fucked-up thing out on our own. Dating's hard enough without knowing what to do with gay dating. Can't talk to our parents, can't talk to our friends, and we can barely talk to each other."

"I dunno," Kory said. "I wasn't that good at dating girls, either."

"Course not. Your heart wasn't in it. Well, your dick wasn't in it." She flashed a quick grin.

He opened his mouth to argue, but he couldn't, really. "I guess not."

She waved her good arm, the wing trailing over his sheets. "So you'll make up with Blackie or not. If you want to, just call him."

"I can't," Kory said. "He said we needed some space." He couldn't bear the thought of going to Samaki and trying to talk and being pushed away again. Besides that, he was still mad at Samaki for judging him so quickly, for not giving him more time to figure things out, and for walking out on him. And there was a little voice in his head saying that those things they'd said couldn't be taken back, and maybe the whole relationship was ruined now. "He's just so...so used to it. He doesn't care if everyone knows about us." Because the Starbucks cup was just sitting there, he picked it up and took a sip. The latte was cold, undrinkable.

He'd expected Malaya to be on his side, after her experience with her father. "And you do?"

"Well...yeah."

She smirked back. "Why you think I ended up in the hospital?"

He stared at the cast as she held it up. "Uh, because your homophobic asshole father caught you looking at Vogue?"

"Wrong." She pointed the magazine at him. "If he didn't know I'm gay, he could've caught me looking at this and he wouldn'ta cared."

"But he found out. You said he caught you and Jen..."

She laughed. "You think he'da caught us if I didn't want him to? I'm not that stupid. And he is."

He shook his head. "Why?"

"I thought you understood about life," she said, looking down at him. "No point sugarcoating it. Y'are what you are. If the world can't deal with it, fuck 'em. But don't hide it. That's just wishing, pretending it ain't true."

"So you'd rather get beat up than just keep your private life private?"

She held up the cast again. "This heals faster."

"Right." He snorted, and looked down at the mat.

Malaya shrugged. "Okay, well, I need a smoke. I'm gonna head upstairs."

"I thought you quit."

She grinned at him. "Old habits. You coming to lunch?"

"I guess," Kory said. She nodded and waved, gliding through the door.

He heard movement over his head, and looked up, and something clicked, something Nick had said. It wasn't much help now, but it gave him something to do, and in the meantime he could dig through his boxes for a notebook and try to write some poems. Maybe someday someone would understand the way he felt.

At first, his old church felt like nothing more than that: old and uncomfortable. He'd gotten up at six in the morning to catch the series of buses here, and he kept yawning, sitting way in the back. He hadn't seen his mother arrive, and was deliberately not looking at the place where she normally sat. She wasn't who he'd come here to see. He'd waited outside and come in late, sitting far in the back so she and Nick wouldn't notice him.

The feeling of the church changed when Father Joe stepped up to the altar. With his first words, Kory felt a small shiver and the comfort he hadn't felt in months, the feeling of belonging. He closed his eyes, listening to a well-known story about the Pharisees, and their love of laws, how they had tried to catch Jesus in contradictions by questioning him on the law, but that he rose above them.

Kory sang all the hymns, but didn't go up front for communion. When the congregation started to file out, he pulled the hood of the sweatshirt he'd borrowed from the Rainbow Center up over his head, and bowed as though in prayer. The pose started as disguise, but as he remained stationary, listening to the easy conversations of the people walking past him, it became genuine. In school, the scents of the students battled in the small classrooms, established pockets that met in chaotic fronts in the wide, low halls. Here in the church, the high roof allowed the scents of the congregation to mingle freely, and the old aromatic wood contained and supported them. Everyone had room. Instead of being pushed together and tense, they were able to keep their own distance and commingle pleasantly. He felt somehow that that was significant.

A hand fell lightly on his shoulder. He looked up into the soft brown eyes of Father Joe. "It's good to see you again, Kory," he said.

"I thought," Kory said, "you might need some help with the hymnals."

They sat together at the front of the church, the books piled between them. "I remember that sermon from years ago," Kory said. "I think I understand it a little better now."

"I didn't choose it for you," Father Joe said, "but I did feel that it would be right as I was preparing this week. When I saw you in the back of the church, I knew why."

Kory's ears came up. "You think it applies to me?"

"Well, it applies to everyone." Father Joe smiled. "But I think it has particular insight into your problem."

"You think so?"

"Jesus's first law was love. When he spoke to the Pharisees, he told them that the laws they loved so much were made for the weakness of people."

"But aren't we supposed to fight our weaknesses?"

Father Joe shook his head. "We had this conversation before. I don't think that love is a weakness."

Kory turned that word over in his head, until Father Joe broke the silence. "I read your essay."

"Any suggestions? I can still change it."

Father Joe's horns bobbed as he nodded. "Your essay is difficult because you're attempting to demonstrate proof of that which we take on faith. But it's not uncommon, and you go about it well. I notice that you reference C.S. Lewis, which is a nice touch, but your essay is still missing something." He looked at Kory, who remained quiet. "You ask, 'Does God love me?' You spend a good deal of space talking about the elements in your life that support or counter that proposition. But I can guess at what prompted this question. And that you don't talk about."

Now he waited for Kory to answer. Kory sighed. "No, I don't."

"I think that shows."

Kory stared down at the stone floor of the church and pressed his feet against it. It was chilly under his pads. "I just didn't want to tell everyone in the admissions group..."

He waited for Father Joe to say, "I know," or something like that, but when he turned, the priest's expression was patient, expectant. He lowered his ears. Phrases like "about my friend" and "about my situation" rolled through his head, but the solemnity of the church and the sheep's deep brown eyes drove them out. He thought about Malaya's words, about hiding, and took a breath. "That I'm gay."

The word hung between them, echoing up into the rafters. The saints continued to smile, the candles continued to burn, and the Lamb on the cross looked down at Kory with sympathy. He heard the echoes die, and looked up to the rafters, where the wood that held so many scents and secrets now held one more. The beams were strong; they held.

Father Joe nodded, the only change in his expression the faintest hint of a smile, turning up the corners of his mouth. "But it is a part of you. And what, in the past year, has been the best evidence that God loves you?"

Violet eyes and black fur. "Samaki," Kory whispered.

Malaya came to see him that evening as he floated in the pool. She took a seat on his bed with an ease that had become familiar already. "Still upset about your fight?"

Kory shook his head. "I called him on the way home and left a message. Told him I was sorry and that I didn't want space, I wanted to be with him so that we can work things out. I still don't know why I'm scared to go live with him, but I'll figure it out with him."

Her good wing rattled. "Jen asked me to move in with her."

"Just now?" Her housing problem might be solved after all.

She shook her head, slowly. "A week before Dad caught us."

"Why didn't you?"

"It was too much. I wasn't ready for full-on dykehood yet."

Kory's tail glided back and forth in the water, creating ripples that spread up his chest and lapped against his chin. "Are you now?"

"Maybe. If the right girl came along, which she won't."

"You don't think so?"

Malaya grinned at him. "She doesn't exist, see? So she can't really come along. I'm stuck liking girls without a girl to like."

"You'd be better off with Jen than with your father."

"Not really," Malaya said casually. "She used to hit me too. The only difference was she'd say she was sorry and kiss me afterwards."

"Ugh." Kory closed his eyes. "You need to find someone who'll treat you nicely."

Her wing rustled, and she let out a sigh. "I'm fine on my own."

The sharp trill of the cell phone pierced the silence. Kory splashed out of the water, scrambling to the little device. He registered Samaki's number before flipping it open. "Hello?"

The moment dragged on. He knew that it would be okay, but he had to hear it to quiet that last doubting piece that said that Samaki would have reconsidered, would have found someone else, would have decided that he wasn't worth the trouble. The fox's voice, gentle and affectionate, was music to his ears. "Hi, hon," Samaki said.

He gave Malaya a huge smile and a thumbs-up. She smiled back, got to her feet, and padded quietly from the room.

212

OCEANS

"Surprise," Samaki said, dragging a large box out of the back of the car, with Ajani's help. His breath puffed white into the afternoon breeze. "I got it," he told his brother as the end slid out from the seat. "Go get the one in the trunk."

"Oh, you didn't," Malaya said, crowding beside Kory to read the label on the box that said, "6' Norway Spruce."

"Mom insisted," Samaki said. "We had this one in our attic, not doing anything."

"It's great," Kory said. "I'll have to get Nick to get my ornaments for me." His smile faded, but only slightly.

"Great." Malaya groaned. "Enough Christmas spirit to choke on. December twenty-six, this all comes down." She shook her wing at all three of them, which slid her grey flannel wrap far enough down to expose her forearm.

"Hey," Samaki said, "you got the cast off."

"Good as new." She showed off the arm, turning it back and forth before pulling the wrap back over it.

"How'd you break your arm?" Ajani asked, holding the box from the trunk. "I broke my arm once fallin' off my bed."

She glanced at Kory and Samaki. "I'll tell ya later," she said, reaching over to ruffle the fur between the cub's ears. "When you're older."

"I *am* older," he said indignantly.

Kory nudged Ajani. "What's in that box?" he said.

"Oh, decorations." Ajani pushed one flap open with his muzzle, his tail wagging. "Some ornaments and scent-pines."

"I'm gonna have to burn incense," Malaya said.

"Nah," Kory said. "Their noses are more sensitive than ours. You probably won't be able to smell the pine."

"I can smell it from here," she said.

"Me too," the black fox said. "Let's get inside. We'll get the wreath later."

Kory led the four of them into the converted townhouse, helping Samaki steady the Norway Spruce. "Don't say anything," Samaki said to Ajani in the lobby. The cub was looking around the lobby, nose wrinkling.

"But it smells funny."

"Probably not to Kory."

Kory shook his head. "Just smells like wood to me." He looked over the pitted wood paneling, the cracked frame of the cupboard that housed the mailboxes for the six apartments, and the grime on the plaster toward the ceiling. "It's not the cleanest place, but we can afford it for now. My online tutoring will help." The black fox paused in his inspection of the lobby when he noticed Kory looking at him, and smiled.

"And it's good to be out of the Rainbow Center," Malaya said, saying the name in a sarcastic sing-song voice.

"We're going over there later to help out," Kory said. "Margo still asks about you every time I see her."

"Tell her I'm fine. Tell her this place is a million times better."

"Oh, come on," Kory said. "The Center wasn't that bad."

Malaya snorted. "At least the neighbors here don't tell me how much I'm loved every time I turn around."

"What are the neighbors like?" Samaki asked, following Kory up the stairs. Ajani trailed behind him, nose still wrinkled, with Malaya following.

"The people across from us are a mongoose family. Ki-yo, I think their name is. One of them is about our age."

"Shara," Malaya called up behind him. "He's cool."

"And we've seen the bear who lives in 1A, but he doesn't talk to us much."

"That's nice," Samaki said after a moment. "It looks like an okay neighborhood."

"If you like drug dealers," Ajani said. Kory heard a soft cuffing sound, and a "shhh!" that he presumed was from Samaki.

"I love 'em," Malaya said. "They know where all the best coffee shops are."

Kory laughed and heard Samaki echo his laughter as he turned the key in the door marked '2B.' The sensation of walking into his own apartment still felt new and strange, even two weeks into it. He breathed in the smells of the apartment—his apartment—as the others walked in, turning the key over in his fingers before sliding it into his pocket.

Ajani put the box of decorations down and walked over to the sofa. He fingered the patched material, gazing at the old TV, the worn coffee table, and finally out the window at the graffiti-covered brick. "This looks like grandpa's place," he said to Samaki, who had taken a small decorative box, red with green stripes, out of the larger one.

"Don't be rude," Samaki said. Both Kory and Malaya saw him look from the box he held up at Kory.

"The couch is probably that old," Malaya said, swinging up to the bar over it and hooking her feet through it to hang upside down. Her face came down almost to Ajani's. "Boo," she said, grimacing.

Ajani laughed and clapped his paws, eyeing the bar. "Cool!" he said, and clambered up onto the sofa. "Can I do that?"

"I don't think so," Malaya said, folding her arms and rattling her wings. "I bet you can't."

"I can do it," Ajani insisted, hopping up and down on the couch. Kory took advantage of the cub's distraction to slip into the bedroom.

Samaki paused to watch Ajani and then followed Kory, closing the door behind him. "You worked it out so you get the bedroom this month?"

The bed, old and worn, was clean enough that it had picked up Kory's scent, even after only a week. He sat on it and smiled at Samaki. "Malaya said that since I have a boyfriend and she doesn't, I can have the bedroom for the time being."

"She doesn't want a boyfriend, does she?" Samaki smiled, turning the long box over in his paws to reveal a gold seal on top of the red and green stripes.

"Well, actually she said since I have hope and she doesn't." Kory chuckled. "Also since she sleeps upside down hanging from a bar and not in a bed."

"That sounds more like her."

Kory leaned back against his tail. "So that's a good thing about having my own place." The moment he said it, he wondered if he'd pushed too hard. Their argument over his living situation had technically ended before Thanksgiving, but tension lingered every time the subject came up.

Samaki's ears flicked. He nodded, his smile faltering only slightly. He fingered the lid of the box he held, drawing Kory's attention to it.

"What's that?"

Samaki opened it. "A couple things." He pulled out a faded Santa Fox, made of construction paper and dangling from a bit of green yarn. "I made this in second grade. Mom thought you—we—should hang it up here."

Red construction paper formed the suit, glued over orange paper that made up the tail and muzzle. He had two ears, colored heavily with black pencil on the orange paper, between which a red hat was set. The tail, too, was colored orange paper, scribbles of white crayon still holding a faint waxy smell. Cotton balls lined the red paper to form the trim of the suit.

Turning it over, Kory saw a child's writing on the back: "Samaki Roden, Miss Gerfy's class." He smiled. "It's cool. I love it." The connection between it and the fox standing in front of him was almost palpable for a moment. He looked around the walls to see where they might hang it.

Samaki took a folded paper out of the box. He held it awkwardly, ears flicking back. "And Mom made me promise to read this with you."

Kory peered up and saw "Your health" and "sexually transmitted" on the brochure. His own ears folded down, a hot flush rising in his cheeks. "We covered all that in health class."

"I know," Samaki said. "We did too. But she knows you have your own place now, and she worries. You know how moms...how she is."

Kory had a flash of his mom handing him a brochure on disease to read with his boyfriend, the image so incongruous that he couldn't restrain a laugh. "I like your mom. Should we get it out of the way?" He patted the bed beside him.

Samaki did sit down then, his tail resting beside Kory's in the familiar way. They looked down at the brochure. "We don't have to read it out loud, do we?" Kory asked.

"No." Samaki held the paper between them. "Just let me know when you're done."

It wasn't one of the ones the Rainbow Center stocked, though the material was certainly familiar to Kory. This brochure explained things in rougher, simpler language that seemed aimed at a younger audience. He read the material about same-species diseases, which he and Jenny had gone over, and then said, "Done," so that Samaki could flip the paper over and they could read about cross-species diseases and the ways you could get them.

"We don't really do any of this stuff," Kory said, pointing at the list. "That, sometimes."

"And I'm fine with that risk because I'm pretty sure you're not seeing anyone else behind my back," Samaki said.

Kory slid his finger down a few more items, and then stopped. "I wouldn't mind trying that one."

Samaki nodded, giving Kory a smile. "We will."

The door cracked open just then. They heard Malaya's, "Hey, hang on," and then Ajani's high voice.

"Are you guys kissing?"

Samaki laughed, and folded the brochure. He pecked Kory on the cheek. "Not any more."

"Can I come in?"

The door opened enough for his little red muzzle to poke through before Kory said, "Sure."

Samaki tilted the box toward Kory so that the otter could see the three wrapped condoms in the bottom, then dropped the brochure on top of them while Kory was stifling a giggle. Ajani, looking around the room, didn't notice Samaki closing the box.

"This is smaller than our room," he said, edging between the bed and dresser. "Did you move these from your house?"

Kory shook his head. "They came with the apartment. And there's only me living here. You've got Samaki and Kasim in your room."

"Look, the paint is peeling here." The cub pulled a big flake of it off the wall.

"Hey," Samaki said, half-laughing, "don't do that. Kory'll get in trouble."

Ajani's ears flattened, then came back up. "It was already loose," he said. "Anyway, it'll be just me and Kasim when you move in here, right? I already called your bed."

"That won't be for a while," Samaki said. "Beginning of the summer."

"I wanted to call it before Kasim," Ajani said, now looking out of the window. "Is that a drug dealer?" he asked, pointing.

"I doubt it," Malaya said from the doorway. "They're nocturnal."

"Is he giving someone something?" Samaki asked.

"No," Ajani said, "but people keep giving him money."

"Oh, is he a raccoon?" Kory got up to stand beside the cub. "That's Joe the Jokester. He just tells jokes all day for spare change."

"Really? I wanna see him! Can we see him when we go back down? Please?"

"All right, all right." Samaki laughed. "How much does he charge per joke?"

"Whatever you've got," Malaya said. "He's not picky."

"Pickled, maybe," Kory said. "You're staying for dinner, right?"

"Depends." Samaki raised an eyebrow. "Are you cooking?"

"Ha," Malaya said.

Kory grinned back. "We don't really have anything to cook. How does McD's sound?"

"Great!" Ajani wagged his tail. "Mom never lets us go there."

"Let's hurry up, then," Malaya said. "I have to be at work in half an hour."

"How's the job?" Samaki asked. He and Kory followed Malaya and the skipping Ajani back into the living room.

"Oh, wonderful," Malaya said. "I get paid to tell stoned hippies where to find the Anarchist Cookbook."

"What's 'stoned'?" Ajani asked.

Malaya and Kory looked at Samaki, who said, "Kind of like drunk."

"Except from the drug dealers?" Ajani asked.

"Yeah." Samaki shook his head. "How did you figure that out?"

Ajani wagged his tail proudly. "They play those "don't do drugs" ads alla time during Yu-Gi-Oh."

"Glad you're listening." Samaki ushered his brother out the door, Kory behind them as Malaya locked up.

After lunch, Kory, Samaki, and Ajani walked Malaya to the bookstore, then picked up the wreath from the car. In the lobby of Kory's building, they ran into two of the mongoose family, the mother and a young girl. "Ah," the mother said, smiling at the wreath, "I thought I smelled Christmas from your apartment. You're Kory, right?"

Kory nodded. "We're decorating. My friend brought over some decorations."

"I'm Samaki," the fox said, extending a paw, "and this is my brother Ajani."

"I am Nani Ki-Yo," the mongoose said, taking his paw gently, "and my daughter Jenny."

Jenny and Ajani looked at each other and nodded acknowledgment. "Nice to meet you," Samaki said. "I was wondering what Kory's neighbors would be like."

"Come for dinner sometime," Nani said. "Let me know, Kory."

Kory promised to do so. "They seem like nice people," Samaki said once they were back in the apartment.

"I haven't really talked with them much," Kory said. "I guess Malaya met the son, Shara, and I met Nani a couple days ago."

"We should take her up on that dinner." Samaki unpacked the artificial tree and started setting it up. Ajani busily laid out all the ornaments, tail wagging.

"Yeah, sometime when you're over," Kory said noncommittally. He didn't mind getting to know his neighbors, but he couldn't help wondering what they would think of a gay couple.

The tree was pretty with the ornaments on it, even for an artificial one. Kory and Samaki hung Santa Fox in his bedroom near the dresser, stealing a warmer kiss as they did. Coming back into the living room, they were greeted with the overwhelming scent of pine; Ajani had hung all the scent-pines near the tree, right next to Kory's doorway. "Malaya's going to kill me," Kory laughed, but he left them up. The smell already reminded him of Samaki and Christmas, two of his favorite things.

They took Ajani to the Rainbow Center with them for the afternoon, where Kory gave Margo an update on the apartment and Malaya's job. Ajani got bored after only a couple hours and started to whine, so they had to leave the upstairs hallway half-painted.

"See you next weekend," Samaki said.

"And Christmas break after that." Kory couldn't wait. It promised to be the first quiet time he'd had in a long time.

"You and Nick are coming over for Christmas Day, right?"

"If you're sure..."

Samaki mock-glared at him. "Stop asking. It's a family holiday, yeah, but you're family."

"We have fruitcake!" Ajani yelled, strapping himself into the front seat Kory had just vacated.

"Oh, okay, if you have fruitcake..." Kory grinned and waved. "Thanks for the decorations. See you next week."

At school, things had settled down since the week Sal had exposed Kory's relationship. Though Kory and his former best friend still maintained a stony silence toward each other during the fifteen minutes they sat next to each other in homeroom, the rest of the school treated the news as old hat, at least, as far as Kory could tell. Even Geoff had moved on, in a remarkably short time, to other amusements than teasing the two of them. Kory kept a low profile, perfectly content with this state of affairs, aware of how quickly it could change.

Only Perry continued to skirt Kory. The last session of their college prep meetings was supposed to be this week, but Kory had finished his applications and sent them out, and without his mother's nagging insistence on attending the class, he saw no reason to waste his time on it. Mr. Pena had seen Kory in the hallway twice since the session he'd missed and hadn't said anything, so apparently he agreed.

So the only time Kory saw Perry was when he walked into English class, before he sat down. The wolf never met his eyes, and waited until he was gone before getting up. Kory told himself that he hadn't really liked Perry much anyway. That eased the sting of rejection.

In fact, things had settled down enough in that week before Christmas that when Kory noticed that Sal's muzzle was swollen, he broached the silence. "What happened to your face?" he asked.

The other otter continued to stare straight ahead as if Kory hadn't spoken. Then he reached up to touch the cut on his muzzle and said, "You talking to me?"

Irritated, Kory said, "Unless there's someone else in here with a fat lip."

"You could have one if you want."

"Fine." Kory stared forward at their homeroom teacher, a middle-aged spectacled bear, and waited for the bell to ring.

He mentioned it to Nick on Wednesday, when they went out for pizza, but Nick was more interested in talking about Christmas at the Rodens'. "Do you think they'll have the candied peppers again?"

Kory laughed. "Maybe. I don't think that was just a Thanksgiving thing."

"I think I can stay the whole afternoon and evening this time. Hey, are you coming to Christmas Eve Mass?"

"Yeah." Kory chewed thoughtfully. "I want to try to bring Samaki. And Malaya."

Nick inclined his head. "I guess you know her better than I do."

Kory laughed. "I don't think she'll enjoy it. But I want her to meet Father Joe."

"I want to come sit with you guys."

Kory shook his head. "You should stay with Mom."

"I know." Nick sighed. "I'll come say hi after." He indicated the last slice. "You want that?"

"Go ahead." Kory grinned. "How's swimming?"

"Fine," Nick crammed the slice into his mouth. "Mfth."

"Fifth in sophomores or the whole team?"

"Whole team." His brother swallowed. "I beat out Reg last week and coach moved me up."

"Hey, cool, congratulations."

Nick shrugged. "So Samaki's okay with you having your own place? Is he gonna move in there too?"

"Beginning of summer. It doesn't make sense for him to move before school's over."

"You guys still going to the prom?"

Kory picked up his soda and took a drink. "I dunno."

"When are you gonna decide? Isn't it in April like ours?"

"I'm not sure. We haven't really talked about it in a while. But we got our college applications done. Have you started looking at colleges?"

Nick grinned at him. "Depends where you go."

Kory felt warmth in his chest. "Don't limit yourself that way. You gotta go to the best place you can."

"I know," Nick said. "But I figure you will, too."

Kory's application to Whitford had been completed quickly and mailed the same day. The applications to Forester and State he'd taken more time over, worked on with Samaki back and forth, and still he didn't know which they'd be attending, with his current financial situation and Samaki's ongoing one. "What's right for me might not be right for you."

"Yeah, yeah." Nick slurped the rest of his Coke. "Just go somewhere with a swim team."

After dinner, they took the bus to Kory's place and spent a happy hour hanging the ornaments Nick had brought from home. If Malaya hadn't been at work, Kory thought, she would have thrown up her wings and grumbled, and indeed, when she did see the added ornaments, she said, "As if the pine scent wasn't bad enough. You know, I have to sleep next to those things."

"That one's been mine since I was five," Kory said of the gaudy snowflake Nick had hung right over the arm of the couch.

"Explains a lot," the bat said, but she didn't move the snowflake, even though Kory noticed it was just below her eye level when she hung upside down to sleep.

Samaki liked the ornaments too, when he arrived to pick Kory and Malaya up for Christmas Eve Mass. "Lot of church this year," he said.

"For you." Malaya hadn't put a coat on and showed no sign of being ready to go, even though Kory had talked her into saying yes the night before.

"Come on," Kory said to Malaya. "We're not making you go in the morning, too. Father Joe is really cool."

"I've had enough fire and brimstone to last my whole life," she retorted, her eyes fixed on "Frosty the Snowman."

"He's not like that, I told you."

She waved a wing at him. "Frosty's just about to get melted by the magician," she said. "I love this part."

Kory started toward her, but Samaki held him back. "If she doesn't want to go, let her." When Kory hesitated, he said, "Come on, it's Frosty. If you weren't so into this church, I'd stay and watch it."

"Next year," Kory said to Malaya, shaking a finger at her. She raised a wing as they left.

They crunched through the snow to Samaki's car. "So what changed?" the fox asked.

Kory slumped down in the front seat. "She got a card from her father, forwarded from Rainbow Center. I don't know why Margo sends those things along."

"She has to." Samaki started the car and pulled away.

"I know." Kory stared ahead at the city. The streets remained well plowed; that first snowfall had been only a couple inches. Still, it looked to him as though the streets had finally received their Christmas decorations. Even in his dirty downtown neighborhood, the snow frosting every awning and lamppost softened the cityscape's harsh browns and greys until the street glowed in the twilight. This was the first time Kory found the sight of his new neighborhood peaceful and soothing.

"What did it say?" Samaki asked.

Kory shrugged. "She wouldn't show it to me. It was a Christmas card, but knowing him, it was like, 'Don't bother enjoying the season of our Savior's birth because He hates you'."

Samaki shook his head. "I can't understand how she survived sixteen years with him."

"She almost didn't."

The silence following that remark was only broken by Kory's directions as they approached the church. "We can park in the lot back here."

Samaki pulled the car into an empty space. The two of them padded through the parking lot to the church entrance, where a trickle of people were filing into the church. As they turned onto the sidewalk, Kory spotted his mother's car, parked right near the front of the lot. His steps slowed enough that Samaki turned to look at him. "Nothing," he said, and kept walking.

The fox looked shrewdly at the cars and then back at Kory. "You going to be okay?"

"Yeah." Kory smiled and shoved his paws into his jacket pockets. "You're going to like Father Joe."

"I haven't talked to a priest in years," Samaki said.

"Well, the last guy we had here you wouldn't have wanted to talk to," Kory said. "But Father Joe is great."

"I can't wait to meet him."

Samaki followed him to the last pew, the only one that was nearly empty. The fox gazed around the church, his tail hanging down next to Kory's. They didn't brush them together, but the proximity of the warm black fur calmed Kory. He loved Christmas Mass and he wanted badly for Samaki to love it as well. The fox had told him that their church's Christmas celebration was a raucous, happy community gathering, and Kory was worried that the fox wouldn't like Father Joe's restrained service. Even though the holiday crowd was larger than at a normal Mass, the bustle and pre-service chatter still sounded tentative, subdued in the enormous space.

"Do I have to do anything?" Samaki whispered. "Or do we just sit here and listen?"

"There are a few responses," Kory whispered back. "I'll point them out in the book."

He opened up the hymnal just as a family of muskrats pushed onto the pew beside them. The twelve-year-old daughter was holding a portable game with headphones, which she played without a break as she walked up to Kory and sat down. The mother and father were having some discussion about Christmas dinner and relatives showing up. Samaki made a show of studying the hymnal, but Kory saw his ears flick toward the muskrats.

"Are there a lot more of your family showing up for Christmas than Thanksgiving?" he asked the fox.

Samaki shook his head. "Aunt Suma and Uncle Mike and my cousins will probably stay home, and my Uncle Ant is still back in Africa."

"Uncle Ant?" Kory giggled.

"He was the only one of the family born here, so they called him Anthony to try to fit in, but Mom thought he looked like an ant crawling around, so she called him that." Samaki grinned. "He's a black fox too."

"What's he doing in Africa?"

"Business connections," Samaki said, and then the service started.

The muskrat girl didn't put her game away until her mother slapped her, which was a good five minutes after Kory wanted to. With that distraction gone, he focused on the service and watched Samaki's reactions. They said prayers together, with Kory pointing out the appropriate responses, and sang Christmas carols. The muskrat girl, it turned out, had a beautiful voice, and loved the carols, but sat sullenly through the rest of the service.

Samaki smiled throughout, so that by the time Father Joe got around to his sermon, Kory's worries had vanished and he paid full attention to the sermon, a new one to him. Father Joe said that the true gift of the three Wise Kings was their journey, like the old saying "it's the thought that counts." They could have sent messengers with gifts, as was the custom, but they gave of themselves to bring the gifts to Mary and the baby Jesus. "So, this Christmas," he concluded, "we should give of ourselves, and be sure to appreciate the gifts that others give of themselves."

The muskrat girl was eyeing her game again. Kory saw that Samaki was smiling, and his tail did swing over to brush Kory's when Father Joe made that statement. "I like him," the fox mouthed, sending happy prickles through Kory's fur.

After the service, they sat quietly while the muskrat mother dragged her daughter out, the game already in her paws and flashing. Kory knew that Samaki was waiting for him to get up, but he was used to waiting until most of the congregation had left. He felt peaceful, sitting there while everyone else was leaving, and today, he also felt a little apprehensive, not wanting to meet the eye of anyone he knew while he was sitting with Samaki.

He saw a skunk in a thick coat and recognized one of his neighbors. He raised a paw as the family filed past, but got no response. Perhaps they had just not seen him. He kept his eyes down after that.

When the noise of movement had died down, he looked up and saw that the church was mostly empty. His mother and Nick had filed out past with the others. "Come on," he said to Samaki. "He'll be greeting in the foyer."

They hung back quietly just behind the large doors until most of the people in the foyer had dispersed. Father Joe had met Kory's eyes and beckoned him forward as the last of the crowd, a porcupine family Kory recognized but had never spoken to, walked out.

"So this is your friend?" the Dall sheep said as they approached him. "I'm Father Joe." He extended a hand.

"Samaki." The fox grasped the hand and shook, smiling. "I loved your sermon."

"Thank you. It's a pleasure to meet you finally." Father Joe looked back to Kory. "I was hoping you would attend."

"I wouldn't miss it." Kory smiled and nodded his head toward Samaki. "I get to go to his service tomorrow morning."

Father Joe inclined his head toward the fox. "Which church is yours?"

"Eastern Baptist, on Twenty-Fifth and Chestnut."

"I know it by reputation only. A good one, of course." Father Joe beamed.

"Kory!" Nick appeared from outside, grinning, and threw his arms around his brother. He was chilly from the outside air.

Kory returned the tight hug, full of warmth from the service and from seeing Nick. "Merry Christmas," he said.

"Ah, save that for tomorrow," Nick said. But his bright smile said he understood.

"When are you coming by?" Samaki asked.

Nick stepped back from his brother's embrace. "I figured around 2 or 3. Can you pick me up at the shopping center?"

"Sure."

Father Joe smiled. "I'm glad you'll be together on Christmas."

Kory nodded, but before he could say anything, a familiar voice called, "Nick."

Everybody fell silent. Kory turned toward the door, meeting the eyes of his mother. She stared at him, and then he saw her eyes flick past him, to Samaki. They hardened. "Nicholas," she repeated. "We're leaving now."

"Celia..." Father Joe began.

Her expression stopped him. "Merry Christmas, Father," she said coldly.

For the space of several breaths they stood, caught in a web whose lines of fear and anger Kory felt he could snap with just the right words, if he could find them. Samaki stared at the ground. Nick's tail curled behind him as he swayed from one foot to the other.

Kory couldn't believe how much older his mother looked. Her eyes were pinched nearly shut, her muzzle screwed up as though smelling something distasteful. Samaki breathed behind him, reminding him of her comment about the fox's musk. His own eyes narrowed, but he wasn't sure she even noticed. "Nicholas!"

Nick remained stubbornly at Kory's side. "I want to say Merry Christmas to Kory," he said.

It looked as though she might order him to come. Her eyes flicked to Father Joe. She opened her mouth and shut it again, arms crossing. "Then say it and let's go," she snapped. "I want you in the car in five minutes."

She seemed inclined to stay and watch them, until Samaki spoke. "Mrs. Hedley," he started, but at his words she turned quickly on her heels. "Merry Christmas," he called, but she ignored him, striding out of the church and out of sight.

The silence that followed her departure was heavy, but not uncomfortable. "That's what makes it so hard to forgive her," Kory said to Father Joe.

"Your forgiveness," the sheep said, "should come from your own heart, regardless of her actions."

Nick had been staring after his mother, and now turned back. "Can I go home with you tonight, Kory?"

"You shouldn't," Kory began, but Nick cut him off.

"I don't want to go home with her. How can she...why?"

Kory shook his head, turning instinctively to Father Joe. The sheep nodded agreement. "Go with your mother, Nick," he said. "Imagine how hard it would be for her to lose two sons."

"You don't have to live with her," Nick grumbled.

"And you do," Father Joe said. He smiled. "Merry Christmas, Nick."

"Merry Christmas, Father," Nick said. "And Merry Christmas, you two. I'll see you tomorrow."

"See you, Nick."

They stood there with Father Joe after Nick walked out to join his mother. Kory sighed. "I hope he doesn't get in trouble for that."

"It's Christmas," Father Joe said. "A time of forgiveness."

"I hope so." Kory glanced at Samaki.

The fox took Kory's paw in his and squeezed. Kory flinched at the public contact, but Father Joe's brown eyes held nothing but smiles.

At Samaki's insistence, Kory spent Christmas Eve with the Rodens. Malaya declined the invitation, saying it would be refreshing for her to spend a Christmas peacefully alone, reveling in the secular commercialism. Kory started to say something else, about not letting other people ruin Christmas for you, but Malaya cut him off with a wave of her wing. "I'm fine," she said. "Jesus, just go already."

Mrs. Roden had certainly prepared enough food for an extra guest; the dinner table was piled with a roast, two different chutneys, a sweet potato dish that Ajani and Mariatu had cleared out before Kory was done his first helping, a sort of vegetable stew that went over couscous and was apparently Kasim's favorite, and a chicken and kidney bean dish with diced onions that Kory decided was his favorite. He told Mrs. Roden so.

"Oh, I just threw that together," she said, her russet muzzle breaking into a wide smile. "I had leftover chicken and some beans and onions." Her ears flicked as though she were embarrassed.

"It's wonderful," he said sincerely.

He barely had room for dessert, a choice between mince pie with ice cream or a thick chocolate bread with a cream sauce. A lifetime of one-dessert rules restrained him to just the chocolate bread, but Mrs. Roden caught him eyeing the mince pie. She slid a piece onto his plate before he could protest, which he wasn't inclined to do anyway. "You're a growing boy," she said, her eyes sparkling.

"Thanks," Kory said, and in return made her beam again with the praise he gave to both.

After dinner, the family sat together in the living room, where Mr. Roden lit candles and turned on the Christmas tree lights. They sang a repertoire of Christmas carols, by the end of which Kory had lost his self-consciousness and was singing as loudly as any of them. Then, as they sat around sipping wonderful, rich, creamy hot chocolate from their mugs, Mr. Roden rummaged under the tree and started to pass presents around.

"Santa hasn't been here yet," he announced to the younger cubs, "but you get one present each tonight from your mother and me, and then we'll see what Santa brings tomorrow."

They squealed and grasped at the brightly-colored boxes he handed them. To Kory's surprise, Mr. Roden handed a blue-and-silver-wrapped box to him as well, a broad smile on his vulpine muzzle. "Merry Christmas, Kory," he said.

Samaki was grinning. "Oh," Kory said, suddenly worrying that he hadn't brought anything. "You didn't have to..."

Mrs. Roden waved a paw. "It's Christmas," she said simply.

He waited until the younger cubs had opened their gifts. Ajani had gotten a small figurine of some comic book hero, a scary-looking coyote; Kasim had gotten three packs of Digimon cards; and Mariatu a vixen princess doll.

"Go on," Mrs. Roden urged him and Samaki. "Open yours."

Kory waited until Samaki had revealed a thick book of the Best Journalism of the Year, and then opened his box, claws tearing the wrapping away to reveal a basic tool set, hammer, screwdrivers, pliers, wrenches. "Oh, I need this!" he said.

"I told them," Samaki beamed, his tail wagging against Kory's.

Mr. Roden smiled. "No house should be without proper tools."

"Thanks!" He picked up the small gift card on the wrapping with his name on it and turned it over, smiling at the oddness of seeing his name in Samaki's parents' cramped writing.

Mr. Roden took his wife's paw, their tails swishing contentedly as they sat back on the couch. Kory had never opened presents on Christmas Eve, but still, it reminded him of happy Christmas Eves with his mother and Nick, when their troubles were all blanketed by the delight of the season and they could talk happily together, sitting by their own Christmas tree with the snow glistening outside. They had water-borne ornaments, little Christmas-tree and reindeer floats that bobbed along the surface of the pool, caught the lights, and sparkled in a way that Kory had always found magical. Even after he'd lost some of his youthful delight in Christmas, he'd always loved the decorations and trappings. One Christmas, Nick had scattered tinsel on the water with the ornaments. His mother had scolded Nick, but had waited until after the holiday to clean it up, and oh, how pretty it had been. Kory and Nick had sat on the bridge with only the Christmas lights on, watching the sparkles in the drifting silver strands below.

The tinsel on the Rodens' tree blurred in his eyes. He wiped them with a paw and looked around to see whether anyone had noticed. Only Samaki was looking at him; everyone else was watching Ajani's coyote figure attack the princess doll, making Mariatu squeal in indignation.

"You okay?" Samaki asked softly.

"Yeah." Kory nodded, and then he was back here in the present, the memories receding. "Let's see that book."

They looked through the book together, and then it was time for bed, the younger cubs going willingly for once. "Kory," Mrs. Roden said, looking down from where she was following the three eager cubs, "we thought we'd put you in a sleeping bag in the boys' room, if that's okay."

"Sure." He grinned at Samaki as the two of them headed up. "Should I tell her we read the brochure?" he whispered.

Samaki elbowed him, his ears flattening. "Don't even!"

They set up his sleeping bag on the floor, pushing aside a pile of comic books and clothes so that he could stretch out. Ajani and Kasim helped, with Mariatu standing in the doorway, looking jealously on. "I want to sleep here tonight too!" she said. "Wanna sleep with Kory."

"You don't want to stay with us?" Mrs. Roden said, smoothing out the sleeping bag. "Are you sure?"

She was looking at Kory and Samaki. Kory said, "I think we could make a little room for her over there."

"Yeah," Samaki said. "She's small, she'll fold up, right?"

"No!" she squealed. "I don't fold!"

"Sure you can." Samaki indicated a space about a foot square between his desk and the side of his loft. "I bet you could squeeze into there."

"Mommy!"

"Sammy's just teasing you, Mari," Mrs. Roden said. "Go get the blankets from your bed and we'll set them up here." She started clearing away a pile of toys.

Ajani watched her with bright eyes from his top bunk. "Why doesn't Kory just sleep up with Sammy?" he asked. "Then there'd be plenty of room."

"Oh," Mrs. Roden said, "I don't think Sammy's bed is big enough."

Kory looked up, not wanting to meet Mrs. Roden's eyes. "I'm fine on the floor," he said, and thankfully, Ajani disappeared back into his bed and didn't pursue the matter.

Mariatu's head ended up a foot or so from Kory's when they were all in bed. Above them, the silhouette of Samaki's muzzle peered over the loft. "Good night," the fox said. He blew a kiss down to Kory.

"Night," Kory said. He raised a paw to his lips briefly and returned the gesture.

"Kory," said Mariatu softly.

"Hmm?"

"What do you think Santa will bring me?"

"I don't know." He turned onto his side to look at her. "What did you ask for?"

"She asked for a pony," Kasim said scornfully. "Like we could have a pony here."

"I dunno," Kory said. "Santa can be pretty creative."

Ajani laughed. "I know something about Santa this year."

Samaki said, "Ajani," warningly.

"I won't say it," Ajani said, but now Mariatu wanted to know.

"What?" she said. "What about Santa?"

Kory thought of one of the stories he'd told Nick. "Ajani knows how Santa gets into houses that don't have chimneys."

He saw Mariatu's eyeshine as her eyes widened. "We don't have a chimney," she breathed, as if just realizing it.

Kory told her the story of how Santa learned to walk through Christmas trees, so that as long as you had a Christmas tree, you could count on a visit from Santa. "Because Christmas trees are all connected in the Christmas forest," he said, "which Santa knows how to get to. So if you don't have a chimney, Santa will just land on your roof, step into the Christmas forest, and step around your Christmas tree to deliver your presents."

"Wow," Mariatu breathed. Kasim and Ajani were also leaning over their beds to watch him. He looked up to see Samaki's broad smile.

"All right now," Kory said. "Time to go to bed, or Santa just might pass this house by."

"He won't," Kasim said, but his face slipped back obediently with the others.

Mariatu said, again, "Kory?"

"Shh," he said. "Go to sleep."

"I'm happy you're here," she said, and her eyes slid shut.

"Me too," Samaki whispered down to him. Kory blew him another kiss, and closed his eyes.

Morning seemed to come almost immediately. He was awoken by Mariatu scrambling over him to get to the door. Ajani and Kasim's covers lay in a disordered heap on the floor, the lower bunk visibly empty, the upper one silent. Kory got up to his elbows in time to see Mariatu's tail disappearing out the door. He turned to see if Samaki were up yet, but there was no sign of the black fox.

"Samaki?" he whispered.

No answer. Yawning, he got to his feet and stood near where he'd seen Samaki's head, repeating the black fox's name. Still nothing. He set one paw on the loft ladder and climbed up far enough to see the lumpy outline of Samaki's sleeping form under the blankets. He climbed a little further up and grabbed the fox's hind paw.

"Psst," he said.

Samaki jerked awake. He turned, blinked, and smiled at Kory. "Morning," he said.

"Merry Christmas." Kory smiled.

Samaki sat up and leaned forward. Kory met him for a warm kiss. "Merry Christmas," the fox said. "And what a nice present."

They kissed again, and Kory slid his paw up the fox's leg. Samaki curled his tail around, and then a noise in the hallway broke them apart. For a moment, they looked sheepishly at each other, and then Kory said, "We should probably go downstairs."

The scene in the living room was at once familiar and strange. Kory could clearly remember running to the tree with Nick to open his presents, but they hadn't done it for years, and there had never been three of them all whispering loudly to each other at once. Mr. Roden, yawning on the couch, waved to the two of them as they came in. "You're late," he said softly.

"Mom sleeps in," Samaki explained to Kory in a whisper. "Dad's Christmas present to her."

"For a little longer," Mr. Roden said. "Have a seat if you don't feel like diving right in."

Kory preferred sitting on the couch, so he and Samaki watched the cubs empty out their stockings and root through the contents. Here, again, Kory felt a familiar yet strange twinge. Each cub had a full stocking, full of candy and small trinkets like superballs. He and Nick used to get stockings full of "small" things like headphones and video games. And the pile of presents, now he looked at it, hadn't grown appreciably from Santa's visit, as his family's did. But the cubs seemed to be enjoying it just as much as he and Nick ever had, sniffing at all the candies and exchanging them, all three little tails wagging in glee. When they'd woken up a little more, Samaki fetched his stocking and another one which Kory was surprised to see had his name on it. They shared the candy with Mr. Roden, who seemed particularly fond of the peanut brittle.

Church was a revelation to Kory, who'd been taught from childhood never to raise his voice during a service. Despite Samaki's repeated exhortations, and the loud, joyful congregation, he could not bring himself to sing at the top of his lungs. The preacher, a wolverine with a booming voice, sang that this day was Jesus's birthday, a day to celebrate His love. And then he said something Father Joe had never said: "Sing with love, and sing it loud!"

His reticence didn't prevent Kory from feeling happy inside. The younger cubs seemed to enjoy church a lot more than he remembered liking it at their age, though, he thought, if he and Nick had been allowed to make a lot of noise in church, they likely would have been more enthusiastic about it from a younger age as well.

Back at home, the cubs could no longer be kept from their presents and fell on them as soon as they'd loosened their church clothes. To his embarrassment, Kory had another present from the Rodens in addition to two from Samaki. He had only bought a couple presents for Samaki, and even though the Rodens waved off his half-hearted protests, he resolved to do something nice for them. Even with the new expenses of living, he thought he could figure something out.

Like for Samaki, he'd written out his rainbow poem, the one that Samaki said had drawn him to Kory, in calligraphy and put it in a nice wooden frame he'd found at the thrift store. Samaki loved it. He'd gotten Kory a small gift card to the bookstore near his apartment, "where we can go pick out something to read together and harass Malaya," and a hand-crafted wall-mounted shelf. "Made it in shop," he confessed.

"It's beautiful," Kory said, and nudged Samaki to open his other gift, a Starbucks gift card. "After we pick out those books, we can go get coffee." Samaki laughed, and they settled back onto the couch to watch the rest of the present opening. Kory felt the warmth of family around him, and it wasn't hard to let himself sink into it.

After most of the presents had been opened, Mrs. Roden padded to the kitchen to start Christmas dinner, while Samaki and Kory helped Mr. Roden clean up. Kory's cell phone rang just as he was breaking down a small cardboard box for the trash.

"Merry Christmas, Nick," he said as he picked up the call.

"She says I can't come," Nick said, miserably.

"What?"

His brother sighed. "I asked her when I had to be back and she said she'd made plans to go see Aunt Tilly, and that I have to go along with her."

"Oh." The warmth of family drained away from Kory. "Can you come over later?"

"We'll be gone all afternoon. You know she's just doing this because of yesterday."

He saw Mr. Roden and Samaki glance at him. Ajani looked up from his action figure as well. Kory held up a finger and walked out into the foyer. "Just because you talked back to her?"

Nick hesitated for so long that Kory wondered if the call had been dropped. "Nick?"

"It's not that," Nick said. "You don't know?"

"Did Father Joe talk to her?"

"No." Nick hesitated again, and this time when he spoke, he spoke in an urgent whisper. "It's because...she was thinking about asking you to come home for Christmas dinner. But she saw you bring Samaki to church, and seeing the two of you together, talking to Father Joe...she thought you were rubbing it in her face."

"She said that?" Kory had to unclench his paws.

"Yeah, pretty much." Nick made a noise that could have been a growl, or a sigh of frustration. "Sorry, Kory. I really want to be there."

"She thought that was about *her*?"

"I gotta go. We're leaving in ten minutes. Merry Christmas, Kory."

"I wish you could be here too, Nick," he said, realizing too late that he'd lost track of the conversation in his anger at his mother. "Merry Christmas."

Samaki appeared in the doorway, watching Kory stare at the cell phone in his paw. "Is Nick coming?"

Kory shook his head. "My mom..." he said, and then thumbed through his phone's stored numbers. "I'm going to call her."

"Maybe you should wait," Samaki said.

"They're leaving in ten minutes," Kory said. The familiar number glowed on his cell phone screen, a relic from his past staring at him. He stared at it, hating it, and then jabbed his thumb at the Talk button. *Connecting...*

Samaki hung back as Kory put the phone to his ear. It rang, once. Silence. Maybe she knew it was him and wasn't picking up. No; they had no caller ID on the land line. It rang again, and then he heard his mother's voice, pleasant and slightly out of breath. "Merry Christmas."

He snapped, "Why do you think everything is about you?"

He heard her breathing, but she didn't answer. He said, "I wasn't thinking about you at all when I took Samaki to church."

He couldn't hear her breathing anymore, just silence. He took the phone from his ear and saw a flashing "00:32," telling him the exact second she'd hung up. He hit Call Again and heard nothing but rings this time, and then his mother's pleasant voice on the voicemail. "Hi, you have reached the Hedleys. Nobody is here to take your call right now, but if you want to leave a message for Celia or Nick, we'll get right back to you."

Beep.

Kory snapped his phone shut. Breathing heavily, he leaned against the wall of the foyer. Samaki came back into the room, stopping a few feet away. Kory kept staring at his phone, and then forced himself to shove it into his pocket. He didn't understand why he suddenly felt a lump in his chest, pressure behind his eyes.

"We're having lunch in a few minutes," Samaki said quietly. "How did it go?"

"She took me off the voicemail," Kory said.

Samaki tilted his muzzle. Kory shook his head. "I mean, I know I don't live there. I just..." He stared down at the floor.

The fox came over to him. "You okay?" He put a paw on Kory's shoulder.

"I guess." Kory didn't want to burden Samaki with his problems, and moreover, he was afraid that if the fox hugged him, that expression of love would make him break down completely. He forced a smile onto his muzzle. "It's Christmas, right?"

Violet eyes full of sympathy looked back at him, and he almost broke down anyway. Samaki smiled, and nodded, and they went in to lunch.

The food was delicious as usual, but even through the friendly banter, Kory's mood was subdued, and for once he was glad to get home to the peace and quiet of Malaya. She didn't seem at all perturbed at having spent Christmas alone, nor did she force him into conversation. They ran out to McDonald's, ate a quiet meal, and then Kory went back into his room to try to work on homework. But he sat for an hour with his history book open to the same page, seeing his mother's phone number flashing on his cell phone, hearing the tension in Nick's voice, hearing her calm voicemail message that went on as if he'd never existed.

Fine, he decided shortly before ten o'clock, the window outside flickering with Christmas lights, headlights, and broken streetlights. If she wanted him out of her life, then he would be out and stay out. He wasn't sure what that would entail that he wasn't already doing, but it felt good to make the resolve, and it enabled him to finally turn the page in his history book.

Nick got away and visited for a few hours the next day. Kory didn't ask how he'd gotten away, and Nick didn't volunteer the information. Nick told him about the visit to their aunt's place, and Kory surprised Nick with some of the candied peppers he'd saved from the Rodens'. Nick had gotten Kory a small iPod shuffle, an expensive and surprising gift. He didn't want to accept it, but Nick's expression when Kory opened the box was so earnest that he didn't have the heart to refuse. Nick, for his part, loved the DVD set Kory had gotten him of the three surfer movies starring his favorite teen otter actress.

They had rigged up Kory's computer to show the first movie on the TV and were halfway through it when Samaki came over. He snuggled up next to Kory on the couch, while Nick and Malaya lay on the floor ogling

Jessica in the revealing swimsuit. Malaya was the first to say, "She's got great boobs," and after a grin at Kory, Nick confessed he liked her legs and tail better. After that, Kory and Samaki started to chime in on the relative merits of the parade of sexy guys she met on the beach, and by the end of it all four of them were laughing. Kory found himself a little warm, and a brush of his paw against Samaki's pants as they got up told him the fox was, too. But it was okay, surprisingly comfortable after the first swell of embarrassment had subsided.

They ordered Afghani food from the small café across the street as a holiday meal. Nick hadn't tasted it before but pronounced it delicious. This, Kory thought, looking around the table, this feels as much like family as the Rodens did yesterday, as much as I ever felt at home. There was a warmth inside him that had nothing to do with food.

Nick took the last yogurt-covered dumpling and gulped it down in two bites. Malaya was eating a slice of thick bread, slowly. Samaki nudged the last piece of chicken kebab toward Kory, with a grin. Kory waved a paw. "I'm full," he said, and Samaki didn't need any more encouragement to take it back. Nick grabbed another slice of bread himself and then sighed, looking at the clock.

"I should get back," he said, taking small bites of the bread and chewing slowly.

Samaki trailed his paw down Kory's arm. "Want a ride, Nick?"

"Hey, that's right. We could drop you off," Kory said.

Nick's ears perked up. He chewed a little faster. "Sure!"

On the ride back, he talked about wanting to explore Kory's neighborhood more, pointing out the silent shops in their ghostly white robes. As they approached Kory's mother's neighborhood, Nick fell silent. Kory didn't have to guess at what was on his mind.

They drove him almost all the way to Kory's house, stopping a block away to say their goodbyes. "Pizza on Wednesday?" Kory said, and Nick gave him a thumbs up as he trudged back through the snow.

They watched him get to the front door of the house and inside before pulling away. "Is he going to be in trouble?" Samaki asked.

"Probably." Kory felt the weight of the familiar neighborhood and turned his gaze inward, looking at the scratched upholstery of the glove compartment and dashboard. Even so, he could feel the presence of the houses he knew, the one that used to be home at the center of them.

Samaki stayed quiet until they were back on the edge of the downtown, and then he said, "It was nice spending the time with Nick."

"Yeah," Kory said. "Glad he liked the Afghan food."

Samaki nodded. "There are good things about your neighborhood. Drug dealers aside."

Kory checked to see whether the fox was teasing him, but Samaki was staring straight ahead at the snowy road, both paws on the wheel. "Malaya likes it."

Samaki chuckled. "I like Malaya, but I wouldn't take her recommendation. I think the filth makes her feel edgy."

Already, the snow from a few days ago had been tinged grey, even in the light of the streetlights. Kory pushed back his defensive reaction and said, "Probably. I don't mind it, though." He saw an overturned trash can, the striped tail of a raccoon protruding from a pile of blankets. The grimy windows of the nearby storefront barely reflected their headlights.

Samaki pulled into a parking space and turned the car off. Kory looked at the fox, smiling. "Have time to come in for a bit?"

"A bit, yeah." Samaki turned toward him, his smile white in the dim light. "I can stay the night."

Any remaining traces of melancholy vanished. Kory felt his ears perk straight up. "Really?"

Samaki nodded, grinning. "I guess that puts us on a schedule of, what, once a month?"

Kory laughed and unbuckled his seatbelt. "Until summer."

"Better than nothing," Samaki said, as they got out and he followed Kory up to the apartment. Kory didn't have to see the fox's tail wagging to feel his anticipation, as keen as his own. They'd barely gotten the door closed behind them when they fell together in a kiss, making Malaya snort.

"Get a room," she yawned as they scampered, giggling, into the bedroom.

Kory still wasn't used to sleeping naked, much less with a warm, soft fox in the same bed. After their initial, quick pawing, they found that neither of them could get to sleep, and in an hour or so they were both hard and panting, ready for another turn. They played with putting the condoms on each other, finding the sensations different. "At least it's easier to clean up. But I'm going to be sore in the morning," Kory giggled in the warm afterglow of his second climax.

Samaki kissed his cheek. "You'll be ready for number three in the morning," he said, and then, finally, they were both exhausted enough to fall asleep, curled up cheek to cheek, tails draped over each other's hips.

On the Friday before Kory's birthday, he got a pleasant surprise when he arrived home. On his bed was a thick envelope bearing the State University logo in the upper right hand corner. Malaya had left it there with a small handwritten note that said, "Guess this is good."

It was. The first thing he pulled from the ripped envelope was a letter congratulating him on his acceptance to State. The rest of the envelope contained a variety of forms and brochures that he would need to have in order to enroll. He glanced through them and then tossed them aside. At least, he thought with some comfort, their fallback plan was in place.

The pictures of State campus didn't look all that bad, actually. Low brick buildings dotted a green hillside by a lake. On another page, three rats and a pair of porcupines chatted in a sunny, open park. An entire two-page spread was devoted to athletics, with State's star football player from last year dominating. He shuffled through the pictures of students walking around, all looking happy to be there. Idly, he browsed the course catalog, skimming the English classes. They looked interesting enough, he supposed, though of course it was hard to tell just from the description.

He wanted to call Samaki right away, to share the good news and ask whether the fox had also received his letter of acceptance, but Samaki would be just sitting down to dinner now. Because he was now taking driving classes after school in addition to riding the bus for an hour, Kory didn't walk through his door until after 5. Well, he would tell him in a few hours when they had their regular call.

It wasn't worth his time to fill out the forms; he was still waiting for responses from Forester and Whitford. He did notice that the tuition asked by State was well within his means, especially since he'd qualified for limited financial aid. That reminded him that he would be paying for his college himself, and he felt a brief flash of self-righteous triumph. It would serve his mother right if he ended up going to State because that was all he could afford. That thought gave him conflicting guilt and pleasure, so he set the forms in a drawer and started working on homework.

Samaki had gotten his acceptance the same day. The two of them looked through the brochures together on the phone, admiring some of the buildings, laughing at one particularly silly picture of a marten who looked altogether too happy to be going to class, and talking about which dorm they would end up in. Kory hung up thinking that, really, it wouldn't be so bad going to State. Not with Samaki.

On the morning of his birthday, he walked through the doors of the school as he always did, knocked almost off his feet a moment later by a charging, grinning, Nick. "Happy birthday," his brother said, thrusting a card at him.

Kory laughed. "You're getting stronger. Workouts going good, huh?"

Nick shoved him. "G'wan, open the card."

"I'll wait 'til the party. You're coming this weekend, right?"

His brother's ears folded back, and his tail stopped its restless movement. "I can't. There's an away swim meet."

"Ah, that's right." Kory patted Nick on the shoulder. "Don't worry about it. I'll still see you for pizza tomorrow night."

"Yeah, but I wanted to give you this on your birthday." Nick's ears lifted somewhat. "Open it!"

Inside was a cute card signed by Nick, and a $25 gift card for online music. Kory smiled and hugged his brother. "Thanks!"

"Happy birthday," Nick said again, and waved as he ran to homeroom.

The only other acknowledgment that it was his birthday came when he stopped by the driving teacher's office to set up an appointment to take his license exam. Mrs. McKay kept him five extra minutes, telling him what an important milestone this was, how he was now an adult with adult responsibilities, encouraging him to read up on the local elections so he could vote responsibly in the primary, stressing what a tremendous responsibility it was to be allowed to drive a car, and so on until Kory made up an excuse and fled, the word 'responsibility' ringing between his flattened ears.

He had convinced Malaya, over the course of the previous week, to come to the birthday party the Rodens were throwing for him that weekend. Worn down to her last protest, she finally said, "I'll go, but if you want someone to laugh and play games..."

"I wouldn't have invited you," Kory said with a grin.

"Fair enough. But I'm working 'til 3 at the store, so I'll catch the bus over later."

Samaki picked Kory up at eleven on Saturday. By noon they were enjoying a simple but delicious informal lunch. Mrs. Roden had made sandwiches of a soft flatbread, reducing the spice in her dressing for Kory. He, Samaki, and the younger Rodens munched happily away while Kory selected games for them to play. It didn't feel like a birthday party to him, even when Mariatu kept putting a party hat on him, because he was just having fun with Samaki's family the way he always did. Apart from Malaya and Nick, he couldn't think of anyone else he'd want to be there to make it a Party.

The bat rang the doorbell a little before four. "Oh, good, we can have presents now!" Mrs. Roden said, smiling as she ushered Malaya into the living room.

Kory looked up from the Sorry! board to see Malaya grinning, one hand held behind her back. "You didn't have to," he said, surprised.

"I didn't mean to," she said. "But sometimes shit happens. Sorry!" Kory had shaken his head quickly and Samaki had jumped to cover Mariatu's ears.

"I heard that word before," Mariatu said dismissively.

Samaki raised his eyebrows and took his paws away. "You know you're not supposed to say it, right?"

Mariatu nodded. "Jenny Adams got in trouble for saying it and she had to go up in front of the class and write 'I will not use dirty words' a hundred times and the teacher said next time someone uses that word they get their mouth washed out with soap."

"I don't think Mom'll use soap," Samaki said.

Malaya grinned. "So anyway, I happened to find this as I was leaving, and then I ran into your postman on the way up the walk," she said to Samaki, revealing the two large envelopes she held in her right hand.

Mrs. Roden shrieked and then clapped her muzzle shut. A moment later, Kory saw what she had seen: the large "Forester University" logo in the upper right corner of each envelope.

"Mom!" Mariatu protested, holding her own ears now. The other cubs looked wide-eyed at Kory and Samaki as each grabbed one of the envelopes and tore it open. They read from their letters, each seeing the words the other was saying and jumping ahead.

"We are delighted to inform you--"

"--accepted to the Forester University class of--"

"--continue our tradition of diversity and excellence--"

"--response by March 1 in order to begin processing--"

"--new student orientation August 23rd—Mom!"

Samaki's letter fluttered to the ground as his mother, unable to restrain herself, threw herself on him and hugged him. A moment later, to Kory's surprise, he got a similar embrace. He returned her nuzzle and grinned as she jumped back, clapping her paws together. "What about the financial aid?" she asked Samaki.

He bent to pick up one of the other pieces of paper. "Here it is. *Pleased to inform you...as long as you meet certain academic standards...*" His eyes shone as he looked up, first at his mother, then at Kory. "Full ride."

His mother shrieked again, said, "Oh, let me call your father!" and then dashed from the room.

Samaki grinned after her, his tail wagging. "What about you?" he said, turning to Kory.

Kory sifted through the rest of his papers until he found the tuition one. "I qualify for some aid. A couple grants...looks like I've got about half of it paid for. I can make up the rest with the money from the online tutoring, and a work-study program." Hope swelled in his heart. "I can actually do this. Without...on my own, I can do it."

Ajani's little tail thumped the carpet. "So you're going to school together next year?"

Samaki reached out to ruffle his little brother's ears. "Looks that way, huh?"

Kory felt as though a door had finally opened, allowing him to see down the corridors of the future. He couldn't keep the smile off his face. "Wanna work on our acceptances?"

The rest of his presents, though nice, were an anticlimax. There was ice cream, and cake, and later, a delicious dinner followed by more cake. Once the younger cubs had gone to bed, Kory and Samaki sat up with Mrs. Roden, going through the packets they'd been sent: the maps, the forms that needed to be filled out, the course catalogs, the brochures for each of the on-campus dorms, and the listing of student groups.

"Look," Samaki nudged Kory, indicating the "Forester Lesbians and Gays" line on that last page.

Kory read the description. "Sounds all political."

"Might just be a place to meet other people," Samaki said. "And somewhere we could hold hands in public."

That would be nice, Kory thought. He tried to imagine the room full of students, boys holding hands with boys, girls with girls, he and Samaki in the middle, their paws clasped together, unremarkable. "We can maybe go once, check it out," he said.

A car rolled to a stop outside. "Your father's home," Mrs. Roden said, getting up from the table. "Let me put some coffee on. Kory, would you like some?"

"No, thanks."

"Some hot chocolate then." She didn't wait for an answer, but swept off to the kitchen.

Samaki put his paw atop Kory's, let it rest there warmly. "So...speaking of holding hands..." His eyes met Kory's. "You decided yet about the prom?"

Why not? He had just been thinking about how this family was all he needed, except for Nick, how comfortable he felt here. His reservations about going to Samaki's prom seemed distant and silly. Why wouldn't he trust the fox and believe that it would be okay, that nobody would laugh at them, or threaten them, or jump them outside the prom?

Still, he'd never gone out with Samaki as a couple, like that. He hadn't gone out as a couple since he and Jenny had gone to a dance with their friends at the Top Hat, a seriously lame club for teens. That hadn't been the best of experiences, and he was happier with Samaki in private.

But still, Samaki really wanted to go. And at the moment, the most important thing to him was to see Samaki's violet eyes light up.

"Yeah," he said. He squeezed Samaki's paw, and smiled.

The eyes did light up, Samaki's black ears stood straight up, and he lifted his muzzle and smiled back broadly. "You'll go?"

Kory nodded. "Yeah," he said again. "Yeah, I will."

Samaki leaned forward and kissed him, and didn't pull away even when they heard his parents come in. It was the best birthday Kory could remember.

"Good for you," Malaya said when he told her the next day. He'd stayed over at Samaki's, but she'd taken the bus home, refusing all offers of a ride with the assurance that she actually liked riding the bus. The Rodens didn't believe her, even when Kory assured them after she left that it was true.

"You think so?" Kory hadn't thought about the decision much until now. He was starting to wonder whether it had been a mistake. Of course, he was committed, so there wasn't much he could do about it, but that didn't stop him from worrying.

She had dropped from her bar onto the couch when he walked in, flipping agilely over in mid-air. Now she was sitting with her wings spread over the back of the sofa, looking up at Kory as he leaned against the kitchen counter. "Sure," she said. "I mean, why not, ya know? Fuck the system."

"The system?"

"The boy-and-girl system. The establishment. Toss me a Coke?"

Kory reached into the fridge. "This isn't a political statement," he said, as he lobbed the can to her.

"Sure it is." She popped the top and guzzled a good third of the can.

Kory folded his arms. "No, really. I only said yes because I want to go with him. I feel like..." He hesitated.

"You love him?"

"I feel like part of his family. So why not? I mean, he thinks it'll be fine. We won't get attacked or anything."

She burped, and settled back. "Doesn't matter what you think it is. It's definitely a statement. How many other gay couples you think will be there?"

"None." The thought depressed Kory. He looked down at the dirty kitchen floor, rubbed his upper arms with his hands, and tried not to think about it. The idea of making a political statement, of deliberately calling attention to himself, made him feel weighty and exposed. The air seemed very dry around him. "I'm going to go swim for a bit. Wanna come?"

Malaya laughed. "Dunk myself in water? On purpose?"

"Fine." He managed a grin. "The municipal pool sucks anyway."

It did, but it had been there that he'd met Samaki, a memory which came flooding back to him the moment he stepped into the locker room. Right there, by the dryers, he'd seen the sleek body, a tangible shadow with a bright white patch at its center, and another between its legs, drawing his eye for reasons he hadn't understood then. He stood, lost in the memory, until he noticed that the chubby older skunk standing at the dryer was looking askance at him. Ears burning, he turned back to his locker and slipped his swimsuit on quickly.

The water, warm and comforting, felt as natural as if he'd never left it. He swam lazily through the deep pool for a while, dodging guppies with ease and staying submerged as long as he could. A shadow thrashed toward him and he ducked instinctively out of the way as a wolf cub struggled by. The first time he'd met Samaki, it had been as a shadow in the water, hurtling toward him and sending him into the wall to avoid it. In the end, he hadn't been able to avoid the shadow or the brightness at its heart. He swam to the surface and rested, elbows on the edge of the pool, watching the wolf make his way laboriously to the other side.

Lots of non-aquatics here today. He watched them splash through the pool while the otters, beavers, and the lone mink flowed gracefully around them. It was rare for him to feel comfortable and confident; when he wasn't at the pool, he was thrashing around in an element he hadn't had enough training to navigate. But there was a small female wolf swimming with grace and ease, and in the other pool, a pair of middle-aged bobcats who looked like they'd been born wet, proving that one could adapt to a new environment. And two red fox cubs who reminded him of Ajani and Kasim surfaced only long enough to shake water from their ears before diving below again, while their mother watched tolerantly, reading a book from the poolside peanut gallery.

That's what he and Sal'd called it, all the years their friends were coming to the pool. At Caspian, the peanut gallery was a level above the pool floor and included a sandwich counter. Here, the parents sat in plastic deck chairs arrayed around a pair of vending machines. A mother wolf and raccoon were talking to each other and staring into the pool. Kory followed their gaze, but couldn't see any raccoons near where they were looking, and the only wolf there was the sleek female wolf who looked too old to be a daughter of the one on the chair. Maybe they were talking about something and just looking toward the pool? No, their muzzles moved back and forth as they talked. They could be watching the thrashing wolf cub, maybe?

Or they could be watching the bobcats, one of whom sat on the edge of the pool with his legs in the water, leaning down to the other. Kory glanced back at the wolf and raccoon and saw that they were indeed staring fixedly at the couple of bobcats.

Couple? Now he looked, he noticed the intimacy of their closeness, a couple inches closer than mere friends would sit, more solicitous than colleagues. They could be brothers, maybe. Or they could be partners.

The wolf cub, who had been on the other side of the pool, now launched himself past Kory, splashing and giggling, toward the bobcats. He was only a few feet away when the female wolf called out, "Remy! Remy!"

He stopped in mid-splash, lost his momentum, and disappeared under the water. The bobcats turned; Kory slipped off the wall, ready to swim over there, but the cub resurfaced a moment later and dog-paddled over to his mother. She leaned forward on her chair. "Don't play over in that end where I can't see you," she said, though the pool wasn't that crowded. Kory saw her eyes flick to the bobcat couple as she said it.

They had turned back to each other, and the one who was out of the water was massaging his calf. They hadn't noticed anything unusual about the wolf calling her son away from them, but Kory had. Part of him wanted to swim over there and ask her what she thought was going to happen to her son if he swam near a gay couple, and whether she'd known that he'd swum past a gay otter just a second before. Part of him wanted to slink back to the locker room and get out of here. So he let himself slip below the water, let its buoyancy hold him up, let its warm thickness block out the rest of the world.

Is that how it would be at the prom? Chaperones calling their children away from him and Samaki? How long would they be able to ignore it? At the prom, he wouldn't be able to just dive into the water to escape, not unless the gym floor opened up like in "It's a Wonderful Life."

The doubts resurfaced later, when he saw the bobcat couple in the locker room, already dry and changing. They weren't being affectionate, and nobody in the room was paying much attention to them. But as he watched them, he gradually saw their intimacy as a negative impression, all the deliberately casual actions leaving a void between them. It reminded him of walking through the city with Samaki.

He stepped into the shower and lathered up his fur with the shampoo he'd brought, getting the water and other scents out of it. So what would be the point of going to the prom? To be stared at? What would that prove?

Get a grip on yourself, he said. The prom's going to be all kids, and kids who know Samaki. He's probably out at school. There's no reason it should be a big deal. You've talked to Father Joe, and Samaki's parents, and Nick, and Sal...

And Sal had been okay, until he hadn't been. Kory pushed that memory aside, rinsing off and stepping out of the shower. Maybe he was making this all too difficult. He'd already agreed. What kind of boyfriend would he be if he backed out now? Likely it would be fine. He just had to trust Samaki and do his best not to think about it.

Fortunately, he had his driving test to keep him occupied for the next couple weeks, and Malaya didn't bring up the prom again during that time. She did ask what good it was to have his license if he didn't have a car, but Kory had a ready answer for that one. "Samaki has a car, and if I save up some money this summer, I could buy a used one."

"Public transportation is cheaper and way more fun," Malaya said.

"You can't smoke on the bus," Kory pointed out.

She grinned at him. "You don't smoke."

"If I get a car, you can smoke in it as long as you keep the window open."

She rubbed her chin. "Okay. Point." She opened the practice manual again. "You better keep studying, then. What is the speed limit on a residential road where no sign is posted?"

The written test proved to be the easy part. Kory only missed the questions about insurance and an obscure parking law. He still felt nervous, because the questions had been so easy and the driving test was yet to come.

They'd promised him a 2:15 spot when he'd arrived at one, but at 2:30 he was still sitting in the waiting area, and the ocelot behind the counter hadn't so much as glanced his way. He wanted to ask her when he'd get his test, but the line at her counter never went away. Just when it had gotten down to one person, three more would march up.

Kory wasn't feeling all that comfortable waiting. He'd made his appointment at the downtown DMV because it was walkable from his apartment, but the convenience now seemed less important compared to his uneasy feeling. A wolf who kept scratching at his side wandered back and forth, seemingly without a purpose, his patched green jacket stained and frayed. When he came close to Kory, the otter could hear low mumbling, but couldn't make out any words. The smell of the wolf made his nose wrinkle, and then he worried that the wolf had seen it. And two seats over from him, a young marmot was smoking next to his overweight father, both dressed in plain white t-shirts and jeans with holes in the knees.

Silly of him to feel uneasy, he thought. After all, these were his neighbors now. He knew they were poorer than the people who lived near his mother. It was just that seeing it close up, looking at the shy young ferret holding the baby and wondering if she were any older than he was, looking at the grey fox with the twisted, useless paw, made him uneasily aware of all the advantages he'd had that they didn't, and made him feel guilty for having them, even if he didn't have many of them any more. Would the ferret be going off to college? Would the marmot? He fixed his gaze back on the ocelot at the desk and tried not to think about those questions.

What seemed like an hour later, he looked up at the clock and found that it was only 2:40. Frustrated, he grabbed one of the pamphlets they had lying around and buried his nose in it, trying to read, but unable to get past the title, Handbrake Handy Do's And Don'ts. Instead, he tried to review in his mind the driving lessons he'd taken with Mrs. McKay. Three-point turns. Check your mirrors before starting out. Check your mirrors regularly while driving.

A familiar voice caught his ears. "...can't believe this is taking so long."

He caught a glimpse of a pale green dress and the faintest whiff of skunk, along with a musky perfume. Along with the voice, the scent clicked into place for him: Flora McGuister, one of the other students in his driving class. For a moment, he debated whether to say something, but the decision was made for him.

"Kory?"

He put the pamphlet down and looked into Flora's black-and-white muzzle. Behind her, an older skunk, obviously her mother, was looking disapprovingly at the ocelot behind the counter. "Oh, hi," he said.

She plopped down beside him. "I didn't know you'd be coming to this DMV or we could've come together." He opened his mouth to answer, but she gestured at the older skunk, still standing. "I stay with my mom on weekends and my dad during the week so I can take the bus to school. But I wanted to take the test with my mom. So do you live down here too?"

"Uh...yeah," Kory said. "I—we moved a couple months ago."

"Cool. You go to some of the shops down here? There's that bookstore on Badger Square."

"I've been there." The bookstore was right near Rainbow Center, much closer to there than to here or to his apartment. He glanced at the ocelot. She'd just called the marmot up to the counter. He was sure he was next.

"I love that whole area. The thrift shop is great. I found this amazing purse there." She held up a small purse, green leather covered with yellow spangles.

"That's cool," he said. "I've been to the thrift store a couple times."

She looked up and down his shirt and pants. "Don't buy clothes there, though."

"I might." He'd actually been thinking about it. "I don't know if I can get away with it."

"I'm sure you have a good fashion sense," she said.

He blinked, not sure he'd heard her correctly, but before he had a chance to ask her anything, the ocelot behind the counter called, "Kory Hedley."

"See ya," he said, lifting a paw as he got up.

She waved back. "Good luck!"

His tester, a bear who crammed into the passenger seat next to him and said nothing more than, "Let's go," made him nervous from the start. Besides that, he was still worrying about what Flora had said. He'd only known her in passing until the driving class. Of course she could have heard what everyone else in the school knew, but did she mean that he had to have a good fashion sense because he was gay? Or did she think he had a good fashion sense because of how he was dressed?

He realized he hadn't checked his mirrors since getting into the car, and did so quickly. For the rest of the test, he tried to focus on the bear's grunted instructions. He only got confused once, when the bear told him to turn and he went right instead of left, into a shopping center. The bear ticked off a mark on his clipboard but didn't stop the test. And when he got to the end, he glanced over to see the large paw writing a "9" on the board.

His spirits soared. 9 points off was a passing grade, easily enough to get him his license. He wished Flora were still sitting in the waiting room when he got back in, because he wanted to tell someone right away and the DMV didn't allow cell phone use inside. All through the final paperwork for his provisional license, he fidgeted from foot to foot, and when the ocelot had handed him the paper and told him his real license would be in the mail in two weeks, he practically sprang out the door, his thumb on the phone.

"I got it!" he crowed the moment Samaki picked up the phone.

He could picture the fox's grin without having to see it. "Yeah!" Samaki yelled back. "When do you want to take our car for a spin?"

Kory beamed. "How about tonight?"

Eight hours later, when Mr. Roden had come home and given Samaki the car, the fox dropped the keys into Kory's paw. "Don't crash it."

Kory grinned, to hide the nervousness he found himself feeling. "We can just go down to the river, if you want."

Samaki's teeth flashed in the light of the streetlamp. "What do you want to do down by the river?"

"Just drive there." Kory sat in the driver's seat and put his paws on the steering wheel as Samaki slid in beside him.

"Aww." Samaki closed his door.

Kory checked and adjusted his mirrors, looked for the location of all the signals, and adjusted the seat so his shorter legs could reach the pedals. "You want to do something out there when we have a nice warm bed to come back to?"

"Point," Samaki said. "I like brushing in bed better anyway."

"Me too." Kory turned the key in the ignition. He'd driven before, but this was his first time without an adult, and it was Samaki's car. He turned the key, gave the car a little gas, and promptly stalled the engine. Face warm, he tried again, and got it rolling on the second try.

Once out of the main downtown area, he managed to relax, unclenching his paws from the steering wheel and feeling tension he hadn't realized was there drain out of his arms. Samaki directed him down to the small park by the river, remaining otherwise quiet. Kory supposed he remembered what it was like to drive for the first time, though on their first drive down to the river, the fox hadn't seemed nervous at all.

But Samaki was like that, more confident in unknown situations, at least on the outside. Kory had only seen him really nervous on the night he'd confessed his attraction to Kory, the first night they'd slept together.

In the darkness of the parking lot by the river, Kory stopped the car and exhaled, turning the key and letting his head lean back. "Very nice," Samaki said, and leaned across the seats to kiss Kory's cheek.

Kory turned his head and met the kiss with his muzzle, his tongue brushing the fox's and then curling around it warmly. Their paws met, fingers interlocking, holding each other tightly. He felt again the safety and security of the fox's embrace, the warmth surrounding them like water when they were together like this. When Samaki tried to pull back from the kiss, Kory pressed forward, not wanting it to end.

But eventually, it did. Samaki's eyes sparkled in the dim light of the car. "Sure you don't want to get out?"

Kory grinned. He could feel the pressure in his groin urging him to do just that, but, "we've got a bed to go home to," he reminded Samaki and himself.

"True enough." Samaki dangled his paw behind the driver's seat, brushing it along Kory's tail.

Kory rested his own paw on the fox's thigh, looking out at the shadows around the parking lot without seeing them. "So what's the prom going to be like?"

"You know what proms are like. Some lame theme, some lame music, a bunch of kids dancing. Drinking in the parking lot afterwards. The beginning of a new generation of public school students conceived that night."

"You guys don't get sex ed?"

Samaki laughed. "If you want to call it that. The 'state-approved' sex ed is basically 'don't let your filthy bodies touch each other until they've been washed clean by the purity of marriage.' We call it 'sex propaganda' in the journalism club."

"Oh," Kory said. "They pass out condoms in my school. It's like, we know you're going to do it anyway, so you might as well be safe."

Samaki nodded. "My mom says that's how schools should do it." His paw slid up and down Kory's tail, making the otter shiver. "Course, they don't even mention anything about couples like us."

"Yeah, not in my school either." Kory sighed. "So do I have to get you a flower or something?"

"A corsage?" Samaki grinned. "Sure, I'd like one. Don't get anything smelly."

"I'll get a rose and dip it in perfume." Kory giggled and squirmed as the fox's paw tickled his tail. "Okay, okay. What about a tux?"

"We can rent those. I'll find a place. We'll go get fitted in April."

Kory looked out at the night again. "It's getting a little chilly. Want to get back?"

The fox withdrew his paw and brushed Kory's groin. Kory felt the pressure on his hardness through his pants, pressed up into it. Samaki chuckled. "Very much so."

They barely said hi to Malaya upon getting back to the apartment, tumbling through the living room into the bedroom. Kory heard her mutter, "Boys," as he closed the bedroom door, Samaki's paws around his waist undoing his pants already.

They fell to the bed together, the last remnants of their clothes shed moments later. Samaki stroked Kory's hardness warmly up and down, fingerpads sliding along the hot flesh with gentle passion. Kory took the fox's erection in his own paw, savoring the heat as they kissed again and again, bare fur to bare fur, pressed as tightly together as if they'd been away for months.

Feeling the warmth of the fox's tongue, Kory came to a decision and broke the kiss, pushing the fox onto his back and grinning. "Tell me if I'm doing this wrong," he said, sliding down the trim body, nuzzling the white chest ruff, the tight black stomach, and then the white patch of fur between the sleek, muscled legs, which parted as easily as Samaki's muzzle had, allowing him to crouch between them.

"You're doing fine," Samaki murmured. His tail twitched against the bed, paws working into the sheets.

Kory brushed his muzzle against the dark shape of the fox's shaft, lying hot and ready against the white fur surrounding it. He touched it tentatively with his tongue and then licked more confidently, remembering how Samaki had always started with him and trying to imitate that.

In moments, the fox moaned encouragement, his shaft bouncing up under Kory's licks, and Kory hesitated only a moment before plunging his muzzle down over the whole thing.

It was cooler than he would have thought, but then, the inside of his muzzle was warm. He tried, again, to remember how Samaki had pleasured him with his muzzle, but the best he could remember was to keep his teeth well away from the delicate skin. Samaki didn't seem to be complaining at all about the way he was doing it, so he kept on, and only grazed the fox with his teeth once.

The problem was, Samaki didn't seem any closer to finishing. After a few minutes of the warm shaft sliding up and down past his lips and tongue, Kory's jaw was starting to ache. He let the fox slide out of his muzzle and licked his damp lips.

Samaki lifted his head and smiled. "That's great," he said.

"Can you finish that way?"

"It might take a while," Samaki admitted. "Try using your paw."

"I know I can do that," Kory said, wrapping his fingers around the slick warmth. He was pleased by how well lubricated it was, the ease with which his paw slid up and down.

"Rrrrurf," Samaki said, panting. "I mean, with your muzzle on the end. If you want to."

"Oh." Kory bent back down, letting just his lips cover the fox's tip while his paw stroked.

That was easier on his jaw, and more fun. Samaki made some whining noises he'd never heard before, and in what seemed like no time, the fox's well-muscled legs were tensing, his back arching, his tail bristled out. Kory suddenly felt apprehensive, and lifted his muzzle away just in time, as his paw drew the fox's climax from him, getting coated in the sticky mess as he pumped away.

"Sorry," he said as Samaki lay back, panting, on the bed. He lifted his paw and reached for a towel to wipe it off.

The fox grinned. "For what?"

Kory licked his lips, which were still very wet. "I wanted to, I just..."

Samaki patted his paw. "Don't worry about it," he said. "It still felt good."

That didn't completely drive out the guilty feelings, but it did let Kory relax. He smiled as he finished cleaning Samaki's fur, dragging his claws across the fox's damp stomach. Samaki rested only for a couple minutes before pushing Kory down to the bed and straddling him, taking Kory in his paw and stroking gently. Kory had been half-afraid that Samaki would take him in the muzzle, as if to show what a better boyfriend he was, but the fox simply slid his warm paw up and down with that nice familiar motion until Kory cried out and bucked against Samaki's weight, feeling his body shudder and spark, the warm rush that had built in him exploding free.

Guilt and worry were gone, nothing left but the fading warmth inside him, replaced by the warm black fur at his side. The fox's slender muzzle nuzzled his, their paws twining as they sank together to the bed and fell asleep.

On his way to the bus stop Monday morning, he was lost in reminiscing about Saturday night, resolving to try to let Samaki finish in his muzzle next time, when he vaguely registered a car pacing him along the street. He looked over and saw Flora's black-and-white muzzle grinning at him. When he waved, she gestured at him to get in.

"I was honking, like, forever," she said. "You musta been really lost in daydreams. I get like that sometimes, but it can be dangerous walking around the streets here. What were you thinking of?"

"Uh, school," Kory said, willing his sheath to fall in line with his story. "What's up?"

"I passed! I mean, obviously. So Mom let me take the car in this morning. Want a ride to school?"

He hesitated, more because it was a change to his routine than for any other reason. Flora said, "I know it's cold, but we can keep the windows open if you want."

"Oh, no, I don't mind," Kory said. "Sure." He got in next to her. Really, the smell of skunk wasn't that much worse than the odor of fox in Samaki's car.

"This is so much fun." Flora checked her mirrors twice before pulling away from the curb. "My mom let me drive with her in the car, but this is the first time I've been on my own."

Kory checked the car clock. "We're gonna be really early."

"Maybe not," Flora said. "I wanted to give myself a lot of extra time to be careful. My mom wanted to come with me, but she had to work early, so I'm going to drive to her office over lunch and she's going to drive me back to school." She came to a full stop at the stop sign and waited as someone else came to a stop and then continued through on the cross street, rolling slowly forward and checking both ways until she was completely clear of the intersection.

"You could've gone before him," Kory said.

"I know. I have time, though. I don't want to get in an accident." She answered without any irritation, speeding up slowly. "I'm mostly worried about merging onto the freeway. I did it a couple times with my mom, but never at this time of the morning. Have you driven on the freeway?"

Kory nodded. "But only late at night. And only once."

"Did you go driving with your mom at all? My dad wouldn't take me. He doesn't want me driving. He thinks it's dangerous." She snorted.

"No," Kory said, craning his head back to check the traffic they were merging into.

"I noticed she wasn't at the DMV, or maybe she was just in the bathroom, but my mom asked why you were there by yourself. I thought I heard you weren't living with your mom any more but I didn't know why."

Kory turned forward and fidgeted with his book bag. "Uh, well, it was just...she's going through some stuff..."

"I don't want to pry," Flora said. "I was just wondering if, you know, you moved in with your boyfriend or what."

Kory's fur prickled all over, as though he'd walked out into the winter air directly from soaking in the pool. He felt his breathing quicken. "We take the Second Street exit to get to school, right?"

Flora looked ahead and nodded. "That's how I usually go. I'm sorry, if you don't want to talk about it or if you just broke up or something, that's cool. I don't want to be a pain, just talking. I know when I broke up with Kel I just wanted to talk to anyone about it. Did you break up?"

"No," Kory said, "it's..." He felt trapped, and wished he hadn't gotten into the car.

"It's cool," Flora said. "I saw you guys together downtown in the fall. He's pretty cute. But he doesn't live downtown?"

"No," Kory said. "You saw us?"

"Sure," Flora said. "I was running an errand for my mom, and you brushed muzzles with him and then got on the bus. You had to stand almost on tiptoe. It was cute."

Kory wasn't sure he could recognize Flora half a block away, let alone however far away she'd been from him at the time. He tried to recall all the times he'd gotten onto the bus after volunteering at the Rainbow Center, and whether there'd been a skunk nearby for any of them. "He's just a friend."

"That's what I thought," Flora nodded. "I mean, maybe he was European, right? They brush muzzles all the time. But then when Vera said Geoff Hill was making jokes about Sal being your boyfriend, I said, oh, I bet that was his boyfriend."

Kory knew Vera a little better than Flora, a plump weasel who liked to talk almost as much as Flora did. She'd been one of the ones he hadn't talked to since his outing at school. Through the almost-nauseating feeling of his private life lying out in the open, something nagged at him. "Wait a minute. You didn't hear it from Sal?"

Flora shook her head. "He hangs out with those tech school kids." She slowed on the off-ramp, taking the wide right turn onto Second Street.

"Oh, geez." Kory put a paw to his muzzle.

"What?" she said, stomping on the brake and turning in alarm to face him. The car slewed to the left, snapping her attention back to the road. She grabbed the wheel and over-corrected, sliding right on the slick road and coming to a stop fifteen feet short of the bottom of the ramp. "Don't do that!"

"Sorry!" Kory's heart was pounding, though it had been only a minor slide and they hadn't been in any danger.

Flora inched toward the light. "What's the matter?"

"Nothing," he said. He couldn't figure out how to ask her whether she'd been the one to out him at school or not, if it was her innocent word that had turned Geoff Hill's rumors from speculation into fact. "I just, uh, remembered that we had another bunch of homework problems to do."

"Oh, I'd forget my homework all the time if my mom didn't give me a PDA. I have to enter all my homework and it syncs with a website and she checks it every night and sends me e-mail to make sure I'm working on it." She chattered on all the way to the school, while Kory replayed his conversation with Sal in his head, desperately searching for an admission of guilt. The words of several months ago, fluid and slippery, refused to accommodate his need.

As usual, Sal ignored him in homeroom, but this time Kory didn't let it go. The effort it took to break the months of silence surprised and saddened him. "I want to talk to you after school," he said.

"Ooh la la," Geoff Hill said behind them.

Sal turned to the raccoon. "Shut the fuck up," he hissed, and then looked at Kory. "Both of you."

"Mr. Lafferty," Geoff called, raising a paw. "Sal used the f-word."

The bear looked up from his desk and sighed. "I didn't hear it."

"I did," Geoff said.

Mr. Lafferty looked at Sal. "Did you curse at Mr. Hill?"

Sal folded his arms. "Yeah," he said. "He was asking for it."

With another sigh, the bear pulled a paper from his desk. "All right, that's one detention. Come to this room after final period to serve it."

Kory had a flash of inspiration. He turned to Geoff Hill. "You're a fucking asshole," he said.

The raccoon raised his paw again, and Kory sat back in his seat, grinning at Sal.

Detention was served in their homeroom, but without assigned seats, so Sal sat on the opposite side of the classroom from Kory. After an hour of quiet study time, Sal sat and waited for Kory to leave until Mr. Lafferty told them both to get out. Kory got up at the same time so Sal couldn't avoid him as they left. "I'm sorry," Kory said.

"You think I care?" Sal said.

"I don't know," Kory said. "I just don't want to be mad at you if you didn't do what I'm mad about."

Sal turned, one paw on the outer door. "Didn't seem to matter to you before."

"You never told me otherwise!"

Sal just looked at him and walked out towards the parking lot. After a moment, Kory followed.

"I apologized! What's the problem?"

Sal didn't even turn, just waved a paw back at him. "Forget it."

Frustration mounting, Kory almost turned around right then. He'd been mad at Sal for so long that it would be easy just to go back to that, to let everything settle back where it had been. But the uneasy nagging feeling that had started that morning in the car with Flora had been growing all through the day, and he knew himself well enough to know that it wouldn't just go away, that he would feel it every time he looked at Sal. "Stop being such a fucking asshole!" he yelled.

Sal turned and looked coolly at him. "Shut up."

"Then stop being a self-righteous prick." Kory had intended to stand his ground, but the next thing he knew, he was lying on the ground, gasping for breath, clutching his stomach where Sal had punched him.

"Stay the hell away from me," Sal said, standing over him and pointing a finger down at him. "It's bad enough I get in fights about you every week, I don't want to have to listen to your fucking apologies. You had your chance, you knew what had happened without even asking me. Well, fine. I told everyone, you happy now?" He lifted his head. "Hey, everyone!" he yelled to the empty parking lot. "Come look at the faggot!"

"Fights?" Kory gasped.

"Go home," Sal said. "Stop trying to be friends again. It ain't gonna happen."

Kory struggled to get up, but by the time he got to his feet, Sal's car was peeling out of the parking lot.

He didn't tell anyone about what had happened. Nick and Samaki had long since given up asking if he and Sal would make up, and Malaya had never asked to begin with, so nobody Kory talked to was likely to ask. The punch in the stomach left no physical damage, not like he'd seen on Sal's muzzle.

What he did do was ask Flora, when he saw her in the hallway, whether she knew of any fights Sal had been in. Her odor got stronger, or maybe it was just the ventilation in the hallway bringing it to his nose. "Look," she said, "it's nothing to do with you anyway. It's just the way those kids are."

"What kids?"

"Oh, come on." She motioned for him to walk with her. "I can't believe that we can see 'Queer Eye' on TV—I used to love those guys—and there are still people who think that—well, I don't know what they think. It's stupid. They're stupid." She looked sideways at him. "Nobody really cares, you know that, right?"

Kory shook his head. "I care."

"Well, of course, but I mean, it doesn't make any difference. I mean, to most of the kids. I mean, to the ones who really know what's what. You know, like me and Vera and Marci, and Rick Novis and Chris Carkus..."

"Chris Carkus knows who I am?" Kory snorted.

"Sure. Now he does. Anyway, just because these kids are acting like grade-A dipwads doesn't mean anything."

"What kids?"

"The tech kids," Flora said. She'd stopped at a classroom. "This is my class. Look, if you want to talk about it, let's meet downtown this weekend, okay? I'll come down to your area if you want."

Kory was slated to go to the Rainbow Center Saturday morning. He gave Flora his cell phone number and told her to text or call him Saturday afternoon. "Promise," she said, and dove into her class as he scurried to get to his on time.

He and Samaki were just propping up the new set of bookshelves they'd been varnishing to dry, while the kids washed the brushes, when Flora called. Kory fumbled for his phone, leaving Samaki holding the shelves, and arranged to meet Flora at the Starbucks by the thrift store.

"I thought that was our place," Samaki said teasingly as they got the last piece of scrap wood under the shelves. "Now you're meeting strange women there?"

"I told you, it's just something from school." Kory forced a grin.

"Can I meet her?"

"What," Kory said, "don't you trust me?"

Samaki glanced at the kids, whose backs were turned, and then brushed a finger along Kory's stomach. "I trust you," he said. "Just thought I could tag along, but it's okay, I can go home."

They were outside the center and walking toward Samaki's car before Kory managed to resolve the struggle in his mind. Samaki had turned to say good-bye to him, but he said, "You really want to come along?"

The fox considered this question, or at least appeared to. "Yeah, sure. If you're okay, I mean. I don't want to force you..."

Kory shook his head. "She already knows, and she saw you once."

"So the secret's out."

They'd started walking through the slushy snow toward the thrift store. "Actually," Kory said, "I think she's the one who outed me at school."

"I thought Sal did that."

"Me too. But he...I don't know now. I don't know whether he did or not."

"But you think this girl—Flora?—might have?"

Kory nodded, slowly. "She said she saw us here, getting on a bus. And she talks a lot. I'm sure she didn't think about it."

Flora sat at a table in the corner, alone. Kory suspected that the rest of the patrons were avoiding sitting near her in the close and stuffy Starbucks, because it didn't seem likely that Flora would have chosen to be so isolated. If it bothered her, though, it didn't show; she greeted them with a cheery wave and beamed at Samaki.

"So nice to finally meet you," she said when he introduced himself. "I'm Flora, Flora McGuister, I saw you once from a ways away. You're even cuter in person. Kory's very lucky."

"Thanks." Samaki grinned, and even Kory couldn't help a smile. "Nice to meet you, too."

"You guys want to get drinks?"

"I'll go." Samaki stood. "Your usual?"

Kory nodded. Flora reached over and patted his arm as the black fox walked toward the counter. "He knows your usual. That's so nice."

"Yeah." Kory glanced around the coffee shop.

"Oh, nobody's watching," Flora said. "Nobody cares, not down here. That's why I love this area. It's so *diverse*, you know?"

Privately, Kory thought that Flora probably wasn't a great judge of what people cared about, and people certainly seemed to care about her scent down here. "So, what did you want to tell me?"

Her muzzle twisted into a grimace. She took a sip of her drink, which Kory couldn't identify over the strong musteline scent, and set it down. "People are stupid," she said. "You just shouldn't pay any attention to them."

"I know that already," Kory said. "But Sal's my friend—he used to be, anyway—and I want to know what's going on with him. And he won't tell me."

She sighed. "I guess from what I heard...now, keep in mind this is from Gregory Barton, and I don't know him all that well, only his brother is one of the vo-tech kids. They don't get along great together, but his brother did tell him a couple things, and then I had to ask him one more and I'm not sure he got it right, but..." She took a breath. "Anyway."

Samaki walked back to them with two steaming cups. "Hot chocolate, full fat," he said as he placed one in front of Kory, "and nonfat hazelnut latte," as he sniffed the other and sat down, cupping it in his paws. He looked from Flora to Kory. "Sorry, go ahead."

Flora played with her own cup, sipping and then moving it from paw to paw. "I was just telling Kory about the vo-tech kids. I guess when they found out about Kory being gay, they started giving Sal a hard time. And it stopped for a little while, but then one of them...Bobby something...started making these photoshopped pics of Sal's head on naked guys. And he's in graphic design, so they were pretty good. And then lately he got hold of some of your pictures, too, Kory, so he's been making pictures of you and Sal in porn and passing them around."

Kory felt a moment's uneasiness at the thought of his face on pictures, but it wasn't as bad as he'd thought it would be. He saw Samaki watching him. "That seems pretty tame."

Flora nodded. "But from what Greg said, they're just not letting up. And Sal isn't helping; he keeps reacting to it and getting in fights. I guess even the guys who used to be his friends pretty much leave him alone now."

"Poor guy," Kory said. Samaki sipped his latte and said nothing.

"It's just stupid," Flora said again. "Nobody in the rest of the school is giving you a hard time."

"I was always pretty much alone," Kory said. It occurred to him that what Sal was apparently now living was Kory's own nightmare, as if he'd left it behind in Sal's house when he moved out and it had fastened itself to the other otter. He thought about Sal saying that they wouldn't be friends again, and thought he felt echoes of that same fear Perry had shown. Since Christmas, the wolf had approached him once or twice, but Kory couldn't shake the memory of the cringing, whining conversation they'd had, so he hadn't encouraged the wolf's efforts.

She turned to Samaki. "Are you out at your school?"

The fox tilted his paw from side to side. "I don't wear pride jewelry, but my friends know."

"And they don't care, right? They don't start fights and make nasty pictures?"

Samaki shook his head. "They're cool."

"I thought you were, like, out out," Kory said.

Samaki shrugged. "I don't make a big secret of it."

"Didn't you date a guy in your class for a while?"

The fox's ears flicked. He glanced at Flora. "We didn't walk down the hall holding paws."

"Okay," Kory said. "Sorry."

Now Samaki smiled. "Don't worry about it."

Flora changed the subject to their driving experience, and soon they were comparing notes on the various cars they'd driven and Kory was teasing Flora about how long it had taken her to drive into school. It was only because Samaki had to leave to get home for dinner that they managed to stop Flora's happy chatter before the store closed.

Samaki walked Kory back to his apartment on his way back to the car. They were a few doors away when they ran into Nani Ki-Yo, struggling with two large grocery bags.

"Let me take one of those," Kory said, taking the closest one from the little mongoose.

"Oh, thank you," she said, adjusting her glasses and seating the other bag more comfortably. "I am lucky to have run into you! It's been a little while since we've seen each other." She wagged a finger. "You still have not come over for dinner."

"I'm sorry," Kory said. "With school and everything, it's been busy."

She peered at Samaki. "This is your friend who helped you move in, I think."

"Yes, Samaki," Kory said. "We were just getting coffee, and he was walking me home."

"A pleasure to see you again, Samaki," she said.

Kory saw Samaki looking at him, but couldn't figure out from the fox's neutral expression what he was thinking. He tried to brush his tail against the fox's, out of sight behind them, but the fluffy black tail swung away. "Good to see you again, too," the fox said. "How is your family?"

"Oh, fine, fine. Thank you for asking." She opened the door to the building and walked inside.

Kory stood awkwardly for a moment. "Well, I'll see you next weekend," he said. "For our tuxes, right?"

"Yeah." Samaki smiled at him, but the violet eyes didn't light up with the smile. "Looking forward to it."

The only thing Kory could think of was that Samaki was upset about having spent so much time with Flora, but that didn't make any sense. He mentioned it on the phone the next night, but Samaki said he'd just been tired, and he did cheer up over the course of the week. When they met the following Saturday at the Rainbow Center, he smiled and joked with Kory, and everything was fine until they went to the tuxedo rental store.

The store had mannequins for only two body types: short and tall. Kory got fitted with a standard black tux that was tight across the stomach but fit well in the sleeves, while Samaki opted for an all-white tux. They got matching violet cummerbunds, at Kory's insistence that Samaki's eyes were prettier than his and deserved to be matched.

Standing in their tuxes while the ferret salesman scurried between them, checking the fit of each suit, Kory looked in the mirror and saw the two of them standing together. It might have been the first time he'd seen them in that way, the tuxedos matching them so that they really looked like a couple. He saw Samaki look into the mirror as well, and in the mirror their eyes met, Samaki looking at Kory's reflection while Kory looked at the fox's. Samaki smiled, tracing a paw down the elegant line of his white jacket, the black fur stark and beautiful against the white cloth.

"You look better than I do," Kory said.

"You look great."

The ferret popped up between them, stretching to place a paw on each shoulder. "You both look wonderful!" he exclaimed. "A lucky pair of girls you have."

Kory saw the shadow flit across Samaki's muzzle, his whiskers curling back as his mouth curved down. The familiar panic that this ferret would find out about them surged in his chest. He nodded and said, before the fox could comment, "Yep."

Samaki met Kory's eyes. "I'm not taking a girl to the prom," he said quietly.

"Oh?" The ferret was scribbling down the information about both suits. "Well, don't worry. As handsome as you are, you won't be alone for more than ten minutes."

The fox opened his mouth to answer, but Kory forestalled him. "No, he won't," he said. "So, uh, how long do we get to keep these for?"

"You want them more than one night?" The ferret looked up from his pad. "We have a special, rent for two days, get one free."

"No," Kory said, "I mean, do we have them for twenty-four hours, or what?"

The ferret explained the terms of the rental, handed them their slips, and waved them cheerily out of the store with a bright, "See you Saturday!"

Outside and walking back to the car, Samaki was silent. Kory felt the weight of his disappointment or disapproval, but rather than let it sit this time, he decided to say something first. "What was the harm in just going along with him?"

"What do you mean?" Samaki wasn't looking at him.

"What does it matter what he thinks?"

Samaki paused, then looked up from the car door. "I don't know. Why does it?"

Kory's paw rested lightly on the passenger door handle, but Samaki was making no move to unlock the car doors. He looked back at the fox over the roof. "It doesn't."

The fox's violet eyes held his for a moment before he heard the click of the lock. The black head disappeared below the roof as Samaki got in, and reached over to unlock Kory's door. "So why," he said as Kory got in, "shouldn't we tell him the truth?"

Kory pulled his door shut with a prickling feeling in his chest. This argument was not going to end quickly, or well. He thought about just ending it, letting it go, but he wasn't sure Samaki would agree to let it go. The image of the two of them standing together in their tuxes, fresh in his mind, reminded him of the promise he'd made to talk out their issues. Wasn't this one of those issues? "What business is it of his?" he said as they pulled out of the parking space and onto the street.

The car remained silent until they stopped at a red light. Samaki tapped the steering wheel with one finger and said, "Why don't you want him to know?"

"I don't care if he knows. It's just easier."

Samaki didn't say anything to that word, but Kory saw his eyes narrow, and forged ahead. "It doesn't always have to be difficult. I want to enjoy being with you, not always thinking about who knows and doesn't know."

They turned a corner onto a busy street. "We're going to the prom next weekend," Samaki said. "Is that going to be a problem, who knows and doesn't know?"

"No," Kory sighed. "I just mean..." He trailed off. He wasn't sure how to put it any more clearly than he already had. And he wasn't sure how much Samaki's insistence that the world acknowledge their relationship was going to continue, nor how much it would bother him if it did.

It was already five by the time they got to Kory's apartment. Samaki hesitated as Kory got out. "Want me to come in?"

"I don't want you to be late for dinner." Kory smiled and kissed his muzzle. Samaki kissed back, but the argument was still there, though restrained. It had been between them for a long time, he thought, as he waved at the retreating car. The apartment was part of it too, he realized as he walked into the lobby. But that had worked out okay. Maybe if he just ignored it, things would be all right.

Malaya asked him what was the matter, when he didn't respond to her teasing about the tuxedos. He just said, vaguely, "I've got homework to do," and retreated to his room.

The prom started at 6:30. In exactly one week, they would be getting into their tuxes, maybe changing together here in this very room and playing with each other as they got dressed. He adjusted his pants. That image appealed to him, but then they would be going out in their tuxes, into a crowd of other students. They would be dancing together, the only gay couple in a sea of boys and girls, all staring at them. Kory held his head. He wanted badly to do this, for Samaki, but the more he thought about it, the more he wondered whether he would be letting Samaki in for a last month of school like the one Sal was having: fights, taunting, teasing. Not to mention worrying about what might happen at the prom itself.

He made a stab at his math homework. When he looked up from finishing one problem, the clock read 6:40. One week from now, they would be starting their first dance, maybe. Could he ignore the eyes staring at them from all over the room? Would people give them a wide berth? The image of the two of them dancing in a small open space in the center of the dance floor stuck in his head and refused to leave.

An hour later, when Malaya stuck her head in to ask if he wanted some dinner, he'd only completed one more math problem. He shook his head distractedly. "I'll just make some ramen or something."

"That's all I'm doing," she said. "Shrimp or veg?"

"Oh. Shrimp, please."

She squinted at him. "Sure you don't wanna talk about it?"

He shook his head, and waved a paw at the math book. "No, it's okay. I need to think this stuff through."

She gave him a long look, and then said, "Okay."

The images tormented him through the rest of the evening. He ate only half of his ramen, forgetting the rest until it was cold and gummy. Malaya looked at him from the couch as he threw it out, silently. He thought she was going to say something, but she just bent back to her own books. She'd started to take some books home from the store to read, mostly in gay and lesbian studies. Tonight, she was looking through a biography of R. Carmine, the poet whose lines were inscribed on the plaque in front of Rainbow Center.

How nice it would be, Kory thought, if everyone could "gather without fear or hate," just by proclaiming it so. If he could rip the plaque from the Rainbow Center and bring it to the prom, and thus make the dance as safe as the Center, he would run down there right now and tear at it 'til his fingers bled.

The next morning, he rolled over and looked at the clock. One week from now, he and Samaki would be waking up together in this bed, preparing to go to church. He'd started going to a downtown church some Sundays to save time, but next week he'd planned to take Samaki back to see Father Joe.

Father Joe. He sat up slowly. There was plenty of time for him to catch the bus and go out to see Father Joe this morning. If nothing else, it would be nice to be back in the familiar embrace of his childhood church. The downtown one smelled strongly of the incense they used to cover up the rot of the ancient beams, and the stench of alcohol from some of the less privileged members of the congregation. Kory viewed his attendance there as a way to strengthen his soul. He had talked to some of those members of the congregation, establishing an acquaintanceship with one or two of them. He kept their misfortunes in mind when cataloging his own troubles, but none of them had to deal with ostracism. None of them, as far as he knew, was gay.

He thought about that on the bus, rumbling through the sleepy Sunday morning past the homeless people, out into the places where they were kept off the street. Down in the city where he lived, Sunday mornings were slow but alive, a city just waking up. He passed a fox curled up near a heat vent and wondered whether what he was going through was really as bad as that fox, stuck without a home and maybe without a family. And then the bus crossed over Kittering Blvd., swooping under the expressway, and stopped at a station with flowers planted out front, whose inside didn't smell of three different kinds of urine. Kory waited there for his connection, and when it came, he stepped up into clean air-conditioned smell.

Out here, where he'd grown up, Sunday mornings were quiet, indoor times. People woke up with their families and only ventured out for church. Indeed, as he drew nearer to the church, more and more cars appeared on the road, until the small block where the church rose above all the other buildings looked like it was rush hour, with so many cars jockeying for absolution. He got off the bus a block away and walked through the cool late spring morning past white snow-covered houses, prim lawns and small offices to join the throng entering the church. There was no smell of alcohol here, no wood rot. These people weren't homeless, or poor, yet they still attended dutifully, as much in need of spiritual help as the unluckier downtown residents. He watched them from his now-customary position in the back pew, seeing the congregation with new insight.

A familiar coat flickered in his peripheral vision. He ducked down and watched his mother pace slowly to the front. Behind her trailed Nick, his head fur slicked down, shoulders bulging under his church blazer. Obviously he hadn't been given a new one yet. Neither of them had noticed Kory.

They sat near the front, in a spot he could see while kneeling. The back of his mother's head bowed as soon as she sat down; he knew from experience that she wouldn't lift it until Father Joe asked for the congregation to stand. Was there a sheen of silver on the fur between the ears, a small streak, or was that just a reflection of the light streaming through the windows? He couldn't look away. His mother had been going to church for years. Had it helped her love? Had she really understood what Father Joe meant, the way the people downtown understood that there was something better, something to strive for? Or was it just to make her feel better about herself?

He closed his eyes, pushing the uncharitable thoughts aside as Father Joe welcomed them. The Dall sheep's familiar voice washed over him, comforting, asking him for the responses he knew by heart. But whenever he opened them, they seemed drawn to his mother's head, stirring up thoughts that distracted him from the service and ruined his sense of belonging. She didn't look like she missed him at all, he thought, and then: I wonder if she still hates me.

By the end of the service, he'd missed large chunks of it, lost in ruminations and feeling the anger at his mother swell again. He heard Father Joe say, "Go with God," but rather than wait while the crowd filed out, he got up and left immediately. There was nothing Father Joe could tell him about what to do; he hadn't been able to help Kory's mother understand him, and Kory couldn't keep running to him with his problems anyway. He knew he had the support of God now, but God would want him to at least try to work his problems out on his own.

He leaned his face against the bus window, brooding all the way back. He couldn't help feeling angry at his mother; it felt like a wasted trip. Not only hadn't he talked to Father Joe, but he hadn't even been able to remember most of the sermon. Why had his mother had to sit like that, reminding him of the night he left, of the last time he'd seen her in the church? He should go to the prom with Samaki. It would serve her right.

Knowing that that was not a good reason didn't help clarify his thoughts any. He tried to imagine himself, a week from Sunday, having gone to the prom. How would his life be different? What if some other Flora McGuister saw him and thought that, hey, it was all right to be gay, but flaunting it was another matter? Would he be, instead of coming home from church, in a hospital bed as Malaya had been? Would he be visiting Samaki in the hospital? He shivered, pulling his jacket more tightly around him. There were plenty of stories on the Internet about gay teens being harassed, especially at public events.

Stop it, he told himself. Imagine the happy side of it. We go to the prom, we dance, nothing happens to us. We laugh afterwards about how silly all my fears were.

Doesn't sound too convincing, does it?

He sighed. I have six days to decide, he told himself, even though he knew that he'd already made his decision.

It took him most of those five days to figure out how to tell Samaki. He put it off and put it off, hoping he might change his mind, but on Friday night as they talked online, he realized that he couldn't let it go any further. Because they would be spending Saturday night together, Samaki was staying home, but would pick up Kory to go to the Rainbow Center, after which they would go get their tuxes and go to the prom.

Looking forward to it. :) The fox had said that once a night all week. Kory felt his heart clench. He couldn't do this. He'd just have to suck it up and go to the prom.

YT? Samaki typed.

Yeah.

You ok?

Kory took a breath. *I'm scared*, he typed. Maybe if he made Samaki understand how badly he felt, the fox would sympathize, would let him off the hook.

Aww. I'll keep you safe.

266

He stared at those words for several minutes, then finally typed, *Not worried about that.*

His phone rang, making him jump. He knew who it was without even looking at the number.

"Isn't this costing you?"

The fox's voice was low, guarded. "What are you worried about?"

He searched for the right words. "It just feels like we're making a statement, getting in people's faces. You don't know how the other kids will react."

"Who cares? Have you been reading stories off the Internet again?" Kory could hear tension below the forced playfulness. He sighed.

"No," he said. "But you know how I feel about being out in public."

"Mm-hmm. You didn't think this was a private prom when you said yes, did you?"

"Of course not." Why couldn't Samaki be more understanding?

"So what's changed?"

"It's tomorrow, that's what's changed," Kory burst out.

Silence greeted that remark. Kory waited, each second feeling like an hour, and when he couldn't bear it any more, he said, "I just...I'm nervous. I don't know."

"So what would you like to do?" Samaki asked. "What would make you feel better?"

Kory didn't answer. Samaki persisted. "Wear masks? Do you want to dress up as a woman?"

"No," Kory said, and took a breath. "Can we maybe go out to dinner instead of the prom? Just a nice night out privately? We can still wear the tuxes."

There. It was out. He waited for Samaki's answer, hoping it would be more accommodating than he thought it would be. The fox had waited for this prom for so long, and now Kory was threatening to yank it away. Even replacing it with a nice, formal night out was probably not going to be good enough.

"You really don't want to go to the prom with me?"

"It's not that it's you," Kory said. "It's..."

"It's all the other people. It's being seen in public again."

"Yes."

"But it's not about me. It's about you. You don't want other people to see that you're gay."

Kory couldn't think of anything to say to that. He held the phone to his ear, thinking about Father Joe, about Flora, about Perry, about Sal, and about Nick. If only he could predict how people would react, it would all be easier. When he had overcome his initial fears about telling those closest to him, he'd been able to gauge their reactions as he talked. What had unnerved him about his outing at school was the idea that everyone was watching him, judging him, behind his back. But he wasn't worried about Samaki's classmates judging him tomorrow night.

"I'm worried about what might happen to you."

He knew as soon as he'd said it that Samaki would say, "But I'm not worried about what happens to me, so you shouldn't be," and in fact, the fox did say that, almost word for word. It didn't please Kory that he knew Samaki that well; it frustrated him because he didn't have an answer for it.

"I know that," he said, to stall. "But I am anyway."

"Why?"

"I don't know! Because I don't want you to get hurt."

Kory didn't know why the silences were more painful than words, but every time Samaki wasn't talking, he wanted the fox to say something, anything. Finally he heard a sigh. "This is hurting me worse than anything they could do."

A vise clamped around his heart. He felt pressure behind his eyes, and squeezed them. "I don't want to hurt you," he gasped out.

"I don't want to force you to go with me," Samaki said. "If you really don't want to."

"I want to," Kory said immediately. "Just...it's just..."

"If you want to," Samaki said, "then we can leave from the Rainbow Center tomorrow. If you need to talk about it, we can talk about it then."

"I don't know if that will help," Kory said, tears leaking out around his fingers.

"I don't know what else I can do," Samaki said. "I want to be with someone who wants to be with me..."

"I do!" Kory yelled.

"...and isn't afraid to be out in public," the fox finished, as though Kory hadn't spoken. "I thought you knew that."

"Yeah," Kory said, "I know it, but..."

Samaki waited, and then said, "But what?"

"It feels..." he groped for words, which was frustrating in and of itself. He was more used to having too many words crowding his mind. "There's so much out there that we can't control, people who hate us just for being together. You haven't seen that. You've got great friends, a great family, you've always been accepted. It's always been easy for you. I don't want you to get hurt when something happens."

"You think it's been easy?" Samaki's voice had grown sharper. "Did I tell you about getting punched when I was thirteen just for resting my head on another boy's shoulder? Did I tell you about Alex Henderson, whose mom wouldn't let him hang out with me anymore when I asked if I could kiss him, even though he said no and we didn't do anything?"

"No," Kory whispered. "Why didn't you?"

"Because there's enough hate and fear out there already. Things are getting better. I just didn't want to scare you."

"But why do you still want to go through that?"

Samaki's response came after a second of silence. "We can't let them intimidate us, can't let them tell us how to live."

"See?" Kory said. "You want to be a symbol, you want to be in their faces. I just want to be with you."

"I want to be with you, too," Samaki said, this time immediately. "I want everyone to know how much I—how much I want to be with you."

"Isn't it enough that I want to be with you too?" Kory's cheeks were now damp. He could feel the tears leaking into his voice as well, no matter how hard he tried to keep them down.

"It's not that," Samaki said. "Don't turn this around. You know how I feel."

"You know how I feel, too." Samaki didn't answer. "So why is this so hard?"

"We shouldn't be doing this over the phone." The fox sounded tired.

"I'm sorry." Kory's voice sounded small and weak to himself. He wondered whether Samaki was crying, too. Maybe the fox was better at hiding it than he was.

"Let's talk at the Rainbow Center."

He sniffled, and nodded. "Okay."

"I'll see you then." There was a long pause. "I love you, Kory."

Kory worked against a sudden blockage in his throat. The pressure of tears seemed to have doubled, swamping his head and tongue. If he said, 'I love you too,' was that meaningless, a rote response? But how much worse would be to say nothing? He wanted to say it, but he'd wanted it to be meaningful, and now he couldn't think of any way to say anything that would let the fox know how he really felt that wasn't either ignoring what had just been said or mechanically responding to it.

"I…" he said, and then choked back a sob.

"Bye," Samaki said, quietly.

The line went dead. Kory said, "Wait!" but the fox didn't answer. He hung up the phone and stared at the picture of Santa he hadn't taken down from his bedroom wall. Had Samaki misheard and thought he'd said, "bye"? What had he been going to say, when he started? He wasn't even sure.

He grabbed a tissue and blew his nose. Had Samaki said that just to convince him to go to the prom? Or had it been reassurance that it would be okay either way? He threw the tissue away, looked up, and saw Malaya in his doorway, her small snout wrinkled in embarrassment.

"I heard," she said, indicating the open bedroom door. "I mean, a little. And you're..." Her fingers began to point at the tissue, then stopped as though she realized it wouldn't be polite. "Um, you okay?"

Kory shook his head. "I don't know," he said.

"Well, I, uh, you know, I never had a girl I was so into that she made me cry," Malaya said. "Not just with words, anyway. But if there's something you wanna talk about..."

Kory shook his head. "I don't think so. Thanks."

"Sure. You know where I am." She turned, stopped, and turned her head. "Look, for what it's worth, I think you guys will work it out."

"Thanks," Kory repeated.

"And if you don't, you're a good guy. You'll find someone else."

That failed to raise Kory's spirits as no doubt she intended it to. He smiled weakly and grabbed another tissue.

Even though he turned out the lights early that night, he didn't get to sleep until well past one in the morning, tossing and turning and replaying the conversation over and over in his mind. What had Samaki meant with that 'I love you'? What had he thought Kory had said in response? What had Kory meant to say in response? What did he want to say? What would he say tomorrow at the Rainbow Center? He played conversations over in his head a million times:

"I love you, so I'll go with you." "Well, if you're not comfortable, I don't want to force you."

"I'll do it even though I'm afraid." "I'm so lucky to have found someone so brave."

"I love you, too, Samaki, but I'm not ready to go to the prom." "That's okay, Kory, we'll just go to dinner."

"I just can't do it right now." "That's okay. I can be patient."

"I'm sorry." "That's okay. We love each other. That's what matters."

"I'm sorry." "That's okay."

"That's okay."

But then...

"I love you, too, Samaki, but..." "If you love me, why won't you go to the prom?"

"I just can't do it right now." "Will you ever? I can't sit around and wait all my life."

"I'm sorry." "Me too. I thought we had more."

"I'm sorry." "If you were sorry, you'd go with me."

"I'm sorry." "Good-bye."

"Good-bye."

His conversations kept coming back to that good-bye, those frightening two words. What frightened him most was that the more he thought about them, the more he wondered if that would be for the best. Would Samaki keep pressing him to expose their relationship in public? No matter how many times he told the fox he was uncomfortable, it didn't seem to matter. Maybe he'd be better off finding some nice closeted boy who didn't mind remaining closeted.

Who wouldn't have a keen mind, a bright spirit, and soft violet eyes that, more than anything Father Joe had preached, made Kory believe in God.

Then maybe he should change, he should get over his fear of exposure. He forced himself to play the image of himself and Samaki dancing at the prom over and over in his head, but his stomach churned just as fiercely the twentieth time as it had the first. And when he finally managed to sleep, his rest was plagued by dreams of running through alleys and abandoned buildings with Samaki at his side while angry mobs yelled and shot after them.

In the morning, he felt as though he hadn't gotten any sleep at all. He stumbled through breakfast, grunting monosyllabic responses to Malaya's questions until she stopped asking them. The clock inched inexorably toward 8:30, when he would have to leave to start walking to the Rainbow Center. In his weary fog, he felt it would just be easier if he stayed home and avoided the entire situation. It would be safer, for sure. He wouldn't be risking having those terrible conversations that ended with "good-bye." He could just claim to be ill—at this point, that would only be a half-lie—and he and Samaki would get through this.

But the thought of basing the rest of their relationship on even that half-lie (more than half, if he were honest, because his condition was directly a result of the situation he was trying to get out of), the certainty that the problem would come up again, and, beyond that, a need for coffee, drove him out the door. Malaya shrugged on her jacket and walked out with him silently when he said he was going for coffee, but said nothing on the way to Starbucks, sucking on a cigarette she'd lit up as soon as they were outside and blowing the smoke carefully away from him.

Memories hit him as soon as he walked in: their first drink together, the daily stops on the way to the Rainbow Center, the taste of his first latte, Samaki trying the different flavors before settling on hazelnut. Kory stopped and breathed in the sweetness of the coffee and pastries, but they seemed fainter today, harder to capture. He followed Malaya to the counter and stepped in front of her when she deferred to him.

"Tall black coffee," Kory ordered, and then said automatically, "And a grande nonfat hazelnut latte."

"I don't want that," Malaya said.

Kory shook his head. "It's for..." He stared at the barista, a young ferret with piercings in her small ears and through her lip. "What do you want? I'll get it."

"Coffee," Malaya said. "Small, whatever you call that here."

"Another tall coffee," Kory said.

"Room for cream?"

Malaya shook her head. Kory paid for the coffees and took his, inhaling the deep, rich aroma. He didn't drink coffee often, but it seemed like the right thing to do this morning. Starbucks reminded him, always, of Samaki. If they broke up, he wouldn't be able to go into one again and face the overwhelming press of memories. That thought nearly brought him to tears again.

His coffee was too hot to drink, but the smell alone opened his eyes, cleared his head. He took Samaki's latte when it was ready and followed Malaya outside. She didn't follow him as he turned left, toward the center, but she did say, "Hey."

Kory stopped and turned. Malaya made a face. "This coffee sucks."

He shook his head. "Sorry."

"Fuck, don't apologize, you didn't pick the beans. Listen, it sucks right now because I'm in the mood for something strong enough to knock me on my ass. This wimpy-ass gourmet coffee..." She sipped it. "I dunno, it's like someone told a cup of hot water about coffee."

When he just nodded and started to turn again, she said, "Kory. It's not bad coffee. And it's sure as hell better than no coffee at all. You know?"

He shook his head. "Mine's too hot to drink."

She stared back at him. Slowly, she raised her free wing to him. "Take care of yourself," she said. "If you don't like the coffee, then, y'know, don't drink it. There's always places to get more. Maybe you aren't ready to drink it yet."

Kory stared down at the steaming cup. "I think I really need it today, though."

"Don't burn your mouth." She sipped hers again. "Fuck, this sucks. I'll see you tonight." She turned back toward home, lighting another cigarette.

The coffee was almost drinkable by the time he reached the Rainbow Center. Lost in his thoughts, he didn't notice the shadow in the corner of the porch until he was at the door, when it spoke.

"Is that for me?"

Samaki slid toward him. Kory nodded and handed the latte over.

"Thanks." The fox sniffed. "You're drinking coffee?"

Kory nodded. "Didn't sleep too well."

"Me neither." Samaki sipped the latte. "I didn't want to talk in there. I mean, I thought we should talk out here first."

Kory stepped back from the door, leaned against the wall. The sight of the fox was sharpening his senses more than the coffee was, every part of him waking some memory in the otter. The paws curled around the Starbucks cup like they'd curled around Kory's arm or tail; the soft black fur whose texture he knew almost as intimately as his own; the long tail whose soft touch he sometimes felt even when the fox was nowhere around; the slender muzzle whose heat he knew well. He bent his muzzle to his coffee and took a sip, wincing at the bitterness.

"Did you make a decision?" Samaki said finally.

"I don't know." Kory took another drink, more because he was holding the coffee than because he wanted it. "So, I guess, no."

Samaki's lips curved slightly. "We are running out of time."

"I know," Kory said. "It's not easy." The coffee was still hot, and the taste it left behind reminded him of the smell of burnt nuts. On the street in front of the center, an otter strolled by, gave them a curious look, and moved on. It was early enough that the street was mostly empty, still.

The fox shook his head. "Nobody ever said it would be."

"But it should be." Kory's voice was getting louder. "I know I shouldn't care what all those people think, but I do. I know you can take care of yourself, but I still worry about you. If something happened to you because of what we did..."

"Then it'd be my decision," Samaki said. "You're not forcing me to take you to the prom. I'm asking you."

Hearing the hurt and anger in the fox's voice just made things worse. Samaki wasn't even making any movements toward him. The fox leaned against the brick windowsill on which he'd rested the latte Kory'd bought him, one paw in his pocket, the other tapping the brick gently. His muzzle was down, but he looked up when Kory said, "Can't we just go out to dinner?"

"Sure," Samaki said. "Where would you like to go? The alley behind the Rainbow Center? Your bedroom? Somewhere else where nobody will see us?"

Kory cringed. Samaki sighed, his muzzle dipping back. "I'm sorry. It's just...if we can't go to the prom together, then when? I mean, I've already told a couple of my friends that you're coming. I was really looking forward to showing you off."

"You told friends?" A little relief crept into the stabbing, paralyzing hurt. The image of them dancing all alone while people stared retreated. If Samaki had friends, at least they would have some allies.

"Well, sure. I don't just go to school and sit in classes and not talk to anyone," Samaki said. "Nobody I really hang out with after, but a couple kids I sit with in class. Couple guys on the track team."

"Oh, yeah," Kory said. "They'll be at the prom?"

"Sure." Samaki smiled. "Everyone's going to be there."

"Oh." Kory took another drink of coffee, which at least was cooler now, but wasn't doing anything to help the churning of his stomach.

"It'll be fine," Samaki said. "You remember I told you about that guy who graduated last year? He brought his boyfriend to graduation and nobody said anything."

"At the end of the year," Kory said. "We've still got a month of school to go. And he didn't go to the prom."

"This isn't about me," Samaki said. "Is it?"

"I'm worried about you," Kory said, though his mind was shrieking, *he knows, he's right!* "I mean, we'll be at college together for four years, right? Why is this so important now?"

Samaki cocked his head. "There's always a 'later'." he said. "If we don't go to the dance now, when will it be important enough to go? Our senior year of college? Our tenth anniversary?"

"I promise, I'll be able to. I just need a little more time." In his stomach, the knot loosened just a bit. Surely his promise would help, would be enough. He leaned forward.

Samaki chewed on his lip, meeting Kory's eyes. Kory tried to smile, realizing that his breathing had accelerated. He closed his other paw around the coffee cup, craving its warmth though the chill of the morning was barely noticeable on his nose and ears. "You really think...like, in a year?"

Kory nodded, barely able to let himself feel the first stirring of relief. They were over the hump now, and things were going to be okay. Samaki leaned closer. "If not...Kory, I don't want to do this, but I don't want to have this conversation again when we move into college. Will you try?"

Emotion blocked the words from Kory's throat. He swallowed and forced out the words, "I have to. I don't want...I don't want to walk away from you. I..." But he couldn't get the last two words out that he needed to and wanted to.

Samaki nodded, his eyes regaining a little of their life. "I don't want to walk away from you, either," he said. "But if you're going to be one of those guys..." He glanced at the door of the center. "Remember Jeremy?"

"The skunk from last summer? What about him?"

"When I talked to him, that time after his mother came to yell at him..." Samaki lowered his head, fidgeting with his claws. "He was crying, said he wanted to be straight, that he just wanted to walk around with a girlfriend like normal people. That's what he said: 'normal people.' He was a little better later, but there was always a little fear, a nervousness about being gay in public."

"You think I'm going to be like that? Why?" Comprehension hit him even as he asked the question. "Because my mom wanted to put me in one of those camps too? Because she blew up at me?"

"No!" The fox's head snapped up.

"I moved out," Kory said. "I don't even worry about her now."

"I know."

"She has nothing to do with this." His voice felt tight and hard.

Samaki stepped forward. "I know," he repeated. "I know. I'm just saying, I think of Jeremy at times like when you didn't want to come live with me, or when you tell your neighbors that I'm a 'friend,' or when you play cute word games with the guy in the tux shop."

"None of them need to know..." Kory started.

Samaki cut him off. "Yeah, none of them need to know, but they don't need *not* to know, either."

"What if the tux guy was like, some kind of religious nut?"

Samaki shrugged. "We'd get our tuxes somewhere else."

"You know what I mean."

"What? What if he followed us out of the mall, and stalked us, and shot us? That barely ever happens. We're in more danger of being run over every day." He waved toward the street.

"I know." Kory stared down at the plastic lid of his coffee. "It's not that, exactly. It's just...I can feel them judging us. Like Flora, when she found out, it was just all about me being...being gay. It wasn't who I was."

The fox made a noise that was half-laugh, half-cough. "So you're worried about the tuxedo store salesman knowing the real you?"

"It sounds stupid when you say it like that."

"How would you say it?"

The fox's gentle voice reassured Kory somewhat. "I don't know. It's just a feeling. It's not him specifically, it's everyone. I feel like if people know I'm gay, that's all they'll ever see in me."

"That's their problem." Samaki's tail flicked hard against the wall below the window. "Didn't Father Joe say that this is an expression of God's love?"

"I don't wear a cross, either." He sighed. "Maybe I'm just a more private person than you are."

"No question," Samaki said. "The only question is whether that's going to be a problem for us."

"I already said I'd try. Within a year."

"Another year," Samaki said.

Kory nodded. Their upcoming one year anniversary loomed the weekend after the prom, two weeks before graduation. He was terrified now that they wouldn't make it. They'd only mentioned it a couple times in passing, more excited about the prom—that is, Samaki had been more excited about the prom. Kory hadn't even been allowing himself to think about the anniversary until the prom were over. "I'm sorry," he said. "I promise to try. I really do." He looked away from the fox, to the sidewalk where a mother skunk walked slowly to let her young kit keep up. He tottered along, taking baby steps, just learning to walk. Kory watched him pull his paw away from his mother, then grab at her again when he lost his balance, while she cooed encouragingly.

"I guess that's all I can ask." Samaki stepped toward him and reached out, closing both his paws around Kory's, pressing the otter's fingers against the warm curve of the coffee cup.

Kory smiled, until he happened to catch out of the corner of his eye a movement on the sidewalk. The mother skunk and kit had stopped right in front of the Center to fix the kit's shirt, and the mother was just straightening, her muzzle turning toward them. Without thinking, he stepped back, pulling his paws out of Samaki's. A moment later, he realized what he'd done, but it was too late.

Samaki stared at him, then looked down at the sidewalk. His muzzle lowered, ears flat. "I gotta go cancel the tuxes," he said. "Tell Margo I'll be here next week."

"Wait," Kory tried to say. All the relief he'd been feeling drained out of him, leaving his stomach clenched, heat and shame pulsing at the back of his head. The fox ignored the guttural noise that didn't quite sound like a word, just raising his paw.

"I'll see you next weekend," he said, walking down the stairs and away, in the opposite direction from the skunks, now moving away from the center.

Numb, Kory watched the white-tipped black tail swing out of sight. He placed his coffee on the window ledge next to where Samaki had left his, and sank down onto the porch, his back against the wall. *Stupid, stupid, stupid!* Maybe he really was like Jeremy, one of those kids who would never be completely right. Maybe it would be better for Samaki just to break things off, so Kory wouldn't continue to hurt him.

No, he was better than that.

You think? said a small voice in his head. *Doesn't look like it from where I'm sitting.*

I can get better, he told himself. It was just an instinctive reaction. I didn't mean it.

Exactly. That's what's really inside you.

He hadn't had this animated a conversation with himself since the time he'd been trying to figure out why he was attracted to a young male black fox in the first place. It's not really inside me, he said stubbornly. It is, but it's just how I've been brought up. I can unlearn it.

Really?

And there was the doubt. Was any of the stuff he'd told Samaki true? Was it about being judged? Or was there some lingering shadow of his mother, some shame at other people seeing that he was gay? He held his head in his paws and rocked back and forth, the knot in his stomach spreading to his chest and throat.

He heard the door open. Margo's voice said, "Kory?"

He struggled to his feet, wiping his eyes. "Oh," he said, and stood there stupidly.

"Are you okay?"

"Yes," he said without thinking, and then, when his brain kicked in, "I mean, no. I'm feeling kinda sick."

"Well, don't just stand there, come on in!" She put an arm around him, trying to bustle him into the house.

The plaque caught his eye: *Beneath my roof, let all gather without fear.* He balked, twisting out of Margo's hold. The squirrel staggered against the door frame. "I'm sorry," Kory said. "I don't think I can go in. I mean, I think I'll just go home."

"Are you sure? You don't look well at all."

"I can make it," he said. "Only, can you throw those away?" He gestured toward the coffees.

Margo moved to pick them up. "Of course."

He didn't have to fake the paw to his stomach or the pained gait as he descended the steps and moved through the fog of his thoughts, people and buildings blurring past him. He thought he saw Samaki half a dozen times, and each time set his thoughts whirling afresh, digging the tracks deeper without reaching any conclusion.

He stayed in his room for most of the weekend, avoiding Malaya, eating ramen noodles while she was at work and keeping his door closed when she was home. When he did boot up his computer, he stayed offline, using it only for homework and not even connecting to the 'net. On Sunday, bleary and exhausted from another night spent tossing, turning, and crying, he went again to his mother's church. The temptation to talk to Father Joe was strong, but he asked himself whether he'd be running to someone else every time he had a problem. That drove him back to the bus stop without even catching the tall sheep's eye once the service was over. What would he have told me, anyway? he brooded. Face your fears. Some other trite, useless aphorism. It was one thing to force himself to take a dive off the deep end, or go see a scary movie. Those were concrete things, done once and over. How could he face this formless, gnawing dread that went on and on?

Sunday night, finally, he slept. On Monday, with a full night of sleep behind him, his thinking became clearer. The situation wasn't as bad as he'd thought. They hadn't broken up, after all. Samaki had agreed to give him more time, and Kory was determined to make use of that time. How he was going to do it, he had no idea, but he was sure that in a year, he could get to the point where he could hold Samaki's paw in public, or at least on the Rainbow Center porch.

He only became worried when Samaki missed their Monday call and picked up on Tuesday just long enough to tell him that he had a lot of studying to do and couldn't talk. On Wednesday, another form from Forester arrived, asking whether Kory wanted to sign up for the mentor program. He mentioned the form on Wednesday when he called Samaki.

The fox took a while to answer. "I got it," he said. "Didn't really look at it, though."

"I don't think we need mentors," Kory said. "Do you?"

"Nah," Samaki said. "Thing is..."

The silence started to gnaw at Kory's nerves. "What?" he said.

"Well, I asked my Dad about going to State. I mean, there'd be a lot less pressure on me to keep my grades up, and Kande's there and all. I can still accept up to end of June."

Kory felt as though he'd been yanked out of a warm pool onto cold, dry tile. "State? But...you're going to Forester. With me."

"I'm just keeping my options open." Samaki spoke quietly. "We could still see each other if I'm at State and you're at Forester. Weekends, like we do now."

This was his fault, all his fault, Kory knew. "I guess," he said, unwilling to start the whole argument over again. "If that's what you really want."

"You know better than that," Samaki said, and Kory couldn't think of any response.

The following Wednesday, Nick stopped trying to get Kory to tell him what was wrong long enough to give him another bit of news, once they'd finished their pizza. "Whatever it is that's wrong," the younger otter said, "this isn't gonna make it better." He fished for something in his pocket.

"What now?" Kory couldn't think of anything their mother could do to ruin his life further, but he supposed he hadn't put as much time toward thinking about it as she might have.

Nick handed him two pieces of paper, tickets to Kory's graduation ceremony. "Here. You got four, but I'm only allowed to give you two. She wants to come to your graduation."

This made Kory sit up straight. "What? Why?"

Nick scowled. "Said something about a public event and I wasn't to say anything to anyone about our situation." He snorted. "Like there's anyone who doesn't already know."

"Great." Kory rubbed his eyes. "That's just what I need. Do I have to talk to her?"

Nick spread his paws. "I hope not. I don't wanna be around if you do."

"No reason you should be," Kory said, "because there's no reason I need to talk to her."

Nick rested his head on his folded arms, eyes down, ears flat, and his voice when he spoke was unusually soft. "Don't make a scene," he said. "Is Samaki gonna be there?"

"Yeah," Kory said, and then, "Maybe. I think he will."

Nick peered up, lifting his round ears. "You think? Is that what's going on? You guys broke up?"

"No. I mean..." He sighed. "I did some stupid things."

"So apologize."

Kory shook his head. "I don't know if it's that easy. When you do the same stupid things over and over, it doesn't work when you apologize any more. You know?"

"No," Nick said, "but okay."

"You never did the same stupid thing twice?"

Nick grinned. "No. But tell me what you did so I can avoid it."

Kory leaned back and closed his eyes. The smell of the fishy pizza and the pizza joint itself had taken on a familiar, comfortable air over the past year. It wasn't quite like popping up in the pool of their house to talk to Nick, but at least it was close. If there were people at the other tables, their conversations were drowned out by the music, so Kory assumed his own were likewise private to him and Nick. "Just...be sure that if you're going out with someone, you really let them know how important they are," he said.

Nick was quiet for so long that Kory cracked one eye open to look at him. Nick noticed, and smiled. "I can't believe you wouldn't let him know that, the way you talked about him here."

"It's hard to explain," Kory said.

Nick shrugged. "If you don't want to, that's cool. So anyway, I guess I won't come over to ride to graduation with you. She wants me to go with her." He lifted his head. "Is Malaya coming?"

"I doubt it." Picturing Malaya dressed up and sitting through a graduation ceremony brought Kory closer to laughing than anything else in the past week and a half had. "It's not really her thing."

"Yeah, I guess not." Nick pushed his chair back. "Well, I oughta go study. See you Saturday, then?"

"See you Saturday," Kory said. "I can't wait for Sunday."

He felt obliged to invite Malaya, who masked her disdainful look a second after Kory had already seen it. And that night on the phone, he had to beg Samaki to come before the fox promised he would, so that when Kory hung up, he was very close to calling Samaki back and saying, "Look, if I have to beg, it's not worth it." But he wanted the fox there, especially if his mother were going to be there too. So he chewed his lip and studied for his tests and went to sleep.

Everything he did that week had been done under the stress of fighting back his fears about his relationship, but he felt he'd done well enough on his exams. The fear remained after the last "pencils down," all through the year-end assembly where various school officials blathered on about something pointless. Finally, at two, high school was over for the year, over forever.

Kory took the bus back to downtown, but didn't want to go back to his apartment. His bedroom had begun to feel suffocating, with all the reminders of Samaki around to feed his worry. He cast around for something else to do, and realized that it had been a while since he'd had a swim.

The municipal pool was empty enough that he was able to close his eyes and float in the warm water without too much disturbance. To his dismay, even the water wasn't able to calm him enough to make him forget about the possibility that Samaki would go to college at State, that Kory would lose the fox for good. He knew he didn't want that, but he couldn't convince himself that he was strong enough to deserve him, let alone keep him. Face your fears, he told himself again, and again he couldn't think of how to do that.

After graduation, he thought, then what? Would Samaki still be moving in? He certainly hadn't mentioned it since their argument on the porch of the Rainbow Center. Kory found that he'd stopped expecting it, and that realization weighed him down even more heavily. But it might be for the best. Would Samaki want to hold paws on the way to the Starbucks? At the little café where Kory and Malaya sometimes ate? On the bus? He closed his eyes, tired just thinking about it.

Running through the list of activities that made up his life brought the realization that it wasn't so bad. He enjoyed Malaya's company, he really did. He had finished well in school, after that rough stretch where he'd bounced from Sal's place to the Center to his own apartment. He'd gotten into Forester with enough financial aid to afford it. He wanted badly, very badly, for Samaki to be part of that world, but as the water relaxed his muscles, calmer thoughts crept in to dull the tension. Maybe, Kory thought, maybe I should be thankful for this time I've had, for all that Samaki's shown me about myself. If I can't be part of his world, I can go out and find my own now. Like...like a tugboat pulls a ship out to the ocean, then has to let it go.

He laughed at himself. What a stupid analogy. The unexpected, spontaneous laughter lightened his spirit. He and Samaki would always be friends, he knew that with a certainty as warm and buoyant as the water around him. Could he get by without Samaki as a boyfriend? Tension fought back against the calming water. He wouldn't like it, but yes, he could, if he had to. His world wouldn't end. He'd given up his home and most of his friends, and he'd clung to Samaki because the fox was the reason he'd given it all up. Did that mean he couldn't also give up the fox? Malaya always said that there were other boys out there, and even though Kory knew there wouldn't be any as special as the black fox, there was probably one who was a better match for him.

In the locker room, he looked at himself in the mirror, picturing another shy otter standing next to him, the two of them content to keep their relationship behind closed doors. The hum of the dryer distracted him from his reverie, calling back the memory of Samaki standing there, warm air blowing through his fur, that first time, over a year ago. Sadness blurred his sight and the memory, and drove him out into the warm almost-summer air.

Face your fears, he thought again.

Haven't you just done that?

He stopped on the street, so suddenly that the person behind him grazed his elbow pushing past. Was he still afraid? Of losing Samaki, yes, but mostly, he now felt sad. He'd played out the worst-case scenario and emerged on the other side, bruised but whole. There were plenty of people online who'd lost their lovers—true loves, first loves, best loves, all sorts of loves—and they'd survived. If necessary, so would he.

These thoughts remained with him as he moved through the sea of people flooding the downtown on Friday afternoon. He saw families, couples, friends, and loners like himself; foxes, otters, skunks, bats, lions, wolves, several kinds of antlers visible blocks away, bobbing above the crowd, raccoons, armadillos, and more species too numerous to count. None of them took much notice of him as he slid through them, just another face, a young otter moving along his own currents back to his home.

"You feeling better?" Malaya asked when he walked in and poured himself a glass of water instead of going back to his room immediately. She was curled up on a chair by the open window, resting her cigarette in one hand on the sill and blowing smoke through the screen.

"A little." Kory sat on the sofa, leaned back, and looked around the small place. "This is our place," he said.

"My bedroom." She grinned at him. "You just figuring that out?"

He shrugged. "I'm figuring a couple things out." He told her about the argument, and his thoughts on Samaki.

She took a long drag on the cigarette, exhaling the smoke in a slow stream. "That's pretty smart," she said. "Level-headed. I was wondering if you'd get there."

"You were trying to tell me," he said.

She nodded, but didn't say anything else. He watched her, curled dramatically across the chair arm like a film noir heroine, trickles of smoke rising from the cigarette. "What?" he said, finally.

She shrugged. "I hope it doesn't come to that. But it's good you'll be okay if it does."

"You hope it doesn't?"

She shook her head. "I like him. You guys seem to work well together. Look out for each other, you know? But if he wants to march in pride parades and you don't, then I dunno, maybe you're better off just being friends."

"Thanks," Kory said. "I thought you'd have something wiser to say."

"Me?" She snorted smoke. "I'm the one who went back to live with my father and ended up in the hospital, remember? Whose entire experience of relationships reads like an episode of 'COPS,' who's working a dumb job in a bookstore rather than go to high school. You think I know how things work?"

Kory shook his head. "You know at least as well as I do."

She waved a hand, scattering smoke. "I'm just better at faking it. That's something you suck at."

"Thanks. I appreciate that."

She arched one eyebrow. "You're gettin' better."

He grinned, briefly. "Not enough to help."

"Do you want to go march in parades and do all that?"

"I don't know." He sighed. "I want to be with him, that's all."

"So be with him. Who cares if you hold hands or not?"

"He does."

She sucked on the cigarette, but held the smoke in her mouth, letting bits of it escape as she talked. "I mean, the great unwashed, the drones, the...what did you call them, muggles."

He laughed. "You work in a bookstore and you still haven't read Harry Potter."

"Optimist bullshit." She waved out to the street. "Anyway, whatever you call them, out there. Who the fuck cares what they think?"

"Tell it to Brian Dallas."

Malaya frowned, and stubbed out her cigarette. "Who's that?"

"Skunk who got beat up at Forester by a couple football players. Because he was gay."

She rolled her eyes. "I bet he was a flamer. I'm sick of those assholes ruining it for the rest of us."

Kory folded his arms, settling back into the corner of the couch. "So because he was a little out there, he deserved to get beat up?"

"Sure." Without the cigarette, she seemed to go limp, as though she'd been flung across the chair and left there, but her voice was as sharp as ever. "Flame on in front of football players all you want, but it's like going into a church and yelling that there is no god, or going into Finster's Café and asking for a venti mocha frappucino. You got the right to do it, but you gotta choose your spots and be prepared to deal with the blowback."

"So you are on my side."

One eye regarded him fixedly. "I'm always on your side, Kory. Except when you're being a mo'."

"You think Samaki's being unreasonable."

"Sure. But so are you."

"Me?" He curled his tail around the leg of the sofa, anchoring himself to it.

She nodded. "You want him to change, he wants you to change. Just like Jen wanted me to change."

"And that didn't work out."

"Well, I didn't really want Jen to change and I wasn't interested in changing for her, so no. Plus she wanted me to change into someone who was okay with cheating and gettin' knocked around. I spent years trying not to change into that, so no dice."

Kory loosened his arms and tail, shifting uncomfortably. "Yeah, I guess not. So who's right?"

"Right? Hell if I know. You both are."

"But you just said..."

"Look, he didn't ask you to come to a track meet and kiss him in the locker room, did he? It's just that you guys are comfortable in different ways." She glared at him. "And don't start that crap about maybe not being gay. I can hear through walls, you know."

Kory's ears flushed. He turned his suddenly warm face down to the floor. "I wasn't gonna," he said. "I think I'm over *that*, anyway."

She grinned at him. "That'll make it easier for you to get another boyfriend. If you want one."

"Yeah." He stared at his feet and rubbed the webbing between his fingers.

"Don't worry about it," she said. "You're cute. You'll find someone."

"I'm what?" He lifted his head to stare at her.

She pointed a bony finger at him. "Tell anyone else I said that, I'll put spiders in your bed."

The next time he talked to Samaki, though, he felt his peaceful resolve melt away.

"I really want you to be there," he said.

Samaki sounded tired. "I already said I'd come."

"I know," Kory didn't know why he was pressing the point. "I just wanted to make sure you know I'm really looking forward to you being there."

"I know," Samaki said softly, and then, a moment later, "I'm really looking forward to it too."

Kory hung up unconvinced that he'd gotten his point across, but unsure how to proceed without annoying the fox. After all, he'd agreed to come, he'd acknowledged Kory's plea of affection; what else could Kory do?

The following night, Samaki sounded more animated, telling Kory about his own graduation, scheduled for the Sunday afternoon after Kory's, and one of his classmates' plans to wear nothing under his graduation robes. "You wouldn't do that, would you?" he asked.

"Would you?" Kory asked.

"I will if you will."

"It's almost worth it," Kory said. "But what if I start thinking about you up on stage and everyone, y'know, sees it?"

"I'd be the only one looking at you. There's going to be, what, a hundred kids on the stage?"

"A hundred forty-eight," Kory said. "But my mom'll be looking at me too."

"We don't even get to go on stage. All four hundred of us have to just sit in the audience. Then we go up row by row as our names are called."

"Lucky," Kory said. "I have to sit on stage for an hour, then another half hour after we get the diplomas while Mr. Pena goes on about the future and all that crap."

Samaki snorted. "Is he that college prep teacher? The one who was making fun of State?"

"Yeah." Kory started to say something about State, then decided he didn't want to bring it up. "Anyway, after that there's the graduation pictures, and they say it'll go fast, but when we had our yearbook pictures it was only supposed to take an hour and it took half the day."

"Fancy." Samaki chuckled softly. "We get one class photo. Otherwise it's DIY."

"Wish our whole thing was DIY." Kory lay back on his bed and stared at the ceiling. "Wish it were over. I'm looking forward to graduation being done with."

He waited for Samaki to say something about moving in. "Yeah," the fox said. "Me too."

"Malaya and Nick and I are going out to dinner after," Kory said. "Hope you can make it."

"Of course," Samaki said, without hesitating. "Wouldn't miss it."

That was all Kory had to hold onto as the Saturday approached. He hadn't even dared make a comment about 'brushing,' and neither had Samaki, but at least he felt secure in their friendship, and could look forward to the dinner. He spent some time preparing his arguments and pleas, but the conversations he played in his head no longer had the frantic desperation they had from the night of the prom.

"I understand if we can't be together."

"I want to be with you if you want me."

"I think we can work it out, but if you don't..."

The biggest problem was that most of the lines, as he rehearsed them, put the burden on Samaki to make the decision, and even as Kory savored the relief they afforded him, he recognized guiltily that they were a little unfair. *Not so unfair*, part of him said. *After all, wasn't Samaki the one who'd made the decision in the first place?* He threw the question back and forth, but hadn't come to any good resolution by Saturday morning, when the sun streaming through his window woke him to the last day of his high school life.

To his surprise, when he walked out into the living room, Malaya was dressed and standing by the door. "Please tell me we're stopping for coffee on the way there," she said, yawning. "Even Starbucks."

He stared. She was wearing her nicest shirt and the jeans with only two small holes in them. "You're coming?"

"If I'm invited. Might as well see someone's graduation."

"Promise not to embarrass me?" Kory's tail curled happily.

She grinned back at him. "No."

They rode the bus together down to the school, transferring at the hub between downtown and the suburbs. Kory broke the silence when they'd gotten on the last bus. "Weird. This is the last time I'll be taking the bus to school," he said.

Malaya fiddled with the buttons on her shirt. "I don't remember the last time I did. I just remember the first time I didn't."

"How long has it been?"

She glanced at him. "Since the hospital."

"Oh. Right." He straightened his own clothes self-consciously. "You were still going 'til then?"

"On and off. Dad made me go when I moved back home. Not so much when I was at sunshine central."

Kory watched the suburbs roll up around them, the now-familiar transition. "It wasn't so bad, really."

"Easy to say now you're done. What did you really get out of it other than a place on a stage with a hundred other obedient little moppets?"

"I learned some things, that's for sure."

She chuckled, dry and short. "The real valuable stuff you didn't learn in the classroom."

Kory recognized some of the cars that crowded the streets as they approached the school, students driving themselves to the ceremony or being dropped off. The parents didn't have to show up for another hour, but many of them probably would sit out in the audience and talk with each other until the official start.

He gave Malaya both her ticket and Samaki's, and called Samaki to tell him to look for the bat when he arrived. The fox said "Okay, driving," and hung up—one of the rules his parents had laid down was "no phone while driving."

"See you in there," Malaya said. "Get in your uniform and hop on that assembly line." Kory smirked, waving as he followed the line of students into the school.

Inside, the scene could best be described as organized chaos. Teachers tried to gather the students into alphabetical groups, but friends crossed group lines to chat and laugh at each other's robes. Kory stood with the G-H-I-J-K group and got his robes on with barely a word to anyone else. Across the cafeteria, he saw Perry struggling into a robe that was one size too small for him, at least; in the next group, Sal was already dressed and talking to one weasel Kory recognized from the vo-tech crew. He tried to catch Sal's eye, but the other otter turned pointedly away.

One person did catch his arm as they started to file out to the auditorium. "Kory!" Flora's excited scent assaulted him. "Is your fox boy going to be here?"

The wolf in front of Kory flicked an ear back, but didn't turn. In front of him, Geoff Hill was laughing about something with another raccoon and appeared not to have heard. "I hope so," Kory said in a low voice. "He said he was on his way."

"Spiff!" Flora grinned at him. "Good luck! Don't fall asleep!"

He laughed, but it turned out to be a real concern. The principal droned on about the future, and then the two valedictorians struggled through painful speeches. Beverly Anderson's was particularly tedious, a long analogy about Columbus crossing the ocean and how they were all standing now on the shore of a brave new world. Kory kept himself occupied by looking for Malaya and Samaki in the crowd, but he actually spotted his mother and Nick first. Nick yawned three times while Kory was watching him, looking stiff and wrong in his suit. His mother was similarly rigid, keeping her eyes focused on the speaker. Nick met his eyes and grinned once or twice, but his mother never, that he saw, looked in his direction.

He finally saw Samaki and Malaya right after the principal started announcing names, when everyone around was fidgeting from the warmth in the room and the concomitant rising odors. Relief infused all the scents as the first row of students got up to accept their diplomas, and when Chris Carkus, the six-foot tall stag who captained the football team, got up from that row, Kory saw the bat and fox in the space his antlers had been obscuring.

They were watching the stage, heads turned towards each other. Samaki looked pleased, as best Kory could tell from so far away. Then he lost them again, as some parents started to stand up to take photos of the diploma ceremony.

If the initial speech had gone by too slowly, the ceremony seemed to fly. In no time, the principal was calling, "Hedley, Kory," and shaking Kory's paw as he handed over a rolled piece of parchment tied with a ribbon. Then Kory was sitting next to the same kids on the other side of the stage, some pretending to smoke their diplomas, some unrolling them to read the message that their actual diploma would be arriving in a couple weeks, some flipping them from paw to paw, and some just holding them in their laps and staring vacantly ahead. Flashes continued to pop as the student body moved through the process, each in turn, until the principal was ushering "Zane, Bradford" off to the left stage and introducing Hilltown's mayor.

The mayor, a lean vixen, said a few words about—surprise—the future. Finally, Kory thought, but no, it turned out the principal had a little more to say, and then Mr. Pena had to make his own remarks, and after that the vice-principal got up and said in a choked voice how wonderful it had been to have known all the seniors and how sad he was to see them go, while Geoff Hill and his raccoon friend sniggered to Kory's right. And then, finally, mercifully, it was time for them to stand up and file out through the auditorium, while the juniors and sophomores in the band mangled "Pomp and Circumstance" not quite beyond recognition. Flashes strobed until it felt like a sedate rave, through which Kory saw Sal's parents waving to him and to Sal, Malaya and Samaki waving to him, and his mother, watching the procession without expression while Nick smiled from behind her.

The tide of students accelerated as they reached the exits, bunched up just before the doors, and then burst through out into the field behind the school, where some of the thicker-furred species were already pulling off their robes. Kory was warm, too, but he left his on, knowing he'd just have to put it back on for the photo later. Some of the kids were tossing their mortarboards into the air, others had met their parents already. Kory had not set a meeting place with anyone, so he floated through the sea of eggplant-colored robes and jubilant expressions and kept an eye out through the crowd, panting in the heat of the June sun.

Malaya and Samaki found him first. The bat punched him lightly on the arm, while Samaki stood back and grinned. "You deserve an award for sitting through that," Malaya said. "I thought I was going to die. I know I say I want to sometimes, but for the record, I never want to be bored to death."

"Pretty cool," Samaki said. "Congratulations."

He offered a paw, but Kory pulled the paw toward him and embraced the fox in a powerful hug. "Thanks," he said, as the fox's arms closed tentatively around him, then tightened. "You helped."

"Me?" Samaki nuzzled him and smiled, and for the first time in a while, Kory saw the smile light up his eyes as well. "You did all the work."

"Yeah, but you kept me on track, and made me look forward to study sessions." The fox's ears flicked and his grin widened.

"Always glad to help," he said. "You earned it all, though." He, not Kory, was glancing at the other students standing a few feet away in all directions, but everyone else was occupied with their own animated conversations. To Kory's left, an ermine and a skunk were covertly passing a flask back and forth and tossing back gulps of whatever was inside.

"Can the sweet talk," Malaya said dryly. "I'm chokin' up here."

Kory turned to say something to her, but was interrupted by the shouting of Mr. Pena. The fox had cupped his paws in front of his muzzle to project. "Students! Can I have your attention?" Everyone turned to face the tall teacher. "We're going to be lining up for photos in the same rows we were sitting in on stage. Row one, over here to my right, please, and row two, get ready behind them. Parents, you should be in line with your kids so we can get all these photos taken quickly."

"You're like, row three, aren't you?" Malaya said, as everyone went back to their conversations. The ermine handed the flask to the skunk and walked toward the photo stage. Beverly Anderson was already posing with her parents and what looked like her younger sister, all four black bears so portly they barely fit on the stage. Three flashes later, they made way for a family of cougars.

Kory nodded. "I guess I'll head over in a bit. What are we doing after?"

"Well, if you haven't had your fill of long, tedious spectacles, the new Oliver Stone film is playing. Or we could see that robot movie with the explosions."

"Definitely explosions," Kory said, and turned to Samaki.

The fox nodded. "I'll take explosions over Oliver Stone any day."

"Can you give us a ride back to the apartment so I can change?" Kory fingered the robes.

"Aw, you're not going to wear them all day?" Malaya stepped back, pretending to size up his outfit. "You look better than that kid." Up on the photo stage, a tall, gangly fox was having his photo taken with his much shorter mother. His ears couldn't quite line up straight, he had a serious overbite, and his robes had slid to one side. His mother reached up to adjust them between photos.

Kory laughed, shortly. He still couldn't see his own mother anywhere.

"Mom took the car back home," Samaki said. "But those do look good on you. Even if you did wear clothes underneath."

"How do you know I did?" Kory raised an eyebrow.

"Pant legs." The fox pointed down at Kory's feet.

"Dang. Should've rolled them up."

Samaki smiled at him, and Kory felt again the emotion, the spark of healing. The argument might still be there between them, but so was everything else, and on this bright, sunny day, even in the throng of students, the shadow of the argument had receded.

"Row two, start to line up please," Mr. Pena called. "For those of you who have been asking, Mrs. Holly is going to get the yearbook done in the next two weeks, so you won't have to wait long." Vera Donovan, Flora's weasel friend, climbed up on stage with an ancient weasel and a younger sister. Vera pressed the billowing robes down, holding her paws on her hips as each flash illuminated her.

"You don't have your yearbooks yet?" Samaki tilted his muzzle.

Kory shook his head. "We never get 'em 'til summer."

"That's weird. We pick 'em up the last week of school. How do you get everyone to sign them?"

"I guess just whoever we see over the summer." Kory shrugged. He could count the number of times he'd seen people from his high school class the previous summer on one paw.

Malaya was looking at Mr. Pena. "I bet it's these pictures. The parents want pictures of graduation. It's not for the kids."

"It's just always been like that," Kory said. "I dunno why."

A compact brown shape in a white shirt piled into Kory, hugging him. "Hey, happy grad!"

Kory stumbled, grinned, and hugged Nick back. "Thanks." He looked around.

"She's waiting by the photo line." Nick made a face. "I told her I wanted to put my suit jacket in the car 'cause it was so hot. What are you guys doing after?"

"*Robots in disguise*," Samaki intoned.

"Cool. Can I ride with you guys?"

Samaki shook his head. "But I could call Mom. I bet Ajani and Kasim would want to see the movie too. Maybe she could come out here."

"Can we all pile into the car?" Nick rolled up his sleeves.

"None of the seniors are going to be impressed by your muscles," Malaya told him.

Kory grinned. "Some of them might. Don't flex around Flora."

Nick punched Kory's arm. "Cut it out."

Kory feigned injury, grabbing his arm where Nick had hit it and moaning, "Oh, ow, I think it's broken!" He held it out to Samaki. "Make sure it's okay?"

The fox extended a black paw and took Kory's arm, feeling along it with the other paw. "Feels fine to me. Maybe just some bruising."

Kory met Samaki's smile and didn't say anything. The touch of the soft fingers on his arm evoked memories and feelings, warming his inside as the sun was heating up his fur. He wanted to tell the fox he was sorry for everything, even knowing that wouldn't solve the argument, but he could see understanding in the violet eyes, more beautiful in the sunlight than he'd ever seen them, and he knew he didn't need to speak the words.

"Guys?" Nick said.

Malaya shushed him. "They're having a moment."

"Oh."

Samaki released Kory's arm, and grinned at them. "It's okay. We're done now."

"Row three," Mr. Pena called. Behind him, Bill Farley, a scruffy coyote who was the school's reigning stoner, got up on stage with his mother. He'd put on a pair of circular purple glasses, and when a few of his friends yelled, "Farley wasted!" he broke into a wide, sleepy grin and held up two fingers in the peace sign, leaving them up through all three flashes. His mother, tall and narrow, kept a paw on his shoulder, looking fixedly off into the distance, and didn't protest.

"Comb your fur," Malaya said.

Kory stuck his tongue out at her and mussed up the fur between his ears deliberately. "She can make me pose with her, but she can't make me look good."

Samaki eyed Kory. "You can't make yourself look bad, is the problem."

"Hey, I'm not..." He grinned at the fox, feeling the warmth rise to the back of his neck again. "Only way I look bad is standing next to you."

"Oh, for God's sake," Malaya said, as Nick grabbed Kory's paw and said, "Come on."

"We'll meet you on the other side of the stage," Samaki said. "Look pretty."

"Fat chance." Kory wandered toward Mr. Pena's right, where the rest of his row was milling around. He took his spot in line, looking at the back of Xilly Grace and wondering if he might be lucky enough to get up on stage and have his photo taken before his mother showed up.

He saw movement on the periphery of his vision and knew it was her from the scent. She stood beside him without a word. They watched the family of foxes get their pictures taken, and then Xilly and her father and brothers walked up the short wooden steps and arranged themselves, a happy family of smiling cougars. On the other side of the stage, a small knot of students led by Flora had gathered, cheering each student as his or her picture was taken. The rest of the sea of fur dotted with eggplant robes seemed mostly indifferent.

"Congratulations," his mother said tightly.

Kory just nodded, not sure of what to say. His mother went on. "I'm glad to see you in church. Alone. I wish it were every week."

"It is," Kory said. "Just not there every week." He pondered whether to antagonize her further by telling her he sometimes went to Samaki's church, decided it was pointless.

"Better than nothing."

The first flash came from the stage. "You don't have to be in this picture," Kory said. "I'm fine by myself."

"I raised you and put you through this school," his mother said.

He saw the movement of her head, and noticed the Jeffersons nearby, and Sal's parents. It didn't make any sense to him that the Jeffersons were here. The wolves had three daughters, all grown and off to college. Then Mr. Jefferson waved to him, and Kory understood that they were here to see him. Unreasonable anger rose in his chest. After kicking him out of the house, his mother was showing him off like a trophy.

He remembered Father Joe's words: forgiveness should depend not on her actions, but on your heart. Well, Kory's heart was not very forgiving at the moment.

His mother seemed to read his mood. "All you have to do is act polite for five minutes. Not even that." Following the third flash, Xilly and her family descended the other side of the stage, leaving it empty.

"Kory Hedley," Mr. Pena said. The short, rotund chipmunk behind the camera waved them onto the stage, crouching behind his camera again.

Kory followed his mother up onto the stage. On the opposite side, he saw Samaki, and Malaya, and wondered why Nick wasn't with them. Just the two of them, he thought, and then Nick came charging up the stairs behind him.

"Nicholas, where's your suit?" his mother said sharply.

"In the car."

The Jeffersons were smiling at them. Two more of his mother's friends from church stood beside them, raising cameras to take their own pictures. Flora and her crowd of cheerleaders said, "K-O-R-Y, yay, Kory!" Malaya looked bored. Samaki looked...

"Go and get it right now."

The chipmunk raised his head. "Ma'am, we don't have time, there are other families waiting."

Kory met Samaki's eyes. The fox smiled, gave him a thumbs up, and looked away. "I'm terribly sorry," his mother was saying. "I didn't know he was going to leave it there. It'll just be five minutes. Nicholas, go."

"Ma'am, would you mind stepping aside so another family can get their photos taken?"

Mr. Pena stepped in at this point. "Wait, I have to make sure the order's correct on the sheet." He looked reproachfully at Kory.

It's not my fault, Kory wanted to tell him. My mother has this obsession with looking good. But he remained quiet as they stepped down off the stage and let Zoe Hemmecher and her parents, grandmother, and four younger siblings all bounce up onto the stage, long ears waving.

Three flashes. Nick came back, jamming his fists into the arms of his jacket. His mother brushed down the fur between his ears, straightened the jacket, and then stood back to look at him. She sighed and turned to Kory, reaching out a paw to touch his robe. He brushed it away, surprising himself with the quickness of his reaction.

Her eyes widened and nostrils flared for a moment, and then she turned to the stage. "Fine. Look however you want."

She and Nick strode up onto the stage, and after a moment, Kory followed them. Her words rang in his head.

The chipmunk went through his litany with the definite weariness of someone who knows he has another seventy or so to get through. "Okay, everyone, nice pose. Kory, you want to get in front here?"

His mother grabbed his arm, shoved him forward. Flora and her friends weren't cheering, but he could hear them talking: "that's Kory, we already did him." Beside them, Samaki and Malaya were smiling. "So what," Flora was saying, "let's do it again."

She got her friends going again, with a cheer of "K-O-R-Y!" Someone else on stage was saying something, and the photographer was giving them

some instructions, but Kory kept hearing other voices in his head, drowning everything else out.

"It felt like you sent it out into the world to find me."

"I'm just figuring things out."

"Nobody else knows what's best for you."

"You kept me on track."

"I love you."

"Look however you want."

"I love you."

Nick, now, was tugging at his robes. "Kory."

He looked around. The photographer said, "Finally. Please look at the camera, nice smile."

To their left, Geoff Hill and his family were waiting to get onto the stage. The raccoon's father, as big and burly as he was, laughed at something Geoff had said. To the right of the stage, Samaki's muzzle was tilted very slightly. Everything melted away around that one face, that look that he knew well: the fox had seen that something was bothering him and wanted to ask what. In that moment he felt suspended, floating in time, as though the world were holding its breath and waiting for him to make a decision.

"Kory," the chipmunk said with more exasperation. "Camera's here. Nice smile. Think about no more school!"

But of course, there would be more school, in the fall. Forester University, and Samaki, and Kory realized that Beverly Anderson had it wrong. They hadn't just crossed the ocean; they had only just arrived at it. The ocean was what lay ahead of them, the wide unknown. None of them knew what awaited them on the other side, or how many would even complete the journey. They didn't know how long it would take, or in fact have any but the barest idea how to cross it at all. What Kory knew, the only thing he knew for sure and certain, was who he wanted to be at his side when he crossed.

"I'm sorry," he said, scrambling to his right and down the stairs. "I'll be right back." His mother yelled his name, the photographer choked off a curse, but all he heard was the pounding of his feet on the stairs and his heart in his chest.

He stopped in front of Samaki, panting from the exertion. The fox's violet eyes widened, his ears lying back. "What's the matter?"

Kory reached for his paw. "Come on."

"That's for your family," Samaki said. He pulled his paw gently away. Flora and her friends were watching, but Kory ignored them.

"That's for the people who are important to me."

"Nobody else brought a girlfriend or boyfriend up," the fox pointed out.

Kory put his paws on his hips. "So now you're worried about what other people are doing?"

He saw the startled laughter before Samaki repressed it. "You don't have to do this."

"I want to do this. Nobody else got kicked out of their home, or had to deal with Jeremy and Malaya, or had to figure out where to go to college without their parents. You think my mother cares whether I graduate?"

"She's there on stage," Samaki said.

"And you guys didn't have to 'deal with me'," Malaya chimed in, glaring.

"She just wants to look good for her friends."

Samaki nodded. "Just go back up and take the picture. We'll take our own after."

Kory hesitated only a moment. "No."

"Don't do this just to get back at her."

Kory shook his head. "I don't give a damn about her. Please." He took the fox's paw again.

Behind him, he heard Flora and one of her friends both say, "Go on up!" and "Get in the picture." Their support heartened him, cinched his resolve. Samaki was still wavering.

"If you don't," Kory said, "then I'm not getting my picture taken."

"You really want this?" Samaki asked. His voice, soft, matched the shine in his eyes.

"Yeah." Kory didn't know how else to say it. He tugged at the black paw, and this time, the fox followed him.

His mother had, of course, watched the whole thing, and when Kory stepped back onto the stage with Samaki a step behind him, she had her paws on her hips. "Kory James Hedley," she said, "this photo is family only."

"Really," Kory said. "Then it should just be me and Nick, shouldn't it?"

"He," she jabbed at the fox, over his shoulder, "is not part of our family."

"I remember you telling me I wasn't part of your family anymore, either," Kory said. "Doesn't that mean you're not part of mine?"

She leaned close, hissing, "You have always been a willful, ungrateful brat. But I will get this picture, and I will not have it ruined by that..."

Her voice trailed off. "By that what, Mom?" Kory asked, putting a sarcastic accent on the last word. Behind her, he could see the Hills and the family behind them watching avidly. "By that fox? By that friend of mine? Or did you have another f-word in mind?"

"If you have any decency," she said, and it took Kory a moment to notice that she was looking up at Samaki, "you will leave the stage right now."

"Kory..." Samaki said apologetically.

"Don't go anywhere," Kory said. "If anyone is leaving, it's her."

"I raised you for eighteen years..."

"Seventeen and a half," Kory said. "And then you decided you didn't want me any more. Just like Dad."

"Don't you dare compare me to him. I stayed behind when he left..."

"Maybe you should've let me go with him," Kory said. His heart pounded.

She glared at him. He couldn't remember ever seeing her look this furious, even on the night she'd told him to get out. Her eyes were narrowed, ears flat back against her head, and the line of her mouth was a slash of rage. "If I had known how you would turn out, I would have."

Kory let the responses bubble to the surface of his mind and swallowed them all. He walked past her, beckoned Samaki to his side, and posed. "Samaki's in the picture with me and Nick." He looked straight ahead at the camera, and smiled.

The fox did not look comfortable at all, but he managed a smile. Nick crept around to the other side of Kory, stealing awed glances up at his brother, his smile a mechanical fixture on his muzzle. The chipmunk ducked back behind the camera. Kory felt his mother's breathing behind him, and noticed out of the corner of his eye that the Jeffersons were whispering to each other. They weren't alone. The sea of students and parents that had been largely ignoring the stage were now mostly focused on it, at least as far out as he could see.

Flash. He blocked out the sight and focused on the camera. "One more," the photographer said, "big smiles everyone." He must have been saying it out of habit. Kory couldn't imagine that his mother was smiling, but the chipmunk didn't call her out as he had Kory.

Another flash. "Okay, last one coming up, almost done. Just hold still, biggest smile because you're done with these in three...two...one..."

Flash. The afterimages had barely started to clear before the chipmunk was yelling, "Next!"

Kory followed Samaki down the stairs and heard Nick behind him. Malaya was there, and so was Flora, to Kory's surprise. He was only vaguely aware that his mother had not come down on their side of the stage before Flora was slapping him on the shoulder.

"*So* cool, Kory," the skunk said, grinning up at him. "You rock."

"Thanks," he said.

Malaya couldn't quite hide her disdain for the perky skunk. "You got balls, I'll say that."

"The way you told her off..." Flora beamed. "So romantic."

"You heard?" Kory felt his face flush.

Malaya cut in. "Not everything, but it was pretty obvious what was going on. She took off the other side of the stage like her tail was on fire soon as the last flash went off."

Flora leaned in to Kory. "Did she really kick you out?" she whispered.

Kory nodded, just as Geoff Hill and his family came down the stairs. "Hey, Hedley," Geoff sneered. "That your *boyfriend*?"

Kory only saw the grimaces on the muzzles of his parents—directed at him, not their son's behavior. Next to him, Samaki was looking his way for guidance, but he didn't know what to do, how to respond. He couldn't make himself say anything rational, and he couldn't tell Geoff to piss off, not with the raccoon's parents standing right there. He felt the creeping feeling that he was going to let Samaki down again, but this time the feeling didn't have time to take hold before Flora piped up. "Yes, Geoff, so you can stop chasing Kory now. He's taken."

"Fuck you, stinko," Geoff snarled, clearly surprised at the attack from that quarter. He stepped back and Kory could see his tail bristling.

"Geoffrey!" his mother said, steering him away from them. "Language!"

"Yes, *Geoffrey*!" Malaya called after them. "Listen to your mother, *Geoffrey*!" The raccoon's stiff back and tightly wound tail told them he heard the taunts even if he didn't respond.

"Malaya!" Kory said, laughing. "You don't even know him."

"I know his type." She shrugged. "Used to live with one, remember?"

Kory nodded, looking at the fox beside him. Samaki tilted his head in a familiar gesture: not quizzical, this time, but resigned, a warm smile creasing the black fur of his muzzle. "There are always going to be Geoffs around," he said. "But there'll be Malayas too, and Nicks and Floras and Margos."

"I gotta go get in line," Flora said. "Hey, Kory, party at Vera's tonight. Bring Samaki if you want."

"Okay," Kory grinned. "If he wants."

"We'll see." The black fox fell in beside Kory as they walked away from the stage, Malaya and Nick trailing them. As they walked through the crowd, Kory saw a few people glance at him and turn away, but more of them gave him a smile, a thumbs-up, a high five, a wag of the tail.

"Why'd you do it?" Samaki asked as they walked. "I mean, I know what you said, but...were you planning this?"

Kory shook his head. "She's so focused on appearances, it disgusted me. Then I realized that that's kind of what I'm doing to you. I didn't want to be that guy. I don't want to be her son, not like that." Samaki's ears lowered, and his smile lost some of its brightness.

"I didn't mean to make you feel that way," the fox said.

"No, it's okay," Kory said. "I was. If you hadn't reacted, I'd just go on doing it. And if...if that's what was important to me, then we shouldn't be together."

The smile flickered back to life. "That would suck."

"Agreed." He flicked his tail across the back of his leg to brush Samaki's. "That's what I decided up on stage. She told me to look however I want, and I just thought, I want to be with you."

"If you need to barf," Malaya said behind them, "let me know so I can get out of the way."

Kory half-turned, but she'd been talking to Nick. "I think I can manage," he said, and Kory saw the big grin on his brother's face. Nick winked at him and looked up at Malaya. "You?"

"I'll hold it in," she said. "I've seen worse. But you two might want to tone it down."

"Maybe you should just hang back," Samaki said. "We're having a moment here."

"Are we?" Kory grinned at him.

"You bet." The fox glanced round. "If we weren't surrounded by your friends and hundreds of strangers, I'd kiss you. Can you wait 'til later?"

"How far to the bus stop?"

They laughed together, and then Vera ran up to give Kory a big hug, demanding to know the whole story and reiterating Flora's invitation to her party, and she was just the first of half a dozen people to ask Kory what he'd said to his mom, wanting to meet Samaki, and in the middle of one of the stories, Vera pointed up to the stage and said, "Look!" They all turned and saw Kenny Vinson, the mink, kissing his squealing girlfriend as the flash burst across them. "See what you started?"

But the strangest thing of all was meeting Chris Carkus on the edge of the field as Kory, Samaki, Malaya, and Nick were finally leaving the school field. His shadow towered over them, even Samaki, antlers jabbing at the sky with every step. His gaze swept over them and settled on the older otter. "Hey. Kory, right?"

Kory blinked up at the towering figure. "Yeah."

The elk extended a hand. "Congrats."

"Thanks." Kory shook it, bewildered.

Chris looked at him, around at his friends, lingering on Samaki, and then back at Kory, nodding. "Good to see you standing up for yourself. Take care."

"Thanks," Kory said again. "Uh, congrats to you too."

The elk smiled, raised a hand, and walked off. Nick stood at Kory's side, watching him go. "I didn't know you knew Carkus," he said in an awed whisper.

"I don't," Kory said. "I think that's the first time he's ever talked to me."

"Well," Malaya said, "looks like you escaped serious injury this time. Next time you decide to hold an impromptu pride demonstration, give me a little warning, wouldja? I'll wear my leather." She lit a cigarette and took a long drag.

"You shouldn't smoke," Nick said. "It's bad for you."

"Lots of things are bad for you," Malaya said, "one way or another. Don't make 'em any easier to give up. Eh, Kory?"

Kory gave her a bland smile. "I have no idea what you're talking about," he said.

"So what now?" Samaki said. "Mom said you're all invited over to our place, but I told her we might be going back to your place. There's Vera's party later, too." He grinned at Kory.

"I've got some money," Nick said. "We could go out to eat."

"You buying for all of us?" Malaya said, nudging him.

"Matter of fact, I am," he said. "Except the ciggy. That has to pay its own way."

She laughed, and to Kory's surprise, she dropped the cigarette and ground it out. "Okay, okay."

"Kory," Samaki said, "it's your day. What do we do?"

They all looked at him. He shook his head, brushing his tail up along Samaki's again. "I've made enough decisions for one day," he said. "You decide. I'll go wherever you want."

"Then," Samaki said, "it doesn't really matter where we go, does it?"

"Nope." Kory took the fox's paw and touched his nose to the tip of the black muzzle. Samaki's breath warmed his whiskers, the fox's scent warm, happy, and comforting, and for that moment, the whole vast ocean of the world was shut out and it was only the two of them, floating together. "Not at all."

EPILOGUE

Gene, the Resident Advisor, had gathered the students from the first floor of Capri House in the lounge area. Kory and Samaki sat side by side on an old green couch under a row of open windows that looked out over the green Mall in the center of campus. Despite the warm breeze that trickled in through the windows, the room was warm and stuffy, with a strong smell of disinfectant, and the ringtail was hurrying to get through his remarks.

"So those are the rules of the dorm," he concluded. "Now let's go around and introduce ourselves. I'm Gene, I'm a junior here studying electrical engineering, and I grew up outside of Millenport. I love sea scallops, and yes, that is a hint if you're thinking about trying to bribe me. Next?"

"My name's Allison..."

"My name's Diana..."

"My name's Mark..."

"My name's Samaki. I'm a freshman from Hilltown studying journalism. My family emigrated here from Africa, and my sister Kande and I are the first two to attend college."

Everyone clapped. "Where's she going?" Gene asked.

"State."

"Well, congratulations." The ringtail looked over at Kory.

"I'm Kory," he said. "I grew up in Hilltown too. I'm a freshman studying English. I think. And I, uh..." He paused, trying to think of something interesting to say about himself.

"He writes poetry," Samaki said. "He won a contest."

"Oh, very cool," Gene said. "So you guys know each other? Did you go to school together?"

"No," Kory said. Samaki was watching him, but he knew there was no pressure in the fox's look. Samaki was letting him say as much as he was comfortable with. Well, he'd always heard that in college you could reinvent who you were, and what better place to start than here? "We almost went to the prom together, but I backed out."

The students around them looked a little more interested. Across from them, a leopard who'd been lounging alone in a chair suddenly sat up straighter, wide eyes darting from Kory to Samaki and back.

Gene nodded. "Cool," he said again, and moved on. "Next?"

The leopard's name was Kalili, from Capo, and he was studying political science. After they'd all introduced themselves, Gene said, "Let's get outside and enjoy the summer while it lasts. Remember, floor meetings every Monday night. I'm in room 31. Anything you need, any questions you have, let me know."

Kory and Samaki strolled together along the trees of the mall, taking in the buildings. The sunset tinged the brick and marble with fire, filtered through the shadows of the leaves. Some students strolled by, while others hurried, making Kory think lazily that he would soon enough have things to do just like them, that he was already part of their world, this new world. The air smelled fresh and clear, full of an electricity that made his fur tingle. The world felt limitless, waiting for them to set out upon a course of action. "Want to explore?" he asked.

"Tomorrow, maybe," Samaki said. "Right now I'm just drinking it all in. I can't believe I'm here. That we're here."

"I know. Me too." Their tails touched again. Kory thought about everything that had brought them to that place, from the collision at the pool to the Rainbow Center to Christmas to their apartment to his graduation. It seemed incredible to him, looking back, that he could have navigated it all to arrive at this place, here, with the black fox at his side. If ever Father Joe wanted a parable to demonstrate the existence of God, he thought, he could just take that story and tell it.

"I'm still sore from last weekend," Samaki said, rubbing one arm.

Kory laughed. "Me too. Who'da thought Nick would have so much heavy stuff?"

"If the rest of the swim team hadn't shown up, we'd be a lot worse off." Their minds were obviously moving in the same direction, because Samaki's question a moment later echoed Kory's thought. "You think your mom's okay?"

"I hope so," Kory said, sincerely. He'd seen her only once during the move, stumbling red-eyed from the bathroom to her bedroom. She'd ignored him, but since then he'd felt the first stirrings of pity for her. Father Joe still held out hope that Kory would be able to forgive her. Maybe pity was the first step, Kory thought. "I'd be more worried about Malaya. I think Nick's going to try to get her to give up smoking."

"If anyone can," Samaki laughed, but his sentence was interrupted by someone striding up beside them.

At the person's soft cough, they both turned to see Kalili. "Hi," he said, looking back and forth from one to the other. "I'm Kalili, I'm on your floor..."

"Sure, we remember," Samaki said, smiling.

The leopard blinked as though this were unexpected. "Well, say, I don't know if I got this wrong, from listening to you guys back there in the dorm, but, um, don't get offended but did you say you were going to the prom... together?"

Kory and Samaki grinned at each other. "He asked me," Kory said, "and I backed out. I wasn't so confident then."

"So you are...I mean, you're..."

"Boyfriends," Samaki said.

The leopard's fixed, polite smile broke down, until he looked like he might cry. "You're gonna think I'm pathetic," he said, "but I didn't think there'd be anyone else here..."

Kory patted him on the back. "We were just gonna get some dinner," he said. "You want to join us?"

"Can I?" He looked nervously from one to the other. "I just wanna talk...it'd be so great to talk to someone..."

"Sure," Samaki said. "Glad to meet you. Come on."

Kory brushed his tail against the fox's as they walked on, Kalili at their side starting to ask questions about how they'd met. "There was a poem in a newspaper," Samaki started.

"That wasn't any good," Kory said. He and Samaki wove their story together, laughing and remembering, as the sun turned the leaves to gold, the cloudless sky stretching overhead like the surface of a vast, bright ocean.

About the Author

Kyell Gold writes anthropomorphic erotica from an undisclosed location rumored to be in California, where he lives with his partner.

His work appears regularly in Sofawolf Press's *Heat*, Bad Dog Books' *FANG* *(www.baddogbooks.com)*, and his own LiveJournal *(kyellgold.livejournal.com)*.

His work has won three Ursa Major Awards: *Volle* for Best Novel of 2005, *Pendant of Fortune* for Best Novel of 2006, and the short story "*Jacks to Open*" for Best Short Story of 2006.

Waterways is his first novel set in the "Forester" Universe, where his next collection of stories is also set.

About the Artist

John Nunnemacher, a.k.a, "Cooner," has worked as an animator on television and feature productions; as a lead art director on interactive software; as a layout and production manager at a monthly business journal; as a character designer and illustrator for various products; as a storyboard and comic book writer and artist; and as a caricaturist at a major theme park. He also worked at a tech support call center for three weeks. He has lived in Pennsylvania, Florida, California, and Texas.

More of his work is available at *(www.griffinparkstudio.com)* and at *(www.furaffinity.net/user/cooner)*

John is currently a freelance artist, working in the home he shares with an otter of his own, as well as their rescued dog, Casey.

About Sofawolf Press

Sofawolf Press was founded in 1999 to provide a venue to showcase great writers of anthropomorphic fiction and to promote the genre to a wider audience. The Press' flagship publication, ***Anthrolations***, a literary anthology of short stories, is now in its eighth issue.

Since its debut, the Press has added to its lineup other magazine-length anthologies, novels, shared-world anthologies and other novel-length collections, comics and graphic novels, artists' sketchbooks, and calendars.

The Press continues to seek out new and creative ways of expanding its offerings of printed creations.

Please see our website *(www.sofawolf.com)* for a full list of titles available from Sofawolf Press. Thanks for reading!